CURRENTLY

SARAH MENSINGA

For Stephen

First Edition published by:
Chattersketch Press

Cover design and book design by Sarah Mensinga
www.sarahmensinga.com

PART ONE — SANDE

MAAM IS DEAD.

I'm glad I didn't see the webbed jaguar bite her neck or the Saltpool men put spears through the animal while trying to save her. And I'm very glad I didn't hear her use what was left of her life to beg those men to take care of me.

But if I'd been helping her crack open waterpods instead of catching squid crawlers with Gren, maybe I could have done something. Maybe I could have screamed or thrown a rock to scare the jaguar away. And if nothing else, I would have comforted her.

That's the worst part. Maam spent those last moments thinking she'd failed me. I wish she'd spent them in my arms with me singing her a night song. I would have even lied to her and told her that Gren had found a way to keep me safe.

And it wouldn't have been a sinking-rock lie, it would have just been a floating-seed-pod lie because now the ocean has arrived, and here's Gren, trying to make sure I don't drown or freeze or starve.

We're standing together at the Varasay gates, for the mountain city is where deeplanders shelter while the ocean passes by. Plenty of other villagers are here too, gathered in a disorganized muddy line with their belongings piled on wagons. The Teeterwood rises up on either side of us, and it's as if those drybark trees have lined up to enter the city too. The cold rain keeps spattering down as well. It's already soaked through my wildwool jacket and fernflax dress, and it makes my skin feel like something rotten I've slipped into.

Sometimes when the tide arrives, it brings storms with it—angry temper-tantrum storms.

But even though I'm shivering and feeling prickly, I like the weather today. I'm just as upset as those swollen, twisting clouds, and because I can't let my worries out in a mess of tears, I like that the sky is howling and fretting on my behalf.

Gren holds my hand tight as if my fingers are fish trying to slither free. She's a Saltpool elder, or I suppose she is *the* Saltpool elder if one villager were to matter more than the others. And because the city priests often do what she says, and a few even bring her nice things like salt-sugar bars and rare spices from the trade routes, she thinks she can convince them to let me into the city. My name isn't in their record books, which is the main problem, but I'm not a criminal like my maam. I just grew inside her, that's all.

"This won't work. They look mean," I tell Gren, watching the Gray Straps register other villagers and assign them barracks units. My friend Sande says the Varasay guards are named after the belt they wear. Today though, those gray belts hide beneath black, oiled-canvas coats that make the guards look like puddle beetles—the nasty kind that sting you. A few of them carry the thick record books that list all the births and deaths in the deepland villages, and fathoms, do I wish my name was written in those pages.

"Oh come now, stop trying to squirm away." Gren tugs me forward. "I always say you can't drink from a waterpod you haven't broken open."

Gren likes giving advice like that, mixing her thoughts up with old sayings. And although I do stop wiggling backward, I still can't bear to keep watching the Gray Straps as they move closer and closer toward us, working their way along the line of villagers. Instead I twist around to look at the ocean. There aren't any trees growing directly below us, so I have a clear view of the tide spreading out impossibly far, covering everything I know with shimmery blue. You'd think so much water would scare me more, but the wandering ocean is a familiar threat. I know that it will always come in the winter and then leave in the spring. What might happen now at the gates is much more unpredictable.

Not far behind me in line, Sande stands with his parents. And when I look at my friend, he gives me a crooked smile and shouts, "Hey, don't worry, Nerry. If those uppies won't let you into the city, I won't go in 'neither!"

His parents would never allow him to face the rising water, of course, but I like Sande because he says things like that.

"What's your name?" I hear a Gray Strap ask Gren. "And what's the name of your village?"

I turn around and find that a guard has reached us, record book in hand.

"Well, I'm Gren Tya Favis," Gren says in a voice that only trembles a little. "And I live in Saltpool with many of these folk." She nods to the people around us. "It's the village on the currentways side of Coral Lake."

"Yeah… I, uh, know where Saltpool is." The Gray Strap looks through his book, hunching over it, surely trying to keep it dry. After turning a few pages, he makes a mark with a charcoal-and-kelpwood pencil. "And the girl?"

"Yes, so this sweet child…" Gren pulls me against her colorful, very-patched seacotton robes, and I like that they smell like a cookfire. "Her mother was banished from the city while pregnant, poor thing. I don't know what her crime was, but you know, my heart just went out to her. Anyway, the poor dear died two sunedges ago, so I took in her child." Gren hesitates and squeezes me closer. "Please just list her with our village. I promise you she is a good girl and quiet as a diver rabbit. No one will ever notice her. She is helpful and hardworking too—she can already bundle dried herbs so much better than I can. And I promise I'll see to all her needs."

The guard crouches down, pulling back his canvas hood to see me better. His face is kinder-looking than I expected, all wrapped up in a soft, frizzy beard. "Ah, I've seen you and your maam from the wall. All of us Gray Straps have… I've always been worried for you, hoping you'll survive the tide. I'm sorry your maam is dead."

"I am sorry too," I say, feeling a warm flicker of hope. Sande says all uppies have hearts of ice, but maybe this man is different. My maam was different.

"So… it sure sounds like you might be able to help us." Gren sways, surely looking around for other Gray Straps who might be listening in.

The guard sighs. "I wish I could, but you know the Threegod priests and their rules. Anyone caught sneaking her into the city would be banished for at least a tide, and the girl would never be allowed in at all, no matter what happened."

My flicker of hope fizzles out.

But Gren tightens her thickly knuckled fingers on my shoulder. "Wait... what do you mean by 'no matter what happened?' *Is* there a way for her to enter the city? A proper way?"

The guard stands back up, tucking the record book into his coat. "If she ever marries a deeplander, she can be registered. Sometimes folk bring in drifter brides."

"But Nerene is only eight tides old," Gren says. "She's far too young to marry, and there's no time to wait. Her mother kept her safe, so she'll be easy pickings for landrunners if she's alone. And who knows what the criminal bands will do to her, and there's also the cold..."

The Gray Strap's mention of marriage, though, reminds me of a patchy, not-quite-thought-through plan I had a few days ago. I'm not used to talking to strange adults and certainly not uplanders, so I turn to Gren. "Member when the Narroes adopted that baby from Pirock? There was a ceremony, and the priest sent a letter to the city to change the record books. What if you did that? What if you adopted me all official, with papers and everything?"

It seems like a good plan to me, but Gren makes a despairing sound, and the Gray Strap frowns as he wipes rain off his beard.

"I suppose you've had your two children?" He looks questioningly at Gren.

She nods sadly. "Daughters, a good twenty tides ago."

His shoulders drop. "Yeah, that won't work then. Even if the priests agree to adoption, they'll want it to be someone who hasn't had their two. But maybe another family might be willing..." He trails off at the slapping sound of quick, wet footsteps, and I don't have to look to know Sande's coming toward us. I recognize his happy, skipping run.

"We'll do it!" he tells the guard. "My family, the Olins. We'll adopt Nerene. My maam can't have another baby anyway." He leans forward as if sharing a secret but then keeps talking just as loudly. "She's been praying and praying to the Water Goddess. She says Threegod don't listen, so she may's well try someone who will, even if it's—"

"Sande, shh, quiet," Gren says in her firmest voice. And even I know you can't talk about the Water Goddess so high up the mountain. Deeplanders aren't supposed to worship her anymore.

Sande's hands curl into fists. "All I'm saying is they'll adopt her. I'm sure of it. You just wait here, and I'll go tell them what they're gonna do."

He splashes off and soon returns with his parents, big Trennet who often gives me extra food and skinny Bessel who always looks like she's wincing in pain. Both of them wear hooded, finely woven wildwool coats, and as they hurry over to us, Bessel is quick to say, "Look, I don't know what my son has been telling you, but we can't adopt this girl. Threegod hasn't blessed me with a second child yet, but I have faith it will happen."

"Oh come now, Bessel," Gren pleads. "If we leave her outside the city, she'll die."

"That is upsetting, it is." Bessel lowers her voice to a whisper. "But let's be honest, this is her mother's fault, not ours. This girl's fate is not our responsibility."

Trennet, Sande's father, looks at me sadly as if I've already been torn apart by landrunner teeth and claws. "Yet if we save the girl everyone will think highly of us. It would also make a rousing fireside story."

"I don't care about stories," Bessel says, adjusting the sash around her waist with swift, sharp tugs. "Besides, isn't there a family who's a better fit than ours? How about the Tayvers? I hear she's barren."

"The Tayvers are young, only just married," Gren says. "You haven't had a child in eight tides."

Bessel's hard face seems to harden even more. "Other women have gone longer and still given birth."

"Please, be reasonable," Gren says in her wheedling and sugary yet still insistent way. "You don't need to mother the girl. Just let the priests think what they need to think, and I'll take care of the rest." She nudges my shoulder and winks at me. "And you'll take care of me in return, right Nerene?"

It's strange that Sande isn't arguing with Bessel too. But looking around, I realize he's not even standing with us anymore. "Where's Sande?" I ask.

Yet even though I've asked the question, all the adults look at me as if I also know the answer. And after a moment, I realize I do. "He's hiding," I say, turning to the sopping Teeterwood trees. "He said if I can't go into the city, he won't go in either."

Ten Years Later

CARNOS TURNS TO ME. "Did you look for him?"

I wish he wouldn't ask such dumb questions because of course I didn't help search for Sande. He was hiding to save me.

"Oh but the rest of us looked," Gren says, eyeing me. She knows it was a stupid question too, and what does that say about my future husband? "Sande was in the Teeterwood, though, so there was no finding him 'til he wanted to be found. We searched through the whole night, and the ocean kept rising up and up, closer and closer. Finally Bessel gave in, and she and Trennet adopted Nerene. As soon as it was all official, little Sande came strolling out of those drybark trees. I'll never forget the way he was grinning like a bubble fox who'd caught a mudhopper. Bessel whipped him of course, but our Nerene was safe."

"Well good." Carnos nods. I think he's approving of the adoption, not the whipping, but with his blank expression, it's hard to be sure.

"I don't understand though," he continues. "What does that story have to do with our wedding?"

Gren manages not to roll her eyes or cluck her tongue, but she does strum her fingers on the stone she's grinding dried beetles on. "How 'bout this... here's a simpler version; Nerene was adopted by the Olins so she could shelter in Varasay. And even though she's always lived with me, the Olins'll have to present her for marriage at the city gates. The Gray Straps will expect that."

Carnos' brow is still crumpled in confusion, and I try not to be frustrated. I've always known that his many good qualities: kindness, bravery, and honesty, come with a certain simplicity.

"Bessel hates Nerene, of course," Gren explains further. "But she'll cooperate."

Carnos turns to where I'm sitting in the shadow of a kelp tree, giving myself blisters as I pluck drowned beans out of their tough hulls. "I don't see how anyone could hate you," he says.

As sweet as that is, I nearly say, "Just think about it for a moment," but I hold my sharp words in. If Carnos did think about it, though, he'd know that I counted as Bessel's second child, therefore she was forced to have the procedure and could never carry a baby again.

"I know that woman, and I don't trust her," Carnos's mother, Itanda, says. She's sitting beside me, also in the shade. The Kaelnos family is from far away Riversborn, but they arrived in Saltpool yesterday so they could travel up the mountain with us. Itanda looks a lot like Carnos with wide shoulders, thick eyebrows, and dense hair. She makes a heavy, disapproving sound as she tightens a neat, red stitch on our wedding gift, a thickly woven seacotton blanket.

"Oh don't worry, Bessel will cooperate." Gren dumps powdered beetle shell into a bowl. "She won't risk getting herself in trouble. Besides…" Gren smiles at me. "Since your Carnos is taking our Nerene off to live in Riversborn, I'm sure Bessel will do everything she can to help."

And what Gren doesn't say is that the true reason Bessel wants me gone is that she surely suspects how much I mean to her son.

But what does Sande think of my betrothal? I have no idea. I haven't even seen him since last tide, for he's been working at the motorliner track house.

If only I could marry him, but because of his childhood stunt to save my life, as far as the city priests are concerned, he's my brother.

Wind makes the canvas tarp covering the top of our stone hut ripple and dance. We've already removed our kelpwood roof, shutters, and door just like we do every tide so we can use the wood to build wagons. Usually I enjoy these final nights in our partly unmade home so long as it doesn't rain. The night air flows more freely around our sleeping mats, and I like how the soft, leafy shadows meet and part on the canvas overhead.

Tonight though, I just can't seem to fall asleep. In the morning we'll say goodbye to our village for the winter and begin the difficult journey up the mountain. And when we reach the city gates, I'll be married to Carnos. I was hoping I'd see Sande before we left. I want to let him know why I'm getting married, and it seems crueler, somehow, if he doesn't know about my wedding until after it's over. But he hasn't returned from the track house yet. And when I walked over to his parent's hut this morning, Bessel told me that he probably wouldn't be traveling to Varasay with the rest of us; he'd be riding the motorliner.

"Believe me, I'm not happy about it either," she said. "We need his help pulling our wagon, but apparently there are still some final shipments coming in. As if I care about the uppy harvest."

So here I am, lying on my sleeping mat, wide awake. It doesn't help that Itanda is snoring and sprawled between Gren and me, and it doesn't help that I just keep *thinking* about everything. It's like my mind is running in wild circles. More time passes, at least an hour, and still not tired, I get up. Quietly slipping out of our hut, I creep past the Kaelnos's wagon, which is piled high with their belongings. Carnos and his brother Marl sleep beneath it, and they don't stir as I tip-toe by. Just as softly, I creep through our village, built on the sloping banks of Coral Lake, and I soon enter the kelp forest. Thankfully both moons are also awake so there is plenty of light. Nima, the larger moon, is round and full, while smaller Moro is just a timid crescent skimming the dark kelp trees.

Most villagers would never enter the jungle at night, and most of them shouldn't. But I have two snappers tucked into my sandals, and I'm pretty good at using the sleeper darts. Gren and I often go on overnight trips to gather herbs.

Roots slip over my feet, it's as if they're trying to trip me, and my thoughts slow me down too.

Is marrying Carnos the right choice? He's nice enough, but I certainly don't love him. Whenever I share my doubts with Gren, though, she always says something like, "Your Maam would like him. She wanted you to be safe, and he'll do that—take care of you. He's like a boulder that doesn't move while the ocean passes by."

Not far off, a bird calls out in a lonesome way. It's not a song I recognize, but that often happens. Creatures are misplaced by the tide and can't find their way home. I always feel bad for them.

I soon arrive at the dead boat—where I tend to go when I need to think. Most deeplanders are afraid of it, for they believe it's full of death shadows, so it's a good place to be alone.

The metal skeleton of a steamship probably once carried an uppy family around the tide, but now it's covered in shell barnacles and wave-crest vines full of frilly green leaves. The wreckage has never frightened me though, and I've always felt safe here. Maam and I used to sleep in the rusted hull when I was young because the criminal bands thought it was haunted too. And when she died, Sande and I came here to escape our chores. We would often play sirens, with one of us pretending to drown the other with irresistible wavurl powers.

And more recently, we created a baby here that broke a lot of rules.

Or would have.

I settle onto the soft grass and fold my legs, a snapper ready in my hands just in case.

If only Maam were still alive, and I could talk all of my worries through with her. Last tide, when that little life was growing inside me, I felt like her death shadow was always with me, watching over me, and sometimes… judging me.

I wanted to be brave like her, even if it meant being banished, and Sande had courageous-yet-reckless plans to save our child too. He thought we should hike away from Varasay mountain and hope we'd find drifters, the Sea Spread's lonesome farmers, before the ocean came to swallow us. He also suggested that we even try to walking to another mountain city, although I don't think anyone has ever survived the lengthy trip.

When Gren finally found out about our situation, because in desperation I told her, she said the village healer could make me a poisoned drink. "It will make you sick for a sunedge—very sick—but the infant will leave you."

And that was tempting too. The Threegod priests would never need to know. No one in the village would need to know.

Sande would be safe.

I'd be safe.

And we'd have a second chance.

The leaves rustle. I lift my snapper, stretch back the resin, and I'm about to send a dart flying into the shadows when a person steps out of the trees. It's Sande—really Sande.

"You weren't at Gren's," he tells me. "I thought I might find you here."

And then together we say, "I couldn't sleep." And it feels silly to speak in unison—so childish.

I leap up and race across the grass to hug him. Forgetting my unhappy news for a moment, but maybe he already knows. "Bessel said you'd be riding the motorliner to Varasay."

"I thought so," Sande says. "But they had enough help already. I wanted to see you when I arrived in Saltpool this afternoon, but Maam put me to work right away." He holds onto me tightly and seems bigger and stronger than I remember—surely because of hauling so many crates at the track house. But he doesn't kiss me, so he must know I plan to marry Carnos. Bessel probably told him.

I pull away. "Let me explain."

I can't read his expression. He doesn't look angry, which is confusing, so feeling bewildered, I stumble through my reasoning.

"You and I obviously can't get married—I'm listed with your family in the city records. And I'm of age now… and Carnos is a good match. But that's not just it. After what happened between us, we need to make sure that never happens again, and… and you're smiling. Why are you smiling?" It makes me angry, actually, because none of this is funny. I'm all knotted up inside.

Sande's smile widens. "Nerry, you don't have to marry *Carnos Kaelnos*." He says my betrothed's name in a deep voice and does an impression of Carnos looking off suddenly as if spotting a long-tailed deer.

"Sande…" I step away from him, not in the mood to be teased.

"What I mean is," he continues. "I have a plan—a way for us to leave Varasay."

"Leave?" I frown, wondering if he'll try to convince me to search for drifter boats again.

But Sande flashes an even brighter and more cheerful smile. "I've made some uppy friends at the track house, and I've learned a lot about the Sea Spread."

"Uppies can't be trusted," I say instinctively.

"Oh no, this has nothing to do with trust." Sande laughs. "You know how uppies like to brag? Well, it turns out uppies who've traveled the tide brag far more than the rest. Take a look at this…" He pulls a rectangle of paper out of his vest and unfolds a printed grid with uppy writing on it. Neither of us can read, so I'm not sure what he's showing me until he flips the paper over. There's a map on the other side.

"It's the Sea Spread." Sande runs his hand over it. "The whole world from top to bottom. I found it in the track house, and I've been asking questions and learning everything I can about it since. I think we should go here." He points to a small dot. "Ellevah. It's not close, but from everything I hear, we'll be happy. All sorts of people live there, there aren't many rules, and it's supposed to be beautiful and peaceful."

It's like Sande's a child again, ready to hide in the Teeterwood to make sure he gets his way.

"But traveling's not—"

"Just hear me out." Sande points to another dot. "You've heard of Beth, right? The closest city currentways? They aren't nice to their deeplanders, but the priests aren't allowed to punish anyone either. There's a king there instead of a chancellor, and a different set of laws. All the mountain cities are different, and we can explore them all. We just need passbooks and some courage, and we'll be free."

He makes it sound so easy, but deeplanders in Varasay aren't allowed to travel the tide.

Sande tucks the map back into his vest and wraps an arm around me. "Come on pretty Nerry, run away with me." Then he kisses me on the mouth, and I let him because, fathoms, I've missed him.

I didn't have to make a difficult decision about the baby last tide. Before I chose between banishment with an infant or a poison that would empty my insides, and before my stomach was too big to hide, I started to bleed. The baby seemed to know it wasn't welcome, and while I cried in Gren Tya's arms, it left me—she left me, all on her own.

This tide I have to make a decision, though, and even though I adore Sande and would much rather marry him, I also know how dangerous running away is. My mother broke Varasay's laws, and the city didn't hesitate to punish her. Despite my feelings, I have to be a boulder that won't move while the ocean passes by.

"I'm marrying Carnos." I step away from Sande. "I'm sorry."

He frowns. "Do you really want to live your whole life with that amphib? Wouldn't you rather take a risk with me?" He holds out the map again and points to a different dot. "See that tiny mark? That's Varasay." He then lifts his hand to the mountain looming over us. Varasay City glitters at the top, and at night it always looks like those distant rocks are covered with stars. "It seems so big, but it's just a speck on the map. The rest of the world, the Sea Spread, is much bigger. There's more than this, Nerene. More than Varasay."

I know he wants me to keep arguing because he is good at convincing people to change their mind.

And if I was going to argue with him, I'd say I want the safe life my mother longed for and never had. And although I wish I could share a life like that with him, it can't happen, and it hurts, yes, but I've accepted it.

"I'm marrying Carnos," I repeat, and I turn away from him and the husk-like dead boat. For once it doesn't seem like a comforting place. "If Gren wakes up, she'll be frightened and wonder where I am. I need to go home."

"You're not just marrying Carnos. You're giving up." There's an unfamiliar edge to Sande's voice.

Fathoms, he can be so charming, but he can also be so frustrating. He acts like it's easy to upend traditions simply because we don't like them. He acts like there would be no consequences.

"You gave up last tide too," Sande says. "Admit it, you did. I know you lost our baby, but if you hadn't, you would have gotten rid of it."

Now I feel like something has wrapped itself around my neck. Maybe there really are death shadows here. I turn to face him again although I'm further away now. "I hadn't made up my mind."

He gives me a look that's somehow searching, angry, and fond all at once. "I love you enough to risk everything. How much do you love me?"

I want to say that true love can't always rush recklessly forward but sometimes must endure and sacrifice. Yet I'm anxious about marrying Carnos and unhappy that I had to think about the baby again, so instead I say what Sande needs to hear. How much do I love him? An immense amount, of course.

But what I say out loud is, "Not enough."

I BRACE MY BACK against the wagon, pushing until my boots slip on the loose, gravel roadway and I have to scramble for better footing.

The tide gleams below as it seeps into our village. I see shallow pools on the plains, which I know will deepen through the day. By nightfall all that water will churn up and over the kelp trees, swallowing every cliff and cave on the lower slopes.

When the tide comes, we're usually already halfway up Varasay Mountain like we are today. But I've heard stories of elders misinterpreting the stars, of people waking up to drenched sleeping mats, and of frantic families wading to the mountain road, forced to leave everything behind.

"Would you like some water?" Gren Tya offers me a tin cup.

I shake my head and continue to strain against our wagon, which is piled high with dried amphib meat, waterpods, clothing and all sorts of belongings. This tide we're sharing our wagon with the Therins and Rinians, which also means we're sharing the task of hauling it up the curving road. At the moment, it's my turn to push, along with Cara Rinian and her uncle, Newis. Meanwhile, Gash Therin wears a leather harness and pulls up front. Unless you're very old, very young, very ill, or very pregnant, everyone in Saltpool helps haul the wagons to Varasay City.

"And are you thirsty, dear?" Gren offers the mug to Cara, who nods.

The Rinians and I tried to convince Gren to ride on our wagon this tide, but she refused. And now here she is, still trying to help. I understand that she doesn't want to be a burden, but I worry about her. Each tide, the climb from Saltpool to Varasay seems to drain her more.

"One of these winters, I should be polite and stay in Saltpool to welcome the sirens," she often jokes. And lately it seems less like a joke and more like a plan she's trying to feel braver about.

At least she's not pushing the wagon this time.

Like every year, the final sunedges of fall were a blur of labor. My fingers are still puckered and green from pickling the harvest, and my arms are scratched from crating wild hens, setting visconey traps, and gathering the last few waterpods growing in the deepest parts of Coral Lake. I spent three days disassembling the roof, door, and shutters of our hut, and then I dragged all that kelpwood over to the Therins so they could use it to build the wagon I struggle against now.

I also spent a day packing Gren Tya's stone-lined cellar with everything we aren't allowed to bring to Varasay, like butchering knives or amphib poisons. No matter how carefully I tuck and fold our belongings in oilskins, though, and no matter how meticulously I seal every seam with wax, I know the roaming ocean will breach at least one of those packets. After the tide passes, something is always ruined.

Last year it was my snapper darts. The year before it was our best ax.

For once though, I welcomed the exhausting winter preparations because they stopped me from thinking too much about my wedding.

I look for Carnos, but instead I see Sande further down the road. It's not his turn to push the wagon his family's sharing with Saltpool's healer, so he's walking with a dozen of Bessel's reed mats slung across his back; mats she'll sell at the barracks market. He looks at me for a moment—no, not at me, at my throat. He's surely noticed I'm not wearing my black shell necklace anymore; the one he made for me.

I haven't left a gift for the sirens in a long time, but I did this morning. I spread the necklace out on the windowsill of Gren's hut, and I know it will be gone after the tide passes.

The Threegod priests hate it when we leave gifts for the sirens. They say it's a form of Water Goddess worship, but a lot of the villagers do it anyway. I doubt many deeplanders believe sirens exist, but there's something comforting about keeping up our traditions. It's also a small, satisfying way to disobey the Varasay priests.

When I was small, my mother always hid trinkets in the dead boat and then told me that the sirens left them during the tide. We'd hunt for those treasures each spring, barefoot and muddy, and it was one of the few times I ever heard Maam laugh.

Leaving that necklace wasn't as difficult as marrying Carnos will be, but it still feels like an important step because it's something that can't be undone.

At dusk, our village stops for the night. We huddle around cookfires for a while and then make up beds inside the wagons for small children and beneath the wagons for everyone else. The deeplands have been getting chilly, but the air is even colder on the mountain, and there's also a bitter, constant wind. After sharing a simple meal of shell beets and crab with Gren, I put on my wildwool jacket, woven muffler, and knit hat, and then I wrap us in all the blankets we own.

"I'll miss you, you know," Gren whispers as we lie there shivering.

"You won't have to," I say. "I'll visit you every sunedge. I already told Carnos I will."

"You think so now," Gren says. "But when a young woman marries, everything changes. It should, though, and it's for the best."

It's not the cold that bothers me after that, it's those two terrible words—*everything changes.*

We reach Varasay the next morning and line up at the city gates, alongside the needle-covered trees of the Teeterwood.

Carnos stands near us with his mother and younger brother, and their wagon. His fur-trimmed cloak makes him look wider than he already is, and every so often, he gives my mittened hand an encouraging squeeze that grinds my knuckles together and makes my insides clench.

Around noon, the Gray Straps begin letting villagers into the city, but as always, it's a long process. They have to account for every deeplander, record harvests, search wagons for illegal items, and then assign us barracks units. I shiver as we wait. Not only is the wind relentless, but we're also standing in the shadow of the Laeros Light God Temple, which stretches high above the city walls.

For as long as I can remember, the temple has been under construction, appearing to grow beneath the scaffolding and tarps each time we arrive at the gates. The fluttering canvas shell is gone this tide though, and instead, pointed archways and slim pillars stand stern and tall. It's a beautiful building, but it must look out of place among the factories and housing towers of the lower city. I can only imagine it was built in this part of Varasay because the rest of the city is already so crowded.

My feet are stiff and numb when I finally hear a priest call for deeplanders who wish to marry.

About twenty people step forward with their families. Most of the couples are young, but there's one older pair. I wonder if they lost their spouses to illness and are remarrying, for only uplanders are allowed to divorce.

Sande's parents stand beside me, and I tense when the priest asks if I'm their daughter. Yet Gren was right to assume Bessel would cooperate. Sande's mother nods yes, says my full name, "Nerene Keel Olin," and confirms that we're all from Saltpool. His father, Trennet, goes as far as patting my arm and whispering, "Congratulations!" He and I have always gotten along, though.

I fight the urge to look around for Sande because I shouldn't care how he's reacting to Carnos and my registration. I know I'm making the right decision, whether he likes it or not.

Once the priest records all the engaged couples' names, it's time for the wedding ceremonies. Carnos and I follow him through the gate, and the only comforting thought I have is that at least our wedding will be over quickly. We'll walk to the small K'Gar Storm God temple near the wharf, the priest will recite a few Threegod prayers, and then we'll all be assigned barracks units.

But once we're through the huge city gates, the priest doesn't head for the docks. Instead he strides toward the impressive, gleaming doors of the new Laeros Temple, his robes swinging out behind him.

Fathoms, are Carnos and I going to be married in there? I stare up at the huge towers and polished carvings. The thought of being married in such a massive building makes me feel like somehow my union with Carnos will be even more unbreakable and eternal.

The other couples exchange excited smiles, and Carnos crushes my hand again. I'm so stunned, though, it hardly hurts. The familiar sounds of the lower city seem muffled too: the rumble of automotors, the drone of people in the street, the constant hiss and roar of the currentways desalination plant. I suddenly wish I had the familiar weight of Sande's black shell necklace around my neck, and I also feel a twinge of panic that the necklace really is lost forever. What was I thinking?

The temple is even more impressive inside with shiny brass decorations and countless electric lights that look like glass flames. Almost everything else seems to be made of creamy marble: the intricately carved pillars, the smooth floors, and even the many benches.

"Women over here please!" a priestess calls, her hair hidden beneath a tight-fitting hood.

She leads us brides into an oval room, and moments later a flurry of other priestesses enter and undress us as if we're small children. Then we take turns climbing into four copper bathing basins that stand on the far side of the room.

"I'd 'ave gotten married just for this bath," sighs one of the brides.

"Yeah, my sister's gonna be jealous," agrees Himmia, who's from my village. "She got married last tide, and it was just the same-old, nothing-special wharf wedding."

I'm probably the only bride who would rather have a same-old, nothing-special wharf wedding.

"Ooo, I hope we'll get to stay here for our wedding night!" cries a girl who, aside from her ample curves, seems too young to be getting married.

"Don't be silly," Himmia says. "It's a temple. Wedding nights aren't for temples. Wedding nights are for…" She hums in a playful way that makes all the brides laugh—except me. No one seems to notice my silence, though.

Then it's my turn. I'm told to climb into the basin furthest from the waiting brides. After three days of hiking up the cold mountain road, the hot water feels wonderful. I wish I could simply stay in the washbasin relaxing and soaking and perhaps skip the wedding altogether. Unfortunately a priestess begins washing my hair with soap that smells like uppy perfume, and her touch isn't exactly soothing. She seems determined to scrub every last grain of traveling grit from my hair.

The same priestess soon hurries me out of the basin and hands me a towel. Once I'm dry, she has me dress in a yellow robe that looks a lot like hers—although hers is hooded. Then she pulls my hair into a tight, straight Varasay braid.

After that I'm approached by a different priestess who holds a book and mechanical uppy pen. "I need your name and village."

"Nerene Keel," I say. "I'm from Saltpool."

She flips pages. "Ah… here you are… Nerene Keel Olin marrying Carnos Kaelnos from Riversborn." She makes a notation. "And you know about the procedure, yes? Once you've given birth to two children, you must report to Varasay City, even if the tide is out."

I nod again, thinking about Bessel. I've heard the procedure is painful, and every now and then, some poor woman gets an infection afterward and doesn't recover.

28

I also hate that the uppies constantly remind us about it as if we'll forget. They even hang posters in the barracks. The one I hate most shows a pretty woman holding two babies looking pleased as Gray Straps drag an ugly woman with three babies from the city.

When all of us deeplander women are clean and dressed, one of the priestesses leads us into the main worship hall. It's an impressive, intimidating space. The ceiling is a busy combination of stone arches and orange and yellow panes of glass, and we're surrounded by rows of identical benches that could surely seat several hundred worshipers. Only a few uppies are here now though, and they look at us impatiently as if our weddings are performances that should entertain them—but aren't. Fire burns bright in four hearths too, and somewhere I can't see, a musician plays a somber, sluggish melody on chimer bells.

I wonder what Sande would think of all this. He's always hated that the uplanders flaunt their wealth when we deeplanders have so little. I suppose it bothers me too, although I know things could be much worse. I don't remember my life with Maam that clearly anymore, but I still have some unhappy memories: the criminal bands hurting her, how cold we'd be when it snowed, how hungry we'd get —and worse, how thirsty. I remember one winter, Maam was unconscious for a whole day, and I thought she'd died. Then there was the winter when a velvet wolf stalked us, and we could never sleep at the same time.

Still thinking about Maam, I watch our grooms gather on the far side of the worship hall. They stand beneath a glittering, embroidered banner that depicts the immortals of Threegod: Laeros, Shale, and K'Gar. The banner above us women shows the defeated Water Goddess. I think she's supposed to be gravely injured, but to me she looks as if she's staring furiously over at Threegods, ready to rally and fight again.

Carnos catches my eye and nods.

I make myself smile in return, pulling my lips across my teeth. It's not fair to compare my feelings for him to my feelings for Sande. Carnos and I hardly know each other—our pairing only happened because Gren and Itanda's mother are childhood friends. As Carnos and I experience life together, I'm sure we'll develop some sort of loving bond. Or at the very least, I'll probably never have to talk him out of a reckless plan. He seems to have an abundance of good sense.

"All rise for the High Priest of Laeros!" a deep voice calls, and as the handful of uppies in the hall stand, an elderly man appears on a raised dais. He must be at least ten years older than Gren Tya, and he looks as if he's about to collapse beneath the weight of his ornate, many-layered robes. Like everything else in the temple, his garments are cream, gleaming gold, and copper, and surely he's meant to look as if he's blazing with sunlight. Instead I find myself thinking of the annoying orange jellycrabs that cling to our fishing nets, the ones that smear slime all over my fingers when I try to pick them off.

"Blessed are these deeplanders," the priest says, his words reverberating through the hall, surprisingly loud and strong. "May the favor of Laeros, K'Gar, and Shale be upon them."

The slippers the priestesses gave us to wear are so thin I feel like I'm standing barefoot. Pain shoots up through my tired ankles.

Hopefully this ceremony won't take long.

But despite his frail appearance, the High Priest has plenty of strength to talk about the new temple: how it's taller than all the other mountain city's temples, how it symbolizes Varasay's devotion to

Threegod, and how on clear days, one can see Beth, the neighboring mountain city, from its highest tower.

I dig a finger into the collar of my robes, trying to loosen them.

The High Priest then drones on about marriage and how having our weddings in the city represents the ongoing friendship between uplanders and deeplanders.

My collar really is far too tight, and why did they make us stand so close to a hearth? Is no one else uncomfortable? I look around at the other brides, but they all seem fine. They're either listening politely to the High Priest or trading smiles and winks with their betrothed.

Fanning my face with both hands, I'm vaguely aware of the High Priest telling the complicated story of how Laeros became a god and how he joined forces with K'Gar and Shale to defeat the Water Goddess when she tried to flood the world.

Sande probably thinks I'm already married. He and his parents have surely been assigned a barracks unit by now and are unpacking. I imagine Trennet and Sande dragging parcels up from the wagon while Bessel arranges cookware in the tiny alcove behind the door. Usually Gren Tya and I would be doing the same thing, and although the Rinians promised to help her until Carnos and I reach the barracks, I hope they aren't too busy with their own belongings.

This tide, though, I won't share Gren's barracks unit. I'll share one with Carnos, and in a short while, I'll be expected to do something there I don't really want to do.

I can't imagine it will be anything like it was with Sande, lying in the soft seagrass beneath the dead boat. Instead I find myself thinking of the wild dogs that sometimes mate with our village mutts on the dust plains. It's a horrible, stomach-turning thought, and once I think it, I can't push it out of my mind.

Even Gren was trying to give me advice last night. "It might not be pleasant at first. Just allow him to be persistent."

Persistent. My robes feel heavier and hotter than they were a moment ago.

I look at Carnos. He's watching the High Priest enraptured. His robes are too short, and the hem hangs a hands-width above the floor. The priests probably weren't able to find slippers to fit him either, for he's barefoot.

I clutch my middle, close my eyes, and lower my head. All of this will be over soon—even the part in our small barracks room on the thin cot.

"Nerene Keel Olin and Carnos Kaelnos!" a priest calls.

I look up, and it's as if I've been in a dark hut for hours rather than simply shutting my eyes for a moment. Gray spots blur the hall, and I'm still blinking my vision clear when a nearby priestess directs me to the dais.

At least Carnos and I will be married first, and I don't have to wait any longer. I breathe deeply in and out, and I feel like I'm leaving Sande's necklace on the windowsill of Gren's hut all over again. I'm sure that once I marry Carnos, I'll have second thoughts. But that's exactly why I have to do this. It can't be undone, and then I'll be safely married, and Sande and I will be out of each others' reach forever.

There's no swelling tide below me and no heavy wagon to push, but somehow climbing these dozen marble steps seems far harder than hiking up the mountain road. Carnos walks slowly beside me, matching my pace.

When we reach the High Priest, he takes us both by the hand. Up close he looks even older, with loose skin like fur oyster flesh and mucus in his eyes. "In the warmth and clarity of Laeros Light God," he booms, his breath smelling of springwine and the white stuff that grows on underoots when they're stored for too long.

I look over at Carnos, at his nose that looks like it has been broken at least once, at the freckles that seem so strangely arranged on just his chin, and at his large mouth that seems to have no teeth until he smiles very wide. Soon that face will press against mine, kissing me and more.

"... In admiration of the perseverance of K'Gar Storm God..." the High Priest continues.

I wonder if Sande will leave Varasay on his own, stow away on a ship, and explore the Sea Spread. If he does, he will probably never return. I'll never see him again.

"... And in the protection of Shale Stone God's eternal strength..."

If only another Saltpool family took pity on me ten tides ago. If only Gren could have adopted me. My vision blackens as if I've shut my eyes again. I imagine running down the mountain road, diving into the tide, and swimming through the cold shadows until I find my necklace.

"Do you pledge to be loyal to each other, second only to your devotion to Threegod?"

"I do," Carnos rumbles, his eyes on mine.

And then it's my turn to speak. Yet when I open my mouth, no words come out.

Instead my breakfast of pigeon eggs and greenberries surges up, splashing across the High Priest's robes and spattering the brand new marble dais.

"Looks like this is it, barracks building ten, Unit 34-C." The Gray Strap gestures to a steel door. Bare metal shows beneath chipped green paint, which shows beneath chipped red paint.

"Thank you," I say, still feeling queasy. And it's not just that I vomited an hour ago, I'm not married. I should be married. I planned on being married.

The Gray Strap grunts in reply, crumples a paper that surely had my barracks unit number written on it, and trudges off down the dark corridor.

Gren is probably sleeping, resting from the climb, so I don't knock. Instead I ease the door open, hoping the hinges won't groan.

But the handle is jerked out of my fingers, and the door opens from the inside. I look up to find Sande's mother, Bessel, staring at me, cooking knife and partially-peeled shell beet in her hand.

"What are you doing here?" she demands, and oh no, the Gray Strap who assigned me to this unit must have simply looked up my family in the city records.

Behind Bessel, Trennet and Sande also look at me in surprise. Trennet seems to be busy arranging reed mats on an upper bunk, and Sande's sitting cross-legged on a lower bunk surrounded by carving tools. I think he's sorting them.

"Someone made a mistake," I say, trying to avoid Sande's gaze. I've already spent too much time thinking about him today.

Their barracks unit is identical to the one Gren and I lived in last winter, with a tiny window, two bunk beds, and a narrow strip of shelving supposedly large enough to hold an entire family's belongings. I see the shelves here are already stuffed with fernflax thread for Bessel's weaving and bushels of food, such as underoot and savorpears. More food, tools, and clothes are crammed beneath the cots, behind the door, and piled on the empty fourth bunk.

"I'm so sorry," I stammer. "I told them I always stay with Gren. Do you know where her unit is?"

Bessel squints. "Why would you stay with Gren? Why wouldn't you stay with your husband?"

I look past her to Sande. His eyes are also full of questions.

"I didn't get married," I admit.

"Why not?" Bessel presses, her voice hardening, sharpening.

"I was sick," I tell her.

Sande's mouth curls up at the corners as he moves two mallets into a kelpwood chest.

"Why would it matter if you were feeling sick?" Bessel's face reddens.

35

"No, I wasn't *feeling* sick," I say. "I *was* sick—all over the High Priest of Laeros."

Bessel gasps.

Sande chuckles.

And I grimace. "Does anyone know where Gren Tya's unit is?"

Sande's eyebrows fly up as if suddenly realizing something, and he peers out from where he sits on the lower cot. "You can't stay with her."

"What? Why not?" I ask.

He smiles the sort of bright smile I rarely see him use in Varasay. It's the sort of smile he wears while wading on the beach, hiking around Coral Lake, or I suppose those few, daring times with me near the dead boat. "Since you got married—or were supposed to—the Gray Straps made Gren share a barracks unit with the Rinians." He looks at his parents. "I guess Nerene will have to stay here." His glittering eyes then return to me. "How disappointing."

Bessel rounds on Trennet. "No, this can't happen. I won't let this happen. I will not feed this girl or have her underfoot for three months."

"*Ack*, Bess, we'll figure it out." Trennet looks at me softly. "Nerene, I'd love to have you stay with us, but perhaps another family would be… a better fit."

Bessel nods so curtly her frizzy knot of hair bobs. "Yes, you've got some experience caring for old people, and there are certainly other elderly folk in the barracks. Go on, go to the arch house and sort it out."

"I'll come with you." Sande springs up from the cot.

Bessel doesn't miss much though. "Sande, I need you here."

"And I'll be fine on my own," I say, edging out the door.

36

"We'll be back before you know it." Sande grabs my hand and pulls me down the corridor before his mother can argue more. "So what really happened?" he asks as soon as we're in the stairwell. The Olin's unit is on the top of their barracks building, three floors up. Bessel must hate that.

"It happened just like I said, I felt hot—I was probably tired from the climb. And then by the time I'd cleaned up, the ceremony was over. A different priest finished the rest of the weddings."

Sande stops halfway down a flight of stairs. "So now will you admit it?" he asks quietly, even though there's no one around. "You don't want to marry Carnos."

"Yes, I do."

Sande raises a single eyebrow. "Your stomach doesn't seem to want to."

I push past him and keep walking down the stairs. "I didn't mean to be sick, and besides, nothing's changed. The priests say Carnos and I don't need to wait for the next tide. We'll just have to pay for our wedding, and as long as we don't mind getting married in a small temple—which is fine by me—it'll only cost fifteen paper shells. I'm sure Carnos and I can raise the money at the barracks market."

Sande keeps grinning at me. "All right, while you save money to marry someone who makes you sick, how 'bout I save money to buy us passbooks? I already have a few paper shells from working at the motorliner track house."

"Don't, please," I tell him because I don't want to know it's possible to run away. It's hard enough to make this decision.

Sande's smile vanishes. "Nerene, I won't stay here if you marry Carnos. I'm leaving no matter what."

I was afraid of that. "I'm just trying to protect you from… well, you can be so rash…"

Sande frowns. "Are you saying you're trying to protect me from *myself?*"

And no, that's not it, but I can't say anything else because a group of unfamiliar deeplanders are now clunking up the stairs with baskets of clothing and a crying toddling. People will still be arriving late into the night, especially from the villages that are further away from the mountain.

We can't really talk freely outside either, the steep lanes between the barracks buildings are full of deeplanders either unloading wagons or disassembling them for storage. We walk quietly, and I suppose I'm fine with that. I am a little worried about what Sande might do to get his way, but at the moment, I just want to know where I'm sleeping tonight. Hopefully Gren and I can be assigned an empty unit. I know she'll be disappointed that I haven't married Carnos yet, but I think she'll be relieved too. I'm sure she'd rather live with me than crowded in with the Rinians.

Sande walks in a bouncy, cheerful manner, and I try to ignore him as we make our way up the steep roads, through the barracks market, and over to the arch house. A tall fence runs around all the barracks buildings, and the arch house is the only way through it. The gate there has never been locked—at least not that I can remember—and I think its purpose isn't really to keep us deeplanders trapped but to remind the rest of Varasay that we aren't really like them.

There are five Gray Straps on duty, and they're all busy. Two are in the left wing of the arch house, sorting out arguments between new arrivals. Not all deeplanders get along, and there are several families who hate sharing the same barracks building. The three other Gray

Straps are assembling a wooden structure outside. I assume it's the platform for the Chancellor's annual tidewater speech, which will probably happen tomorrow morning. Sande and I wait for several moments, and then I catch the attention of a female Gray Strap. Even though she has two gunnerifes on her hips—the frightening, mechanical weapon of the city—she has a dainty look to her that I hope means she'll be understanding.

"Excuse me," I say, stepping into the arch house. "I'm in the wrong barracks unit. I always stay with a Saltpool elder named Gren Tya. I help her cook and clean and run her market booth. I was supposed to get married this tide, but I didn't, so now I'm assigned to the wrong unit."

The Gray Strap woman glances out the window of the arch house.

It seems like I'm losing her attention, so I speak faster. "Could you please put me in a unit with Gren Tya? My name is Nerene Keel."

Now the Gray Strap is staring at me without much of an expression. I think I overcomplicated my explanation, so I take a deep breath to start again. But before I speak, she says, "Do you have a unit assignment?"

"Yes."

"Who are you staying with?"

"Her adopted family," Sande offers politely, and I want to step on his foot.

"Then I don't see a problem." There is a clatter outside. It sounds like the platform has collapsed. The woman's eyes flick over to the window again, and her eyebrows lower.

"I always stay with Gren," I say, feeling like I'm floundering. It would be unthinkable to stay with the Olins. Bessel hates me, and

Sande doesn't hate me enough. "Gren needs my help," I add. "She depends on it."

"Then check on her daily." The Gray Strap pushes past me and heads out the door, shouting, "No, I said that goes on the *left* side. Is that the left side? I think that's the I-wasn't-listening side."

"I know how to solve your problem," Sande whispers as we head back outside. "It's rectangular and has pages."

I don't answer. I just stare at the barracks buildings—our prisons for the winter. All twelve of them stand in neat rows of four, yet from here they look uneven because they're built on such a steep slope. The setting sun makes one side of the tiled rooftops burn bright orange while the other side simmers dusty red.

"Nerry, I *am* sorry… mostly sorry," Sande says gently. "I don't like it when you're upset, and I wish you'd just trust me. I know we—"

He stops speaking abruptly, which is strange, so I turn around. I find him staring at the wooden platform, which the Gray Straps have finished assembling, podium and all. They're now hanging a large poster on the wall of the arch house. I'm used to seeing posters in the barracks, images that remind us to be in our homes before curfew or images that encourage us to visit the Threegod temples, but none of those posters are this large or colorful. It seems to show a factory with deeplanders lined up outside of it. There are also bright red words on the bottom that we can't read.

"Hey, what does that say?" Sande asks the nearest Gray Strap.

"This? Says, 'do your part.'" The man glares at us. "Yeah, just you deeplanders wait."

COLD WIND SEEPS through my wildwool jacket the next morning as I stand with Carnos to hear the Chancellor's tidewater address. All the villages surrounding Varasay Mountain have arrived now, and almost two thousand of us are crowded into the barracks market, a cobblestone-covered plaza near the arch house. The sun is bright and cheerful but unfortunately not strong enough to warm us, and I hear a lot of the deeplanders around me complaining about how tired they are. It always takes a sunedge or two for everyone to get used to sleeping in the saggy barracks cots again.

"Are you feeling better?" Carnos asks as we watch a shiny, black automotor park on the other side of the fence.

"Yes," I say.

He was so kind to me yesterday on that dais—worried I would faint and wanting to carry me down the steps. Then later, as we walked back to the barracks, he was concerned that I'd be sad about our postponed wedding. He may not be a complex person, but he is kind. I should hurry up and marry him.

It's not Chancellor Noble who climbs out of the automotor. It's someone younger and skinnier, wearing a striped, gray uppy suit.

Does Varasay have a new chancellor?

As troubled murmurs move through the crowd, my thoughts turn to Gren Tya. I tried to visit her on my way to the plaza, but she was still sleeping.

The young uppy man climbs onto the platform and stands behind the podium, which is draped in the Varasay colors of silver and aqua. He gives us an indulgent wave as if we're cheering rather than staring, and now that I can see him more clearly, he does look like the Chancellor. He has the same burst of dark hair, scattered freckles, and prominent nose. He also looks just as ridiculous as the Chancellor often does in his expensive uppy finery. The silliest part of his outfit are the black tassels on his shoulders. I'm sure he thinks they make him seem strong and Carnos-like, but I think it looks like some of the strange creatures that live in the deepest, darkest parts of the tide have attacked his jacket.

"Greetings citizens of Varasay's lower plains," the stranger says, and his voice is oddly loud. It must have something to do with the thin, metal contraption on the podium. Uppies do love their gadgets. "I am Giron Noble, and I am Chancellor Fess Noble's son. My father asked me to speak to you this tide, and I was extremely honored. Not only do I have a deep respect for deeplanders—" here, he pauses for laughter that doesn't come— "it's also my job to arrange the details of your stay, and I've been working tirelessly on improvements." Giron now applauds and smiles at us as if we should clap along.

No one does.

Rather than let his clapping fade away pitifully, Giron seems to think it best he end with a showy, loud, double clap. It makes his sound device crackle and hum. He then keeps speaking, and what he says sounds rehearsed. "For countless years, Varasay has graciously provided you with homes and the opportunity to sell your goods while the tide passes. I'm sure you are aware that our city has become more crowded, and Mount Varasay, stubbornly, will not grow larger. Every tide it's more challenging to keep your barracks homes available for you. Therefore, since we here in Varasay City are generous hosts, we ask that you deeplanders be generous guests."

Somewhere behind me, I hear Sande mutter, "Giving them two-thirds of our harvest and all of our landrunner kills is already pretty generous."

I bristle and look back at him. I didn't realize he was so close.

He winks.

"I've always said that deeplanders are a proud people who don't want charity." Giron's voice bounces off the brick walls of barracks buildings two and three. "But there is something you lack that I would love to offer you, which is… an education."

There is mild, hesitant applause because most of us know that if an uppy offers something that sounds too good to be true, it's surely too good to be true.

Giron smiles in a stiff, toothy way that I think is meant to be kind. "So I've come up with a solution. It will give you a chance to repay us for housing you and a chance to learn new skills that will enrich your lives. I've asked my people to use the phrase 'win-storm.' It's like windstorm but with win instead of… well, you understand.

43

So now I invite all of you to experience a 'win-storm' with me, for every deeplander between eight and sixty-five tides will be awarded a factory job!"

"A factory job?" I echo.

"Awarded?" Sande grumbles.

Giron steps back so we can better see the poster hanging on the arch house wall. "So here, take a look at this. I know many of you can't read, so it says 'do your part' there on the bottom. And right now I'm promising you that I will 'do my part' to make sure you always feel at home in Varasay. I wish you calm waters!"

An uproar of conversation ripples through the crowd, and people shout out questions like, "What about the barracks market?" and "How much will we be paid?" and "How will we care for our children?"

"At least we'll be able to pay for our wedding more quickly now," Carnos says with an uncertain happiness.

But I only feel dread. I've seen tired factory workers in the lower city. I've heard about the ugly accidents that leave people without arms or legs.

"Please! Please. Don't everyone shout. I'm happy and prepared to answer questions." Giron smiles so wide his molars are visible. "Now I've thought through the age requirements carefully, so either your older children or your elderly will be free to care for your infants and toddlings. Parents can also request alternating day and night shifts. The barracks market has an even simpler solution; rather than operate daily, it will only be open on K'Gar third day, which coincides perfectly with your sunedge day of rest. And there's no need to concern yourself with shell papers or coins. To simplify things, your earnings will be put into a fund that will pay for the rent and upkeep of the barracks buildings. See? I have thought of everything."

Again he claps and seems to expect us to clap too. Again we're silent.

At least Giron's factory jobs will give me good reason to frequently leave the Olin's barracks unit. When Sande and I returned last night from talking to the Gray Straps and told Bessel I'd have to stay, she stormed off to the arch house to try and solve the problem herself. Of course she had no more success than we did, and she hasn't spoken to me since.

"What if we don't want a job?" Sande shouts. "What if we refuse to work?"

But Giron doesn't hear him or at least pretends not to hear. Instead he gives a hasty run through of the usual reminders about the procedure, curfew, and that we're required to visit the Threegod temples every sunedge. When Giron's finished, he adds a final, firm comment that sounds less polished than everything else he's said. "You deeplanders should be thankful. It's a hard truth maybe, but if we didn't let you into our city, you'd drown. Know that a lot of uplanders, loud uplanders, think life would be easier if you didn't exist. I'm trying to protect you." He then climbs down from the podium, shooting us a disappointed, somewhat irritated look. Perhaps he really thought we'd appreciate his work assignments. Maybe in some confused way, he believes he's helping us.

I think we might welcome jobs in the lower city if they were optional and we could save our pay. But I don't think many people, deeplander or uplander, like changes that are forced on them, especially changes that don't seem fair.

After Giron leaves the barracks with his four burly guards, a Gray Strap tells us that we'll have to line up in the market this afternoon to be assigned jobs and that those who arrive early will have more options. Since Giron took his voice-enhancing device with him, the Gray Strap's words are nearly drowned out by the rising hum of discussion.

"He didn't answer me." Sande glares at the poster. "I want to know what happens if we refuse to work. Will they banish us?"

"Let's not find out," I say.

Carnos's mother, Itanda, tucks her dark curls beneath her knit hat. "I think it'll be interesting to learn about Varasay's mechanical wonders. Those gadgets could make our lives easier. I'd like to drive an automotor up the mountain road instead of pushing a wagon." She doesn't look at me while saying any of this, and I suppose she's surely not happy with my weak stomach during the temple wedding.

Sande shakes his head. "They won't teach us what they teach other uppies. They'll show us how to do one thing, which will probably be something boring, like tightening a bolt, and that'll be it. I know how those factories are."

Carnos turns grimly to me. "Nerene, it will be difficult to marry. I don't know how we'll raise the money if we can only sell our goods at the barracks market every…" I see he's counting days in his mind. Three days for each god, so…

"Ninth day," I say gently, helping him out. "Well, if we have to wait until next tide, we'll wait."

"It'll be hard to save money for anything," Sande says. And I know he's thinking about passbooks.

We part ways with Carnos's family because they are in barracks building seven which is to the right. Building ten, our building, is on the left.

"This is how it starts," Sande says. "I got paid at the track house… maybe I won't next spring."

I was thinking that too, but I say, "At least Threegod doesn't approve of slavery." Perhaps there is an upside to the Threegod priests being so powerful in Varasay City.

"They'll find a way around that. Why do you think Giron says we're getting paid even though we'll never see money? It's already slavery, it's just slavery in disguise. The uppies say they don't want us here, but they also refuse to let us travel the tide. What does that tell you?" Sande picks up a rock and throws it against a nearby brick wall. He then turns to building ten's entrance, an arched opening that leads to the stairwell. When I keep walking, he says, "You're not coming in?" He grins and adds, "I bet you want to visit more with my maam."

I smile and shake my head. "Sadly I need to check on Gren."

She's in building twelve, and I'm glad that at least her unit is on the ground floor. The Rinians aren't home, and I guess they're still at the barracks market talking with other deeplanders about work assignments. I'm also pleased to see that although Gren's skin is ashy and she's tucked beneath several blankets, she's sitting up and wearing her favorite dress—the purple one that she's sewn a lot of dream markings on. Whenever deeplanders have prophetic dreams, we stitch images on our clothes to remind us of the details.

"Oh no, don't look at me like that, Nerene," she says and then coughs. "You know how the climb gets to me. Give me another day, and I'll be up and running around the market. Now as for you, seems like you're bringing me some bad news."

I nod, cringing because I have plenty of terrible things to share. "Did you hear what happened with Carnos?"

"Do you mean, did I hear that you two didn't get married?" Gren waves her bony hand at me. "News travels fast when you vomit on a priest."

47

I flush. "Bessel thinks I have a nervous condition."

Gren snorts. "Bessel couldn't find a rotten fish if it were stuck up her nose."

"I'm still going to marry him," I say. "Sande and I just have to find a way to pay the temple fees."

"Sande and you?" Gren tilts her head.

"Carnos and I," I correct myself. "You know what I mean."

"I know what you said," Gren laughs, but it quickly turns into another coughing fit that leaves me worried.

"Can I make you some tea?" I ask, looking around for the Rinian's kettle. In such a small unit, you'd think it would be easy to find, but I'm surrounded by stacks of honey candles. The candles are what the Rinians sell in the barracks market, just like how Gren and I sell dried herbs, the Narroes sell carved kelpwood spoons, and the Olins sell woven reed mats. The candles certainly take up a lot of space, but at least they smell pleasant.

As I search for a kettle and then decide to use a cookpot to heat water instead, I tell Gren about the factory jobs. Thankfully she won't have to have one because of her age.

"Now isn't that a cockled idea," she says. "What's everyone going to eat by the time the tide drains out?"

I hadn't thought about that, and she's right, it'll be tough. We deeplanders sell our goods for uppy money when we first arrive in Varasay, but by the time the tail-end of the ocean passes, we're usually trading our wares for tinned vegetables and meat instead. No matter how much food we haul up from the deeplands, it never lasts through the winter.

Gren sighs in a thin, wispy way. "At least I'm good at making little ones do what they're supposed to."

Yes, Gren is wonderful with children, but I have trouble imagining the frail woman on the cot chasing wild toddlings or wrestling uncooperative babies into clean nappers. I sit on the edge of her bed and hold her hand. "You took wonderful care of me."

"I did." She smiles at me with crinkly eyes. "And perhaps this old shell still has a pearl in her yet."

I'm not sure what she means, but hearing her use one of her wise-old-lady phrases is reassuring. It's a sign she'll get better.

"Go find that blue tin of mine," she says. "You'll have to dig around under this cot, but you know the tin I mean. That Mernor Rinian probably shoved it all the way to the back, even though I told him to put it where I could reach it."

I do as she asks, and yes, I know the tin she's talking about. We usually store our rarest herbs in it, like moss sage and silvany weed, because it can be locked.

Gren takes the key out of a buttoned pocket on the front of her sweater and opens the tin. As I expect, there are dozens of little cloth bags of herbs tucked inside and some stoppered glass bottles too. Carefully removing the contents and placing them on her knit blanket, Gren then pries up the bottom of the tin. "Ooo, a secret compartment!" she tells me, looking smug. "Oh, huh… I forgot I had a snapper in here. Well, you should take it too."

She hands me a thin leather pouch on a cord.

"Gren!" I can't believe she risked smuggling a snapper into the city. Paralyzing darts certainly aren't allowed in Varasay.

"If you're working in a factory, you should have some bite 'round your neck," Gren says. "Who knows what might happen in those places."

"I can't risk getting caught with this," I say, but Gren wiggles her bony fingers as if flicking my concerns away.

"Just don't let anyone see it. I always have one on me." Next she pulls out a sealed, waxed canvas wallet. "Now this is what I was looking for; plenty of paper shells and coins. I've saved them up over the years, and it's more than enough for your wedding."

I turn the wallet over several times and then examine the delicate money inside. It's soft, almost like fabric, and there are images of different shells printed on each bill. There are also about a dozen coins. "I can't take this."

"You can, and I'm going to make you." Gren noisily shuts the tin. "We both know what happens when you're in reach of Sande. You must run from trouble, Nerene." She chuckles. "Run all the way to Riversborn."

I laugh too, but it's good advice. I caught myself listening to Sande's breathing as we fell asleep last night. And not only was I paying too much attention to the even, steady sound of his breath, I also longed to slip out of my bunk, cross the cold, concrete floor, and join him under the wildwool blankets. And of course I didn't do it, wouldn't do it, but wanting to is still a problem.

Tucked in the middle of the paper money, I find a stiff rectangle of cardpaper that has glossy uppy letters printed on it. There is also a symbol that looks like a weapon with three spikes. "What's this?"

Gren glowers at the cardpaper. "Oh that. I got it from some uppy tide merchant… He wanted to buy a child. Can you believe it? I said, 'no sir, all you'll get from me is dried rain mint.'"

I sit up straighter, surprised. "Buy a child? Whatever for?"

"I'm sure it wasn't to be kind to it," Gren says darkly.

How odd. Tide merchants usually don't visit our market either, for there are so many other markets closer to the wharf. Yet I suppose there are also plenty of Gray Straps near the harbor, and this type of man probably wanted to avoid them.

It's also odd that Gren has kept this cardpaper for all these years. I'm about to ask her why, when she says, "Throw that away, won't you?"

"Of course," I say. But I'm troubled by her story, and as I tuck the cardpaper into my jacket pocket, I've already decided to keep it.

I sit and talk with her until the Rinians return, and although I'd love to stay longer, there's just not enough room for all of us in a single barracks unit. Leaving their small, temporary home, I step back out into the drowsy winter sunlight and begin to walk over to barracks building seven to tell Carnos about Gren's generous gift. But I only get as far as building ten.

Perhaps I shouldn't spend this money on a wedding, at least not yet.

It might be smarter to wait a sunedge or two just to see how Giron's work assignments affect life in the barracks.

I know Gren is trying to help me, but if food becomes scarce, I may need to help her.

The Gray Straps assign Trennet a cleaning job at the big currentways desalination plant, and his shift starts before dawn. Bessel has to work at a boot factory, and although she says the boots are badly designed and the leather is low-quality, I can tell she's excited about using a stitching machine. "It moves really fast," she tells us after her first day. "It took some time to get the settings right, but then I got so much done. At this pace, they'll have to give me a new work assignment after rest day. I'll have made boots for everyone around the Sea Spread by then!"

As for me, like many young deeplanders, I have to work in a new factory owned by Giron Noble. There are several rumors about why Giron's hired so many younger workers, such as the other factory owners prefer stronger and more mature workers, or Giron thinks young workers have more energy. But I think it's because he still wants deeplanders to consider his work assignments a type of education. If all the youngest deeplanders go to the same place, it will almost seem like an uppy school.

Because of Sande's experience at the deepland track house, he's given a rare opportunity; the chance to choose his job. He can either work at the desalination plant with his pa or at Giron's factory with me. And surprise, surprise, he chooses the factory.

"This way we can keep each other company," he tells me with a smile.

But if Sande thought that working at the same factory would mean spending our days together, he's mistaken. When we arrive for our first shift, we're split into groups of boys and girls. I don't know where the boys go, but us girls are sent up a flight of concrete stairs and told to put on uniforms—pale gray smocks, thin stockings, dark blue aprons and kerchiefs to tie back our hair. Once we're wearing our uncomfortable clothes, we're arranged along what the foreman calls an industry line. On my left, a young girl I don't know must drill holes in sheets of metal using a machine as tall as she is. Those hunks of metal then travel down a conveyance belt to me, and I'm supposed to force rubber tubing through the holes. After that a worker named Amista, who is from Saltpool and is surely only ten tides old, must feed copper wires through the rubber tubes. I ask what we're making, but the foreman doesn't seem to know or care.

"I get paid per crate," he says. "So you better move fast, or I'll make you work a double shift and you'll have to drag all night." Dragging, we learn, means hauling leftover metal scraps across the factory, so they can be melted and reused.

The first day is terrible. The conveyance belt moves too quickly and none of us can keep up. Worse, Giron often strolls around our floor making humming noises of disapproval. At one point he tugs the rubber tubing out of my hand and forces it through the metal sheet himself. "It's like you're not even trying," he tells me.

Our midday break is short, and I scald my tongue trying to gulp down a bowl of soup before it ends. Then we're herded back to the industry line, back to standing on sore feet, and back to hunching over the conveyance belt. The production floor is hot too. Sweat soaks my uniform and stockings.

"I'm sorry I'm slow, but this is hard," says the girl on my left—I think she's from Pirock. The drill she's operating is so large I'm sure it would tire Carnos out.

Once that first horrible day is over, I find out what happened to Sande.

"Oh it's been great," he tells me as we walk back to the barracks. "I've been slicing copper with a giant saw that might chop off all of my fingers." He massages his hands, which are covered in blisters. Some of his sores have even torn open and the skin beneath is angry and pink.

Carnos visits me that night to see how my first day went. The uppies assigned him a job at the harbor, and he'll be moving goods on and off the steamships when they arrive. "Since there are no ships yet, we cleaned out a storehouse today, and it was hard work," he says. "But I can tell it will make me stronger. When we return home, I'm sure I'll be a better hunter."

"I don't think my work will improve me," I say miserably as we stand in the corridor outside the Olins' barracks unit.

"It will give you strength here." Carnos places gentle fingertips on the top few ribs of my chest, which is actually sweet, but then he adds, "You will need a lot of patience when you become a mother." And even though he may be right, I don't like the reminder that the two children I'm allowed to have will surely be with him. I also don't like that my future children will probably have to work in a factory too.

Again I consider telling Carnos about Gren's money. He would surely understand why I want to save it, for if he's anything he's practical. But just at that moment, Sande's laughter floats out of the nearby doorway, and I say nothing.

The next day of factory work is the same, right down to the bland soup, which we eat in a chilly alley beside the factory's cookery. The day after is the same again, and I start to feel as if I'm living a particularly awful day over and over.

On the sixth day, the poor girl on my left cries through her shift. I've learned her name is Selestea. And on my right, Amista curses whenever our supervisor's out of earshot—which is often because of the deafening drill. I'm shocked at how many gritty words she knows.

"Can I switch with Selestea?" I ask our supervisor when he passes by. "I'm bigger and stronger."

"It's not like it's up to me." He doesn't even stop walking. "Master Noble makes those decisions."

And when I ask Giron, he says no.

That night Sande and I trudge into our barracks unit exhausted and ready for some of Bessel's fish stew. She usually has it ready because she's the first to arrive home, but tonight she's just sitting on her lower bunk motionless.

"What's wrong?" Sande asks.

She looks at him with red-rimmed eyes. "Your pa is dead."

THE GRAY STRAPS didn't tell Bessel much, or maybe she was too shaken to ask many questions. All she knows is that there was an accident at the desalination plant, Trennet died, and most likely, no one can reach his body for a few days.

At least a fellow Saltpool villager, Newis Rinian, was also working at the plant, and he's able to give us more details. Apparently an uppy worker fell into a saltwater reservoir—one of the big tanks that stores tide water before processing. The man couldn't swim, for not too many uppies can, and so the workers tried to throw him a rope. Trennet offered to jump in but was told not to. The plant workers said that if the pumps turned on, the man would be sucked down to the bottom of the tank. Someone ran to make sure the pumps were off—they were on clockwork controls—but Trennet didn't wait. Perhaps the man was going under, perhaps Trennet figured he was a strong swimmer who could fight any current, but whatever the reason, he jumped in.

"Well at first everything was fine," Newis tells us, looking miserable. "He swam over to that man and grabbed 'em and was pulling him to the ladder. But then there was this awful rumblin' that shook the whole building—the pumps had turned on. And then... just like that, Trennet and the uppy man—they were gone."

We're told Trennet's body is stuck somewhere in the filtration system and can't be reached until the entire plant is drained. Even more upsetting, we hear uppy workers at the plant are angry about missing several days pay. They blame us deeplanders for shutting down the plant—never mind that it was an uppy who first fell into the tank.

Bessel doesn't cry much, but she also doesn't seem to sleep. All night long, I hear her whispering things like, "How am I supposed to survive now?" or "Why would he do this to me?" As for Sande, he's unusually quiet and unusually still. I was already feeling like an intruder in their barracks unit, but now it's worse. I feel like I'm clumsily standing in the middle of what should be private family grieving.

I'm sad too, though. I always liked Trennet, and it's terrible that he died in such a frightening way. I can't help but morbidly wonder where his body is and how long it took between the dreadful moment he knew he couldn't fight the suction of the pumps and the moment he drowned. I hope it wasn't long.

Plant workers recover Trennet's body two days later, and he doesn't look like himself anymore. Instead he looks like a spongy, gray doll or the empty-eyed statues that stand near Threegod temples.

I help with the grim task of wrapping his remains in fernflax cloth, and then we place him on a litter of woven reeds. Since we can't bury anyone while the tide passes and we don't tend to burn bodies like uplanders, the priests let us float our dead into the currents.

Usually we say our final goodbyes at dawn, but we take Trennet to the harbor at midnight because we have to work our shifts first.

Sande carries the litter through the lower city with his close friend Leej, fellow villagers Newis and Mernor Rinian, as well as Carnos and his brother Marl—who insisted that they help. Bessel follows her husband's body, silent and sad.

I walk even further behind them with a group of Saltpool villagers and other deeplanders who knew Trennet. Gren hobbles along with us too, and although it's good to see her outside, I worry about her. She's still very weak, and it's cold tonight. It hasn't snowed yet, but the air has the icy smell of snowflakes.

A fitful wind tugs at the fernflax wrapped around Trennet's body. It makes me think grim thoughts like perhaps his death shadow is still trapped inside him fighting to fly free.

I haven't been to the wharf yet this tide. Sande and I often watch the first steamships arrive, but I doubt we'll have time for that with our new jobs. The boats won't be here for another few days either since it's not wise to sail too close to the leading edge of the ocean.

And not only is it strange to see the docks so empty, I'm also not used to seeing them at night. Deeplanders are supposed to be inside the barracks fence at sundown. Today, though, we have special permission to be out late. The rows of concrete piers look so lonesome in the dark. Only a few of the electric lights are on, and there are no workers shouting to each other or autohaulers rumbling through.

A priest joins us to say prayers of the dead on behalf of K'Gar, Shale, and Laeros. We gather beside him near a launch ramp that leads down into the black water. There, a small uplander fishing boat waits to tow Trennet's litter further into the tide. The currents wouldn't carry him off otherwise.

The priest recites his prayers as soon as we're assembled, and he speaks quickly as if longing for his warm bed in the temple dormitory.

I'm sure there was once Water Goddess prayers for the dead too, and I wish I knew them.

After the priest says a final, "Praise Threegod," Carnos thumps a hand on Sande's shoulder. "If only I could avenge your father's death. I never knew my father. He died when I was small, and I was looking forward to knowing yours."

Carnos's naive kindness almost makes me smile, but now is probably not the best time for him to befriend Sande. I step forward to intervene, but to my surprise, Sande covers Carnos's hand with his own and says, "If there was a way to avenge my pa, I'd welcome your help."

Bessel weeps as the fishing boat tows Trennet's litter out into the water, and I don't think I've ever heard her cry. There's a hollow, rough sound to it.

I watch the fishing boat move slowly away, its uppy motor growling, and I realize something. I decided to marry Carnos because I wanted to keep Sande and me safe from temptation and safe from punishment. But life near Varasay is perilous no matter who I marry, especially now that we're being forced to work. Trennet followed the city's rules, and he still suffered. I'm also sure he won't be the last to die in the factories.

I think of the wallet Gren gave me and the paper shells inside.

Perhaps it's time to spend that money.

When we return to barracks building ten, I wait for Bessel to use the scrubpits on the first floor, and as soon as she's gone, I climb into Sande's bunk and kiss him all over his face and neck.

"Nerene?" He blinks. "What are you…"

"I have the money we need to buy passbooks," I say between kisses. "Gren gave it to me for my wedding, but I won't let my children work in these awful factories, and I won't watch you die in one. Let's go to that faraway city of yours." I touch his dark brown curls. "Elvah, wasn't it?"

"Ellevah, it's called Ellevah." Sande wipes his eyes, still red from crying. "And yes. Yes! Let's go. I'll get us passbooks." Now he kisses me all over my face and neck, pressing me back onto the rope netting of the cot, folding me up against him. And oh I've missed him and this—

But we can't let it go on. Bessel will be back soon.

So I reluctantly untangle myself, climb down from Sande's cot, and find Gren's wallet under my blankets. Handing the canvas pouch to him, I say, "I hope this is enough money. You find us passbooks, and I'll have Carnos tell me which steamship we should travel on." I feel terrible using Carnos any more than I already have, but since he works at the docks, he'll probably know which ships are in port. He probably won't question why I want to know either.

The next morning Sande seems brighter and more energetic than he's been all tide. He rises early to make us sweet river rice for breakfast, taking care to brown a crunchy crust on the bottom of the pan. Bessel is too miserable to notice his changed mood. She used to spend her mornings gleefully complaining about how our neighbors stored too many things in the shared corridor or boasting about how she could design better boots at the factory where she works. But since Trennet drowned, she hardly talks, and when she's not working, she often stays in bed.

As soon as Sande and I leave for our factory shift, I say, "Do you want your maam to come with us?"

He gives me a grateful look. "I didn't want to ask. I know she's always awful to you, but I'm also worried about leaving her here alone. Maybe if we travel to someplace nicer, she'll be nicer."

I nod, wishing Gren could come too, but of course she can't. It's not just that she's older and ill, her family is here—her daughters and their children. I'll miss her intensely though. As Gren would say, I'll miss her like a shucked clam misses its shell.

I'll miss her like I still miss my maam.

It takes Sande another sunedge to find all three passbooks.

"It wasn't easy," he whispers to me during the only day the uppies now let us sell our wares at the barracks market—K'Gar third day. "I had to go to the UPT merchants, and not the friendly ones—the ones who look like they can crack open waterpods with their bare hands."

"I'm glad you got the passbooks though," I say under my breath, while also smiling at the two uppy women rummaging through my baskets of dried herbs. I wish they'd be more careful and not mix everything up.

"Oh don't buy those," one woman says to the other. "You can get them shipped in from Suthrellon, and they're much cheaper."

"Mine are fresher," I say loudly. I don't know if that's true, but it's worth a try. The more steamships roaming the tide, the less we deeplanders sell.

Thankfully a few regular Varasay customers stop by too. Most of them run cookeries or prepare food for wealthier uppies, and many of them ask about Gren and are concerned when they hear she's ill. One woman, Parsita, even promises to bring by a healing tea that she says can get rid of a cough. "You'll have to pay for it though," she tells me. "I can't just give things to deeplanders for free."

Later that night, while Bessel sleeps, Sande shows me the passbooks he bought.

"I tried to find ones that match our ages," he whispers as we examine his purchases beneath the dim electric lights in the quiet corridor outside unit 34-C. I expected the passbooks to be sturdy and large, like the Varasay record books, but they're remarkably small—only about the size of my hand. They're also covered with soft amphib leather and embossed with various golden symbols that must represent different mountain cities. The first page of my passbook has information written on it that I can't read, and the rest of the pages are mostly blank. I do notice a few ink stamps though—a seapony, a mountain dog, and a star urchin.

"Some cities stamp your book," Sande explains, although then he adds an uncertain, "I think."

I hold the book meant for me. Apparently I'll have to pretend I'm someone named *Voreska Mynd*, and Voreska is twenty tides old not eighteen. "Are you sure that's what this says?" I touch the tiny, printed words. "Those merchants might have lied to you."

"They might have." Sande closes his passbook. "But I think it's a risk worth taking." He runs a finger across my cheek. "There's a girl in Ellevah named Voreska, and I'd like to marry her."

"If she'll have you," I laugh. I don't like the name Voreska, but I suppose I'll just have to think of a nickname.

We also decide not to tell Bessel our plans just yet.

"I know my maam—if she thinks about leaving for too long, she'll get scared and refuse to go." Sande moves out of the soft yellow light and into the shadows.

I nod. "Let's tell her about the trip when everything's ready."

Gathering information about the steamships is as easy as I expect, although I do feel intensely guilty about it. I start visiting the wharf after my factory shifts, and although I cringe every time Carnos proudly introduces me as his betrothed, he does know a lot about the ships.

Because we don't have enough of Gren's money left to travel on a passenger ship, and it would be risky to pretend to be a family of uppies, we'll have to stow away on a boat—at least until we reach the next mountain city. There, I hope we're able to find work so that we can continue our journey more honestly.

I soon find a ship that will be perfect for our escape—*The Sunset's Splendor*. Despite her pretty name, she's a massive shipping vessel—a traveling warehouse really—and she's stocked with specialty foods from around the Sea Spread. According to Carnos, rich uppies love eating fruits, nuts, and meat from distant lands, and they'll pay huge amounts of money for them.

Therefore, if we stow away on the *Sunset's Splendor*, we'll have plenty to eat, and because the boat is so big, there are probably lots of good hiding places too.

However, since the ship is only docked in Varasay for two days, Sande and I must act quickly.

The hardest part is telling Bessel. I worry she'll be afraid to leave, and I worry she'll be furious that Sande and I care about each other as much as we do.

I let Sande handle it, and he wisely doesn't focus on me. "Pa would want you to be happy," he tells her. "He'd want us to have a better life."

Bessel listens quietly, then she examines our passbooks and asks how we paid for them. She hardly reacts when I admit the money was meant for my wedding, and I'm not sure if that's a good or bad sign.

That night we pack our belongings and dress in dark clothes. I feel calm and brave for the most part, but when it's time to say goodbye to Gren, I'm overwhelmed with tears.

To my surprise, Bessel takes pity on me. "How about you two walk over to Gren's unit together?" she says to Sande. "Nerene could probably use the company."

And maybe he was right. Maybe Bessel only hated me because she was unhappy.

"At least Gren's too old to work in the factories," Sande says as we walk down the thin lane between barracks buildings.

"That's true," I sniffle.

I long to tell Gren about our plans, but the Rinians are with her, and there are just too many deeplanders in the corridors of their barracks building. It seems like everyone who lives in building twelve spends their evenings visiting neighbors and sharing food. It's actually quite lovely although not helpful right now.

Gren seems to sense something is happening though, and surely she can see I've been crying.

"I love you, my third daughter," she tells me, and to Sande she says, "Now you take care of her, or I'll haunt you as a death shadow."

"She knows," I say as we walk back to building ten, huddled together because it's now raining. Grumpy winter weather is probably for the best tonight, though. It'll be easier to sneak aboard the *Sunset's Splendor* if the shipsmen don't want to be drenched standing guard.

We soon return to our barracks unit, where we've left our baggage and Bessel, who's hopefully ready to leave. We find her stoking a fire in the small cookstove that's built into the wall.

"What are you doing?" Sande asks. "We already ate."

"Oh I'm not cooking," Bessel says, and instead of looking at him, she smiles at me. "I burnt the passbooks."

I NEVER THOUGHT Sande was like his parents, but I see it now. The Olins will all go to dramatic lengths to either make something happen or to get their way. Trennet jumped into a saltwater tank to save an uppy worker, and now here's Bessel, burning our passbooks.

"What! What? Why?" Sande rushes forward, grabs a poker, and yanks open the oven. I pull aside a reed mat as he scatters burning crumbles of ash onto the concrete floor.

The passbooks are destroyed, though. There's nothing left of them that's recognizable, aside from shriveled, blackened covers.

Bessel calmly closes the door to our barracks unit. "I didn't have a choice, Sande. That girl influenced you like she always does. You were making poor decisions."

By *that girl* she means me.

Sande stares at his mother, speechless, his arms shaking.

"It's her fault I had the procedure," Bessel continues. "And only a mad woman would make herself vomit on a priest just to get assigned to your barracks unit. And now here she is, putting tricky little thoughts into your head about running away. She might as well be a siren, Sande. When you're near her, you don't think straight. It's like she has wavurl."

"Stop talking," Sande shouts. "*Stop.*"

"No, I won't." Bessel raises a hand. "These are things you need to hear. You could have worked at the desalination plant with your father. If you'd been there, maybe you could have saved him, but no, you followed the criminal's daughter to the steamship factory. And now she's convinced you to risk your life, oh and my life too, on a plan that will get us all banished."

"It's not her plan; it's *my* plan." Sande's voice drops so low it sounds like a growl.

"You just think that—that's how deceitful she is." Bessel turns to sneer at me. "I bet your mother was thrown out of the city for the same sort of behavior. I mean think about it, she was pregnant, what does that tell you?"

I've never seen Sande look like he wants to hit someone. His fingers are rolled up tight, and his right hand trembles.

"You should leave," I tell Bessel.

"Oh, would you like me to? Shocking. Well this happens to be my home and my son. It's you who should leave." Bessel steps toward me. "Look at you, so proud of yourself. I know what happened last tide. Marsie the Healer? She said Gren wanted fere poison—and trust me, I know what that's used for."

"Get out!" Sande yells. "Out! Now!" He opens the door, grabs Bessel's sweater-covered arms, and shoves her into the corridor. I get a quick glimpse of her landing hard on her hip before Sande clangs the metal door shut and slides the bolt across.

I've never seen him so distraught, and I'm worried he'll do something rash in the hope of setting things right—but what desperate thing might he do?

"We'll find more money, buy new passbooks," I quickly suggest, wanting to calm him down. But it's such a feeble solution. Gren gave me money that she had saved over many tides. Where would Sande and I find another fifty paper shells? "Or maybe we can travel without passbooks?" But I don't want that, not at all. We'd have to be stowaways for a much longer time, and it would be difficult to legally work in any mountain city. And what would happen if we were caught? Would we be shipped back here for punishment? Probably.

"This is my fault," Sande says, dropping to sit on the bunk that was once his father's. It's still covered with Trennet's favorite wildwool blanket. "I should have known she'd do something like this. She's always been monstrous when it comes to you."

"We'll just have to find another way." I sit beside him and run my hand over the fuzzy knots and braids of the blanket.

"There isn't one," Sande says, and it's not like him to sound so defeated.

I wrap an arm around his shoulders, and together we watch the restless orange remains of Bessel's passbook fire.

Even though Sande was heartbroken when Trennet died, our plan to buy passbooks and run away to Ellevah lifted his gloom. But now that the passbooks are gone, his grief seems to hang on him more heavily than before. It's not that he cries or is irritable, he just never smiles or laughs, and one afternoon I find the map he showed me at the dead boat, the one of the Sea Spread, torn into tiny pieces.

I'm sad too, but what happened will never cut into me as deeply. I haven't recently lost a parent or been betrayed by one.

We let Bessel back into our barracks unit because she has nowhere else to go, and we don't want Gray Straps asking questions. She doesn't speak to us when she returns though, so we don't talk to her either. To be even more defiant, Sande sleeps in my cot, even though there's not much room.

And one night, when Bessel has a late shift, he tries to undress me.

"No," I say, wriggling away from him.

"But nothing matters now," he whispers.

"If I get pregnant, it'll matter."

And as things get worse in our barracks unit, bad things seem to be happening elsewhere too.

A Riversborn man hurts himself in a factory, and although he doesn't die, he crushes his leg so severely in a metal press uppy healers have to cut it off. After that, a stomach illness spreads through an automotor warehouse. Gray Straps quarantine several families because of it, and there are rumors they aren't giving the ill people enough food. Sande then cuts his hand at the factory so badly the foreman sends him home for a sunedge, and Gren's cough deepens.

"Now why are you still here?" She whispers during my next visit, sounding disappointed.

Even though the Rinians are away at their work assignments, I don't want to endanger Gren by telling her too much, so I just say, "Bessel ruined everything."

"Oh, she's got a talent for that." Gren sits up in her cot, her movements slow, her arms trembling. "I want to help. Is there anything I can do?"

"Not unless you've got more paper shells," I joke ruefully. I've brought her some spiced bread, and after putting the wrapped parcel on a shelf, I flop onto the cot opposite hers. "You were so generous, and I... I'm sorry. It was wrong of me to use that money for something else."

Gren's eyes crinkle. "I'd give you more if I could. I just want you to be safe, and I'm usually so good at keeping you safe. I've lost my touch. You know, I saved you one time you don't even know about."

"When was that?"

"Remember that cardpaper you asked about? The one with the fancy letters and the trident?"

I nod and turn so that I can see her better.

"I told you that tide merchant wanted to buy a child. Well, the child was you."

My insides twist. "I don't remember."

"Oh no, you wouldn't. You were still outside the city with your maam." Gren crumples her brow as if struggling to remember what happened. "He heard I was friendly with your mother, so he came to my market booth with all sorts of questions. In particular, he was keen to know what time of year you were born. Anyway, he asked me to sneak you into the city the next tide. He promised to pay me all sorts of money if I brought you to him. But of course I would never do what he wanted, for my goodness, how could I take you from your mother? So to get rid of him, I told him you'd died, and that was that."

"Oh." I'm not sure what to think about her story. Surely there could only be one reason a traveling merchant would want to know when I was born. "Do you think he was my father?"

70

Gren shrugs. "Maybe, or maybe he was hired by your father. But who would steal a child in such a way? It's not like he wanted to help your mother. And Nerene… this man didn't seem like a good person. He had a strange way about him that made me feel wrong inside." She hesitates as if she's not sure how to describe her memories. "It was like my thoughts were sick."

I leave Gren's wishing she hadn't told me about the tide merchant because I'm now full of questions I'm sure I'll never get the answers to. I've also never thought about my father much on purpose because it never seemed like he deserved my attention. Therefore I don't like having to think about him now. I suppose I always assumed that whatever happened to my maam, whatever her crime was, my father was tied up with it or maybe even to blame.

As I walk back to barracks building ten, I take the strange man's cardpaper out of my pocket and turn it over in my hands. The corners are soft, probably from being in Gren's wallet for so many years, but otherwise it looks as if it was printed in a fine shop. I run my fingers over the black letters that are smooth and yet slightly raised. Is my father's name written on this card? Should I even care?

Another sunedge of nine days passes, and although I can't think of a new way to escape the city, I begin to suspect Sande has. He often stops in the middle of what he's saying and drifts off in thought. Also, for the last day or so, whenever I return home from Giron's factory, he's not in our barracks unit where he's supposed to be resting and letting his hand heal. I suppose I'm glad he's working on a new plan—it's better than him being sad and despondent—but

I'm troubled that he hasn't told me about it. That means it's probably dangerous, and what's more dangerous than illegally buying passbooks?

I soon get an answer. A few days after Sande returns to work, we're met at the factory doors by a foreman who tells us to gather in the storage hall—something we've never been told to do before. Feeling nervous, we walk to the cavernous space on the countertide side of the factory, and because it's still largely empty of steamship components, there's enough room for all one hundred and fifty of us workers to crowd inside.

My heart stutters when I see Amista up on a balcony attached to the head foreman's office. "She works beside me," I whisper to Sande.

A big uppy holds her arms, and Giron stands on the balcony too. His striped blue suit and patterned orange necktie look out of place in the grimy room.

Sande and I climb onto a supply crate so we can see better, and I'm so worried about Amista, I slip twice. Even from the far side of the storage hall, I can tell she's crying.

"Why would she be up there?" I ask.

"I don't know," Sande says, but his conflicted look makes me think he does.

We wait for the entire day shift to arrive—about a quarter of an hour—and it's the worst kind of waiting because we can all sense something bad is about to happen. When workers stop trickling in through the doors, Giron moves closer to his voice-enhancing device. I don't like that it's here. If he bothered to set it up, he's put a lot of thought into whatever is happening.

"Well I'm very sorry you're starting your day in here, but we have a discipline situation." He sounds angry, not sorry. "You'll have to work late tonight to make up the time. Anyway, this floor worker, Anisa Frue—"

"Amista," I correct softly.

"—stole from my medicry."

"Kracken," Sande swears under his breath.

"No, I didn't!" Amista twists so that she can shout into the voice-enhancing device too. The uppy holding her arms pulls her back, but she keeps yelling and we can still hear. "I would never do something so cracked. I don't care what's in your stupid medicry!"

"We have to help her," I whisper, thinking about the illegal snapper Gren gave me. I tucked it in the back of my boot, but what can I do with it? I just have the one, and if I knock out the uppy holding Amista, another foreman will simply climb the stairs and take his place. Not to mention, I'll be in horrible trouble.

"Oh stop fussing, of course you're the thief." Giron adjusts his necktie and winces at Amista as if just looking at her offends him. "I know your grandmother is a healer. I also know you visited the medicry yesterday for a burn. You obviously looked around and said, 'Well gee, how about I help myself?'"

"My grandmaam doesn't need your uppy supplies!" Amista shrieks. "She makes her own medicines, and they're way better than any moldwater, syphillin uppy garbage."

Giron's eyes widen, and he's surely not used to hearing that sort of language come out of such a small person. He clears his throat, swallows, and then clears his throat again. "Well, in Varasay we have rules. You stole from me, so I must punish you. And if you refuse to submit to punishment, I will report you to the Threegod Priests. Do you want to risk banishment?" He looks to the rest of us with a hesitant smile as if expecting our support. "Look, I'm on your side, deeplanders, and I am trying to be fair. *No stealing* is fair." He swallows, wipes perspiration from his brow and then nods to the foreman. "Put her on that stool there and give her three lashes."

"No! NO!" Amista wails. She wrenches herself from side to side, but the foreman has no trouble forcing her small body over the kelpwood stool, stomach down.

She hasn't even been struck yet, but just seeing her in such a vulnerable position makes me feel like something has broken into sharp pieces inside my chest.

Another foreman, my supervisor, climbs onto the balcony carrying a whip. He's not tall, but he looks strong.

"Here, why don't you give me that..." Giron holds his hand out for the whip, and I doubt he's volunteered to be kind. Yes, he's probably weaker than any of the foremen, but I have a grim feeling that he wants to personally punish Amista.

Giron unrolls the whip, letting it hit the balcony floor with a soft, leathery slap, and there's a wave of angry movement in the crowd—a silent, horrified protest.

He swings his arm back, looking as if he has no idea what he's doing, and both foremen grimace, perhaps worried he'll miss and hit them. But before Giron cracks that long piece of leather over tiny Amista—Sande shouts, "Hey, I did it! Over here! I stole from the medicry!"

My breath catches in my throat. Is that true?

I am certain that Giron heard Sande, for the hall is quiet and nearly everyone turns to look at us, but he whips Amista's back anyway, and she screams as the leather slices into her uniform. We're on the opposite side of the hall but I can still clearly see a line of red bloom on her dress, and Giron has the strangest expression. He seems to be smothering a smile, and his eyelids are also fluttering as if he's about to faint. I've gutted plenty of fish and skinned countless visconey, but I wonder how much blood Giron has seen in his sheltered, uppy life.

"I said it was *me*," Sande cries, jumping down from the crate. "Punish *me*."

So was this his new plan? Steal from the factory medicry? Or is he trying to save Amista?

Giron seems to share my suspicions. "You just want to protect the girl."

"No, I've been trying to protect myself." Sande shoves his way through the other workers. "I was going to sell the medicine and buy a passbook, and then I was going to leave this miserable city. I don't want to work for free, none of us do. You shouldn't force us."

Many of the other deeplanders murmur in agreement, but not me because I see a foreman near the door pull out a shiny, black gunnerife.

"This is completely just and fair," Giron splutters. "You deeplanders take advantage of us. We save your life every tide and for what? You owe us."

"For all your priests and prayers, you don't know what fair means." Sande keeps moving forward, and he doesn't have to push his way through workers anymore. The deeplanders clear a path for him and offer him encouraging nods and grim smiles. "Besides, we don't owe you anything," Sande continues. "We already give you our landrunner meat and two-thirds of our harvest. We already give our souls to your Threegod not our Water Goddess."

The other deeplanders agree with angry shouts.

Another foreman nearer to me pulls out a gunnerife too. Does Sande see their weapons? Does he realize how much danger he's in?

I wrench Gren's snapper out of my boot and hold it tight in my hand, but I still don't know what to do. The snapper can only put one person to sleep.

Giron shifts to the other side of his voice enhancer as if the thin metal pole will shield him from Sande. "You'd have a different perspective if you were an uplander."

"Yeah, I like to think I'd act differently than you." Sande walks up the stairs as if accepting punishment, but there's nothing about him that looks submissive. At the top of the stairs, he turns to Giron and speaks loudly enough for us all to hear. "My pa just died in the desalination plant. He was only there because of you and your work assignments."

Giron swallows, then stutters while saying, "A-all right, all right, just calm down. I'll let the girl go and you'll have her lashes instead."

The foremen free Amista, and she skitters to the back of the balcony, but Sande doesn't crouch over the stool. Instead he says, "You're running out of room in your city, but you make our women have a procedure that's painful and dangerous. What about the women who live here?"

"Well, there's actually a proposal…" Giron starts timidly, but his words are lost in a roar of agreement and rage from the workers. And now I'm terrified because there's no way this can end well. Even if Sande is whipped, he's been publicly defiant to Giron, and he's admitted he planned to buy an illegal passbook and travel the tide. I wish I could stop this, unravel this. Sande will be banished for sure now—maybe even banished with mutilation, which is a punishment for more severe crimes. I squeeze the snapper. It's hard enough to survive the winter on the thin strip of dry land outside the city walls, but it's nearly impossible if you're missing a hand or foot.

"Whip him," Giron squeaks at the nearest foreman, throwing the length of leather toward the man. "Do it! Now!"

The foreman is twice as broad as Sande, but although he picks up the whip, he looks unsure. Sande isn't exactly being cooperative. He's staring at both of them with his arms crossed. And then with one of his smooth, easy movements, and one of those chilly, emotionless looks that so enrages Bessel, Sande pulls out a shiny gunnerife of his own and points it at Giron. "I didn't just steal from your medicry."

"No! Sande!" I shout.

"My father's dead," Sande yells into the sound-enhancer, tears glinting on his face. "I don't owe you, you owe me, and you owe me a life!"

The Sande I know would never hurt anyone. He'd try to strike a deal and maybe demand that Giron give him money and safe passage to the wharf. But it's almost as if pain and anger have reshaped him. I know he hates Giron, and I know he likes to deal with problems in brash, bold ways, and what's brasher or bolder than killing someone?

But murder is something he can't come back from. It's a black shell necklace that will be forever lost in the tide.

So I raise the snapper because I finally know what to do with it.

I've always had good aim. It's one of the reasons Gren and I have the biggest variety of herbs at the barracks market—we travel further into the kelp forest than other deeplanders would ever dare. We often spend several sunedges wandering through the swaying, curved trunks, using snappers on anything too big to run from.

And so even though I'm on the other side of the storage hall, when I pull the resin back in the snapper tube and let the poisoned dart fly, it strikes Sande neatly in the side of his neck. He has just enough time to look at me and realize I've betrayed him before collapsing.

THE STORAGE HALL erupts with noise and movement. There's
me, frightened and fighting to reach Sande, then there are the other
deeplanders surging toward the foremen, and most alarming of all,
there's a sharp popping sound as foremen fire gunnerifes into the crowd.
Deeplanders fall, but foremen fall too, struck by snapper darts. It seems
Sande and I weren't the only ones hiding forbidden deeplander weapons.

If only I'd known that a moment ago.

With a scraped knee and torn skirt, I reach Sande but can't carry
him to safety. He's not burly like Carnos, and I'm fairly tall, yet there's
still no way I can haul him down the balcony stairs and through the
churning crowd. I can help someone else though. Amista's huddled
near the doorway of the foreman's office, her dress red with blood.
Abandoning Sande feels like I'm leaving my heart pinned to the floor,
but I grab Amista's arm and push, struggle, and elbow us down the
stairs and out of the factory.

It's only then, in the shadowy, cold alley outside, pressing my hair kerchief to Amista's still bleeding back, that I realize Giron was no longer on the balcony and neither was the gunnerife that Sande stole. I imagine the Chancellor's son huddled somewhere in his factory, angry and wanting revenge.

"Run back to the barracks," I tell Amista. "Go to your grandmaam's."

She clings to my arm. "Aren't you coming with me? You have to come with me!"

I try to shake her off, but she hangs on tight. "Amista, no. I can't leave Sande."

"You can't help him if you're caught by the Gray Straps. They're coming now, listen…"

And fathoms, she's right. I hear the distant whine of the alarm attached to the Gray Strap's autohaulers. Someone, maybe Giron, must have used a relayphone to call for help.

This is awful. I'm awful. I've just knocked Sande unconscious and left him to the mercy of the uppies.

"Run back to the barracks," I tell Amista. "Go. Now! I'll follow as soon as I can."

She looks at me with frightened, uncertain eyes, then quick as a ridge cat, she skitters down the alley and vanishes around a corner.

As the wailing sound of alarms grows louder, my panic seems to get louder too. It's like a terrified shouting in my mind and chest as I shove my way back through the double doors, back into the factory. Even though I was only in the alley for a few moments, the situation inside has changed. All the foremen have either fallen or fled, and I'm horrified to see a couple of dead deeplanders too. Some young workers are helping injured friends, but most of them are tearing open crates of what we've made—steamship components maybe—and spilling them onto the ground. A few other workers are smashing windows by throwing wrenches, bricks, and whatever else they can find. Smoke fills the air, and I notice a dancing ribbon of flame near the head foreman's office. And thank goodness, there's Leej and a few other Saltpool boys carrying unconscious Sande down the balcony steps.

I rush over to them. "What can I do? What do you need?"

"A better way to move him would be good," Leej says. "There are barrows near the first floor conveyance belt. Can you get us one?"

I nod, and fighting to ignore the fear pulsing through me, I dash out of the storage hall to where Sande and the other boys worked on the lower level of the factory. It looks a lot like the production floor where I worked, and I spot a few deeplanders sabotaging this area too. Two boy pry open the control panel of a machine and then smash the gears and levers inside. I also see a girl about my age slicing conveyance belt leather with heavy shears.

"Where are the barrows?" I cry. "I need one."

The boys point me to a group of one-wheeled, sturdy-looking carts. I snatch up the metal handles of a barrow, and rolling it clumsily, I hurry back the way I came.

But as I rush down the long passage leading from the factory floor to the storage hall, I hear men's voices in the distance, and my thoughts catch up with me. The Gray Straps must have arrived. It's probably too late to help Sande, and as Amista said, I can't help him if I'm arrested too. With sinking regret and feeling like I'm wasting time and making mistakes at every turn, I abandon the barrow. I need to leave the factory. It's not safe here.

Breathing hard, I change directions and head for the factory cookery instead. There's a door there that leads outside. I know because we always ate our midday meal shivering beside the factory in the alley.

I smell smoke as I hurry outside, and I think about the fire that was blooming near the head foreman's office. Hoping Sande is safe, I dash up the muddy, icy pathway that runs between Giron's factory and a neighboring textile factory, and then I head for the barracks.

Yet when I near the twelve identical buildings where we deeplanders spend our winter, my quick steps slow to an uncertain shuffle. A Gray Strap autohauler stands near the arch house and at least a dozen city guards mill around it. Worse, the arch house gate is shut—which is something I've never seen before.

Huddling near a shabby, lower city housing tower, I'm not sure what to do.

The Gray Straps might let me return to the barracks, although maybe I should lie about where I work. My long wildwool jacket covers my uniform, but do any other factory shifts end right now? I don't think so. It would be too early.

And if I do enter the barracks and the Gray Straps keep the arch house gate shut, I'll be trapped in there and unable to help Sande if he's been arrested.

And yet, out here in the lower city, I have no shelter and no safe place to go.

If Gren were here, I bet she'd tell me to visit one of our lower city herb customers because she always says people make wiser decisions when they are warm and safe. I don't know where any of our uppy customers' homes are, but a few of them run cookery houses and there's always Parsita with her tea shop. I think her shop is near the old K'Gar temple, and although she's not the friendliest woman, she did bring Gren that medicated tea the other day.

I feel numb as I walk toward the old temple, and I worry about Sande. He stole a gunnerife—that alone is reason for the city to banish him. But then he also threatened to kill Giron, which is even worse. I worry about myself too. If I don't return to the barracks now, I might never be allowed to return.

Thankfully Parsita's shop is where I thought it was. I once brought her moss sage a few tides ago, back when we deeplanders ran our market all sunedge long. Her shop is on the lowest floor of a narrow three-story building, wedged between a cobbler's workshop and a carpentry store that mostly seems to sell tide-traveling chests.

There are no customers inside the tea shop, which is a relief, only Parsita and a bearded man who must be her husband. I find them busy cleaning three large brewer kettles.

Parsita looks up as I enter, for the bells attached to the doorknob jingle, and she frowns. "Has Gren died then?"

"Oh no, she's still alive…" and then I trail off because why have I come here? I'm not just here to warm up so that I can make wise decisions—I need help, and deeplanders don't usually ask uppies for help.

But my awful morning at the factory must somehow show in my eyes or maybe Parsita heard the autohauler sirens because she walks around the low cabinet where the brewer kettles sit and says, "You've brought trouble, and I don't want it."

I take a deep, frustrated breath as she moves closer. Gren certainly befriended kinder uppy customers, but I don't know where to find them. "I'm sorry, I'll go."

I turn, but Parsita catches my arm. "I may not want trouble, but we don't always get what we want. You look like you need something hot to drink, that's plain enough. And I think you should drink it where no one can see you, maybe in my storage closet. Gorven, watch the shop."

She leads me into a small room full of shelves, each crowded with jars, tins, and packets. For a moment, I'm afraid she might lock me in and call for Gray Straps. But when she leaves, she doesn't shut the door behind her, and when she returns, she hands me a ceramic mug of steaming tea. Her husband brings us both chairs from the tea shop too.

"So why are you here?" Parsita asks. "And if you think you can lie to me, you may as well leave."

Goodness I thought Bessel was intimidating, but in some ways, I'm glad Parsita is making me feel defensive. I'm fragile and close to tears, but because talking to her is a bit like being prodded with a stick, I have enough rising anger to tell her what happened at the factory with dry eyes.

Once I've finished telling my story, Parsita harrumphs and says, "So what do you expect me to do about it?"

I bristle, but I can also tell she wants an honest answer.

"I need a place to stay and food to eat, just until I know what to do next," I say. "I'll be sure to cook and clean and do any chores that need doing while I'm here. I also need your help finding out where Sande is now."

Parsita's mouth pinches at the corners. "I can help you for three days, and then you must leave. Does that sound fair?"

I nod.

Three days may be fair, but it's not that long.

PARSITA HAS ME work hard in her tea shop for the rest of the day. First though, she gives me old clothing to wear so no one will recognize my factory uniform. She also tells me to unravel my loose braids and then she winds my hair up into a severe city style instead.

I spend the next few hours scrubbing all the floors in her shop as well as the small housing unit upstairs that she shares with Gorven. And then, with my knees still smarting from working on all fours, Parsita has me clean piles of dishes, including plenty of tea mugs. After that, I wash clothes and bed linens in the cellar, and as evening falls, I mend a stack of clothing too, hunched beside an electric lantern. Parsita often walks by to criticize my work, but since she also keeps saying that it's wonderful to get so many chores done, I think she's pleased.

I'm a bit frustrated doing all this work, though, because I wish I knew where Sande was and if he's safe. But I try to be patient because there's probably not much I can do to help him just yet.

It doesn't snow that night, but freezing rain taps and pings against the shop windows, and the countless, icy pellets striking the road outside makes a soft hissing noise that helps me sleep. Parsita has given me enough blankets to stay warm on a floor mat in the back of the tea shop, and as I lie there curled up, I hope Sande isn't outside in this horrible weather. What if he's been banished already?

When I wake up the next morning, it's as if my mind was working while I slept, for I've remembered there's another uppy who might be willing to help me. After filling the big, electric brewer kettles for Parsita, I ask her, "Can you read?"

"Of course I can read," she says with a snort that might be a laugh.

I hurry to the storage room, where my wildwool jacket hangs, and I dig the small rectangle of cardpaper out of my pocket—the one Gren said belonged to the strange tide merchant. I show it to Parsita. "What is this, and what does it say?"

"It's a callercard for someone named Lord Almen Osperacy," she tells me. "He looks to be in the shipping business."

"Do you know him?"

She snort-laughs again. "Why would I know him? Wealthy travelers don't visit lower city tea shops."

Lord Almen Osperacy. *Lord Almen Osperacy.* I run the name through my thoughts a few times to make sure I don't forget it. Lord Osperacy could be my father, I suppose.

Parsita has plenty of early morning customers, and a few linger at the two small tables near the door. By mid-morning though, the shop is quiet. Parsita leaves to visit a lower city market, and she gives me a patched blanket to mend while she's gone. It takes me a few hours to repair the fabric, and as I rip out old stitching and replace it with new loops of thread, I feel the constant, anxious tug of wasted time. Parsita says I can only stay for one more day. How can I help Sande if I'm stuck here?

Thankfully though, Parsita takes our bargain seriously, and she returns from the market not only with brined cheese, fresh fish, and savorpears but also with information.

"Several young deeplanders were arrested after the riot, but I don't know their names," she tells me in the privacy of the storage room. "And that Noble boy's factory ended up burning to the ground. He's alive but seriously injured. Apparently he had to jump out of a window to survive."

Well, at least that's satisfying. Not that I'm one to celebrate suffering, but Giron was far too eager to punish Amista so I'm glad he was punished in a sense too. "What about Sande?" I ask. "Did you hear anything about him?"

"I said I don't know any names," Parsita says, dumping the basket of food into my arms. "Put all this away, will you?"

We eat a plain midday meal of cheese and kelp leaf crackers, then Parsita gives me more work grating cinniflower sticks. "Gorven gets swollen joints these days, so while you're here, you may's well do it."

I grate the sticks for a while, but there is a huge, fernflax bag of them, and I'm sure it will take me the rest of the day to finish. So pretending to use the scrubhouse out behind the shop, I hurry to the wharf with Lord Osperacy's cardpaper.

Ships don't always pass the same mountain cities as they travel the tide. As far as I understand, in many places along the trade routes, there are mountain cities in both starways and skytide directions. Therefore, if steamers must either move with the ocean or run aground and there is only one city far skytide of Varasay, I'm pretty sure there is a good chance that Lord Osperacy's ship is either in port now or soon will be. As much as I want to race to the docks, I move carefully because the roads are steep and slippery with ice. It's windy too. A fitful patchwork of silver, violet, and blue clouds drift across the sky while salty and fishy smells blow up from the shore. The wharf is the only place in Varasay where there aren't city walls and the Teeterwood Forest standing between us and the tide. It's crowded with ships though, some as big as floating cities, and unlike the night we said goodbye to Trennet, there are people everywhere. I don't know where to begin looking for Lord Osperacy, so I head to the warehouse where Carnos works.

I find him pushing a wagon much like the ones we use to carry our belongings up the mountain. And not wanting to be seen by other deeplanders who have work assignments at the docks, I wait until he's alone.

"Nerene!" he cries when I finally approach him, and after putting down the wagon handles, he crushes me into a hug. "We all thought you died in the factory fire!"

"I hid," I say. "Then the arch house gate was locked, and I didn't know what to do, so now I'm staying with some kind uppies." It feels strange calling Parsita kind, but I suppose in many ways she is.

I ask Carnos if there's a place we can speak privately. It's so open and busy on the pier, and at any moment I could be recognized. Carnos nods, his eyes still gleaming happily, and after bringing his wagon to the gangway of a ship, he leads me down a narrow path behind a warehouse.

"Oh my dear bride," he says as we stand in a small diamond of sunshine, the only warm spot between these large buildings. "I am overjoyed—overjoyed! Threegod be praised that you are alive."

I let him hug me again, even though his arms feel like weighty, clinging guilt. "What's happened since the riot?" I ask when his grip loosens, hoping he knows more than Parsita.

The joy on Carnos's face shifts to sadness. His massive hands move to my shoulders, and he says, "I'm afraid things are bad, especially for your brother. Many young deeplanders were arrested—many. Some will be given longer work hours as a punishment, and some must labor in the city when the tide leaves. A few poor maidens will be forced to have the procedure early, and as for Sande…"

My whole body tenses.

"He's to be banished with mutilation."

I can't form words, only a helpless cry. I was afraid of this. Being banished from the city is terrible, of course, I know that from my early years with Maam. But being banished with mutilation is a grisly death sentence. No one survives winter in the Teeterwood if they're missing an arm or leg.

Carnos seems to think this is a good time to wrap his arms around me again, and he's so big, I feel like my grief is suffocating me.

When he lets go, I show him Lord Osperacy's callercard, and I tell him what it says—touching the raised, black letters as if I can read them.

Carnos frowns. "And this man is…"

"Maybe my father," I say while thinking that Lord Osperacy could very well be horrible and evil too. Gren is a good judge of character.

To my disappointment, Carnos has never heard the name, and he also needs to return to work. But he promises to ask around and suggests I wait if possible. So risking Parsita's anger, I stay where I am. I shiver and fret in that sunlit diamond, and I follow it as it slides across the rocky alley, stretching longer and climbing the far wall. I also watch it change from a pale afternoon yellow to a fiery sunset orange. As I wait, a terrible realization comes to me as well; the priests often banish criminals at the end of a sunedge, and the current sunedge ends tomorrow.

Carnos eventually returns with disappointing news. "Our foreman has heard of Lord Osperacy. Yet he also says Lord Osperacy's ship usually doesn't come into port until late in the tide."

So I return to Parsita's tea shop feeling defeated, and of course I also find her furious that I didn't finish grating the cinniflower. She says I don't deserve supper, although when I tell her that Sande will be banished with mutilation, she ladles soup into a bowl and hands it to me anyway.

"I also sent word to Gren," she says. "I told her you were safe—for now anyway."

"Thank you," I say.

Early the next morning, when the sun has yet to rise but the sky is already a pale blue, I wake to a loud *bang, bang, bang!* Someone is pounding on the tea shop door.

I don't risk peering over the brewer kettle cabinet to see who's there because they might see me too. Instead I scurry into the cellar, terrified that the Gray Straps have found me. But Parsita soon comes huffing and creaking down the stairs to tell me, "It's a big deeplander who says he knows you."

Rushing back up, I find Carnos in the front of the shop, breathing heavily, his face both flushed from the cold and shiny with sweat. "The symbol on the cardpaper you have—the one with the three spikes? That same symbol is on a ship that arrived in the harbor last night."

I put on warm clothing, and Carnos and I head back to the docks. The streets are cold and mostly empty.

As we walk, Carnos talks about what he thinks our life will be like once we're married. He believes we'll inherit his grandda's hut, which is near a river. He tells me that the gardens need work, but the soil is good and drains well. He also tells me that he'd like to build a second room on the hut, but only if he finds the right rocks to use for the foundation.

It's still probably unwise to be honest with him about my feelings, but as he continues to talk about our future, it becomes unbearable to listen—here he is still delighted about our betrothal when I nearly ran away with Sande.

So when the shadowy shapes of docked steamships prod their way through the fog, and Carnos tries to wrap an arm around me to "warm us up a bit," I pull away and blurt, "We can't get married."

Carnos stares at me. "Why not?"

"Because you should have a wife who wants to marry you, and I don't…" Oh this is hard, his face is bunching up like his favorite hunting spear just fell into a fire. "I don't think I would be the sort of wife you want, either," I add.

"Of course you are," he says. "You're hard-working and dutiful, and tall and strong."

I don't want to tell him that I care for someone else, but it also seems like the only way to make my feelings clear. "I love Sande, but we can never marry, so I decided to marry you. It wasn't nice of me, and I'm sorry." I say it all very quickly.

The confused expression Carnos wears most of the time intensifies "Are you sure?"

"Yes," I say, and I keep walking. The sooner we reach the ship with that strange symbol the better. And as we move quietly down the steep roads, which are less icy today, I feel sick and sad. Sande will probably die, now I certainly won't marry Carnos, and I might not be allowed to return to the barracks to see Gren again either.

"Thank you for being honest," Carnos says after a long while.

"Thank you for not being angrier," I reply. He is a good person, and I wish I had even the smallest amount of romantic feelings for him. Life would be simpler.

The ship he brings me to does have the weapon-like symbol on it that matches the cardpaper—a trident, I suppose. The hull also has letters painted on it that I suspect proclaim the boat's name. It's a massive steamship too, with many layers of windows, decks, and railings, and there are three huge smokestacks on top that stand taller than any of the nearby warehouses.

No one has lowered a gangway yet, and Carnos has to report for work, so he leaves me waiting alone.

"I hope your father is a kind man," he says.

"I hope so too," I say. "And thank you for helping me." I want to apologize further, but before I can figure out how to put my words in the right order, Carnos gives me a nod and walks away.

Shipsmen in crisp, light blue uniforms lower the gangway roughly an hour later, just as the rising sun chases away the remaining fog. Since I've been waiting huddled on a concrete bollard, my legs don't want to unfold and they are very uncooperative as I limp toward the gangway. I also feel painfully aware of how simple and ragged I look in my shaggy wildwool jacket.

"May I speak to Lord Osperacy?" I ask.

All three shipsmen frown at me as if I'm most definitely a beggar or liar. "What business do you have with our employer?" one asks as if he's already certain I have none.

"You're not welcome here," another shipsman quickly adds.

"Lord Osperacy came looking for me once, and I want to know why," I tell them, feeling frustrated already. I remember Sande saying that uppies who travel the tide are more arrogant than the ones who stay put in mountain cities. The true reason I'm here, of course, is to beg for help, and I sense that will get a swift dismissal from these men, so instead I say, "Lord Osperacy might be my father, and I just learned about it. He gave my grandmaam this." I hold up the cardpaper.

Now the shipsmen look annoyed. The one that first spoke sighs. "I don't know where you got that, but you won't fool us." He tries to grab the callercard, but I take a fumbling step back and hold it close to my chest.

"Get out of here," he says, "or I'll call for your city guard."

I try to swallow my fear. If these men call for the Gray Straps, I'll be in big trouble, but I can't give up now. "Fine, call them," I say. "Abandoning your children is against Varasay law."

The shipsmen exchange glances and mutter to each other, and I hear the name "Douglen" said a few times. Finally one of them says, "Very well then, I'm going to fetch someone who'll expose your scam far faster than you'd like."

And now I'm even more frightened, but I still stay where I am. Two of the shipsmen stand with me, and as we wait, I keep my head up and try to look confident as if I have every right to make demands of a wealthy uppy.

The third shipsman doesn't return, instead a strong looking, square-shaped man of about thirty tides walks down the gangway. He's not wearing a uniform, but rather a dark gray, well-tailored uppy suit. When he reaches the pier, he examines me with half-lidded eyes. "Are you here to steal from my family? Tell the truth."

His family. Is this man related to me? We don't look alike. But as I'm thinking all that through, I feel a strange pressure in my stomach as if I must answer him—as if words are something bitter I need to spit out. "I'm not here to steal," I say.

"Then why are you here?" he asks, and again he adds, "Tell the truth."

Once more, I feel that strange pressure forcing me to answer. I also notice that both shipsmen look amused as if they know I've bumbled my way into a dangerous situation, and they can't wait to watch me suffer the consequences. Horribly, the truth spills out of me in a clumsy, unhelpful way. "The boy I love is about to die, and I think Lord Osperacy is my father—he came looking for me once. So because he's rich, I want him to save my friend."

The thick, short man in the suit inspects me from my knit hat to my muddy boots, grimacing as if he's never seen something so revolting, and when I'm done talking, he looks into my eyes in a way that makes me want to run. "How self-serving of you. Well, my father is *not* your father, I'll tell you that right now. But if he came looking for you, he must have had a good reason..." The man hesitates, apparently mulling something over, and then he frowns. "How old are you?"

This time I don't feel a sickening pressure to answer, but it's also a simple question. "Eighteen tides."

He nods. "When exactly were you born?"

"I don't know for sure. I don't think it was recorded."

"Well… it's unlikely, but I suppose there's a chance. There's no point bothering my father so early in the morning, but I can deal with you. Follow me."

Deal with me. Those words are fairly frightening. And when he tells me to follow him, I feel as if something has grabbed my spine and is forcing me to walk like a puppet. My legs march up the wood and steel gangway whether I want them to or not. I'm also deeply confused. "There's a chance?" I say. "What do you mean? A chance of what?"

But the man doesn't answer.

We're soon up on one of the decks, and even though it's not the highest deck, it's still dizzying. I've never been on a steamship before, other than standing on the wrecked hull of the dead boat— but that hardly counts. The dead boat is tiny compared to this monstrous vessel.

The man leads me through a doorway and then along several beautiful passages, all of them decorated with dark, brinewood panels, seaweed colored rugs, and golden light fixtures.

"You're a deeplander, aren't you?" he asks.

"Yes," I say.

He gives a short, harsh laugh. "Oh she'll hate that."

She? I have no idea what he's talking about. He soon stops and pounds on a door much the same way Carnos banged on the tea shop door this morning.

"Wake up," the man shouts. "I have a present for you."

A muffled female voice answers, "Go away, Douglen! I'm sleeping!"

He pounds again. "Get up or I keep knocking."

I felt strangely compelled to do whatever this man said, but the girl behind the door doesn't seem to be affected the same way. Now I'm even more confused.

The man—Douglen, I suppose his name is—keeps smashing his fist against the door, and a few sleepy faces even peer out of other cabins. Seeing him, though, those people meekly vanish again. I keep waiting for the door to break off its hinges, but it eventually opens, revealing an angry-looking girl with pale skin and black curls. She's also wearing a lacy, luxurious nightdress. "Why are you always so impossible? I'm telling father, you know, and he'll—" But then her eyes flick over to me and she looks wary. "Who is that, and why is she with you? Part of a task?"

"No," Douglen says. "She's for you... maybe. You need a new balance, don't you?"

The girl makes a face. "Not one like that. Make her go away."

"Why don't *you* make her go away?" A menacing smile cracks across Douglen's teeth, and as confused as I am, I sense that he's challenging her somehow.

"Fine." The girl glares at me and shouts, "Get off the ship, you disgusting sludge."

"I'm sorry you're upset," I say softly, wishing this was going better. "I just want to talk to Lord Osperacy, and then I promise I'll leave. Please."

"You have no power over her—none." Douglen laughs again, although it's more like an angry bark, and the girl's face turns red as if she's a toddling about to throw a temper-tantrum.

"No. NO! This can't be! Don't you tell Father." She whirls on Douglen. "I won't have some backward sludge for my balance. I refuse. That would be..."

Douglen's laughter ends with a satisfied sigh. "Hasn't this been a wonderful morning? She didn't even know her birth date. It was *such* a long shot." He looks at me as if I'm a fabulous cut of meat he can't wait to devour. "I'm so glad you paid us a visit. What's your name?"

"Nerene," I whisper, deeply confused about what just happened and wishing I'd never come.

"Well, Nerene," he says. "I think my father, Lord Osperacy, would indeed like to meet you."

DOUGLEN BRINGS ME to a dimly lit, spacious cabin that smells of spiced fin tea—the kind Gren Tya and I make whenever we find rare sinker leaves.

The floor is covered with overlapping wildwool rugs that seem far too pretty to step on, plush chairs surround a small table, and a large desk stands near a row of windows. Through those windows I see Varasay's cramped lower city with its ugly factories and many housing towers. I can also see an orderly ring of bright, square windows above the lower city, surely the mid city I've heard about but never visited.

Now that I'm alone, I wonder if I should try to leave the ship. Douglen seems dangerous, and I remember Gren saying she had felt afraid of Lord Osperacy too.

But I've come this far, and I don't know of any other way to help Sande, so I wait.

A short while later, probably about as long as it would take for someone to wake up and put their clothes on, the door opens and a man enters. He's about fifty tides old, wearing a delicately striped uplander suit with a cream-colored ruff that's held in place with a gold, squid-shaped pin. His smooth steps make me think of the silent players in the lower city market, part dance, part theatrics, and all grace.

"Child," he says, holding out a hand. "My name is Lord Almen Osperacy, and I believe I'm about to offer you a job."

"A job," I echo, stunned because that's certainly not why I came.

Lord Osperacy sits behind a polished desk and invites me to take a seat in one of the fabric-covered chairs. "I hear you have a callercard of mine."

I nod, and the chair I sit on is so soft it's like an embroidered bog. I grip the arms tightly and try not to sink too far in. "My grandmaam had it. She said you came looking for me once."

"It's hard to recall everyone I meet," Lord Osperacy says. And I silently agree with Douglen. This man can't be my father. His skin is too pale, his eyes are a strange, watery blue, and his body is too small and fragile. "How old are you?" he asks.

"Eighteen tides."

"Of course you are." He folds his hands, lacing one set of long fingers into the other. "Although I thought even deeplanders in Varasay had to record births and deaths, and I've checked the records here many times and never found you."

"They do record those things, it's just… my birth wasn't written down," I say. "My mother gave birth alone in the kelp jungle. She'd been banished."

"Ah, now I remember." Lord Osperacy smiles. "You're the criminal's daughter. When I heard about you, I thought you might be a match, but then I was told you were dead. I suppose I could have tried harder to track you down, but it seemed like such a shadow on the horizon that you'd be a good fit anyway. Yet surprise, surprise, you *are* Melily's balance. And she badly needs one."

"What's does balance mean?" I ask for everyone here keeps saying it.

"Melily has the unique ability to control the actions of others," Lord Osperacy tells me. "But her talent doesn't work on you, therefore you are her balance."

I think about how Melily tried to order me off the ship, and how furious she was when I didn't leave.

Lord Osperacy smiles at me again, showing two rows of clean, straight teeth. It's not a friendly smile either, it's a victorious one. "Tell me, Nerene, what do you know about sirens?"

When I think about sirens, I think of the necklace Sande made me, the one I left on the windowsill of my Saltpool hut. It's probably been swept into the kelp forest by now and buried in mud, but a small part of me likes to think green hands picked it up, and that it now rests on the delicate scales of a fish maiden's neck. "My Maam used to tell me stories about them," I say.

"Fanciful stories of half-fish, half-humans I imagine." Lord Osperacy chuckles, gazing up at framed engravings of sirens hanging on the wall—I suddenly realize there are many. "You know, sirens do exist, but not in the way you might think. They're not fish-people who live in the tide, but they do have, essentially, wavurl. You know what that is, don't you?"

I nod. "Wavurl is how sirens summon people into the tide and drown them."

"In the stories, yes, but in reality it's how people like Melily and Douglen control the will of others."

I would think this man was telling me a wild story if I hadn't just met Douglen. Even so, there's a part of me that feels like reality and reason can't be trusted at the moment. Stepping onto this ship has almost felt as if I've stepped into another world.

"Melily is a siren," Lord Osperacy continues. "Yet her wavurl doesn't work on you. Sirens can control anyone except for the rare people who were born precisely when they were, and of course, other sirens."

I nod again, and I'm also surprised that the angry girl in the nightdress who looked to be about twelve or thirteen tides old is actually the same age as me. I watch reflections of electric light slide across Lord Osperacy's shiny desk as I think everything through. There's so much wood on this ship, and so little of it the cheap kelpwood or pressed-reed boards we deeplanders have in abundance.

"I'm also a siren," Lord Osperacy tells me. "Or rather I once was. Unfortunately wavurl vanishes when one grows older."

As I watch his reflection in the desk—an undulating, blurry shape —I think about how Gren said speaking to him made her thoughts feel sick.

"I'm still immune to it though," he continues. "So now I care for others with the gift. First I took in Douglen, then Melily, and one tide ago, I welcomed a young boy named Timsy. It's nearly impossible, you can imagine, for common parents to raise such uncommon children. Young sirens may not have full power until they reach maturity, but they can still be little tyrants, impossible to discipline, completely disruptive, and often dangerous." Lord Osperacy leans forward. "Douglen has two balances, his wife Shara and a man named Jeck. They serve as his conscience and remind him not to misuse his abilities—always a great temptation for sirens. We are a rare group, and the equatorial powers tolerate us so long as we're useful. But if we ever became uncontrollable, they would quickly cut us down. I have no illusions about that.

"Now I've found a balance for Timsy, even though he doesn't have much use for her yet, but I don't have a balance for Melily, and as you can imagine, balances are difficult to find. As I said, we sirens cannot use our wavurl on each other, but Douglen and I do not have time to constantly supervise Melily. She needs a level-headed companion—someone who can steer her away from trouble, someone who can remind her what her responsibilities are. I hope that will be you."

Had this man found me a sunedge ago, I would have had endless questions about these real-life sirens and their wavurl, and I would certainly want to know more about the job. However, right now I'm only thinking about how I can use this strange situation to help Sande. I'm still confused about a lot of what Lord Osperacy has told me, but one thing is clear—I have value to him. "I won't work for you," I say. "Not unless you help me."

Lord Osperacy narrows his eyes. "You realize I'm offering you a wonderful life here on my ship—something you surely don't have." He glances at my ragged clothing and pauses, perhaps to give me a chance to say I've changed my mind. When I remain silent, though, he shifts slightly in his chair, and I get the sense that he's both annoyed and a little impressed that I'm being so stubborn. Whatever the nature of my work for him will be, I'm guessing it requires strength of will.

"So what is it that you want?" he asks.

I tremble because now everything I care about feels as if it's hanging over a cliff. "I want you to save my friend Sande. He's been arrested and is in prison and will surely die. He needs to leave Varasay."

Lord Osperacy looks thoughtful. "Why was your friend arrested?"

"He started a riot and threatened the Chancellor's son," I say, sensing that it's best to be honest about Sande's situation.

Lord Osperacy's eyebrows rise.

"But I care about him," I continue, "And he's not a bad person. The uplanders here are going to banish him with mutilation, and I don't want him to die. Please. If you don't help him, I might as well die myself—I'll be useless to you."

Lord Osperacy's mouth twists to the side in irritation, but I also see a twinge of a smile. "What's his name again?"

"Sande Olin."

The uppy man is quiet for a long time but finally says, "Douglen can handle it, but you'll go with him. I don't want him rescuing the wrong person."

And is it really as easy as that? I close my eyes and let my fear fall away. *Thank you, Water Goddess.*

The soft chair no longer seems like it's trying to swallow me, instead it feels like it's cradling me.

"However—" Lord Osperacy says.

And my fear snaps back into place, rigid and sharp.

"Your friend cannot travel with us." He looks as if he expects me to pay very close attention.

I do, but I also say, "Sande isn't dangerous, I promise."

Lord Osperacy straightens his fingers, splaying them across his desk like bony starfish. "It's not just that. I want you focused on Melily. You are no good to me pregnant. Is there a chance you're pregnant?"

"No." I flush. Not this tide. "But if you save Sande... will we be apart forever?"

"Isn't that better than him dying?"

I nod, swallowing back the threat of tears that aches in my throat. "How will I know Sande's even safe then? How will I know you've kept your word?"

Lord Osperacy smiles faintly. "You may correspond with him using the mail ships."

"But we can't read or write. We're deeplanders."

Lord Osperacy closes his eyes for a brief moment, surely annoyed. When he opens them again, he says, "Then I suppose... you may speak to each other using relayphones when we are in port. But you will have to learn how to read and write. It's imperative for a balance. Melily can teach you."

I hate the thought of being separated from Sande, and I'm afraid of traveling with these powerful strangers, but I came here for Lord Osperacy's help, and now I suppose I have it. I manage a genuine-sounding, "Thank you."

I'VE NEVER BEEN in an automotor before. It growls at me like all uppy machines, but it's not the chugging rattle I so often hear in Varasay's lower city. It's more of a steady rumble, low and deep, and it makes my legs tremble as we travel to save Sande.

I can't see the driver, but Douglen and his wife, Shara, sit across from me. Shara is one of Douglen's two balances, and she seems to be the opposite of him in almost every way. She's tall where he's short, slender where he's boxy, and as far as I can tell, gentle where he's cruel. The fragile, floating fabric of her lavender dress and her pale, shining curls, make me long to bathe and run a comb through my own hair.

As Douglen watches Varasay's lower city pass by the automotor's windows, Shara asks me questions. "Do you have any family, Nerene?"

"Just Gren... she's like a grandmaam," I say, feeling another stab of sadness that I'll soon be leaving her and blinking back tears.

"What are the Varasay deeplands like?" Shara asks.

"Beautiful but hot," I tell her, and it's difficult to have a conversation right now because I'm so worried. Shara seems nice, though. I'm glad I'll be traveling the Sea Spread with at least one kind person. "So… do you have wavurl too?" I ask, still feeling confused about how the Osperacy family operates.

"No, not me," Shara says with a smile. "I'm like you. I was simply born at the same moment Douglen was, so his wavurl doesn't affect me."

I glance at her husband. Although I've had an unnerving taste of his wavurl—I'm still concerned his strange power won't be enough to free Sande. Yet when we reach the checkpoint leading from the lower city to the mid city and Gray Straps ask for our passbooks, Douglen proves how strong his abilities are. He hands the guard his passbook, as well as passbooks for Shara and the driver, and then he says—very casually—"You don't want to see the girl's passbook."

The Gray Strap standing at the automotor window frowns, but after inspecting the three small booklets, he waves us through.

I'm still nervous as we continue on through Varasay's mid city, but at least I can distract myself by looking out the windows. I've never been in the mid city before, few deeplanders have, and it strangely seems even more crowded than the lower city. Even though the houses are clean and well maintained, they're also small and jammed close together on steep slopes. A few homes have gardens out front that might be lovely in warmer weather, but those little squares of dirt are so crowded with Threegod statues and garishly bright banners, it's hard to tell. Bridges sometimes arch overhead, and every so often, we pass buildings that are as large as factories and overly decorated with elaborate window frames and complicated brickwork. I suspect they are schools or healing houses.

We travel through another checkpoint, and again Douglen uses his wavurl to make sure I don't have to show my passbook, and then we enter the high city. Here the buildings surrounding the automotor are even more showy and ornate than the ones in the mid city. Every single home, housing tower and shop seems to have colorful walls, grand entryways, and roofs that almost look like jaunty hats. And between all of these structures are plenty of giant, gilded Threegod statues—some show K'Gar, Laeros, and Shale battling demons while others have them standing hand in hand, and in one sculpture—which I find particularly amusing—each god cradles a baby landrunner.

The automotor stops before a dark purple home with silver pillars and a blood red door.

Carrying a latched case, Douglen leads us up the front steps. After he speaks with a servant at the entrance, we're brought into an enormous room. It's as large as a barracks building, if barracks buildings were hollow inside, and there is an intense arrangement of blue and purple tiles on the floor, plenty of finely-made furniture that seems tiny in the vast space, and curtains made out of enough pearlsilk to dress everyone in Saltpool. There is also an overpowering smell of burning, fragrant oil. I'm a little surprised because I thought we would be going to a prison. Sande surely isn't here.

A servant pushes a man seated in a wheeled chair into the room, and a bolt of fear runs through me—it's Giron. A knit coverlet hides his legs, there is an ugly bruise across his narrow face, and his voice sounds frail when he says, "My father will join us in a moment, Master Osperacy."

This must mean I stand in Chancellor Noble's home, and as I absorb this shock, Giron notices me. "That girl... she worked in my factory. She's a deeplander." His mouth flattens in anger, and he tries to rise from his rolling chair, but whatever his injuries are, they're severe enough to stop him. He sinks back down, groaning in pain.

"She works for my father now," Douglen says lightly as if the news is unimportant.

Giron sucks in a sharp breath. "You can't just take our people."

"Of course not," Douglen says. "My father is giving you something in return."

Giron eyes the latched case in Douglen's hands expectantly, but Douglen doesn't open it. Instead it seems we're waiting for the Chancellor, who arrives a moment later. He looks just like he did last tide when he visited the barracks to deliver the tidewater address. He wears a dark suit with a blue vest that fails to hide his round belly. His thick hair is streaked with gray, but he still has plenty of it, as well as a bushy mustache. He also wears a gold-plated gadget that I think is a portable timekeeper. There are three parts to the little machine, all of them pinned to his jacket and connected with glittering chains that bounce as he walks.

The High Priest of Lacros follows him into the room and that very much surprises me. It's the same old man I threw up on.

The Priest's eyesight, though, must be poor because he doesn't seem to recognize me. Although I suppose it could also be that he simply doesn't remember what I look like—I am an unimportant deeplander after all.

"It's good to see you again, Master Osperacy," Chancellor Noble says in such a stiff way it's clear he'd rather not see Douglen at all. "When I heard you wanted to discuss the release of a prisoner, I called for High Priest Fenelly of Laeros to join us as well—he oversees holy justice in the lower city."

The High Priest bows his head. "As you know, true justice comes from a power higher than our mortal selves. I am simply a representative of that power."

Douglen gives Shara a quick, annoyed look that must mean he's not a devout Threegod follower and then says, "It's a simple matter. We're taking this girl, and we also want one of your other prisoners released to us." He turns to me. "What's your boyfriend's name?"

"Sande Olin," I say softly.

"No!" Again Giron tries to stand, and again he collapses back into his rolling chair, this time muttering several ugly curse words.

I have to admit that as unhappy as I feel right now, I'm glad Giron's miserable too.

"You can't have that deeplander," Giron says. "He stole from me and tried to kill me, and he started a riot that destroyed my factory. He's extremely dangerous!"

"My son is right," Chancellor Noble adds, although he speaks calmly. "We value our friendship with your family, of course. Lord Osperacy has certainly helped me out in some thorny situations, but that prisoner cannot be released. You are welcome to take the deepland girl; my goodness you may take more deepland girls if you like—have your pick—but the prisoner you ask for must be punished. We need to restore peace and order to the lower city."

My stomach twists at Chancellor Noble's suggestion that Douglen help himself to other deepland women.

But Douglen doesn't seem interested. "I know I ask for a lot, which is why my father has sent a token of deep appreciation." He opens the latched case, and because he's standing in front of me, I can't see what's inside. Whatever it is, though, seems to impress Giron, Chancellor Noble, the High Priest, and even the smartly-dressed servants in the doorway. Everyone's eyes widen.

Chancellor Noble brings his hands together. "Generous as that may be, we will not—"

"Come and take a closer look," Douglen says. "All of you."

And even though his wavurl command isn't directed at me, I can feel it rasping painfully against my thoughts. I also watch in amazement as everyone obeys him—Chancellor Noble steps closer with a humiliated blush, the High Priest approaches Douglen with a slow shuffle, Giron grunts in pain as he moves the large wheels of his rolling chair with his hands, and even the servants drift nearer to Douglen with expressions of helpless shame. I suspect they aren't supposed to move from their positions in the doorway unless summoned.

"And now that you can all clearly see Lord Osperacy's gift," Douglen says in a low, rather menacing voice. "Surely you are also reminded of how easy it would be for me to free the prisoner myself, but since my father would like us to remain friends, I hope we can come to an agreement."

"Of course, of course." The Chancellor nods and with a look of defeat, reaches for the case. "We here in Varasay value your friendship too much to quarrel."

Now that Chancellor Noble is holding the case, I see that a golden, jewel-covered necklace lies inside.

The High Priest of Laeros frowns at Chancellor Noble. "Such a valuable trinket should be given to the gods."

And Giron glares furiously, not at Douglen but at me. "Is the deepland girl paying you somehow? I know your power can be bought."

"Hush Giron," Chancellor Noble says, and then he turns to the High Priest. "We'll find a fair way to make sure our city and Threegod both benefit from this generous gift."

Shara smiles faintly as the servants scuttle back to their places alongside the doorway, their cheeks red. And I am tremendously relieved that the Chancellor will free Sande, but beneath my happiness, I'm troubled. The Osperacys are more powerful than I thought, for the most influential people I have ever known just yielded to them.

When we return to the ship, I spend the rest of the day in my new cabin. I suppose I should be admiring the luxurious, pleated curtains, the shiny brass lights and the huge bed, but all I see is how hatefully uppy it all is.

Gray Straps bring Sande to the ship at dusk, and Douglen, with his balance Jeck this time, reunite us on an upper deck.

"Father wants you to be certain that he's honoring your agreement," Douglen tells me.

And as for Sande, he looks awful. His face is swollen and bruised, and a deep cut runs beneath his left eye. Unfamiliar, grungy clothing covers the rest of him and probably hides other injuries. Judging by the crooked way he's standing, I'm sure there are plenty.

I rush forward to hug him—gently—but he stiffens and steps away. "Not now, Nerene."

"Are you upset with me?" I ask, surprised. "Sande, I just saved you."

"You only had to save me because you shot me with a snapper. We could have run. You could have shot Giron instead."

111

I blink, and I'm so shaken by his anger I don't know what to say. I suppose I understand how he feels about the snapper, but I thought by now he'd realize why I shot him. "I couldn't let you kill Giron."

"So you were protecting me from myself again, huh?" Sande says bitterly.

I suppose my attempt to protect him didn't succeed. He was still captured and given a fatal sentence. Still though… "You shouldn't have stolen from the medicry."

"I did it to help us." Sande takes a deep, trembling breath.

"But you also stole a gunnerife!" I cry. "Sande, that was stupid."

"No, it was a risk worth taking. Do you know how much gunnerifes sell for in the lower markets?"

"But you almost shot Giron."

"To save Amista—I didn't think he'd blame her."

I'm speechless because how is this my fault? I just saved Sande's life, and now we have to say goodbye, maybe forever, and he's ruining our last moments with an argument. I suppose Sande probably just spent the past few days enduring beatings and maybe even torture, and I suppose because of that, I can't expect him to suddenly give me a tender goodbye, but…

I hear laughter and turn to find Douglen and his balance, Jeck, sniggering.

"As funny as it is to watch your boyfriend berate you," Douglen says dryly, "finish saying goodbye. I need to bring him to the ship he's traveling on."

I turn to Sande, and even though I'm upset, I still do my best to remember every detail about him. As awful as our final farewell is going, at least he's safe. It's dark, but the warm glow of Varasay illuminates everything I'm trying so hard to memorize: Sande's large eyes, the soft curve of his lips and nose, his jagged mess of curly hair.

I want to say something memorable, something he can run through his mind while we're apart, but before I get the chance, Sande says, "I might be angry, but I also love you, and I'll miss you."

"I love you too," I say.

I step forward to kiss him, but then he says, "You paid for my freedom somehow, didn't you? What are you giving those men?" And his tone of voice makes me flush.

"Not what you're suggesting," I say, although I suppose Douglen could command me to do whatever he pleased and I'd hardly have a choice. Another ripple of fear runs through me.

"That's enough," Douglen calls. "Say goodbye."

"Goodbye," I say, wincing against the wavurl and disappointed that Sande and I are parting like this.

"Goodbye," Sande echoes, and there is still sharp fury in his voice.

Then Douglen makes Sande walk—or rather, limp—away, and a serveman leads me back to my cabin. Once there, I huddle in the center of my uppy bed and let out all the tears that I've been holding in. I'm thankful Sande is alive, but now I'm leaving him and Mount Varasay, the only place I've ever lived. I didn't even get to say goodbye to Gren, and thinking about her in particular, I cry myself to sleep.

PART TWO — MELILY

WHEN I WAKE the room is full of sunlight, and I have a headache.

A girl stands beside my bed, and I suppose she woke me up. She has tan, freckled skin like mine and curling brown hair like Sande's, and she wears a belted, gray dress that has the tidy look of a uniform.

"I'm so sorry to disturb you." She takes a timid step forward. "But Lord Osperacy would like you to dine with the family today. He wants you to get to know Melily before we reach Beth."

Beth. My foggy mind latches onto the name. Of course, Beth would be the first mountain city we'll visit, the closest one currentways. Sande told me about it once, but I can't remember any details aside from the fact that it has a king.

I try to sit up, but unhappiness holds me down, heavy as the tide.

"I can't come to dinner," I say softly. "I'm not feeling well." Whatever my job entails, it surely doesn't require me to be friends with these uppies.

The girl in the uniform is young, perhaps only five tides older than me. "Oh…" She looks down uncertainly. "Lord Osperacy's not going to like that. But I can run a bath for you, and don't you want some clean clothing? I think you'll feel better."

I shake my head, closing my eyes. She's being kind, and I should be thankful, but I almost wish she were behaving more Bessel-like. I want to lash out and fight someone.

"When did you last eat?" she asks. "I didn't know you were here yesterday, or I would have brought you some food. That might be why you're not feeling well."

When did I last eat? I think it was at least one day ago at Parsita's, but now my insides are too numb to feel hungry.

The young woman reaches for the door handle. "Well, I'll bring you some food. My name is Marthes, by the way, and I'm the servegirl for the *Trident's* second deck. If you need something, just press that buzzer over there. And I'll be…" she snaps her fingers, "right here."

Marthes returns shortly with biscuits topped with some sort of peppery fish mixture, and she offers to run a bath for me again. Her polite persistence probably means I'm even filthier than I feel, but I'm too broken to care. When she leaves again, I lie completely still, letting time wash past, formless and endless. I think about how miserable Bessel must feel, and I wonder if she knows about Sande's fate. And I think about Gren, who's surely worried—I hope Carnos told her where he last saw me. I also think a lot about Sande. What would have happened if I'd sent that snapper dart into Giron's neck? If the riot had still broken out, maybe Sande and I could have fled to the docks and simply stowed away on a ship. He had robbed the medicry, after all, and it seems likely that he might have hidden what he stole in the factory. Maybe we could have escaped together. Did I ruin it all with that snapper?

I feel like I've made a bargain with a family of demons too. Wavurl power has only ever been something I heard mentioned in stories, not something real. These people call themselves sirens, but they aren't swimming through the tide, so what are they really?

At one point the ship shudders and rumbles around me, and it feels as if I'm inside the mighty lungs of an exowhale.

We must be sailing out of Varasay's harbor.

And Sande is also leaving or has already left on a ship I don't know the name of—and where is he going?

The windows darken and then grow light again.

Marthes returns with a morning meal of toasted bread, ripe shallowberries, and roast gull. She lingers too, surely to make sure I eat. I pick at the food and swallow a few of the berries, but it all tastes wrong.

It's also strange, so strange, to have someone serve me and treat me like I'm an uppy. I don't like it.

Again Marthes shares an invitation from Lord Osperacy to dine with his family, and again I say I'm not feeling well. I'll do my job and escort this Melily girl around when I must, but I don't want to spend any more time with these frightening strangers than I have to.

I only leave the vast bed to use the washing room, which to my surprise is not like our shared scrubpits in the barracks but, instead, my own private space. It's nearly as big as my cabin, and there's a strange washbasin shaped like a chair to relieve myself in. There's also another washbasin built into a cabinet and a giant bathing tub.

As the sky grows dark once more, my cabin door opens again. Yellow light from the outer passage falls over the foot of my bed like a rumpled blanket.

"I'm not hungry," I say, assuming Marthes has brought more food.

The yellow light widens, and a shadow fills it.

"Get up."

And I do because it's not Marthes, it's Douglen Osperacy. My joints protest, my muscles ache, and the stubborn thoughts in my head seem to shift and resettle as I stand. I feel as if I've either just recovered from a terrible flu, or I've aged fifty tides.

I glare at Douglen.

He wrinkles his nose. "Good Shale, it smells like something died in here."

Marthes hovers behind him, carrying a stack of towels.

Douglen steps further into my cabin. With his wide face, square features, and slab-like hands, he looks as if he'd be more comfortable in a Gray Strap's uniform, not the dark blue suit he wears. And even though he's nearly a head shorter than me, he still looks strong enough to snap me in two. "You know that with a simple command, I could make you throw yourself off the ship. Do you really want me to stay and force you to bathe, dress yourself, and come to dinner?"

I long to slink back onto the bed. "No."

"Good." Douglen looks to Marthes. "Clean her up. You've got an hour."

As soon as he leaves, Marthes meekly says, "I'm sure this will make you feel better."

I stare at the closed door. "I don't like him."

Marthes stiffens. "Not many of us do, to tell the truth, but it's best not to anger him."

The bathing tub is a smaller version of the baths in the Laeros Temple. Hot, salty water pours out of a gleaming spout, filling the shiny ceramic basin. It's so different than the bathing alcoves in the barracks where we deeplanders hastily clean ourselves beneath frigid trickles of water, and if I weren't so upset about being compelled to bathe, I think I'd like it.

Once I'm clean, Marthes swaddles me in a towel and shows me four dresses that belong to Shara. There are also some underthings, stockings, and uppy shoes.

"I'm sure you're gonna buy your own clothing in Beth," Marthes says, smoothing one of the gowns out on the bed. "But Miss Shara says she'll share hers with you until then, so aren't you lucky 'cause she has the loveliest clothes."

The dresses are beautiful, although far too slim for me. The only one that fits is an orange gown made of such flimsy, light material I expect it to tear as Marthes buttons it down my back. The shoes, though, are a little too big.

When I'm dressed, Marthes has me sit near the washing room mirror, which is clearer and smoother than any mirror I've ever seen. She towel-dries my hair and then arranges it into a mound of twisting braids.

On the way to the dining hall, we pass several other shipsmen, servemen, and servegirls. Most of them wear gray uniforms like Marthes, but a few wear black outfits or deep blue. I wonder how many people it takes to operate such a large steamship and how Lord Osperacy pays them all.

We pass through a large dining hall full of elegant tables. Most of them are empty, although a few well-dressed, unfamiliar uppies dine alongside the far windows.

"Who are those people?" I whisper to Marthes.

"Lord Osperacy welcomes other passengers too," she says, and I imagine some of those travelers were the people I saw peering out of cabin doors when I first met Melily.

121

Through the windows beside the passengers, I see the tidewater, smooth and flat. It makes my heart quicken, for I've never seen the ocean this way, with no dry land in sight.

We enter a smaller dining room that has a single, long table in it, as well as a glittering electric light that looks like a cobweb covered with raindrops. Lord Osperacy's already eating, as are Douglen and Shara.

Shara nods at the empty chair beside her, surely inviting me to sit. "That dress looks pretty on you."

I'm too amazed by all the food to reply. Huge quantities of tied bread, smoked fish, and sliced fruit lie in tidy half circles on gold-trimmed platters, and several steaming silver cauldrons stand nearby.

"Welcome Nerene! I hope you've enjoyed your time on my ship so far," Lord Osperacy says as if he has no idea that I've spent the past day and a half sulking in my cabin.

"It's nice," I say stiffly, and I sit beside Shara, feeling like a fish swimming with the wrong school.

A woman dressed like Marthes in a gray uniform and a white hairpiece pours red liquid into my eggshell-thin glass. I look around for the real Marthes, but she seems to have left.

A uniformed man then serves me salted cabbage and squares of roasted meat in a dark sauce. I wonder how I'm supposed to bring the food from the plate to my mouth. The knife doesn't look sharp enough to skewer it, and there are no clay ladles like we use in Saltpool.

Just then, Melily drifts in.

I haven't seen her since we first met, when she was half awake and furious. Now she looks like a child wearing her mother's clothing. A lacy, kelp-colored dress swings around her knees, a necklace of black pearls drips down past her waist, and a band of green velvet tames her curls. It's still strange to think that we're the same age

She sits across from me but doesn't seem to see me. "Ugh, I thought we were going to have lobster. Didn't we have water ox, like, two days ago? Tell me this isn't leftovers—because gross."

I look down at my meal. Water oxen are landrunners. No wonder it smells so good. Aside from fish and crab in Saltpool, we usually just eat stringy amphib.

I try to stab a piece of water ox with a dull knife, but the cube slides to one side. Frustrated, I pick it up and pop it quickly into my mouth.

"Oh Threegod!" Melily says. "Did you see what the sludge just did?"

Shara touches my arm, points to the pronged tool lying above my plate, and softly says, "We use the bigger one for meat."

I nod and not wanting to wipe my gravy-covered fingers on my borrowed dress, I lick them clean.

Melily bursts out laughing. "Ugh, you've got to be kidding me, Father! Look at her! She's like a mountain dog. I can't have her following me around in Beth! What if she barks at someone?"

Jeck, Douglen's other balance, enters the dining cabin just in time to laugh at me too.

I want to throw my useless, shiny knife at them. If only it wasn't so dull. What is it for anyway? Cutting wheatmeal? Slicing water? Only uppies would have something so wasteful and foolish.

Lord Osperacy turns to Melily. "If you don't want Nerene to embarrass you, then you must teach her how to behave. How about you two spend the day together tomorrow?"

Melily opens her mouth to protest, but instead she slumps back in her chair and puckers her lips as if she just ate sour river melon.

Jeck has more to say, though. "You've got your work cut out for you, Mel. Deeplanders are really stupid. I hear it's so damp in the kelp jungle, it rots their brains."

He and Melily laugh.

"That's enough," Lord Osperacy says. "You'll help train Nerene too, Jeck. She needs to know how to use a gunnerife by the time we reach Beth."

A gunnerife? That wasn't part of our agreement. Gunnerifes only cause trouble. In my mind, I see Sande holding that awful weapon again and pointing it at Giron and ruining everything. "Why must I use a gunnerife?" I risk asking.

"Sometimes Melily strains herself while using wavurl, and it can leave her vulnerable." Lord Osperacy plucks a salt shaker up off the table. "It's your job to protect her."

"I wouldn't trust a sludge with a gunnerife," Jeck says, and eyeing me, he cleans his teeth with his tongue. He's skinny and tall, with a soft jaw and mottled skin, and strangely, even though he's dressed as finely as everyone else, there are black oil smudges on his fingers and similar stains on his shirt. It's as if he's been working in a lower city factory. "I mean look at her," he continues. "She can't even eat normally. There's probably only one thing she can do well... or I guess I could say, have done to her."

Anger burns through me, and I jerk my arm without meaning to, spilling the red drink. To my astonishment, the fragile glass doesn't break, but the red liquid sloshes into my lap, soaking my legs through the borrowed dress. It smells like the springwine we drink in Saltpool, so it must be some sort of cohol.

There are no serveworkers around at the moment, so Shara helps me sop up red drink with the fine, foamsilk cloths that I didn't realize were tucked beneath our plates.

"I'm so sorry about your dress," I say, for it's surely ruined.

"It's fine," she says lightly. "I have plenty more." But then under her breath, only loud enough for me to hear, she adds, "Be careful." And I know she's not talking about the stain spreading across my skirt.

THE NEXT MORNING Marthes helps me find Melily's cabin. The petite siren appears at her door with her dark hair curling in all directions and wearing a frilly dressing gown. Seeing me, she frowns. "Oh right, I'm supposed to civilize you."

Melily's cabin is much bigger than mine, with two adjoining rooms and windows that overlook a narrow deck. I'm sure she has a pretty view most days, but today it's raining, and the sky is just as dull and gray as the ocean.

Her room, however, is cheerful looking, with bright blue walls and dark blue trim. Two upholstered benches rest on a thick, circular rug, and there's also a large bed veiled with transparent drapes. I'm most fascinated by her many railed shelves full of landrunner sculptures— some familiar and others not—as well as framed picturegraphs. The only picturegraph I've ever seen is the massive portrait of Chancellor Noble in Varasay's wharf market. He looks so real in that poster, I've had dreams where he tears off the pressed kelpwood and stomps around, crushing market stands.

"Would you like anything before I leave, Miss Osperacy?" Marthes asks.

"You should already know I want some hot seaweed tea," Melily says as she strides away to peer at herself in a round mirror, its frame decorated with carvings of water lilies.

Marthes nods and then leaves us alone. For a while I wait for Melily to speak to me, but when she continues to busy herself at the mirror, combing her short hair, picking at her skin, and dusting her cheeks with pink powder, I walk over to the shelves and examine the picturegraphs.

They're all of young men; most handsome, a few not; some with dark skin, others with light. Some of them wear seacotton suits, like the uppies do in Varasay, while others wear unfamiliar clothing, like cloth bundled around their heads, large hats, or garments of patterned pearlsilk.

I pick up a picturegraph of a man who looks a lot like Sande, although his nose is thinner and his hair isn't as curly.

"Don't touch that," Melily snaps from where she stands beside her wardrobe, a black dress draped over her arm.

Of course I continue to look at it.

"Um, aren't you listening?" she says, her voice wound tight. "I said put it down."

I turn to see understanding spread across her face. Surely she's realizing that I truly am her balance, and her wavurl won't work on me.

Tossing the lacy dress aside, she marches over and yanks the picturegraph out of my hands. "You can't just come in here and paw through my stuff. You'll break something."

"Who is this?" I ask.

"An admirer." She stands on tiptoe and carefully sets the frame back on the shelf. "Actually he's one of my *many* admirers. Father has us travel to so many places it's hard to keep track of them all."

She steps back as if to survey her collection, but she's really watching me out of the corner of her eye. "Which one do you think is the best looking?"

I shrug and point at the picturegraph I was just holding, the one that reminds me of Sande.

Melily moves closer to the shelves. "That's Selaan Waels—obviously the son of Pinser Waels, owner of Waels Equatorial Shipping."

I suppose I don't look impressed enough because Melily exhales heavily.

"Have you even *heard* of Waels Equatorial Shipping?"

I shake my head.

She looks at me as if I don't know how to shuck a clam. "I can't believe Father is actually going to make me take you into Beth. This will be *so* humiliating."

She retreats to the other side of the cabin and scoops up her black dress.

I'm wearing another of Shara's gowns today—one with far too many ruffles. She sent over a new selection of clothing this morning, and again, less than half of the outfits fit me. I'm fairly slender, but not in every single place, and Shara doesn't seem to have any curves at all.

While Melily buttons her dress, I explore her room, almost hoping she'll scold me again. With Douglen making me feel so powerless, it's satisfying to defy someone.

On the other side of her bed, I find a strange contraption that seems to be part polished wooden furniture, part machine, and part large brass horn. Beside it lies a stack of stiff cardpaper squares about the size of uppy dinner plates. The one resting on top has words and pictures printed on it.

"So who was that boy you wanted saved?" Melily asks a little timidly.

I look up from the wood and metal machine. "He's my closest friend."

Melily is now dressed, although she's still pulling on stockings. "Douglen said you were more than friends, *and* he said that sludge boy was really mad at you. What did you do?"

I don't want to discuss Sande with her, so I keep my answer short. "Something he didn't want me to. Is there anything I can do to help you get ready?"

"Don't change the subject." Melily climbs onto the bed, a white stocking hanging from her hand. "Was he your lover? He was your lover, wasn't he? I can totally tell by the way you're doing that thing with your face."

It's still hard to remember that Melily and I are the same age. Even with her painted eyes and elegant dress, she looks and acts so young.

I take a deep breath, sensing I should try harder to end the conversation. "I loved him—love him, yes… but we can never marry."

Her eyes widen. "Why?"

"When I was a child, Sande's family adopted me so that I could shelter in Varasay City while the tide passed. I was never truly part of his family, but because of that, because of what's written in the record books… we can't be together."

"So you're saying you love your brother? That's disgusting." Stockings on, Melily slides off the bed and plucks up a pair of shiny black shoes. "I wouldn't touch Douglen if someone paid me, and we're adopted too."

I fall silent—guessing that trying to explain the details of my relationship with Sande will only make things worse. But talking about him again makes me wonder where he is and how he's doing. I hope Lord Osperacy has kept Sande safe as he promised, and I can't wait to speak to him on the relayphone in Beth just to be sure. I also hope Sande will have forgiven me by then. Just knowing that he might still be angry makes me feel a constant ache.

I idly pick up one of the dinner-plate-sized cardpaper squares. There's a simplified drawing of a young man with bright green eyes on it. His hair rises up from his head like dark flames and then breaks apart into tiny black fish.

Melily rounds the bed. "Oh, do you like Cressit Scale?"

I think she's talking about the young man in the drawing, but I'm not sure.

She rolls her eyes when I don't answer. "Ugh, you don't know who Cressit is either, do you? You are so below. Give it to me."

But I don't. She didn't ask nicely, and I'm still looking at it. There's an opening on one edge of the cardpaper. The whole thing seems to be some sort of pocket, housing a flat, circular disc.

"I said give it to me." Melily tugs the square from my hands. "Good K'Gar, I *hate* having a balance. I have no idea how Douglen can stand having two."

She slides a disc out of the cardpaper and sets it on the contraption beside her bed. She then winds a winch on the side, fiddles with several mother-of-pearl knobs, and to my delight, music wafts out of the brass horn. It sounds far away, like I'm listening to tiny musicians through a long, hollow log, but those are definitely instruments and a real person is singing. I smile and gasp. As much as I want to hate all things uppy, I'm amazed that someone's captured noises in such a clever way.

The music is different than our village narrowstring and clatter-shell songs. There's an irregular drumbeat and something that makes me think of an automotor horn, although the sound is much more controlled and pleasing. I move closer to hear better.

"Yeah, Cressit is amazing." Melily kneels beside the other cardboard squares and flips through them. "The Bay Sisters are fabulous too, and I really like the Craw Trio." She tosses two squares on the bed. One has a picturegraph of women wearing frilly, white dresses printed on it, another is decorated with a strangely exaggerated drawing of three men using a washbasin for a boat.

It's then that I spot another picturegraph lying on the floor, almost beneath the bed. It has no frame, and the corners are bent.

I pick it up. A boy smiles at me. He has dark skin, short hair, and large eyes. "Is this another admirer?"

"No!" Melily leaps to her feet and looks as if she wants to snatch the picturegraph out of my fingers. "That's just Elgin, my old balance."

So she did have a balance once. Maybe he was the real reason Lord Osperacy stopped searching for me.

"He looks nice," I say. There's something about him that's friendlier than the formal portraits on Melily's shelves, something that makes me think he's probably fun to be around. "Where is he?"

Melily's mouth shrinks. "I don't know, and it doesn't matter." She takes the picturegraph from me and tucks it back under the bed—this time far under the bed.

We share our midday meal in Melily's cabin too, and she corrects me as I eat, making me feel as if I'm doing everything wrong.

"Um, you're supposed to cut that with a knife and fork," she says impatiently as I bite into a stack of sliced bread, smoked fish, and creek lettuce.

"But this is easier," I say. "And the knife isn't sharp."

"It doesn't need to be sharp to cut bread." Melily primly dismembers her own bread-fish-lettuce stack. "I can't imagine what it's like to visit the deeplands. It must be like going back in time."

I try to cut the bread the way Melily does, but all the smoked fish and creek lettuce squishes out the side.

Melily frowns. "So after lunch, I think we should go swimming."

That hardly seems practical or safe. "But how will we get back onto the ship? And won't it be cold?"

Melily snorts into her fizzy, pink drink. "Oh good Shale, we're not going to swim in the tidewater, you dummy. The *Trident* has a pool."

I look up, fascinated. "You mean there's a pool of water large enough to swim in—on the ship?"

"Uh yeah." Melily pops a snail-shaped biscuit into her mouth.

I try to look unimpressed, but to be honest, I'd love to go swimming. However when Melily has Marthes bring me one of Shara's swimming outfits, I like it less. "Do I have to swim in clothes?"

Melily laughs harshly like she did with Jeck yesterday. "It's not a bath. Have some shame. No wonder you love your brother."

I really regret telling her anything about Sande.

The pool is square, lined with tiny white and blue tiles, and it smells like saltwater. Surrounding it are huge, throne-like seats made out of reeds, painted white.

"Usually more people are swimming," Melily says.

"More people?" I echo, hoping she doesn't mean Douglen or Jeck.

"Yeah, other passengers." She tosses her robe onto one of the big, reed chairs. Her swimming outfit is pale pink with a large fabric flower on her hip. She also has a matching flower on the cap covering her hair. "We usually have more people traveling with us—uplander people, of course. We were supposed to welcome a new family in Varasay, but for certain *reasons* we left in a hurry." She looks at me as if I owe her an apology.

Melily's a surprisingly good swimmer. She moves easily through the water and dives with the grace of a fishing bird. I'm not sure why, but it upsets me. Maybe it's because uppies already have so many skills and talents. Swimming should belong to deeplanders.

Like Shara's other clothing, her swimming outfit doesn't fit me either. It's too tight, and I can't freely move my hips or shoulders. After a few attempts at gliding through the water, I climb out and glumly wrap myself in a towel.

I want to swim, though. As unusual as this pool is, I long to float on my back, close my eyes, and pretend I'm in Coral Lake. So I do my best to remember where the pool is, counting the turns in the passages, noting which stairwells we climb. Hopefully later, when everyone's sleeping, I can return.

We eat dinner in the ship's dining room again with Lord Osperacy, Douglen, Shara, and Jeck; and to my surprise, two young children in special toddling chairs; a boy and a girl.

"Ugh, I hate eating with Timsy and Dorla," Melily mutters. "Siren babies are such brats."

And sure enough, seconds after we sit down, the small boy cries for a spice dispenser. A weary-looking servewoman gives it to him. He then points and screams for one of the dull knives. The woman picks up a knife and begins to hand it to him too, but Lord Osperacy intercepts it.

"No, Timsy."

"Want, want!" the boy shrieks, and although I know he's misbehaving, and I know small children shouldn't play with knives—even dull ones—I still find myself reaching for my knife.

Thankfully before I hand anything to the child, Lord Osperacy takes my knife and pockets it. "Good evening, ladies. How was your day?"

Melily looks at the ceiling. "Absolutely horrible! Although… I suppose not as horrible as it could have been."

"I'm glad to hear it." The older man fixes his round, slightly bulging eyes on me. "Nerene, after dinner Jeck will give you gunnerife lessons."

I look at Jeck, and the slippery way he meets my gaze makes me lose my appetite.

The lesson on the drizzling deck later that evening doesn't begin terribly, though. Maybe it's because Shara joins us.

"I'm just here to make sure you don't shoot each other," she tells me with a wink.

Jeck starts by explaining how to fire a gunnerife, and then he has me shoot rubber bullets at empty tins he balances on the deck's railing. At first everything about the city weapon is strange, the weight of it and the fact that I can simply pull a trigger rather than stretch resin back, like I would with a poison dart. But it's not too different from aiming a snapper, and before long I'm hitting most of the tins. After an hour or so, I can shoot them so well, Jeck and Douglen start betting which ones I'll send flying off into the darkness.

"I had no idea she'd be so easy to train," Jeck says to Douglen. "We should start a sludge army and pay them with bottle caps or something."

134

I hate the way they talk as if I can't hear them.

I'm left alone to practice reloading while Jeck shows the others a fist-sized mechanical ball he's built. "It's simple," he tells Shara and Douglen. "You wind this crank here, and then you throw it as far as you can. The throwing part's important." He laughs.

I see a flash of silver as his invention splashes into the dark, distant water, then—*boom*—a cloud-like burst of fire appears below the waves.

I scramble away from the railing. What was that?

"I thought Lord Osperacy told you not to make any more weapons," Shara says as the water darkens again and an unnatural, unpleasant smell fills the air.

Jeck shrugs. "Eh, Almen will love them once he figures out how to sell 'em." He tosses another gleaming ball into the darkness, and as I hear another dull boom, I hope no fish or amphibs happen to be nearby.

When Jeck declares me a good-enough shot (and Shara says I'm excellent) Douglen tells me to return to my cabin.

"Wait—aren't you gonna thank Jeck for the lesson?" he asks as I near the door leading back into the ship.

I act like I don't hear him. It wasn't a wavurl command, just a question.

"Stop, Nerene," Douglen says.

And this time he uses wavurl. My hand hovers over the door handle, but I can't move further.

"Turn around."

I don't want to, but I have to.

Jeck sniggers.

"Now thank Jeck for the lesson," Douglen commands.

"Thank you for the lesson," I say softly.

"I think you can do better than that."

"Doug." Shara puts her hand on his arm.

Douglen shakes her off. "She needs to learn who's balance she is, and who's balance she isn't. Now sludge, thank Jeck properly."

I'm not sure what properly means, but my body seems to. As everything in me fights against Douglen's command, I drop to my knees on the wet deck, fold my hands, and say, "Thank you for taking the time to teach me how to fire a gunnerife. You've honored me with this lesson, you've honored your family, and you've honored Threegod."

Jeck chuckles, licks his teeth, and eyes Douglen. "Why don't you make her open her top too?"

"No." Shara darts forward. "Absolutely not." She pulls me back to my feet and glares at Jeck. "Don't start anything."

"Start what?" Jeck shifts a box containing his round, metal inventions to his other arm and wipes rain off his face.

"Lord Osperacy has been trying to find Melily a new balance for years." Shara pulls me to the door. "He risked our relationship with the Chancellor of Varasay for Nerene. If something happens to her or… goes wrong, what do you think Lord Osperacy will do to you? Let me remind you, Douglen has two balances, but he only needs one."

Jeck glances at Douglen. "When it's Shara's monthly time, warn me, won't you?"

Douglen turns to Shara. "Why don't you girls get out of the rain?"

When the ship is dark enough and quiet enough, I creep back to the pool. Patches of shadow cover the large room, and the water shivers with ripples. Outside the big window, the rain has stopped. The dark tidewater spreads out black and vast, and there are no moons, only thousands of stars—just as many as I can see in Saltpool.

I undress and slip into the warm water.

I don't swim like Melily did, diving and splashing. Instead I drift on my back, stretching out my arms and legs, and letting the water fill my ears and soften my hair. The only thing missing is the rustle of windswept kelp leaves and a breeze cooling my exposed skin.

I float until I feel sleepy, and when I start slipping into a dream about gathering herbs with Gren, I climb out of the pool and take a towel from the basket near the windows. For a short while, I watch the star-spattered tidewater, and then I pull on my nightdress and head for the door.

Yet as I leave, I glance at the chairs on the far side of the pool and my insides turn cold. Someone sits in the darkness, silent and still— someone with long arms and legs who looks a lot like Jeck.

Flustered, I pretend not to notice, and I let the door close behind me with an overly loud click. Then I race to my cabin barefoot, and heart thumping, I lock myself in.

IT TAKES US SEVEN DAYS to reach Beth, and when the city finally appears, it does so spectacularly, glittering like a mound of jewels on the tidewater. I can't sleep as the *Trident* sails nearer. So while the sun rises, I peer out my cabin window, and I watch the glowing mass split into two rounded peaks, both of them prickling with thousands of buildings. One of the peaks is taller than the other and both are ridges rather than points. It makes me wonder if the city rests on an old mountain range.

I'll speak to Sande on a relayphone so very soon, and it will be such a relief to know he's all right.

Docking the *Trident* is a complicated process with tugboats and heavy cables. And when the huge ship is finally secure between two concrete piers, I run to find Lord Osperacy.

It doesn't take me long. He's sitting in the dining cabin, reading a folded stack of papers, and drinking salted coffee.

"Can I speak to Sande now?" I ask.

He glances up from his reading. "Probably not."

I take a step backward, not sure what he means.

"Today, though," he adds. "You'll go ashore and buy proper clothing. I need you to be ready for tomorrow. Melily has a task."

I don't like the way he says *task*, letting the word roll across his tongue and then click deep in his throat.

"Can I speak with Sande tonight then?" I ask.

Lord Osperacy sighs and rests the paper he's reading on the table. "Your criminal companion left Varasay on a different ship that is most likely still traveling. When he reaches his destination, and *if* you've been managing Melily well, I'll allow you to speak with him then. Understood?"

I'm sure he would like me to now leave, but I risk asking another question. "Where... where is Sande going?"

Lord Osperacy picks up his folded papers again and says, "He's going where I sent him."

When Shara and Melily appear for the morning meal, Lord Osperacy tells them they'll be escorting me into Beth's high city so that I can purchase clothes. Melily seems happy enough about that ("I love shopping in Beth!") while Shara gives me a kind smile and says, "I'm sure you'll enjoy having your own wardrobe."

We're soon warmly dressed and climbing into one of the ship's two automotors. Lord Osperacy arrives in the hold to see us off, carrying Timsy in one arm and holding a passbook in his other hand.

He reaches through the open automotor window and gives the passbook to me. "I suspect rumors about our visit to Varasay have spread," he says. "Don't draw attention to yourselves."

A real passbook. I hold it like it's made of gold. It feels strange to just be handed one after everything Sande and I went through in Varasay. I wonder if Lord Osperacy bought this in secret or if he really got me land certified. When I flip the leather-bound book open, I see Chancellor Noble's walrus stamp. If it is a true passbook, Douglen must have commanded someone in Varasay to print it. I hope Sande now has one too.

Lord Osperacy also gives Shara some folded paper shells, and then our driver, a young serveman named Brindy, steers the automotor down a metal ramp that stretches out of the *Trident's* hull. We shade our eyes from the bright sunlight as Brindy guides the wheeled vehicle along the pier and over to a roadway. Beth's lower city doesn't look like Varasay's. It isn't a cramped mix of mismatched housing towers, aging factories, and tiny shops. Instead it's orderly and bleak. Rows of tall, identical buildings line thin streets that are otherwise empty—almost like endless barracks.

Aside from a monstrous desalination plant, I can't tell if the buildings are dwellings, shops, or small factories. I occasionally spot groups of people marching in lines.

"Are those deeplanders?" I ask Shara.

She gives me a quick look, pressing her mouth closed.

Melily answers instead. "Beth doesn't put up with sludges. The uplanders here own the deeplands and everyone who was dumb enough to live there."

How awful. I watch a group of women Bessel's age enter a plaster-covered building. Their clothes are plain, without any beads or embroidery, and I don't even see any dream markings.

Something like this could happen so easily in Varasay, especially after the riot. Already the uppies send workers on motorliners out to farm distant, uninhabited lands. Surely sooner or later they'll decide farming our land is easier.

I'm determined to hate everything about Beth, but my anger melts away when I see how beautiful the high city is—at least the currentways side we visit. Unlike Varasay's garish, far-too-ornate high city, the snow-covered buildings here have a sort of quiet elegance. They are tall and lean, with delicate stonework and subtle-but-pretty details, such as arched doorways and hanging, copper lights. The roads also curve like flowing water, and they're paved with dark gray and white stone. The sleek automotors that glide past us seem to move extra smoothly as well, and it's hard to imagine motors grinding and clunking away inside them.

We eat our midday meal in a cookery house that reminds me of the *Trident's* dining hall, except there are far more people and higher ceilings. A fancily-dressed man also plays music on an instrument that looks like a polished, uppy cabinet.

I dread blundering my way through yet another meal, but thanks to Shara, things don't go that badly. She helps me select my dinner from what she calls a "dining list" and demonstrates how to use Beth's double-ended fork. She also shows me how to cut my food into bite-size pieces using the shears tucked beside my plate. Melily, over on the other shore like usual, isn't helpful at all. She spends a lot of time telling us about all the wonderful food she's eaten before and why this food doesn't compare.

To be honest, I'm not sure I like this food either. Shara suggested I order creamy root mash and fish cakes. Although the mash tastes good, it's richer than what I usually eat and feels heavy in my stomach. As for the fish cakes, there's something oddly fragrant about them. It's as if I'm eating a flower or something flavored with uppy soap.

After our meal, the serveman in the automotor, Brindy, drives us over to Beth's clothing district where many brightly lit stores line the streets. Melily dismisses most of the shops as "too first tide," "too tacky," or "too mid city," before leading us into one with a sign shaped like a flutterbee. There, I try on dress after dress after dress. And I'm amazed by the many different types of fabrics, colors, and shapes of clothing there are.

"I like this one," I say, standing before three connected mirrors in a green gown that hangs from my ribs like a waterfall. I love how it swings and wafts out when I twist. It's so soft, too. I feel like I'm wearing flower petals.

"That is very pretty on you, isn't it?" The shopkeep appears in the mirror on my right, cradling an armful of other gowns. She's round and dimpled, and if she had thicker eyebrows, she'd look like Carnos's mother, Itanda.

"Yes, what a beautiful color." Shara joins me at the mirrors too and adjusts the lace on my shoulders. "I don't think Melily or I could get away with that shade of green."

"Um, this is taking *forever*," Melily says from where she lounges in a plush chair. She snaps her fingers at the shopkeep. "I want to try something on too. Find a dress for me."

The shopkeep winces as if someone's pinched her, surely confused as to why she feels compelled to do what Melily says. "Oh, I'm afraid we don't sell children's clothing here."

And even though I haven't known Melily for long, I know the shopkeep just made a terrible mistake.

"What?" Melily sits up straight. "Say that again."

The shopkeep places her armful of dresses on a chair made of coiled wire and silver leaves and looks even more confused. She repeats what she said, word for word, or at least tries to. "I'm so sorry... miss, but we don't sell children's clothing."

Melily stands as tall as she can—which even in her shiny, heeled shoes is not that tall. "You know, it's not nice to insult customers. Maybe I should teach you a lesson to make sure that you don't offend anyone else."

"Melily." Shara reaches for her arm. "There is no need to—"

"Shut up," Melily says.

Shara falls silent. She has to. She's only Douglen's balance and can't resist Melily's wavurl.

That means it's time to do my job. Lord Osperacy doesn't want Melily causing trouble, but how do I stop her? I can't undo her commands, only resist them. "Let's go to another shop," I suggest. "I can buy clothes somewhere else."

Melily ignores me. "So do you own this place?" She strolls toward the shopkeep, her shoes clickity-clacking across the pink and white tiled floor.

"No," the woman says, looking troubled.

"Then listen very closely," Melily says. "I want you to take all the dresses you can carry and throw them in the—"

"No," I say loudly, interrupting her. "Melily, your father will be angry if you do this."

"Uh, I don't care," Melily says, still glaring at the shopkeep who's hunched up as if she's about to be struck.

I feel like I'm trying to reason with a ridge cat. "If we draw attention to ourselves, we'll have to stop shopping, and you said you need new shoes."

"You're the one desperate for attention." Melily puts her hands on her hips. "You're the one flouncing around in dresses you can't afford. You're the one who's just a lucky sludge born at the wrong time."

I take a deep, quick breath. I wouldn't say I'm lucky, aside for maybe the *Trident* arriving in Varasay when it did, but at least I've distracted Melily from using her powers on the shopkeep. "You're right, this dress doesn't look good on me. Maybe you can help me find something better."

I hastily change back into the dress I was wearing before, another gown borrowed from Shara, and emerge to find the shopkeep boxing up numerous items.

"And ah… I'll take that too." Melily points to the green gown I just took off, which hangs over the dressing alcove door.

The shopkeep obediently fetches it and tallies the cost of the items.

Yet before she's through, Melily says, "Never mind the price, just give me everything for free."

"Yes, yes of course," the woman stammers.

"Melily, that's stealing," I say.

"So?" She runs her fingers over the silky top of a fabric-covered box. "You can't stop me."

"Yes, I can." I am bigger than her. "I could pull you out of the shop and make you leave everything here."

Melily's eyes widen because she surely knows I could overpower her. And at the very least, being dragged out of a shop would be embarrassing. Her concern doesn't last long, though. "Yeah? Really? Well go ahead and try. 'Cause if you do, I'll scream and tell everyone who comes running to rip your arms off." She pauses, then maliciously adds, "I'll make Shara attack you too."

Behind Melily, out of her line of sight, Shara makes hurried, lowering motions with her hands, encouraging me to calm her down.

And fathoms, how am I going to control this girl? Her wavurl might not affect me, but what does that matter if it affects everyone else?

So I give in, and it feels like giving up. "You're right," I say to Melily. "I'm not being nice, and I'm sorry. I'm not used to visiting uplander stores."

At least the automotor can only hold so many packages, and Shara manages to convince Melily that we should leave some room for the items Lord Osperacy wanted me to buy.

Still though, surely this shopkeep will be accused of stealing and lose her job, or maybe she'll be punished more severely. I don't know how strict Beth's laws are. And just as upsetting, if I can't control Melily, Lord Osperacy won't need me. And if he doesn't need me, what will happen to me then? And what will happen to Sande?

As we walk across the snowy street to another clothing shop— one Melily thinks looks "too boring"—Shara flashes me a quick, sympathetic smile that seems to say, *it'll get easier.*

I hope so.

I also wonder why Shara married Douglen. Surely she could have been his balance without marrying him, and it's hard to imagine she loves him.

Thankfully Melily behaves for the rest of the afternoon or is at least sulky but tolerable. Even though she tells me that every outfit I try on is ugly or not my color, I still return to the ship with a small stack of parcels and boxes, and I won't have to borrow clothes from Shara anymore.

That evening, I'm the first to arrive in the dining cabin for the evening meal. Shara appears not long after I do, and I'm thankful because I have a question for her. While servewomen arrange dishes on the table, I join Shara by a window overlooking Beth's busy harbor.

"How do you manage Douglen?" I ask. "I don't know how to be a good balance."

Shara gives me a conflicted look. "I wish there was an easy answer. I suppose it helps if I stay calm because if I get upset, he'll get even more upset. But... I can't stop him from doing what he wants to do. I can only offer advice and hope he listens." She then falls silent as Lord Osperacy enters the dining cabin.

He says, "I'm glad to hear you were successful today." And I'm relieved that he doesn't seem to know about what happened at the dress store.

After we eat, though, he calls me to his suite of cabins, back to the carpeted, decorated room where I first met him. Walking around his desk and opening a drawer, he says, "I have something for you."

He then places a gleaming, silver gunnerife on his desk, and says, "Bring this with you tomorrow."

I stare at the weapon's reflective surface and curving handle. Snappers stun and never kill, but gunnerifes are like death you hold in your hand. I don't even want to touch it.

But I want Lord Osperacy to think I'm being cooperative, so I take the gunnerife and say, "Thank you." Yet when I return my cabin, I hide it behind my new underthings, which Marthes arranged neatly in a drawer, and I plan on leaving it there.

MELILY AND I set out early the next morning. It's snowing, but I'm warm in my new fur jacket, soft wool mittens, and felt hat. I'm also wearing new boots, pale ones that fasten with brown laces, a beaded dress the color of a cresting wave, and Marthes fashioned my dark hair into two knots with cascading curls using heated, electric tongs. I look pretty, but not deeplander pretty. I'm uppy pretty, and it makes me feel like I'm wearing a costume.

Before we leave, Lord Osperacy pulls me aside and asks if I'm ready to protect Melily. I know what he's really asking—do I have the gunnerife? I nod yes, even though it's still hidden in my cabin.

"Remember, you must keep Melily out of trouble," Lord Osperacy says. "It won't be easy either. She's strong-willed. You must be stronger."

I wasn't stronger yesterday, so I feel anxious as I climb into the automotor and shimmy onto the soft seat. It doesn't help that all I know about Melily's task is that she's supposed to acquire something.

What that something is or how she'll get it or even where we're headed is still a mystery.

Today Brindy drives us into a tunnel that cuts through the mountain, connecting the wharf to the countertide high city. For a long time, we travel in darkness, with only the automotor's twin driving lamps illuminating the concrete road ahead and the man-made arches above. Eventually there's a burst of daylight, and we emerge onto a roadway. Leafless trees flash past my window, and a smooth brick wall rushes past Melily's side of the automotor. After a while, we reach a gate where we have to show our passbooks to several uniformed men. Like yesterday, the city guard hardly look at our passbooks. I suppose they assume two well-dressed young ladies in a gleaming automotor belong in the high city.

Beth's countertide high city is a lot like the currentways one, all elegance and modest beauty. Brindy parks the automotor alongside an ornate building that's both shorter and wider than the housing towers surrounding it and covered with windows. "When should I return, Miss Osperacy?" he asks, opening the door for us.

"In an hour," Melily tells him, climbing out. She glances briefly at me. "You should stay here with Brindy. You're just going to be in the way."

If only I could stay in the automotor without angering her father. Reluctantly, I climb out too.

Beth is colder today than yesterday. Clumps of snow whirl down from the sky and cling to my shoulders and hair. Brindy drives away, and for several moments I shiver as Melily inspects a pillar covered with paper signs that I can't read. She peels off a yellow square, tucks it into her white-fur jacket, and then turns to face me. "Now listen, acquiring things is my specialty, so don't say anything. If they know you're a sludge, this will be harder."

If acquiring things is Melily's specialty, Douglen must have a specialty too. When I ask Melily what it is, she shrugs. "Oh I don't know, a bunch of dull political stuff like fixing fights and trials, that sort of thing. Douglen makes Father more money, but Father cares more about what I do."

She clatters up the nearby stairs in her heeled shoes, her fluffy jacket obscuring her shape, making her look like a snowball supported by two black sticks.

I awkwardly follow her. I'm not used to my new boots—the soles are slippery and the ankles stiff.

When I reach the top of the steps, I find Melily waiting for me beside a set of brass doors that are flanked by stone dolphin statues. She purses her lips and tilts her head. "Uh, I thought Brindy would return while you were climbing. Threegod, you're slow."

I look up at the building. It seems larger and grander now that I'm standing so close to it, and judging by the half-dozen people entering and exiting through the ornate doors, it must be some type of public hall. "Where are we?"

"Oh right, you can't read. It's Beth's museum."

"I don't know what that is."

Melily partially closes her eyes and flattens her mouth. It's a look I'm getting used to—one that both mocks my ignorance and delights in knowing something I don't. "Museums are buildings where people keep old, expensive things. Shara's obsessed with them, and I think they're boring. It's the sort of place you have to at least pretend to like, though, or everyone thinks you're stupid. Now come on, it's cold."

We enter a round chamber with a domed, blue glass ceiling and a darker blue, tiled floor. I feel like I'm underwater.

A young man wearing an elegant suit greets us. The cool, wintry light shining through the roof paints him blue as well. "Good afternoon! Welcome to the Royal Museum of Beth. Admission today is fifteen shells."

Melily doesn't reach for her handbag, though. Instead she laughs, and the sound echoes through the hall like chimes. "Oh, come on, you're not going to make us pay."

"No, I guess not," the young man chuckles too, looking mildly confused.

"We're here to speak with Sir Saevel Mauricen," Melily continues. "Go find him for us."

"Certainly." The young man shudders as if attempting to shake free of her command, but he still strides obediently over to a small door. "Please wait in the main gallery."

The main gallery is a dimly lit room as large as a steamship. Exowhale bones hang from wires above, and dead animals pose on pedestals as if they're still alive. I see snow bears, fringed bears, striped panthers, long-tailed deer, water ox, gully-pigs, and dozens of other amphibs and landrunners that I don't recognize.

"This place is strange," I say, moving to one side of the hall. I can barely see the wires attached to the exowhale skeleton, and it doesn't seem safe to stand beneath it.

Melily isn't bothered though. Instead she inspects the crumpled paper she tore off the pillar.

After a moment, her eyes dart over to me. And as if worried I'll inspect the paper over her shoulder, she quickly folds it up and stuffs it back into her coat pocket. "I have a big surprise for you after we're done here."

"What is it?" I suspect I won't like it.

Melily's mouth curves into a prim smile. "You'll just have to wait and see."

A few uppies pass through the hall, pausing to view the dead animals and discuss them in hushed voices. Eventually a tan-skinned, white-haired man appears wearing a vivid blue jacket and frothy, gold-threaded scarf. I'm guessing he must be Saevel Mauricen, the man we're waiting for.

Sure enough he walks over to us, looking at me. "Do I know you?"

I suppose I appear to be the eldest and therefore in charge.

Melily is quick to correct him. "Oh, no-no, you don't know her, you know me! You just haven't seen me in ages. My name is Melily Osperacy. I'm Lord Almen's daughter."

"Of course you are! Melily, it's good to see you again." He gives her a quick, formal embrace. "You are so grown up! Is your father well?"

"He's doing wonderfully well," Melily says. "And he also said that while I was in the high city today, I just had to stop by to see your personal collection."

"And of course you must!" Sir Mauricen idly taps his walking stick on the gleaming floor. "I wish I could say it was as impressive as your father's. Does he, perchance, have any new finds to sell?"

"Not this tide—not yet anyway," Melily says. "But he heard a rumor that you acquired some arctic stones. Did you really?"

Sir Mauricen's eyes glitter. "I did!" he says as if sharing a secret. "And they're breathtaking. A friend of mine found them on an expedition to the skytide frozen cities. Can you imagine? Traveling all the way up there?"

I like the friendly crinkles in the corners of Sir Mauricen's eyes. They make him look like the sort of half-rugged, half-refined person who might enjoy visiting Saltpool. I like his walking stick too. The handle is a glass ball with a tiny blue starfish inside.

"You'll have to forgive my office. It's in a terrible state!" Sir Mauricen leads us out of the main gallery and into a chamber lined with painted portraits. The subjects have unfamiliar hairstyles and clothing, but they have the same rounded cheeks and curved features that seem to be common in Beth.

"We just opened a new exhibit," Sir Mauricen tells us. "It's about Oro-Lemah, the Water Goddess, and the many ancient people who once worshiped her. However, the city priests are livid. They say it's an offense to Threegod! Can you imagine? I'm sure Threegod doesn't care about a lost culture and dead religion. Anyway, I've been writing letters to King Renji trying to sort it out. I've got papers everywhere."

I didn't know the Water Goddess's name is Oro-Lemah. Maybe people only call her that in Beth.

"Can we see the…" I falter, not sure how to phrase it. "See the Water Goddess… room?"

Melily sighs. "No, Nerene. We're here to see Sir Mauricen's personal collection, remember?"

"Why don't we see both?" Sir Mauricen smiles at me. "We'll pass right by the Oro-Lemah exhibit on the way to my study." He walks faster, swinging his starfish cane broadly as if it were for decoration rather than support. It makes me think of the way Sande and I carried sticks when we were children. We'd knock them against kelp trees, sending birds flying and rain monkeys skittering up into the higher branches.

We pass through another corridor lined with paintings of harbors and old-fashioned sailing ships, and then we enter a spacious hall containing a statue of a siren that stretches from floor to ceiling, nearly as high as a barracks building. Fins spread out from her dimpled elbows like oddly placed wings, and her legs curl into twin fish tails. Her mouth is full of jagged teeth, and a single beam of electric light makes her glow greenish-gold.

I stare up at her in awe. So this is the Water Goddess or, I suppose, Oro-Lemah. I wonder if there was once a statue of her in our village.

If the real goddess is truly so huge, she could pick me up with one hand.

Keep Sande safe, I beg her with my thoughts. *Please.*

A glass box framed in polished wood rests at her feet. I move closer, and I see a miniature city lies inside, complete with tiny sculptures of people and animals.

Sir Mauricen joins me. "Fascinating, isn't it? That's a scale model of Dovi, one of the greatest deepland cities. Actually, Melily, your father helped me locate it, and we led the first expedition there together. I love how flat it is! Those ancient architects didn't have to worry about limited space like we do."

I lean closer, pressing my hands against the glass. These buildings are so much larger and more intricate than the huts we repair and rebuild after every tide. I wish Sande could see them.

I ignore Melily's folded arms and walk over to another glass box. This one holds fine metal shafts the size of my fingers. Each shaft is engraved with angular patterns and what must be writing, some even have jewels on them. "Are these… snappers?" I ask.

"Why yes!" Sir Mauricen says. "You have a good eye. They are so much more refined than the snappers deeplanders use now."

I prickle because I'm sure we deeplanders could make fancy snappers like these if we had fine metals and jewels.

"So much knowledge was lost during that first tide," Sir Mauricen continues. "So many craftsmen and artisans drowned. Can you imagine what it was like for those people when the water first came? Most of them had nowhere to run. Many of the lowland cities weren't near mountains, you see. There was no way to escape the floods. It was such a tragedy."

"How did the tide start?" I ask. It's a question I've asked before. Gren Tya says the Water Goddess lost her children and asked the ocean to find them. Bessel thinks it's because people are sinful, and the Water Goddess is trying to drown us, and the Threegod priests say the Water Goddess is really a demon who spat venom into the ocean, driving the water mad.

Sir Mauricen grips his walking stick with both hands. "The professors at Beth University teach that it's because our moons aren't equal in size. They believe one was knocked out of position by debris in the stars. I wish I remembered their lectures well enough to explain it in greater detail because their theories are fascinating." He moves over to a table. "Come this way, my dear, you might enjoy this. It doesn't look like much, but it's my favorite part of the exhibit."

I join him at the table. It has a depression in the center that cradles a carved slab of rock.

"We don't know what the writing says—hopefully one day we will—but isn't the art interesting? Here are the uplanders." Sir Mauricen uses his walking stick to point out a group of carved figures who carry spears and stand on a hill. "We were so simple then, hunters mainly. And here are the deeplanders." He points to several people standing among flat, rectangular buildings. A few of them have hints of gold paint on their clothing, although much of it has been worn or washed away. "But who are these people?" Sir

Mauricen points to a few figures standing in a lake. "Fascinating, isn't it?"

"I'd like to see the arctic stones now." Melily follows her comment with a loud sigh.

"Of course, of course." Sir Mauricen turns to her. "Forgive me, I'm just so fond of all this dusty old stuff. I once led all the expeditions to Dovi—first with your father and then on my own, and it was so exciting! It's been years since I've been down in the deeplands, but hopefully, I'll be able to go again soon. Who knows if I have the energy, though!"

He seems to have plenty of energy to me as he jogs up a wooden staircase and nearly sprints down a thin hall. After a few more doors, stairs, and passages, he ushers us into a room with sandstone walls, a circular window, and mountains of clutter. It seems as if someone ran about the place tossing books and paper into the air. Within the chaos, stand countless shelves and glass cases, all crammed with rocks, rusted bits of metal, paintings, stone sculptures, and tattered scrolls.

"See? It's such a disaster. I do apologize." Sir Mauricen tugs on a thin chain, and electric lights that resemble candles flicker on. He then picks up a human skull as casually as I might hold a rock and doesn't even whistle to soothe the death shadows. "We just closed an exhibit on the mining shafts beneath Beth. Much of this was on display and needs to be cataloged."

"What a fascinating collection," Melily says, not sounding remotely interested. "Please show us the arctic stones."

"Ah yes! Just let me get them." Sir Mauricen digs a key out of his bright blue jacket and unlocks a small metal door in the wall. A moment later he pulls out a wooden chest, which he also unlocks.

SARAH MENSINGA

Nestled on foamsilk inside, are what seem to be ice shards pulsing with soft light.

"They're beautiful!" I say.

"They are." Melily sounds surprised. She squeezes between us. "Could a person make jewelry out of these? You're going to give me five of them. Could one be cut and, like, set into a ring?"

"Arctic stone jewelry would be lovely, wouldn't it?" Sir Mauricen says. "I've heard they make some arctic stone necklaces skytide of the equator, but I can't imagine..." He winces as if in pain and touches his head.

I look to Melily, impressed and a bit frightened by how smoothly she used her wavurl.

Sir Mauricen's eyebrows pull together. "I can't imagine how much they cost and..." He steps back from the table and takes a moment to gather his thoughts. He then turns to Melily. "You know, this may sound odd, but I'd love to give you a few of these, perhaps five? It's an extravagant gift, but I was once very close with your father."

"Oh, well thank you so much!" Melily's surprise is almost convincing.

Sir Mauricen holds out the chest of arctic stones with a crooked frown.

She's here to steal. We're here to steal. The reality of it squeezes me around the middle. I feel so stupid. I should have realized what 'acquire' meant earlier. "Is this what you do?" I whisper to her. "Is this what I'm supposed to help you do?"

"Hush, Nerene." Melily gives Sir Mauricen a reassuring smile, and then selects one, two, three of the largest stones and slips them into her handbag.

Sir Mauricen's eyes drift over to me as if he hopes I'll explain what's happening.

I turn away, feeling horrible. All of this is for Sande. This is what I must do to keep him safe.

After Melily selects rocks four and five, she snaps her handbag shut. "Aw, you're way too generous. And now we actually have to be on our way. Show us out please."

"Of course." Sir Mauricen gives his head a little shake. He then puts the chest of remaining arctic stones on a precarious pile of books and leads us out into the corridor.

My cheeks burn with shame, and halfway down the first stairway, I say to Melily, "Is this why your family has so much money?"

She exhales heavily. "Ask your stupid questions later. I'm trying to focus."

And I suppose I've distracted her from whatever she must do to keep Sir Mauricen in thrall because he pivots on the landing and glowers at us. "You've done something to me. Why did I give you those gems?"

"You're supposed to be helping, not making things harder," Melily hisses at me, hurrying down the steps. "Show us the way out, Sir Mauricen, and make it a back door."

His face crumples as he tries to fight her wishes, but he also continues to limp down the stairway.

"You can't control him forever," I say under my breath, and at least I think she can't. "He'll call for Gray Straps."

"You mean he'll call for R.S. Men," Melily tells me. "This is Beth, not Varasay. And no, he won't. I'm not wrinkly old Douglen with fading wavurl. I'm a full-strength siren."

I vaguely remember Lord Osperacy telling me that he no longer has wavurl. That makes me hopeful. If Douglen's powers fade soon, maybe he won't be able to control me much longer. And when Melily loses her wavurl, she won't need a balance anymore—although I certainly hope I won't have to serve her for that long.

Sir Mauricen opens a door, revealing a snowy alley behind the museum. I race outside, my boots punching out crisp footprints. But Melily lingers beside the older man, craning her neck as if she's about to peck him on the cheek. "Forget everything about meeting us," she tells him.

Then leaving him inside, she shuts the door, takes three staggering steps, and collapses.

"WAKE UP," I WHISPER, rolling Melily over so she isn't lying face down in the snow. "Wake up, please!"

I glance over at the museum door, half-expecting Sir Mauricen to barge through it calling for Gray Straps or R.S. Men or whatever the city forces are named here.

Several minutes drag by. Is Melily dying? Is she already dead? I take off a glove and work my bare fingers past her pearly knit muffler to find her neck. But when I touch her warm skin, her eyes spring open, bloodshot and purple around the edges.

I pull back. "Oh thank the Water Goddess! Are you all right? What happened?"

She shudders out a breath. "Making someone forget… it's hard."

"Come on, let's get you up out of that snow." I pull my glove back on and hoist her onto her feet, glad she's tiny and I'm not. This must be what Lord Osperacy meant when he told me that Melily might strain herself.

Snowflakes collect in our hair as we hobble down the alley toward a lively street full of bundled uplanders and creeping automotors. I expect Melily to scold me for distracting her in the museum, but she doesn't. Perhaps fainting softened her temper.

"Doug and Shar keep saying that I need to be more subtle." Melily leans heavily on me. "They say it's better if people don't know I'm commanding them. But it… takes so much focus to do that… and it's especially hard when I have a new balance." She gives me a cloudy look. "Sometimes it's just easier to make people forget they ever saw me."

It doesn't seem easy. She's hanging off me like a springwine drunk or someone sick with a fever. When we reach the busy roadway, I steer her toward the front of the museum. Hopefully none of the uppies slogging past will notice how weak she is, and hopefully Brindy will have the automotor waiting.

"No." Melily turns in the opposite direction, and when I resist she seems to double in weight.

"Yes," I say. "We have to return to the ship."

"But the surprise, remember? I have a big surprise for you." She rummages in her fluffy, white coat and hands me the flier she tore off the pillar. "*This* is tonight."

I can't unfold it one-handed, so I pinch a corner and shake it open. Large, urgent writing covers the yellow paper. I also see the same drawing that was on one of Melily's music squares—the drawing of a young man with flame-like hair that breaks apart into fish. "I don't understand."

"There's a Cressit Scale swingshow tonight! Right here in Beth!" Melily's voice is high and airy as if she's telling me that one of the Threegod forms is about to descend.

"A swingshow?" I echo, confused.

"He's performing!" Melily taps the words on the flier with her mitten. "Singing!"

"We're supposed to go back to the ship," I say firmly. Again I tug Melily toward the front of the museum.

But she's regaining her strength and pulls away. "You don't have to come, but I've wanted to see Cressit sing for forever, and I've never been in the right city at the right time. Father still thinks I can't be trusted at swingshows. This might be my only chance. I'm taking it."

Which means I'll be blamed, and if Lord Osperacy's angry with me, he surely won't let me speak to Sande on the relayphone. Panic flutters in my stomach. I try a different approach. "What about the arctic stones? Your father will want them as soon as possible."

"*Pssht*, that doesn't matter. He won't find a buyer for months. He can wait a few stupid hours." Melily staggers away from me.

I debate running to the front of the museum. If Brindy's there, I can tell him Melily's plans, and he can tell Lord Osperacy or Douglen. But if I leave Melily, I risk losing her for several hours, and it's my job to protect her.

I flick snowy hair out of my eyes and wish I knew what to do. I need to make up my mind quickly, though, because she's already several housing towers away.

With a moan of frustration, I plod after her. Surely Lord Osperacy wouldn't want me to leave her side while she's weak.

Melily waits for me to catch up. "Does this mean you're coming?"

I nod in resignation. "Can we at least ask Brindy to pick us up when this Cressit person's done singing?"

Melily makes a face. "No, absolutely not. Brindy will want to tell Father, and I don't want to spend the night wavurling him. Don't worry, I'll just make someone drive us to the *Trident* later on."

Then as if to show me just how easy that will be, she waves the flier at the roadway until a bronze-colored automotor rolls to a stop, and then she orders the driver to take us to the Cressit Scale swingshow.

As anxious as I am about Melily flaunting her wavurl, I'm happy to climb into a warm auto. I squeeze in beside a scandalized-looking young woman and her three fuzzy black dogs.

Melily glares at her. "Don't ask us any questions."

The young woman opens and closes her mouth a few times, and then says, "Excuse me, you can't just ride in my —"

"And don't complain," Melily adds. "Or talk."

The young woman falls into a red-faced silence. Two of the dogs cower behind her laced boots, but the third betrays her and climbs into my lap. I scratch its ears.

We soon arrive at some place called the Islet Dance Gallery. It's similar in shape to Giron Noble's factory, squat and rectangular, but otherwise much nicer to look at. Tall, colorful windows stretch across the front of the building, patchworks of glass arranged to look like women wearing dresses made of gleaming triangles and diamonds.

As we climb out of the automotor, releasing the woman and her dogs, Melily tells me the swingshow won't start until dusk, so we eat at a nearby cookery house. Just like yesterday, I find it strange to walk into a building, sit down as if it were my own home, and wait for people to bring me food.

Melily doesn't bother reading me the dining list like Shara did, instead she orders us both clam soup and a sugary dish she assures me is so delicious I'll "want to die."

"The only time I've ever seen a swingshow was when the Star Children performed in Lellev," Melily tells me. Her eyes are still

162

bloodshot and swollen from forcing Sir Mauricen to forget about the theft, but she seems to have recovered otherwise. "It was life-changing, I swear. You are going to wake up tomorrow morning and everything will be different."

"Lord Osperacy will punish us, won't he?" I prod the foamy concoction with a spoon, too anxious to eat. I should have run for Brindy. I know that now. I may have lost Melily, but she would have been fine. Then I could have told Lord Osperacy where to find her, and he'd only be angry with Melily, not me—or at least he wouldn't be *as* angry with me.

"I guess he'll punish us. But it'll just be a slap on the hand." Melily takes an ample scoop of her dessert. "Anyway, who cares? Seeing Cressit Scale sing in person is worth changing a few of Timsy's nappers."

But my punishment will surely be worse than hers. "If we return to the ship right now, we can tell Lord Osperacy we were hungry and lost track of time."

Melily rearranges her double-looped necklace. "Don't be such a tadpole. You'll like this, I swear."

I give the frothy pink stuff an angry stir. All I can do now is beg, though I suspect that won't work either. "Melily, please. Your Father will only let me talk to my friend on the relayphone if I do my job well. I just want to know where Sande is and know that he's safe."

Melily listens attentively to me. It seems like a good sign.

"I miss him," I add. "Please, can we return to the ship? I really don't want to anger your father."

"So you're still calling that boy your friend, huh? Because that's not really true, is it?" Melily smirks and blows a cloud of steam off her tea, making it clear I haven't convinced her. And worse, there's sourness in her smirk and a hint of cruelty. "Look, I'm doing you a favor. The sooner you forget about him the better."

Melily doesn't want to pay for our meal, but I manage to convince her to by reminding her that not paying might help Lord Osperacy or Douglen find us. Then we head back out into the bitter cold, although thankfully it's no longer snowing. In fact, Beth looks even more beautiful. It's dark out now and many electric city lights glitter across the ice and snow.

We walk along shoveled pathways to the Islet Dance Gallery, where it's even brighter. Blue and green lights sweep across the front of the building, skipping over pillars and diving briefly into the dark sky to reveal patches of clouds. The images of women in the colorful glass windows burn red, orange, and violet, and garbled music thumps out through the open doors.

Melily grabs my arm and squeals, "I can't believe this is happening!"

"Hey, does anyone need tickets?" shouts a man not dressed as nicely as the many other uppies crowding around the entrance. "The show might be sold out, but I'll getcha in!"

"Give me two." Melily thrusts out a hand.

The man passes her a pair of printed cards, looking both surprised and annoyed. "I want twelve shells for 'em."

"No, you don't." Melily waves the cards at me. "Let's warm up!"

Rhythmic sound swallows us as we pass through the brightly lit entrance. I've never heard anything so loud, with the exception of the machines in Giron's factory. Melily leaves her coat with a woman in a side room and tells me to do the same.

"Will we get them back?" I ask.

"Uh, of course," Melily laughs. "Besides, it's not as if we can dance with them on." She straightens the lace band holding back her dark curls and then leads me into a not-quite-oval, not-quite-rectangular room that is as large as the museum's main gallery. It's mostly dark, but faint light glimmers through hundreds, or perhaps thousands, of sharp glass shapes hanging from the ceiling. Huge, purple-red murals of sleepy-looking, partially-dressed women cover the walls, while uppies sway like seagrass across the floor. I suck in a deep, amazed breath. Everyone here looks like royalty. The women wear richly-colored, sparkling dresses, along with pearl necklaces, feathered headdresses, and high-heeled shoes like Melily's. The men wear patterned shirts rolled to their elbows, shiny vests, and scarves that mimic bunched up leaves.

Melily tugs me through all the luxurious fabric and elaborate hairdos, toward a large platform attached to the far wall. On it, a woman wearing a gold dress stands in a concentration of orange light, singing a song that seems to be about heartbreak and the tide. Behind her, two men play instruments that must be connected to sound enhancing devices like Giron's. And their music is so alive and fresh compared to the cardpaper squares in Melily's cabin. I feel it pressing into my chest, encouraging my heart to beat in time.

The closer we get to the platform, the more people are dancing around us. At first it's just girls tapping fingers on their thighs and young men nodding with crumpled expressions as if they're straining to lift something heavy. But soon we see uppies shaking their hips and shoulders, and a few even lift each other into the air. I've danced before in Saltpool, but those were ceremonial dances for feasts and parting moons, nothing like this.

"Get into it, Nerene! Dance!" Melily cries, twisting as if she's a drenched rag that needs wringing out.

I'm not sure I like the music, it's so noisy and unpredictable, but there is something exhilarating about how hazily it marches around me and, in a strange way, tempts me. I secretly wish I did know how to dance like these uppies because they certainly seem to be having fun. Instead I'm jostled by the crowd, and I struggle to stay close to Melily.

The woman in gold sings a few more songs and then her orange light dims and the music fades, leaving only a steady drumbeat. The uppies roar, happily I think, and surge forward. I feel trapped as I cling to Melily's hand, but the dense crowd doesn't seem to bother her. She grins at me and mouths, "Cressit!"

There's a sudden swell of sound that I guess is music, and a young man twitches his way across the platform. Flashing lights make it difficult for me to see him at first, and all I can make out is his silhouette. The uppies whistle and scream, and I feel a rush of fear because everyone seems to be on the edge of losing control, much like the factory riot.

The flashing lights blend together until they become an intense, white glow shining up from beneath the platform, and now I can see Cressit properly. He's skinny and tall, with a pointy face and a long swath of black hair swept over one eye. He also wears a blue suit that sparkles like a freshly caught fish as he struts up to the voice enhancer. Holding an instrument that looks like our Saltpool narrowstrings, except black and glossy, he launches into a fast-paced melody. Behind him, three men blow into gleaming horns, first pointing their brass instruments to one side, and then moving as a group and pointing them to the other. Another man pounds a collection of drums that gleam with silver and gold accents.

"C'mon!" Melily yanks me closer to the platform.

"No." Now I'm the one digging in my heels and refusing to move. This is already too close to the uncontrolled crowd surging around the musicians.

"Fine! I'll find you after then!" she calls, twisting away.

"Give me your handbag!" I holler over the music. I should at least keep the arctic stones safe.

She tosses her beaded bag to me, and then she's gone. I retreat to the nearest wall, hugging the purse to my heart, looking for a scrap of space where no one will stumble into me, and certain that I'm being a terrible balance. I spot a bench beneath one of the giant wall paintings and hurry toward it. I'm nearly there when a smiling young man slips an arm around my waist and tries to pull me back into the crowd, the moving lights, and the overwhelming noise.

"I don't…" I shout, trying to escape. "I don't want to dance."

"You don't what?" he yells, pointing to his ear.

"My village! We don't dance like this!"

He shrugs, apparently still not hearing me, but he also, mercifully, saunters away.

When I reach the bench, another stranger hands me a drink that smells like something I'd cure hides with. I smile *thank you* and put it beside me, untouched.

Most of Cressit's songs sound the same: lots of horns, lots of drums, and lots of cheerful-yet-aggressive wailing. I try and fail to spot Melily among the churning dancers. I hope it's just because she's short, for without her, I'm stranded in Beth's high city. I have no idea how to reach the Osperacy's boat on my own.

After twelve or so songs, Cressit ends his performance with a much quieter melody about tide pirates. It seems like a song I might actually like; there's something gentle about it. I think the words tell a story, but the uppies are still cheering, whooping, whistling, and applauding so loudly, I can't really hear it.

Thankfully as soon as Cressit leaves the platform, the lights brighten and the crowd thins. It takes me a few frightening minutes to find Melily, and as soon as I see her, I'm glad I took the arctic stones. Her hair sticks up like the Cressit drawing, and she's missing her headband, along with one shoe. Her long pearl necklace is miraculously unbroken, but a torn, lacy shred hangs off her dress.

"That was amazing!" she cries. "Admit it, you're glad I made you come."

"Yes," I say. There's no point arguing now. The damage is surely done with Lord Osperacy. "Let's find your shoe."

It's under a table, lying in a spilled drink. I expect Melily to complain about how wet and sticky it is, but instead she hastily buckles it around her ankle while chattering about the performance. "I just loooved 'Adrift.' The way Marto started it with that drum roll —he's the drummer, you know—it was so… *so*… ! I never thought anything could be that fantastic. Which song was your favorite?"

"All of them," I say vaguely. "Now let's find someone who looks trustworthy, and you can wavurl them to take us back to the *Trident*."

Melily stares at me like I've suggested she eat her stockings. "Are you serious? We're not going back to the ship yet! I'm a siren! Don't you know what that means?"

That because of her, I'll lose Sande. "No," I say softly.

Her eyes sparkle just as brightly as Cressit's blue suit. "Our night's just beginning."

I FEEL HELPLESS and frustrated as Melily grabs my arm and hauls me over to a man standing in front of the swingshow platform.

"We're here to meet Cressit," she says. "Find him for us."

This man is twice as large as Carnos, something I never thought possible. He looks down over his swollen chest as if he'd like to refuse her, but of course he can't. "The singer already left."

Melily narrows her eyes and gracefully gathers up the torn shreds of her dress. "Tell me where he went."

"His… housing tower, I think," the big man rumbles, and then covers his mouth with several massive fingers as if that might stop more words from escaping.

"Take us there," she says.

"I would but I don't know the way," he says, brow furrowed.

I exhale in relief. Now we'll *have* to return to the *Trident*. But then with a grunt of pain, like something is being torn out of him, the giant man adds, "Tarrol, he knows." And he points to a skinny uppy across the hall.

The uppy, Tarrol, wears a white foamsilk suit, and he's busy showing a stack of picturegraphs to a pair of women in matching black furs and glittering dresses. I watch helplessly as Melily skips toward him. And only a few moments later, she and I have retrieved our coats, and we've joined Tarrol and the matching women in a shiny automotor as it cuts through snowdrifts. We're on our way to Cressit's housing unit.

And now I'm not just worried, I'm also sleepy. Melily, though, looks as if she could stay awake all night. She's perched on the edge of her seat, ankles crossed and her gloved hands still dancing on her knees. "Beth's so pretty when it snows, isn't it?"

"Just like a sugar cake," agrees one of the women.

Melily slides closer to me and, surprisingly, drops her head onto my shoulder. "You know, I really thought I'd hate having you as my balance, but now I wish Father'd found you sooner."

It's an odd comment, and I'm not even sure she's being that nice, but maybe because the moonlight on the snow really is beautiful, I momentarily forgive her for all the trouble she's causing.

Cressit's housing unit or "spread"—for that's what Melily tells me housing units are called in high cities—is at the very top of a building overlooking a steep cliff. We ride up to his home in a contraption called a lifter, which is essentially a small closet that mechanically travels up and down a hollow shaft. And although I'm glad we don't have to climb flights and flights of stairs, I still feel as if I might suddenly drop to my death. I cling to a shiny brass bar attached to the lifter wall and squeeze my eyes shut until the box we're in stops rising and the operator opens the doors.

I don't know what to expect as we walk down a thickly carpeted hall lit by golden clam shell lights, but my mind cobbles together an image of Cressit preparing for bed, and I feel embarrassed that we're about to impose. Yet that concern vanishes as we enter another dimly lit space, crowded again with uppies. For a moment I feel as if we've walked back into the Islet Dance Gallery, yet there aren't as many people and they aren't behaving as wildly. Most of the uppies here are talking, laughing, and sipping cohol drinks from elaborate glassware. A few couples dance to sluggish tunes crackling out of an uppy music machine, and on the far side of the room, several people blow clouds of smoke through thin metal tubes.

The room itself is long, with a high ceiling and a group of windows overlooking Beth's sloping streets and the starry tide. Here and there, lights with decorative fabric shades cast glowing pools of red, and the air smells strange—almost like a burning patch of riverbank flowers.

"Ooo, there he is!" Melily squeezes my shoulder. In the few moments I've been looking around, she's shed her coat and found a drink that's in a blue-tinged glass as long as her forearm. Slim loops run down one side of the glass, and I think they're meant to be handles.

"Just look at him," she sighs. "Isn't he absolutely perfect?"

I follow her gaze. Across the room, Cressit rides a current of giggling young women. Occasionally he flips his shiny, black hair to reveal both of his eyes and laughs in a lazy, slow way that makes it seem as if he needs to clear his throat. There is something interesting about him, though, and I don't like that I notice.

"Go on, go talk to him," I urge. As soon as Melily realizes that Cressit is just another uppy in far too fancy clothes, we can return to the *Trident*.

Melily gulps down a large mouthful of her drink, and her cheeks flush. "But what would I even say?"

"I don't know. You could ask him to sing to you, or you could use your wavurl to *tell* him to sing to you." I give her a nudge in the performer's direction.

Melily looks at me as if she's fighting to contain a scream. "I feel like I'm going to throw up. What if I throw up in front of him? What if I throw up *on* him? Let's just walk around a little bit until I feel braver."

"He won't say no to you," I remind her.

But she's already wiggling away and off into the passage on my left. Not sure how else to encourage her, other than to let her drink more, I follow.

Cressit's housing unit is massive. The corridor we're in alone is far taller than it is wide, and it's also lavishly decorated. The paintings on the wall are so skillfully done they look like picturegraphs, and the black floor is so polished it looks wet.

As Melily and I pass a pair of uppies deeply fascinated with each others' mouths, I say, "If you don't want to talk to Cressit today, why don't you visit him the next time you're in Beth? You know where he lives now."

Melily snickers, and it's a laugh that tells me I've misunderstood something she thinks is obvious. "Um, he's in Beth today, yes, but he's not always in Beth. He travels with the tide, performing all over the trade routes. He rents spreads wherever he goes. That's what all the big swingshow stars do."

We enter the cookery, which is sleek and black and so clean I wonder if anyone's ever prepared a meal there. We find several young men refilling their goblets and talking loudly about something called paddlebat. They're dressed a lot like Cressit, with sequined jackets and tight vests, except their hair is short and brushed back as if they've all been caught in a strong wind.

One of them, still talking about how much he hates "pole floaters," reaches over to refill Melily's now-empty glass. While another young man, one with a curly sweep of hair and round middle, leaves the paddlebat debate to offer me a drink.

"I'm fine, thank you," I say, eyeing Melily and her second drink with concern. The glass is very big.

"So are you countertide or currentways?" Curly hair asks. Now that he's standing close to me, I can tell he's older than he's trying to appear, maybe around thirty tides.

I think he's asking me which side of Beth I'm from, so I say, "Currentways," in a cool tone I hope will end the conversation. Then I shimmy away from him and move toward the roasting hearth, a shining, metal monstrosity that could probably cook a whole froth turkey.

"Really? What neighborhood?" he asks, following me. "See, I'm from that peak too. You know much about Zevin Cove? My father renovates houses there."

"Uh... no." I glance at Melily. She's now perched on the food preparation ledge, sipping something orange and bubbly, and giggling at a paddlebat story. I dodge around the man who's trying to talk to me and snag her arm. "Let's go find Cressit."

The passages in Cressit's home form a loop. We pass a luxurious washing closet, several bedchambers, and as we return to the large room where all the people are, I see a door leading out to a snow-covered balcony.

Back in what I suppose uppies would call a gathery room, a pretty girl with dark skin is now singing while two men play stringed instruments. I look for Cressit, expecting to find him still wreathed by young women, but he isn't there.

"When you see him again," I tell Melily. "Just talk to him."

She discards her empty glass on a small, low table. "But what if I say something stupid?"

"Do you think those other girls were being clever?"

That makes her smile, but she also sways. I should have intercepted that second drink. It's time to be firm and get her back to the ship. It's nearly midnight.

I lead her along the windows. We'll just circle the spread once more, and surely we'll find Cressit. But we're only halfway across the room when the uppies around us go strangely stiff, like a startled herd of landrunner deer, and they all turn toward the housing unit's entrance.

I look too, and bracken, six city guardsmen are shoving their way into the spread. Fear grips me. They must know Melily and I robbed Sir Mauricen. This is probably why Lord Osperacy wanted me to carry a gunnerife.

But then people start shouting, "Raid! Raid! R.S. Men looking for subs!" and telling each other to run for the "fire stairs!" I have no idea what those are or where they are, and since we are close to the windows, the easiest thing to do is pull Melily behind the heavy, scarlet drapes.

Unfortunately she won't be moved. "I can easily get rid of Royal Shieldsmen," she snorts and makes her tilting, unsteady way over to one of the city guards. "Um, hey, you over there, take your men and go away."

To my surprise though, the man only snaps his fingers at another guard. "Ugh, Perrin, will you check that one?"

Melily's mouth hangs open as another R.S. Man rushes over and shines a bright, electric torch into her eyes. "They look pretty red," he says.

"I said *leave*!" she insists, but again it has no effect.

And oh no, it's because she's drunk. It must be. Why didn't Lord Osperacy warn me that cohol would affect her wavurl?

With considerable regret, I step out of my hiding place behind the curtains. "Please, my friend hasn't done anything wrong."

"Yeah, you're probably right," mutters the R.S. Man, now pocketing his electric torch. He then shoves a pale bit of paper into Melily's shocked mouth. "We're just supposed to check everyone. There's always lots of substance pushers at these types of parties, and King Renji's sick of 'em." He pulls the paper back out just as quickly and holds it up to the light. "But hey, good news, she's clean, see?"

I don't know what he's looking at, or what the paper means.

"And don't worry," he adds, glancing at another R.S. Man on the opposite side of the room. "The captain said not to arrest curfew breakers tonight."

Melily splutters angrily as he takes her handbag. "Give that back!"

Again the R.S. Man ignores her wavurl command. He clicks the purse clasp open and then frowns into the velvet-lined interior.

The arctic stones. Fathoms!

"Uh, sir?" He calls for the leader of their group. "You should take a look at these. I haven't seen anything like them."

The head R.S. Man inspects Melily's handbag too. "Huh. Why are they glowing like that?" he asks Melily. "What are these?"

I hope Melily can think of a reasonable-seeming answer, but she doesn't even try. Instead she folds her arms and says, "Just wait until you meet my brother."

The leader of the R.S. team snaps Melily's leather bag closed. "I guess this could be some new kind of subs. Who knows what floats in with each tide. Well, bind her. She's gotta come with us."

I open my mouth to offer an explanation of my own, but I struggle to think of one. Surely I can't tell these men that the arctic stones are actually rare gems we stole from the museum. So feeling very useless, I mumble, "I don't think they're dangerous. Please don't take her!" And I hang onto Melily as the R.S. Men wrap her wrists with a long black cord that has strange metal attachments on each end.

"Don't you get arrested too," Melily says, sounding a little more sensible than she did a moment ago. "You have to tell Father something's gone wrong. Tell him my wavurl's broken! Get Douglen! Hurry!"

Another R.S. Man leads her away, and then I have a bright light flashed into my eyes and a piece of strange paper pressed into my mouth—it tastes like rotten fish.

"She's clean," the R.S. Man calls to the other city guards.

I retreat to the windows, feeling helpless, stranded, and amazed that a night I didn't think could get any worse, just did. Melily told me to get help—somehow I'm supposed to contact Lord Osperacy, but I have no idea how. I can't even return to the *Trident* without her.

Once the R.S. Men leave, only about six or seven people remain in the gathery. I suppose most of the guests ran down those "fire stairs" or fled some other way. All the uppies still here are strangers to me. I don't even see Tarrol and his matching ladies or the curly-haired man from the cookery or even Cressit.

Feeling shaky and desperate, I approach a plump young woman who has dark hair and brightly painted lips. "Please help me. My friend's been taken by those men. I have to get her back!"

The strange uppy looks at me kindly. "Aw, night pick-ups aren't processed 'till morning, sweetie. There isn't anything anybody can do right now."

I suppose I must be crying, because the woman puts her arm around me and says, "Oh don't do that! Cheer up! This isn't a big deal. They say it isn't a proper party if there isn't a subs raid. Does your friend use?"

I look at her blankly.

"Take anything? Anemone pills? Sea Star vapor?"

"I don't think so," I say.

She gives me another warm smile. "Then you've got nothing to worry about. Now come with me, Terli looks after her friends."

Terli's idea of looking after me is to deposit me on a plush red sofa with a massive drink. The glass is just as fancy as Melily's was. It reminds me of a mushroom cap perched on two stems that twist and wind around each other.

I stare at the liquid for a long moment, and then I drink the whole thing in one go. It tastes sweet but burns like barnacle peppers once I've swallowed it down. Managing to set the glass on the floor, I slump back into the sofa and let the room spin.

What am I going to do now? How will I get back to the *Trident*?

I suppose I don't have to return. I have my passbook. I could stay here in Beth, find work, carve out a new life.

But that would mean abandoning Sande.

I wish I had another drink.

And then, like something out of Gren's fanciful siren stories, one appears. "You look like you could use this."

I look up in surprise, and although my surprise is dulled by the liquid that just seared its way through me, it's still alarming to have Cressit Scale hand me a drink and then sit on the sofa beside me.

His hips wedge themselves in beside mine and the upper parts of him seem to crush the upper parts of me into the armrest, and I realize it's not that large a sofa.

I expect him to say something about the raid, but instead he smiles that same smile I saw him flashing at the other girls and flips his hair back, revealing green eyes. "Did you enjoy the swingshow?"

I'm not in the mood for this conversation, so I say, "It was loud."

Cressit's smile vanishes for a moment, but then like a fire that isn't quite extinguished, starts curling up again. "Yeah, I suppose so. What do they call you?"

"Nerene Keel." The last time I pressed this tightly against anyone was when I shared my bunk with Sande. Remembering what it felt like to curl up against him sends a pang of sadness through me.

"So tell me, Nerene, are loud noises offensive to you?" Seeing Cressit's sharp jaw and thick lashes up close, I can see why Melily's taken with him. He's handsome like a lot of uppy dresses are pretty —you don't buy the dress because you want to wear it, you buy it to make everyone else jealous.

"Loud is terrible." I feel raw, like an open wound that should be bleeding all over the sofa.

"I apologize."

"You should."

He wants to kiss me. He has that look—half-closed eyes and a sideways twist to his mouth. And I know, I absolutely know, I won't be the first person he's kissed tonight.

But I ache to be comforted, I'm angry with Melily, and my thoughts are spongy with cohol; so I lean over and kiss him. I close my eyes, I think of Sande, and in a bittersweet way—mostly bitter— I'm comforted.

IT'S MORNING. I'm still on the red sofa. Oh no.

Sunlight floods the room, but at the same time, the air is cold—so cold it almost feels like I'm outside. I'm missing my coat, but someone's covered me with a shiny, delicately-woven blanket. I try to pull it to one side, yet it stretches instead of moves, and I feel like I'm trying to unravel a fishing net. With the blanket still wrapped around me, I sit up.

My head feels three times heavier than normal, so I rest my chin on my hands and look blearily around the gathery room. It looks like a storm has gusted through the spread, scattering hats, decorative pillows, a scalloped rug.

Aside from the clutter, though, I'm alone.

Being upright seems to stir up the silt of my memories—R.S. Men arrested Melily, I'm stranded in Beth's high city, and I made the horrible mistake of kissing that singer.

179

And even though my memory of kissing Cressit is fuzzy and far away, as if it happened several tides ago, I still feel a sharp sting of shame and guilt. Sande would be hurt and furious. And even more conflicting, I didn't hate the kiss. Surely that's because it was revenge on Melily, though.

But oh Melily! She has sunk us into such deep trouble.

Shivering, I brush strands of hair out of my face and tug my rumpled dress down. The balcony door is open, that's why it's so cold. Through a nearby window, I see two people talking outside.

Sitting here and regretting a mistake isn't going to set anything right. I have to ask for help or beg if I must.

I rise, and as I do, more foggy memories surface. Did I tell Cressit about Melily's arrest? I think I did. My eyes feel tight and dry like I've been crying too.

I hate that my mind is so sluggish. That cohol drink was far stronger than our deeplander springwine.

I bunch the stretchy, woven blanket up around me as if it were a Laeros Temple robe, and then I follow the path of wintry, outside light, keeping my hand on nearby furniture. The floor seems to slope toward the windows.

I don't know if I'm relieved or disappointed when I reach the balcony door and see that Cressit isn't out there. The men that are outside stand close together, wearing heavy, well-tailored jackets and sleek, brimmed hats. Both of them hold thin pipes, and they appear to be deep in conversation.

"Um, I'm sorry to bother you," I say, my voice sounding gravelly and raw.

The men turn to stare at me as if I'm a gust pigeon or snowflake dove that just landed.

I press on. "I need help. My friend was arrested last night, and I have no way to return to my ship before…"

Before it leaves! I didn't even think about that! Panic swells up inside me.

The men are older than I am. One has a single patch of gray marking his neat beard, and the other has thin lines around his eyes. The bearded one says, "All right, see? This is the perfect example of what I'm saying. We have a post-industrial society now, and young people are the victims of excessive luxury. They just don't know how to contribute to the culture in substantial ways."

The other man blows a stream of gray smoke over the balcony. "Yeah, Beth's younger generation is spoiled, but are they the responsibility of the monarchy? I believe it will be a burden we all must bear if more of these youngsters abandon traditional family structures…"

And he keeps talking, giving me no chance to respond. Not that it matters, I have no idea what he's saying, and it's clear these men are not going to take me to the *Trident*. Are all uppies so self-centered? Sir Mauricen seemed kind, and I wish I could ask him for help. But even if I could find my way back to the museum, he surely wouldn't recognize me.

Feeling both queasy and hungry, I hunch in my blanket and head back inside. I shut the door behind me, hoping the gathery will now warm up, and for a moment, I just stand there, clinging tightly to the curved handle as if it were the only solid thing in the tide.

If Sande were here, what would he do? I'm sure he wouldn't expect the uppies to be kind to him or take pity on him. He'd probably start looking for shell papers or for something else valuable that he could tuck into a pocket and later sell. I don't want to steal again, but—

"Ah, here you are."

I look up too quickly and nearly fall.

Cressit stands on the far side of the room near the entrance. He doesn't look like the polished young man who leaped and bellowed his way through a swingshow last night. Instead he looks like the monster in a children's story whose princely disguise has melted away. His eyes are red and swollen, he wears a dull gray sleeping robe, and his hair either juts straight up or hangs limp.

"Would you like some tangelemon spice water?" He holds out a steaming mug.

I shake my head no. I've had enough unfamiliar drinks.

He hugs the mug to his chest and makes no move to come closer. "I have good news and also some unfortunate news."

I tighten my grip on the door handle, not sure why he would be bringing me any sort of news.

Cressit edges along the wall as if trying to stay as far away from me as possible, or perhaps just far away from the still chilly area around the balcony door. And even more confusing, he speaks to me in a kind voice. "I've spent the entire morning on the building's relayphone trying to locate your friend."

So did I tell him about Melily, or did I tell him about Sande? The memory of kissing him keeps overshadowing everything else. I wish I could shake off my fogginess and think straight. I'd have a better chance of sorting everything out.

Cressit tosses his head, flipping his long, slept-on hair to one side in a way I suspect he's practiced in a mirror. "So I searched, and at first I couldn't find her. Someone said she spent the night in the countertide city cells... and then someone else told me she'd been released—so that's the good news. Unfortunately, I don't know where she is now."

So it was Melily I told him about, and yes of course, once sober she'd be able to use wavurl again. That means she is probably either back on the *Trident* or traveling there. Relief that she's surely safe and distress that I'm not battle for my attention. My thoughts also circle around Cressit's mention of a relayphone—perhaps I can contact Sande. "Your relayphone, is it nearby?"

Cressit nods and sips from his mug. "The housing tower has a shared line for all guests."

"Can I call a friend of mine? A different friend, please?" Sande might still be traveling on the tide, but it's worth a try. He might even be here in Beth like me.

Cressit looks sideways, and I can't tell if he's tired or annoyed that I'm still here. "Would you be using a ten number code?" he says. "The relayphone here is probably not wired for twelve."

"Number code?" I echo in a whisper, feeling lost again.

Cressit nods. "Yes. You need a number code if you want to make a relaycall."

"I don't..." I drift off. I don't understand. I frown, feeling stupid and frustrated. "Never mind."

He's silent for a moment as if he expects me to say more, and when I don't, he runs his fingers through his hair. "I'm going to dress and wash up. Then I thought I'd summon us a ringer. Do you need anything else?"

Yet again I don't understand.

I must look bewildered because Cressit offers an explanation without being asked. "What I mean is, I'll hire us an automotor, and that way I can return you to your ship. I promised that I'd help you."

He says the last bit with a strange punch of surliness as if I've doubted his helpfulness and now he must prove me wrong. He then wades across the cluttered floor to the far passage. "If you're hungry," he says, without looking back at me, "there is food in the cookery." And then I'm alone again.

I realize with sudden dread that I put my passbook in the pocket of my coat, so now I really must find it. As I'm searching, two young people emerge hand-in-hand from another part of the spread and pass me as if I don't exist. I also find three servewomen in the cookery; one of them scrubs glassware in the sink while the other two wipe the preparation ledges with gray rags.

There's a mirror in the washing closet, and looking into it, I see that I'm just as disheveled as Cressit. My hair is jammed up on one side, and sunken, gray circles are under my eyes.

I unravel what's left of Marthes' hairdo, splash water on my face, and rinse out my mouth. Then feeling a little cleaner and more alert, I return to the gathery and thankfully soon find my coat. It's wedged beneath a chair. When Cressit reappears, he looks more like he did last night, wearing shimmery, expensive-looking clothes with his hair brushed down over one eye. "Come on then," he says, pulling on black gloves and walking to the door.

I button my coat. "Why are you helping me?"

He glances at me as if he's not sure how to answer, and then says, "I suppose I feel sorry for you."

I follow him into the corridor, hating his answer. I don't want uppy pity. I suspect he's realized that I'm a deeplander, and maybe he's repulsed that he kissed me.

He is, at least, telling the truth about hiring an automotor. One of the gleaming uppy machines waits for us outside, its mechanical insides rumbling impatiently.

The trip back down to the wharf seems to take a lot longer than it did yesterday when Brindy drove Melily and I up to the museum.

For a while Cressit and I travel in silence, but when we're in one of the tunnels, he says, "So based on what you said last night, you don't like my music."

"It's just not what I'm used to," I say, watching the passing lights flash across his face like a steady swingshow drumbeat.

"So you don't like things that are unfamiliar?" he asks.

I think for a moment. "I liked your last song. I just couldn't hear it that well."

"Ah, interesting. My band doesn't like that song. They say it doesn't fit with the tone of our other music. But I keep insisting we play it, now I'm glad I do." When the next passing tunnel light shines on Cressit's face, he's smiling.

Despite his fancy uppy clothes and manners, Cressit's more likable than I expected. And strangely, I'm getting the same cozy feeling from him that I get from Gren, like he's someone I could trust and rely on—like he's someone I'd enjoy spending time with.

I feel like I'm betraying Sande just by noticing it.

When we reach the wharf, I have trouble finding the *Trident*. The harbor is much larger than I remember, and there are dozens of steamships. For a few heart-crushing moments, I'm afraid the Osperacys left without me, but then I spot the *Trident's* three red and black funnels.

"Thank you," I tell Cressit again, and I find it hard to leave the automotor. It's not only that it's warm and I'm afraid of facing an angry Lord Osperacy, Cressit's been kind to me.

"There's no need to thank me just yet," Cressit says, opening the door nearest to him as the driver opens a door for me. "I'm coming with you."

"What? Why?" I ask as I climb out of the auto.

Cressit hands paper shells to the driver and asks him to wait. "I promised I'd help you, so I'm going to talk to your employer and explain what happened."

"No, that's not a good idea," I say. Surely Cressit will only complicate things with Lord Osperacy, and I'm a little afraid of what Douglen or even Melily might do to him. But he's already walking toward the ship, the wind blowing his long jacket sideways. I wish I had wavurl so I could command him to leave.

Two shipsmen guard the gangway. One of them gives me a cold look and says, "Lord Osperacy is gonna be happy to see you," as if Lord Osperacy is a hunter, and I'm a long-tailed deer. The same man also holds a hand up to Cressit. "No one boards the *Trident* unless my boss says it's okay."

"I only wish to speak with him briefly," Cressit says, offering the man a couple of folded paper shells.

To my chagrin, the money convinces the shipsman to let Cressit aboard. Lord Osperacy, he tells us, is in the dining cabin.

As we walk down through the ship's long, beautiful corridors, I try to send Cressit away one last time. "You really should leave. It's not safe here."

"Why isn't it safe?" Cressit asks.

And I don't know how to quickly explain wavurl, so I don't answer.

We find Lord Osperacy sipping salted coffee and examining tide charts. When we enter, he only seems to see Cressit. "Who are you?"

"Cressit Scale," the singer says. "And I apologize for any complications. Please don't blame this girl for what happened at my spread... I'm a musician and sometimes the parties after my swingshows get a bit too wild. It's entirely my fault."

I watch Cressit out of the corner of my eye, wondering how old he is. He holds himself with plenty of confidence, but his skin is as smooth as mine.

"And I would also like to speak with you about a business proposal," Cressit adds.

Lord Osperacy puts his cup down at once, smiling. "Absolutely, let's do that right now. Would you like something to drink?"

I feel like I've just been kicked, although I suppose things make more sense now. Cressit didn't just want to help me, or perhaps didn't want to help me at all. He must have heard about the Osperacys and their strange talents, and now he wants to hire them.

Lord Osperacy finally looks at me. "Leave us, Nerene. I'll speak with you later."

I'm eager to leave, and feeling betrayed by Cressit who I was stupidly beginning to trust, I move quickly out of the dining cabin. As I pass the singer, he has the nerve to give me a guilty, apologetic look. I flash him an angry glare in return.

I'm not in my cabin for long before Melily drifts in.

She closes the door behind her by flopping against it, and her eyes sparkle like the arctic stones. "So I was taken to jail! Can you believe it? It was so crazy! My powers came back, but slowly of course. And at first all I could do was, like, move other people away from me, but after a few hours, I was ordering all the R.S. Men around. And did I ever punish them!" She stifles a giddy laugh. "What we did in Beth will be hard to top in Noret! We have to find another swingshow to go to!" She gulps in a quick breath. "So how did you get back to the ship?"

187

I suspect she won't like my answer. "Cressit hired an automotor."

Melily peels herself off the door. "What? Why were you talking to Cressit?"

My lips prickle and so do my cheeks. "He was the only person willing to help me." My words come out shaky and high-pitched. I snatch up a brush and force it through my hair.

Melily says nothing, which is odd, so I sneak a look at her.

She's watching me with wide, angry eyes. "You were gone all night. Something happened."

"Nothing happened," I say, because nothing significant did happen and the rest of it I will scrub from my mind.

Melily stares at me for several seconds as if the intensity of her gaze might burn the truth out of me.

"Nothing happened," I repeat. "Cressit used a relayphone to try and find you, and then he brought me here. And I think the only reason he wanted to come here was to talk to your father."

Melily's little body, all knotted up in rage, softens. "He did? Well that's not terrible. Maybe Cressit needs me to *acquire* something! That would be amazing!"

She dashes from my cabin with her eyes gleaming again.

I spend the afternoon trying to sleep, but even though I'm exhausted, I only manage to nap in short spurts. Lord Osperacy doesn't call for me until well into the evening, long after the *Trident* rumbles out of port and long after the ship's relayphone has surely been disconnected.

"Come in," Lord Osperacy says when I knock on his cabin door.

I do as I'm told, heavy with misery.

There's only one light on, the ornate table lamp clamped to his desk, and the windows behind him are dark and mirror-like. Looking up from a stack of paper, Lord Osperacy puts down a gold-plated pen, snapping it loudly onto his desk. Then his round, bulging eyes meet mine. "Did you forgot something yesterday?"

I don't answer. It feels like a trick question. I think he's referring to Melily, and I wonder what story she's already spun for him.

He reaches into a desk drawer and then places my gunnerife on his desk with a dull thump. "When you didn't return, I asked Douglen to check your room to see if you ran away. He found this."

My stomach feels hollow, and I don't like the thought of Douglen rummaging through my underthings. "I'm sorry. I didn't think that Melily would be in danger. I didn't think that I'd need it, and—"

"You always need it," Lord Osperacy says, his voice slicing through mine. "I know you're not a stupid girl. Surely you realize our arrangement is a delicate one. You must take care of what is valuable to me, while I make sure what is valuable to you—that deepland boy —*stays alive.*"

"Yes sir," I murmur.

He loosens the tasseled scarf around his neck, and something about the way his long fingers grip the fabric puts me on edge. "I would rather Melily have no balance than a balance who defies me and cannot control her."

I squeeze my hands together. "I'm sorry. I'm so sorry."

"Because of your… recalcitrance… you will be disciplined. It's not possible to relaycall your friend yet, he's surely still traveling, but even when we can reach him, you won't speak to him immediately. Not in Noret, or Panlo, or the U.P.T. either." He slowly spins the globe beside his desk.

Each mountain city name feels like a separate venomous sting. "Please…" I say. "When can I talk to Sande?"

"If there are no more troubling *incidents*…" Lord Osperacy stops the globe with his finger. "You can relaycall him in the Hill Kingdoms."

The Hill Kingdoms? Where are the Hill Kingdoms? I've never heard of them before, which means they must be very far away.

I hold in my sadness until I return to my cabin, and then I let my tears soak my dress sleeves and bedding. I found it hard enough waiting days to speak with Sande, but now I'll have to wait sunedges or maybe even months.

The next morning, I feel drained and numb as if all my emotions are still sleeping. With the fuzzy sense that I should probably show Lord Osperacy how responsible I can be, I rise early, bathe, and I'm in the dining room before anyone else. Beth is gone. There's no sign of its double peaks, with the countertide side higher than the other. I stand at the large windows and watch the tidewater, listening to the soft tinks and clatters of the serveworkers setting the breakfast table. I can't let what happened in Beth happen again. I have to find a better way to handle Melily.

"Good morning."

I turn, expecting Jeck or Douglen, but it's Cressit who stands on the other side of the table, with a cup of that tangelemon spice water in one hand and a book in the other.

A smile curves the lips I know better than I should. "And surprise, I suppose."

I STARE AT CRESSIT. I should say something, but what? He lied about why he was bringing me to the *Trident* or at least didn't tell me everything—which makes me angry. But in the short time we've spent together, I have the feeling we could be friends—so in that sense, I'm happy. But then I also kissed him, which I feel guilty about, so…

Thankfully just then, Melily enters the dining cabin. "Eeek! It really is you! Father just told me the news!"

Cressit smiles and looks genuinely happy to see her. "You must be Melily."

"Threegod above, you know my name!" Melily tiptoe-jumps, and I notice she's more dressed up than usual. Not only did she put on one of her lacy, fringed dresses, she's also wearing a string of pearls and a headband with a plume of feathers. "Did Marto really get caught with subs?" She stands so close to Cressit I almost expect her to wrap an arm around him. "Is your ship really impounded? Are you really, *really* going to travel with us?"

Cressit lifts an eyebrow. "You make an impounded ship sound like a good thing."

Melily covers her tide-wide grin with both hands and tries to look somber. "I mean, I'm so sorry about that."

Cressit pulls out a chair and sits down. "Well, hopefully we'll sort everything out quickly. Now that your father's made room for me and my friends here, we won't have to cancel any of our shows. A lot of other performers depend on my little ship."

So that's why he's here—his ship is trapped in Beth because of another subs raid. I wonder why he didn't tell me yesterday, but I'm also glad he's not hiring the Osperacys to steal for him or to manipulate a trial or to do something else awful.

Melily sits beside Cressit, tucking her hands under her knees. "You must love traveling on the tide."

"Absolutely." Cressit reaches for a silver teapot. "Who doesn't?"

"Not me," she says. "As in, yes me, I love it too. Like, so much."

"I'm glad to hear it."

"I'm glad I said it."

Not sure what to do with myself, and since I don't want to join their awkward conversation, I sit on the far side of the table. Gray clouds skim the water outside, threatening rain.

"Tell me if you have a girlfriend," I hear Melily command, and that's not a good sign. She's using wavurl already.

I glance over. Cressit looks surprised by Melily's question, but of course he has to answer. "There isn't anyone special."

I try not to pay attention, and I don't like that I'm curious. I shouldn't want to know anything more about him or his private life. I turn back to the windows, back to the foggy weather, and only then do I realize that I've picked up a spoon, and I'm squeezing it so hard my knuckles are white.

Lord Osperacy, Douglen, Jeck, and Shara soon arrive. Eager to escape, I eat breakfast as if I'm in a race. I ignore the kelp tea scalding my throat, and I swallow wheatmeal, brined cheese, and shallowberry cakes so quickly they all taste the same.

Conversation darts and glides around me. Melily keeps complimenting Cressit—he's so clever, he's the best songwriter on the equator, his dining jacket is so fine Threegod must have sewn it. Douglen, on the other hand, says he's never heard of Cressit, which he somehow turns into a boast. He then asks what sort of music 'mountain brass' is in a way that makes it clear it's nothing he'd ever bother listening to. Jeck wants to know all about the women Cressit meets at swingshows—which makes my neck feel hot—and when Cressit doesn't give him a juicy answer, Shara politely asks which mountain city is the singer's favorite.

"Ellevah," he says, "Although unfortunately, I haven't been there in several tides."

Ellevah, that's the city Sande wanted to travel to. I glance over at Cressit and find he's already looking at me.

I swallow a final mouthful of wheatmeal, and oh thank goodness, I'm done eating. I drop my spoon and leap up as if I've been sitting on a cookstove. "I need to... tend to... a walk!" I say far too loudly, and then I dash out of the dining room.

I take my next few meals in my cabin until I learn from Marthes that Cressit isn't eating with the Osperacy family anymore. He's been sitting with his musician friends and other passengers in the larger dining cabin, and she says he only ate with us that first morning because Lord Osperacy invited him.

A disappointed Melily tells me that Cressit also spends most of his time practicing with his band and writing new songs, so perhaps I don't have to worry about him being on the ship at all. I do cross paths with him a few days later in the corridor near the ship's pool, but surprisingly, and I guess thankfully, he seems eager to avoid me too. All he says is, "You said the ship was dangerous. Are you in danger?"

"I'm fine," I say. "I just thought you might not be safe here."

"You don't need to worry about me."

"Well you don't need to worry about me either," I say before hurrying away from him.

And so the *Trident* sails to Noret City, a place that seems small and charming compared to Beth and Varasay. It's full of little stone buildings topped with mossy, kelpwood shingles and a surprising number of drywood trees in walled off, well guarded forests. Selling drybark is apparently the main trade in Noret. After that, we travel to Panlo, a skinny ridge of a city topped with very tall buildings that seem to be made out of dark gray, nearly black bricks.

On each mountain island, I escort Melily off the ship, and on each outing, I obediently take the gunnerife. Fortunately I never need to use it, and just as fortunately, Melily is so enamored with Cressit, she doesn't cause more trouble... or at least, not much. At Lord Osperacy's request, I help her "acquire" an emerald necklace, an ancient, hand-painted atlas, and a few dusty stacks of paper vitally important to one of Lord Osperacy's clients. Meanwhile Douglen arranges a few complicated marriage contracts, "encourages" someone to rewrite their will, and assists in the trial of an accused murderer, forcing him to confess.

When I do see Cressit, it's often at a distance, and he's almost always with Melily. The terrible guilt I felt before fades. We just shared a kiss, that's all, and of course I still care about Sande. I'm sure Cressit's already forgotten about what happened between us, so I try to do the same.

I can't completely avoid him, though. After we pass Panlo, late one evening, several wooden sailing ships mysteriously slip past my cabin window. Even more oddly, they're sailing countertide—and not very many people travel in that direction. I rush to the upper deck to get a better look, and I find Cressit already there.

"Are those drifters?" I ask, staring at the silent ships that are already gliding back into the dark.

Cressit nods. "Yes… and I haven't seen any in a long time." He looks over at me and smiles. "It's supposed to be good luck seeing them, you know."

I nod. Gren always said that too. Drifters are farmers that don't belong to any city. They sail against the tide, and when the ocean ends, they put their ships on stilts and farm the land they wash up on. When the water returns, they pack up and sail across the tidewater again.

"Do you miss your home?" Cressit asks. He's wearing nightclothes like I am, but he had the foresight to grab a jacket too. "Melily told me all about Varasay."

I cringe inwardly, imagining what terrible things Melily might have said. "I miss my village," I say. "But I don't miss the city." I watch the last ship disappear into the darkness and hug my fluttering nightdress close.

"Do you want my jacket?" Cressit offers.

"No," I say, sharp as an ax—as if he didn't offer me his jacket but his hand in marriage.

"You're upset with me." He looks at me closely. "Why?"

If Melily told him about Sande, he must suspect that I regret our kiss.

"I'm not upset with you," I say as the wind makes my hair dance over to him, betraying the rest of me. The truth is I'm upset with myself, but I'm not going to say anything that personal to Cressit, so I just murmur, "Goodnight," and hurry back inside.

By the time we pass the United Peaks of Trellor, a low series of mountain tops crowded with shabby housing towers, I feel as if I've become an uppy machine. I try not to think or feel. I do as I'm told, and I try to keep Melily happy. All I want to do is speak with Sande.

So when Melily swings into my cabin singing, "Guess what? Captain Gedwick says we'll reach the Hill Kingdoms tomorrow!" I almost cry with relief.

"So that means you can relaycall your sludge lover and stop sulking around." Melily leans against my bed, her three necklaces jangling together. Ever since Cressit's been on the ship, she's been wearing her finest jewelry, prettiest dresses, and highest heels at all times.

"I'm not sulking." I look up from the book I'm struggling to make sense of. It's a children's story belonging to Timsy and Dorla. Shara's trying to teach me how to read since Melily grew bored and quit.

Melily smiles wide. "Yes, you have definitely been sulking, but it doesn't matter. I want to tell you something." She tugs the book out of my hands. "And I don't want to talk here. Marthes or Shara might come in and be all, you know... the annoying way they are. Follow me."

She takes me to an unfamiliar door one deck down. Unlocking it, she gives the light switch a twist, revealing rows of railed shelves. I see beautiful furniture, fine brinewood chests, sculptures, and paintings, and all of it is secured with ropes and straps. This must be where Lord Osperacy stores his *acquired* treasures.

Melily closes the door, shutting us inside the crowded space. "I'm going to tell Cressit to kiss me."

I find I'm upset, but I try to ignore the feeling because Melily's fascination with Cressit shouldn't bother me. I take a deep, slow breath.

"You do remember who Cressit is?" she asks, taking my silence for confusion.

"Yes of course, and I suppose I thought you'd have made him kiss you already." As I say it, I find I really do want to know why she's waited. Is she nervous? Does she think using her wavurl to make someone kiss her is wrong? That doesn't seem like something that would trouble her.

Melily's frown narrows to a pucker. "Weeeell." She drags the word out, surely giving herself time to think about her reply. "I was waiting for the right moment. I want it to be, you know, romantic."

She prods a dusty set of springwine cups. As I watch her lift the delicate crystal with a single hooked finger, I think I understand her hesitation. She wants Cressit to want to kiss her.

I feel a sudden, strange tenderness toward her, almost as if she were my younger sister, and I speak carefully. "Maybe... if you wait a little longer, *he* might kiss *you*."

"Why should I keep waiting, though?" Melily sneers, but her eyes are big and vulnerable and seem to be begging me to give her a good reason. "He got a message in Panlo that his ship will catch up with us in Gatreijan. I'm running out of time."

So Cressit will leave soon. That makes me feel a bit sad. But the fact that it upsets me means it's surely for the best. He can clearly stir up my feelings, and before now, that was something only Sande could do, and I preferred it that way. "Well if you wait for Cressit to kiss you, then you'll know he really cares about you." I bring my teeth together, expecting Melily's temper to flare up.

But instead she sets the springwine cup gently back with the others. "So... then... like, how do you make someone kiss you, you know, without *making* them kiss you?"

"I don't think you can."

Melily slumps sideways, knocking a shelf and making its precious contents clatter together. "But I don't know what else to do! I've shown him the whole ship. I've watched tons of his boring practices. I've told him all about Father's travels and even your weird story. I know the words to every single one of his songs. He *seems* interested in talking to me, and he's not resisting when I give him commands. But... he just... I don't know!" She rubs her face, smearing her black eye paint. "Maybe he just cares *so* much about me, he doesn't want to get too involved. That way he won't hurt me when he leaves."

"That might be it," I say, hugging her, and I don't think she gets hugged very often. I have to pull her over to me, and she's all pointy shoulders and elbows. "Or," I go on, extremely carefully, "maybe he's just not the right match for you."

"Of course he is," she whimpers. "He's so beautiful."

He is, and I wish I didn't notice.

For a while, Melily leans against me, uncharacteristically quiet, but then she says, "I guess it doesn't matter. Father will never let me get married anyway."

She's silent for another few moments and then adds, "Douglen got to marry Shara because she's his balance. Father says we shouldn't marry someone we can control, but I know I'll never find a male balance again. And even if I do, he'll probably be ugly and strange, and he won't be Cressit."

"Did you care for Elgin?" I risk asking, thinking of the tattered picturegraph hidden beneath Melily's bed.

She pulls away from me, and I pretend not to notice her tears. "Yes, but also no. Elgin didn't like girls." She stares at the shelves. "I'm going to be alone forever."

I'm not sure what to say. "Maybe it seems like that right now, but—"

Melily flashes me a sharp look, the same one she gives me when she wants me to do something and I refuse. "Stop acting like you know how I feel. Someone's loved you your whole life. You also have… well… *boobs*."

And before I can fumble out a response, she leaves.

I STAND ON the upper deck, watching sunlight spill over the Hill Kingdoms. It creates little arches of orange and gold, and I feel happy for the first time in ages. Today I'll talk to Sande.

The Hill Kingdoms are so different from the other settlements we've visited. These islands don't look like mountain tops but rather like soft, grassy lumps dotting the tidewater. There are no high cities or mid cities because they aren't big enough for that. I don't even see a proper wharf or harbor. The *Trident* simply drops anchor near one of the islands, a place called Pre'Enity, and we take a small, motorized boat over.

I like Pre'Enity at once. And it's not just the unseasonable warmth or the fact that I'm about to talk to Sande—the town is clean and bright and friendly-looking, like a drawing from one of Dorla and Timsy's picture books. The houses are small and made of rocks and pressed reed boards, and the people here have also lovingly decorated them with bright clay tiles, painted walls, and colored glass windows. I don't see any factories or automotors, and perched on a stony hill overlooking the island is a large building with towers on each corner that are decorated with cheery bunches of flags. That's where Pre'Enity's king lives, Douglen tells me.

"Each hill has a stupid little king or queen," he continues, as we climb out of the small motorship and onto a brick pier. "It's ridiculous."

But it's the King I need to talk to. He owns Pre'Enity's only relayphone.

Melily and Shara linger at the tide-side market to shop, and Jeck vanishes into a cookery house with a picture of a siren on the outside —the sort with a fish's tail. Douglen stays with me, though. Lord Osperacy asked him to help me operate the relayphone.

This island is small enough that we can walk from the pier to the King's home, and so Douglen leads me along a path between houses and crowded vegetable gardens. I never feel comfortable when I'm alone with him, but I try to make conversation anyway. "Are there barracks here for deeplanders?" I ask—although I can't imagine where they'd be.

Douglen shakes his head. "Everyone here's the same. They all farm in the deeplands during the dry months, then when the tide comes, they all cram themselves into those ugly, little shacks."

I look around. No one seems to be squeezing into their houses today. Everyone is outside doing chores or talking together.

"What a beautiful house," I say as we near the large building on the hill.

"It's not a house; it's a castle," Douglen says in a condescending tone as if an infant should know such a thing.

The King of Pre'Enity seems to already be on good terms with the Osperacy family because as soon as Douglen gives his name to the guard at the castle entrance, the man ushers us inside. The King greets us moments later in a bright room decorated with paintings of ships, narwhales, and sunsets.

"Douglen Osperacy, it's a pleasure to see you again!" The King is both tall and round. He wears lushly patterned robes, layers of vests, and several gilded shell necklaces. His dark gray beard bristles with braids and the rest of his hair is swept up under a coral crown. "Has your father come ashore? He always has such interesting things for sale."

"I'm sure he'll come by," Douglen says, bending at the waist. "He wouldn't want to miss seeing you."

Not sure what to do, I bend like Douglen and rise when he does.

The King turns to me. "And who is this delightful young lady?"

"She works for my father," Douglen says. "She's called Nerene."

The King takes my hand in one of his massive ones. "Greetings Nerene, I'm King Bevreden, and you are most welcome in Pre'Enity."

"Thank you," I say in my politest voice. He reminds me of the elegant landrunner stags that race the tide—perhaps it's his large, gentle eyes, or more likely, it's the way his coral crown branches out like antlers.

"You'll both dine with us, I hope." King Bevreden looks to Douglen.

Douglen hesitates, surely thinking that I shouldn't be included, but he eventually nods and says, "Of course. We'd be honored."

As Douglen asks about the relayphone, I take a better look at the paintings on the walls. They aren't as detailed as the paintings I saw in Beth's museum; they only have a few colors and the shapes are smooth and uncomplicated. Their simplicity is nice, I decide. The paintings are easy to look at, pleasing even.

A serveman takes us to the relayphone. It hangs in a room with a large window and a rug made of striped jaguar fur. For some reason I expect the relayphone to resemble Melily's music machine, but instead it's a rectangular, brinewood box attached to the wall, covered with levers, dials, and metal knobs.

As soon as the serveman leaves, Douglen pulls out a thin folder that has a coil of wire running down one side. "Wait outside while I make contact. Be ready, though. Decide what you want to say. You won't have much time."

I leave the room, suddenly panicked. I thought I would just talk to Sande the way I always do. But now that I know it can't be a long conversation, my mind feels empty.

Douglen soon calls me back into the room. He puts a metal cup to my ear and points to a copper tube. "It's simple enough. Speak into here."

I press the earpiece against my head. "Sande? Sande, are you there?"

At first all I can hear is meaningless noise, but then a distant voice echoes back at me. I can't make out the words, but I can tell it's Sande, and that means he's alive. Lord Osperacy kept his word. Feeling relieved, I lean against the wooden box. "Can you hear me?" I call. "Sande, it's Nerene!"

For a few moments Sande doesn't respond, but then I hear his voice again, and this time he sounds even further away. In desperation, I look to Douglen. "It's not working! I don't think it's working."

He shrugs. "Could be a bad connection. That happens sometimes."

I turn back to the relayphone. Maybe Sande can hear me better than I can hear him. "I miss you."

Again it takes a long time for Sande to reply, and again his words are garbled and unintelligible. But then all of a sudden, the sound takes shape. Sande's voice is loud and perfectly clear. It's as if he's on the other side of the wall. "—not much, and I work hard. But I'm still alive, Nerene, and I love you, and I'm sorry I blamed you for that snapper."

"I love you, and it's fine," I cry, glad that he's not still angry. "Where are—"

Click.

And silence.

I look down and see Douglen's broad finger on a switch.

"That's enough," he says. "These calls are expensive."

I keep staring at his hand, and then I stare at the relayphone mouthpiece, and then at the horn-shaped part of the device that just held Sande's voice. I feel helpless, horrified. "No! No! Make him come back! I couldn't hear him before. Please, I—"

"Stop complaining and stop yammering," Douglen says, using wavurl to force me silent.

He watches mildly as I cough back anger. He doesn't care—I'm sure of it. He has no idea what it's like to not get his way.

I'm so upset I'm shaking. He may have commanded me to be quiet, but he didn't tell me to stand still. Giving Douglen a furious look, I stomp my sharp heel onto his fancy uppy shoe as hard as I can.

He swears loudly and drives his fist into my stomach, knocking me against the wall. I fold over, strangely shocked he would be cruel in a way that doesn't involve wavurl, and I gasp for breath. Still in his control, I can't speak or cry, but tears blur my vision.

"Uh, is everything all right, Mister Osperacy?" a serveman asks through the closed door.

"Yes, everything is great," Douglen says, giving me a tight smile that's all sharp corners and teeth.

I slump in a sitting position, crossing both arms across my middle. I hurt so badly I feel like I might vomit. Douglen's eyes catch mine like barbed fishhooks. I suspect it's been a long time since anyone's crossed him like I just did. I'm also sure he's not through punishing me.

"Well, I don't want to bother you, but the food is almost ready," the serveman says, still on the other side of the door. "King Bevreden and his family have gathered to eat."

"Good. I'm hungry." Douglen holds an arm out to me. "Give me your arm."

Touching him is the last thing I feel like doing, but I don't have a choice—he's commanded me. I let him help me up as my insides rage in pain.

We return to the room with the painted walls and join King Bevreden, several men, and a handful of beautifully dressed women around an oval table. As the King and Douglen discuss shipping and currents, I sit in agony, trying to remember what Sande's voice sounded like.

He's alive though—and that's what matters most.

Dozens of serveworkers soon enter holding baskets of salt bread and platters of fish prepared in all sorts of ways; smoked, dried, poached, and coated with a variety of sauces and spices. Serveworkers also carry many trays of seaweed cakes and river-rice rolls.

The meal smells delicious. I wish I were hungry.

The serveworkers pile my plate high regardless, and I watch the King and his family scoop a red sauce over their food. Not wanting to be impolite, I reach for a little glass bowl too.

"I like a brave girl," the King booms, smiling at me. "Soaked pepper spice is the hottest sauce in the Hill Kingdoms!"

I suddenly notice all the red sauces are slightly different—some are dark, some light, and the one I have has little seeds in it. "I didn't realize," I whisper. Is it too late to put the bowl down? Everyone's looking at me.

"Oh go on," Douglen says. "Try some."

It's a wavurl command. Unable to stop myself, I spoon crushed pepper onto my smoked fish.

"Don't pay attention to her," Douglen says, wavurling everyone around us, and as people look away and resume conversations, he leans closer to me. "Put more on."

I swallow, tension spreading up my neck and down my back. I glop another spoonful of the blood red sauce onto my fish.

"More," Douglen says.

I obey.

He eases the bowl from my fingers, and with his eyes on mine, upends it over my plate. "Now start eating," he says, and there is both cold triumph in his gaze and an unnerving gleam of pleasure. Marthes did warn me.

Trembling, I bring a small amount of fish to my lips with a pronged spoon. It's all but hidden by sauce. With mounting dread, I put the flakes of fish into my mouth, chew, and hastily swallow. At first it simply tastes like the stormradish sauce we often use in Saltpool, but then a sudden fire blazes on my tongue and sears down my throat. Tears fill my eyes.

"Keep going," Douglen says.

And I have to. The next spoonful is so painful, it's almost as if the skin is being scraped out of my mouth. The next makes me feel like my insides are bleeding. Sweat seems to instantly drench my gown and hair, and I start crying. And because Douglen told them not to, no one at the table looks my way. I thought his powers were supposed to be fading.

Helpless, I keep eating.

"King Bevreden," a serveman enters the room. "The entertainment is here."

I swallow a sob and whirl to see Cressit entering the hall with four of his musicians. They all wear shimmery swingshow costumes and carry musical instruments. They also all bend politely to greet King Bevreden, much like Douglen and I did.

Cressit spots me as he straightens, and I very much hope he realizes I'm in distress. But even then, what can he do? Douglen's here.

I'm not sure if it's on purpose, but Cressit does seem to try to help me. "Douglen," he says. "Your father would like you to return to the *Trident*. I'm sorry I've interrupted your meal."

"Father can wait," Douglen says, watching me eat another mouthful. The pain is so intense I shut my eyes and hunch my shoulders.

"No! Go to your father!" King Bevreden's voice seems to fill the large room. "And then please, bring him back here to me. I can't wait to see what astonishing trinkets and treasures he's selling this tide."

Uttering a final, "Be sure to clean your plate," Douglen departs. As he moves away, I feel his hold on me slip. As soon as he's out of sight, I run from the table, yet I'm still compelled to bring the hateful plate of food. Breaking off more fish with my fingers, I notice Cressit following me, leaving his musicians to set up their instruments. King Bevreden and his court still don't seem to notice what I'm doing.

"What's wrong? What's going on?" Cressit asks me in the corridor.

"Douglen's making me eat this," I manage to say before putting more food into my mouth. Surely Cressit won't understand. I doubt Lord Osperacy told him about Douglen, Melily, and Timsy's siren powers. "Help," I beg, swallowing and crying harder.

"Stop eating," Cressit grabs my wrists. "Stop."

And just that easily, I'm free. Douglen's grip on me falls away, and I drop the plate. Its contents splatter across my boots and the reed mat. Pulling away from Cressit, I spit what's still in my mouth out too, wishing I could also spit out the burning pain. And yet as I wipe my sauce-covered hands onto my skirt, leaving bright red smears, a thought clicks into place.

Cressit undid Douglen's wavurl. There's only one way he could have done that.

"You're a siren."

CRESSIT LOOKS SCARED. And as for me, I clench my stinging fingers and tip forward, breathing in and in—as if I can somehow extinguish the fire in my mouth and throat.

In an anguished haze, I stare at the floor tiles, which are mostly bronze although there a few, scattered bright blue tiles too. And then Cressit crouches down and appears in front of me again.

"Yes, I am a siren. You're right, but you can't tell anyone. Nobody knows." His visible eye, the one not hidden behind his long black hair, darts in thought. "I have to get you out of here."

My stomach wrenches, and I'm pretty sure it's one of those times where vomiting won't give me any relief. I try to say, "All right," but the only sound that comes out of me is a wheezing rasp.

"Stay here," Cressit says. "Just for a moment."

I don't know if it's a command or not, but it doesn't matter. I'm not going anywhere on my own. Everything hurts. I keep gazing at the tiles, imagining flames sizzling beneath my skin. In the distance, I hear voices, faint and unclear—Cressit's talking, then King Bevreden, Cressit again, and then I hear King Bevreden laugh. Their conversation ends with a burst of cheerful, rapid music.

I lurch onto my knees. I'm sure I am going to throw up any moment now. I wish it would just happen. My vision's gone funny, and the patterned floor is dancing. It looks like water's streaming across the passage, washing the little blue tiles away.

A hand grabs my shoulder, and then an arm circles my waist. "Hold on." Cressit pulls me to my feet.

Tears blur my vision as he rushes me through the castle. "She's all right; she just ate something that disagreed with her," he tells someone, maybe a serveworker.

Down a hall, down a flight of stairs, our overlapping footfalls thrum an uneven drumbeat. I see sunlight, windows, a door. My stomach heaves. I cry out in pain.

"Hang on, hang on," Cressit whispers. "We're nearly outside."

Moments later, salty wind cools my bare forearms and face. We race down more stairs, down a steep path, and then Cressit pulls me sideways. Feathery leaves speckled with pink blossoms brush my ankles. They're so tiny, so pretty, and I cover them with the contents of my stomach. Then more food surges up and still more, and oh it hurts just as bad coming up as it did going down.

I fall away from the mess and huddle on the dirt pathway, embarrassed and miserable. Pre'Enity's colorful houses look like a blurry rainbow. I need to clean my eyes and face, but with what?

Thankfully Cressit hands me a scratchy cloth.

I wipe my mouth and fingers, but I don't think I wipe them well enough because when I brush away tears, my eyes burn. I wail.

"We shouldn't stay here," Cressit says. "Can you walk?"

I nod.

He helps me up again, and we shuffle down a brick roadway, back into the town.

"Please, you cannot tell anyone I'm a siren," he says as we head toward the water. "If Lord Osperacy were to find out or Douglen, I can't imagine they'd want me around."

"Does Melily know?" I ask in a ragged whisper.

"No, and she can't—not yet. Actually... she's the reason I'm traveling with you."

But how can that be? Cressit didn't meet Melily until he boarded the *Trident*. I feel even more confused, and I also sway and hug my stomach. I can't tell what hurt me the most, the sauce or Douglen's punch. I wish I were wearing my soft, leather deeplander shoes, not these rigid, uppy boots that seem to catch the lip of every uneven paving stone.

Cressit's grip on my arm tightens. "I just knew something would go wrong today. You being left alone with that monstrous man... Osperacy would have been kinder if he had sent you off with a fringed bear."

So did Cressit rescue me on purpose? More pink flowers grow between the paving stones. I hunch down, locking my arms around my stomach. I feel like I'm holding my insides together, making sure they don't fall apart in charred, fleshy pieces.

"Melily?" I gasp. I want to know more.

"She's..." Cressit hesitates. I think he's debating how much to tell me, or maybe how much he trusts me. "Well, Lord Osperacy kidnapped her—a long time ago." His voice tightens. "I'm trying to bring her home."

I feel like I should be more surprised that Lord Osperacy would kidnap someone, but I suppose I'm not. He's a thief after all. I wish I were able to pay better attention to what Cressit is saying, though, and ask questions. Instead I'm fighting to control my insides.

Cressit leads me down a roadway that's less crowded than the others. But even here, I still see plenty of people. Women look up from the fruit they're peeling with curved knives. Men look up from leather they're stretching and shaping.

And I throw up again. The vomit is a different red now, a brighter red. I realize I still have that cloth bunched up in my hand, and I also realize that it's the sparkly scarf Cressit was wearing—a green length of fabric, shot through with silver. I've completely ruined it.

"This way." Cressit guides me toward one of the houses where a large woman hunches over a beading loom. "Good afternoon. My friend is ill and needs to rest. Could we use your home? And could she also have a drink of water?"

I think these are simply questions not wavurl commands, so I expect the woman to say no.

But she smiles at Cressit as if he's a beloved son, puts the loom aside, and heaves herself onto her feet. "This girl would be better off with seaweed milk if she's got a sore stomach."

She soon settles Cressit and I on a cramped patio overlooking the tidewater. The stone platform we're on is just large enough to support two clay pots bursting with rain mint, silvany weed, and whirl chimes, as well as a cage of gust pigeons and the short, plain bench I'm sitting on. I do my best to ignore the clashing odors of bird droppings and herbs, but the warm seaweed milk the woman gives me tastes like home, and it does soothe my stomach.

Cressit stands in the only patch of free space and leans against a railing that I think is made out of kelp tree roots. He holds a bucket in case I need it, and I'm sure I will.

"How do you feel?" he asks.

"A little better," I say, although my legs are still shaking, and I still feel strangely hot even though we're in the shade. "The King will be sad you didn't sing."

Cressit waves a hand. "He won't mind. Larone and Gaveni are excellent musicians. I just get in their way. So why was Douglen angry with you?"

I don't want to answer his questions when I have so many of my own. "It wasn't about anything important—I just stomped on his foot. Tell me about Melily, though. Why did Lord Osperacy take her? Who did he take her from? And how do you know all of this?"

"I know because it's my fault." Cressit works his mouth over his teeth for a moment. "Her true family thinks she's dead, and she was taken when I was supposed to be watching her. I was a child myself, but I still shouldn't have let it happen. I've been trying to set things right for fifteen tides now, but until recently, I couldn't find her."

Lord Osperacy made it sound as if he were helping people by adopting their siren children. I suppose this makes more sense though... Lord Osperacy does seem like the sort of person who would steal children with wavurl and use their talent to make money.

"Does Melily know about this?" I croak. She and Cressit have been spending a lot of time together.

Cressit shakes his head. "I didn't want to tell her until it was time to leave. I was afraid she might get excited or upset and perhaps say the wrong thing to someone."

I don't blame him. Melily probably would have a tough time keeping a secret. "So…" I feel like I don't know the right questions to ask. "So your village or mountain city… are there lots of sirens there?"

"No, but…" He looks at me carefully as if trying to figure something out. "Or rather yes, there were. It was a small place—far outside the trade routes, and Lord Osperacy was born there too. He left a long time ago, and he took our secrets with him. We're safer when the Sea Spread doesn't know what we can do."

"So Timsy… he's from your mountain city too?"

Cressit nods. "He must be." With a loud exhale, he joins me on the bench. I feel immediately self-conscious about how badly my breath must smell.

"Where is your home?" I ask, wondering if it's Ellevah, the mountain city Sande wanted to travel to and the mountain city Cressit said was his favorite.

But Cressit doesn't answer right away. After a few moments, he says, "Nerene, I think I can trust you. Or maybe I just want to trust you because I never can be honest about who I am. But at the same time, Melily will be in danger if I tell you too much, and you could be in danger, and I certainly will be. Do you understand?"

I nod.

Wind sweeps up off the tidewater, rearranging Cressit's long hair. "When my ship catches up to us, I'll tell Melily, and we'll leave. But if Lord Osperacy hears of my plan, I'm sure he won't want to let Melily go. She's far too valuable to him."

"What about Timsy?"

Cressit tries to smooth his scattered hair. "I'll save Melily first. Then perhaps I can ask for help from my people. You see… leaving our village is forbidden, and I left to find Melily. If I bring her home, hopefully my people will forgive me." He turns my way. "So will you promise not to tell anyone?"

I look down at the white, translucent seaweed milk in my mug. "You could just command me not to."

Cressit's eyebrows drop. It's almost as if I've insulted him or mentioned something shameful. But when he speaks, his words are kind. "That would only work if I stay close to you. And even then, I would never do it." His hands shudder, and he locks his fingers together.

"Well don't worry, I won't say anything," I tell him. And as I look out at the black and green waves chopping up the surface of the tidewater, I think about how happy Melily will be to learn all of this. Her beloved Cressit was actually searching for her for many years. It makes me think about how I'm searching for Sande—or rather how I'll search for him as soon as I'm able.

Cressit's plan could ruin things for me, though. If Melily leaves the *Trident*, surely Lord Osperacy won't keep me on board. He won't have any reason to keep Sande safe anymore either—if Sande even is that safe. *I'm working hard,* Sande said. Working hard where?

"If you take Melily, I'll lose my job," I say.

"With all due respect, it seems like a brackish job."

And there's that uppy arrogance. Of course to Cressit, with his money and freedom, my situation probably does seem like a terrible arrangement. "It's not that I care about the job," I say. "It's that I promised to protect Melily because in exchange, Lord Osperacy said he'd keep a friend of mine safe. If you take her away, the Osperacy's won't need me anymore. That could put my friend in danger—and I don't even know where he is." My body trembles and my insides pitch. "Bucket!" I cry.

Cressit has it instantly in front of me, and I cradle it as my stomach rebels, although nothing comes up.

"Well, that's no problem," he says. "Or at least it's a problem that's easily solved. You can run away with Melily and me, and I'll help you find Sande."

I stare down into the bucket's circular darkness. Cressit's plan does sound wonderful, marvelous. Although how does he know Sande's name? I suppose I shouldn't be too surprised since Melily told him all about me. Although does she know Sande's name? I can't remember.

I will surely feel miserable for days, but when I'm strong enough to walk, Cressit and I return to the pier. The weather was warm earlier, but now I see late afternoon shadows and a cool tidewater breeze makes me wish I'd brought a sweater. As we navigate the kelpwood walkways and pass cookery houses and shops, I look around for Douglen and sometimes glance at Cressit. "I can only imagine what Melily told you about Sande. Did she say he's my brother? Because he isn't."

"I'm pretty sure you told me about him." Cressit frowns. "Or... it could have been Melily, I suppose. She says all sorts of things."

I frown too. It seems strange Cressit would think I told him about Sande. Other than today, we've hardly spoken to each other since that uncomfortable morning in Beth. Melily must have told him.

And just as I'm thinking about Melily, we find her standing with Shara on the pier, waiting for the small motorship that will carry us all back to the *Trident*. And even though I'm glad that Cressit and I have lucky timing when it comes to the motorship, I can tell by the scrunched up expression on Melily's face that she's not happy we arrived together. As we draw nearer, her nostrils flare and she folds her thin arms. "Um, Nerene, you're supposed to be with Douglen. Isn't today the day you relaycall your *lover?*"

Shara, however, seems to notice how weak I am. "Nerene, what's wrong?" She quickly puts down her basket of fruit, which she surely purchased at the local market, and rushes over to me.

I don't know what to tell her, and as kind as she is, I don't think I can say, "Your husband hit and force-fed me."

Thankfully Cressit gives a short, sensible answer. "Something upset Nerene's stomach."

Shara touches my forehead and cheeks and then looks at me carefully. "Is it an allergy?"

"Maybe," I say, wondering if she knows how cruel Douglen is. She must know. How could she not know?

"You look awful. Did you throw-up?" Melily makes another face.

I nod.

"That is so disgusting, but this also works out perfectly." She smiles brightly as if there's no way an ill person could have stolen Cressit's heart. "Shara can wait with you for the motorship while Cressit and I take another look at those bracelets I liked. Cressit? Follow me."

He gives me a quick put-upon look that plainly says his cooperation is just an act and then allows Melily to lead him over to the nearby market stands.

"Let's find somewhere to rest," Shara says. "I'm so sorry you're not feeling well."

We sit down on a low stone ledge near the pier, and as we wait, a series of thoughts shift through my mind, nestling into each other and fitting together. Yes, Cressit probably heard about Sande from Melily. But back in Beth, he knew about Melily's arrest before I woke up, and he knew I had to return to the *Trident* too. Maybe I had a conversation with him about those things the night before, maybe

217

after we kissed, but my memory is so murky. Up until now I blamed that murkiness on the strange uppy drink. But since Cressit is a siren, and a powerful, young siren like Melily, he could have used wavurl to make me forget our conversation.

Beside me, Shara chats about the Pre'Enity market and the interesting fruit she bought, but I keep thinking about Cressit. He had bloodshot eyes that morning in Beth, just like Melily did after she made Sir Mauricen forget about our theft. I hadn't thought much about Cressit's red eyes before. I suppose I assumed they were from poor sleep or too many cohol drinks. But now that I know he's a siren and I'm sure we talked, I'm also sure he told me more than he meant to.

By the time we're back on the *Trident*, the sun has set. Most everyone meets for a late dinner, but I retreat to my cabin. I'm too sore to sit at the table, and it feels like I'll never be able to eat again. I also want to avoid Douglen.

After about an hour, someone knocks at my door. I'm immediately terrified that Douglen has come to hurt me more, but it's only Marthes. "I brought you some broth and tea because Miss Shara said you weren't feeling well," she calls in from the corridor.

Unlocking my cabin door means moving, which is painful, but I manage it. "Thank you."

"So tell me, did your relaycall go through?" she asks as I ease my sore body back into bed.

"Yes, but…" I pause, not sure how much I should say. "I could hardly hear my friend."

"Ugh, isn't that the depths? Well, I've never used one of those relay things, but I hear they are very complicated." Marthes helps me bathe, and after she leaves, I try drinking some broth. It's cold now, but the liquid still manages to reignite the fire in my stomach. So giving up, I click my bedside light off and close my eyes.

But I can't sleep.

My thoughts swirl around Cressit. He was so kind today, and again, I had a strong feeling that he would never be cruel to me. But taking away memories isn't nice. I feel like he's stolen something from me and then lied about it. If I'm going to wager Sande's safety and mine on his promise to help, I have to know everything. I have to be able to really, truly trust him.

I climb out of bed carefully, trying not to disturb my still aching insides, and I pull a long, robe-like sweater over my nightdress. Surely Cressit's still awake, and I'm fairly certain his cabin is only one level above mine. I've seen Melily lingering near his doorway.

I guess correctly. Cressit opens the door when I knock. He's wearing his nightclothes too, and he's also recently bathed. His usually pale skin looks pinkish, and his hair hangs in damp waves.

He looks surprised to see me but only asks, "How are you feeling?"

"Better," I say. "Although I'm still uncomfortable." My knees feel soft and untrustworthy too, which makes it harder to focus on the question I need to ask. "That first night in Beth, after your swingshow. Did you make me forget something?"

Cressit doesn't answer.

I feel even more unsteady. "I know sirens can do that. So did you? Did you do that to me?"

He puts a hand over his mouth. "Threegod," he says in a muffled whisper.

And then there's another long silence that makes me feel tight and anxious and tenser than I already am. Something's wrong. I thought Cressit might be defensive, but this is odd… He looks sick. He looks like he just swallowed a mouthful of that spicy Hill Kingdom sauce.

"You should come in," he says, stepping back from the door.

I hesitate. Surely that's not a good idea. There are no Threegod priests on this ship, but I know all about people assuming the worst. At the same time, Cressit clearly has something important to tell me, and I want him to. Swallowing, I step inside.

There aren't many lights on in his cabin, and it's a larger and fancier room than mine with a sitting area and a desk. I see a few of his stringed swingshow instruments lying in open cases near the round windows, and the clothes he wore today hang draped over a chair.

Cressit shuts the door. "You're right. I did make you forget something."

"Why?" I ask, hugging the sweater-robe tightly around myself. It's strange how I used to feel so comfortable in nothing more than a fern-flax dress, but now without my restrictive, uppy underthings on, I feel exposed.

"I didn't realize you knew Melily that night," Cressit says. "Not at first. And I… The thing is, most girls I meet after swingshows are interested in… so…"

I feel sick. I think I know what he's trying to tell me. Faint light shines through the windows. It paints blue stripes across the folds of his nightshirt. It pools on his cheekbone and on one side of his eyebrow. It concentrates into a pinprick of light in his left eye, leaving his right a pit of black.

"You don't really want to know this, I don't think," he says, and it's almost like he's pleading.

"I do." I sound certain, but I feel so unsure.

Cressit stands still for a short while, as if giving me time to reconsider, and then he takes hold of my shoulders, pulls me close, and breathes a command into my ear. "Remember."

The word settles into me just like Douglen's wavurl. There's a heaviness to it, like a stone in water. There's nothing my mind can do to stop it from sinking in deeper and deeper.

Cressit staggers away from me, and just like Melily after we left the museum, he faints, colliding with the corner of his bed and hitting the floor hard.

Instinctively I move toward him, but my memories are also rushing back. Everything I forgot about that night in Beth returns, and instead of helping Cressit, I drop to my knees and cry.

THERE WAS MORE than the kiss.

The night I spent in Beth's high city unfolds and uncurls from the corners of my mind. Hazy thoughts appear like smoke and then transform into solid, certain, and frightening knowledge.

The kiss wasn't so much a kiss as it was kissing. And as it went on, my reason for pressing against Cressit seemed to change. Our embrace began because I missed Sande and I was angry with Melily, and Cressit was a handsome bandage for my sadness, but very quickly those complicated feelings vanished. All that remained was a pleasant feeling of warmth and a sense that I was enjoying something delicious.

I felt like I could trust Cressit, and even though he certainly wasn't talking, all around the red sofa, wafting through the air, was a promise he seemed to be making—a promise of bliss.

His hand traveled up my leg and beneath my skirt, and usually I wouldn't let someone touch me like that, but I didn't stop him.

And when he said, "my bedroom's down the hall," it felt like a rare and special opportunity. I followed him through his spread, feeling lucky and powerful—as if I were the Water Goddess about to free the Varasay deeplanders or overturn the Osperacy's ship.

And what came next... I undressed without fear, and I touched Cressit without hesitation. This was love, I was sure of it, exciting and pleasurable, and yet at the same time, safe and cozy.

Then he pulled me onto his bed, and we twisted together with an urgent intensity. His skin felt like hot fire and mine cold water. He was on me, surrounding me, inside me.

"Threegod," he moaned.

And I gasped and gaped, and by then I felt like the sirens I always thought were in the tide. I was trapped on land and couldn't breathe, but everything felt so good, air didn't matter.

Then it was over, and we rolled away from each other, exhausted. I felt elated, peaceful even.

But then Cressit fell asleep.

And my contentment seeped out of me as another feeling took its place—a poisonous horror that I had just lain with a complete stranger and betrayed Sande.

I didn't love this singer. I didn't even know him.

Had I been gripped with insanity? Was the uppy drink more powerful than I thought? Could cohol fool a person so completely?

I've always felt frustrated by Sande's impulsiveness, and I was furious with Melily's rash decisions about the swingshow, but now I'd done something far more reckless.

I slid off of the unfamiliar bed, shaking, still naked. And I looked at Cressit, who still lay sprawled across the blankets snoring. And then I began to cry as I searched for my clothes. Snowy moonlight shone through three tall windows, helping me find my dress, but my underclothes, my shoes, my jacket—where was everything?

"Quiet, I'm trying to sleep," Cressit murmured, rolling over.

What a callous comment. Another sob escaped me.

After mumbling a bit more, Cressit sat up. At first he blinked blearily, but then his eyes widened. "You're upset. Why? What's wrong?"

I pulled my dress across myself, tried to answer, and instead sunk down on my knees, feeling crushed by shame.

He slid off the bed and knelt beside me. "Fathoms, you're not... hurt are you? Why are you so upset? Tell me, please."

"I didn't want to come here," I said, hardly able to look at him. "I didn't. And I didn't want to do that with you. I don't know why I did that with you."

Up until then, Cressit wore a kind yet weary expression. But at that point, his face changed. It was like I'd told him the ocean stopped roaming. "You didn't want to lie with me, you mean?" he asked softly. "But you kissed me... and then..."

"I kissed you because I was upset!" I cried, too confused to care about sounding mean. "And now I feel like I've gone mad. At first I just thought you were some spoiled uppy, but then... but then I did all of that. I've ruined everything." Gren Tya always said rich uppies had fragile nerves because they think about themselves too much. Had I caught that illness?

Cressit put his face into his hands. "Fathoms." He wiped his fingers slowly down his cheeks before lifting his head again. "Ugh, this is my fault. I thought you were interested in me... and well, the girls who come to my spread after swingshows tend to be here for only one reason. But you're saying, you didn't want to do what we just did?"

"I didn't even want to go to your swingshow," I said. But this isn't his fault. He didn't force me into his arms. He didn't make me do anything.

"Ah," he said, eyeing me. "This isn't good, and I'm so sorry. How dreadful. When the R.S. Men appeared, the girls I was… spending time with… ran. I still felt like, shall we say, having company, and I saw you. You seemed interested, and it was late, so I skipped the formalities to hurry things along. I shouldn't have. I'm so sorry."

He collapsed onto his knees and buried his fingers in his hair, looking as horrified as I felt. "Fathoms. I… I don't even know your name."

"Nerene," I whisper.

"Well, Nerene, I confess I have a strange talent… I can make people feel things—so sometimes I make them feel good. I've always thought it was a kindness on my part in the bedroom—a sort of generosity—but I see that I went overboard with you. I misunderstood what you wanted."

"So you're a siren," I said, wondering how many of them there were.

Cressit looked at me with deep confusion. "How do you know about sirens?"

"I'm… I…" I'd made things bad enough already. I couldn't confess all my secrets. "I can't say."

"Yes, you can," Cressit said, moving closer to me. "How do you know? Tell me the truth."

And that was most definitely wavurl, although his power didn't feel like Douglen's. Commands from Douglen felt like a rope around my neck, yanking me in a direction I didn't want to go. Cressit's command was more like a gentle-but-persistent nudge I couldn't resist. So sniffing back tears, I told him everything; all about my last tide in Varasay and how I am Melily's balance and how I made a bargain with the Osperacys to save Sande's life.

"Augh, I've made a huge, *huge* mistake," Cressit said. "I know I keep saying I'm sorry, but I really am." Turning on the bedside light, he pulled on his clothes and helped me find the rest of mine. "I'll fix everything, I promise."

"You can't fix this," I said sadly, and by then I sat on the bed with my arms folded. "You can't undo it."

"Not exactly, no," Cressit said, his brow furrowed. "But for you it will be like it never happened."

And I knew what that meant. He planned to clear my memory—the same wavurl trick Melily used on Sir Mauricen. "What if I don't want you to?"

"Trust me," he said with wavurl in his words, as he reached for my shoulders. "It's for the best."

And I suppose he was right for a while.

Now on the *Trident*, with my broken memory made whole, I'm not done crying when Cressit wakes up.

He doesn't say anything at first, he just sits leaning against his bed.

And as for me, I've tied myself into a knot, with my ankles locked together and my arms wrapped around my knees. I'm not a small person, but I feel tiny right now.

After a long while, I say, "How did I get back to that red sofa?"

"I put you to sleep and carried you," Cressit says. "Again, I am sorry, and I was sorry, but I suppose you remember all of that now too." He sits like I do, hunched up and small. "Back in Beth, it felt merciful to take your memory—but now... I realize I tricked you and then lied to you."

I skim through my repaired memory again, especially the parts that burn brightly and make me blush. "You didn't command me, though, not until... after. Are you different from the Osperacys?"

Cressit lets his arms unfold and drop into his lap. "No, but their way uses wavurl like a mallet. I prefer to use it subtly. I can make people feel specific emotions. It's why I'm such a popular performer."

I hate that he sounds proud of himself. My anger rises up again. "That morning in Beth... I thought I could trust you, and that you could become a friend. I felt it. Was that just your wavurl?"

"Probably," he admits. "I often use it without thinking." Cressit shakes his head. "I taught myself to use my wavurl like that with good intentions—I really did. Using direct commands to find Melily felt wrong, and I thought it would be better to bring people to me with music, and maybe they'd have information about her. It also gave me a good reason to constantly travel the trade routes. I just wanted to find Melily, and I didn't mean to hurt anyone." For a moment, he falls silent again. "I have to admit, though, recently... I wasn't as focused on finding her as I should have been. It had been so long, I thought that maybe she was dead, and..." He shrugs, looking away. "I suppose I was enjoying who I was."

"Who you *are*," I say. I've stopped crying, but my sadness feels lodged in my throat.

"I'm not going to be so selfish anymore. I won't. I promise." Cressit kneads the sides of his head, and I heard anguish in his words. I'm not sure I'm sympathetic, though. And what do I do with my memory of that night in Beth? It wasn't upsetting while it was happening, but it's devastating now.

"I could be pregnant."

"You aren't."

The way he says it, so certain, makes me upset. I wonder how many children he's fathered on the tide.

He didn't have to give me my memory back. He could have just told me what happened in Beth—that sort of confession probably would have been harder on him but easier on me.

Cressit must suspect what I'm thinking because he says, "Do you want me to make you forget again? There's still time for that, and—"

"No!" I say, sharp and loud, feeling defensive of my mind. And then I softly add, "But it's not up to me, is it? You could lie with me and make me forget afterward, over and over. I'd never know."

"I wouldn't do that." Cressit stands, holding his arms at his sides, straight and stiff. "And besides, I didn't make you kiss me. You did that on your own." He isn't whispering now. "It was wrong to *influence* you after that, yes, but you can't blame me for thinking that you—" He falls abruptly silent and puts a hand on his mouth. When he speaks again, his voice sounds low and controlled. "I made a mistake—a big mistake. But I want to make it right. Look, if there's an upside to this, it's that I know I did wrong. Tonight is a turning point for me."

"I have to go." I struggle to stand. My thoughts and feelings are still churning. I need to make sense of them and that can't happen here.

Cressit moves to the door, but before he opens it, he stops and looks at me. "I know you're furious, and you should be, but please don't let what happened between us ruin Melily's rescue. When we reach Gatreijan, my ship…"

"Of course I won't say anything. I care about her." I'm a little surprised to hear myself admit it, but I suppose it's true. "You can't take her just yet, though."

He still lingers at the door. "What do you mean?"

"I'm not sure you're any better than the Osperacys, and besides, if you take her, you'll put Sande in danger and me too. If you owe me anything, you owe me patience."

Cressit blinks and wipes his red eyes. "But... I promised to help you. When I take Melily home, you'll leave with us. And since I'll have my ship by then, we can find your friend, Sande. None of that has to change."

"Well I don't want your help. Not anymore." I push past him and out into the corridor.

Back in my cabin, my bed feels too large, and the fernflax sheets refuse to absorb my warmth. Ever since we left Beth, Cressit has been kind to me, and today in the Hill Kingdoms, he even acted like a friend. And yet for sunpeaks, he had secret knowledge of me. I thought I could trust him, but the only person I can truly trust is Sande. And oh Sande, where in the Sea Spread are you? I lie on my stomach, and with my arms folded under my ribs, I shiver myself to sleep.

For the next few days, I avoid everyone, and my stomach slowly heals. Melily badgers me to go swimming with her, but I tell her I'm still not feeling well. I keep my eyes down in the dining cabin, and thankfully Douglen ignores me. He spends his meals like he usually does, talking with Lord Osperacy and Jeck. They debate which trade route will make them the most money, discuss how much time the *Trident* should spend in each mountain city, and suggest ways to avoid the storms that appear on the weather sweeps.

Cressit is easy to avoid. He doesn't eat with us, and he spends most of his time either practicing in the cavernous hold with his band or trailing after Melily and, I suppose, letting her think she has power over him.

I even stay away from Shara. I'm not sure I can lie to her if she asks me what's wrong.

At least Gatreijan is close, only days away, and if Lord Osperacy is true to his word, I'll have another chance to speak with Sande.

Now that I've had some time to think about my last relaycall, I suspect Douglen didn't just end the conversation to be cruel. He ended it because I asked Sande where he was. Yet if I've figured out why Douglen cut our call short surely Sande has too. Hopefully the next time I speak with him, he'll tell me where he is immediately. I probably won't even have to ask.

I stubbornly put all thoughts of Beth and Cressit out of my mind, and I feel genuinely happy when I arrive in the dining cabin one morning to find that we've reached Gatreijan. The city seems to stab its way out of the tidewater—a jagged spike growing larger on the horizon. After my meal of cold shallowberry oats, I'm so busy thinking about what I should say to Sande, I don't notice Cressit waiting for me in the corridor. He snags my arm and bundles me into an empty cabin, hushing me at the same time.

"Don't touch me!" I don't want anyone handling me, especially him.

"Shh! Quiet," he urges, shutting the door. "I just needed to speak with you for a moment."

He doesn't use wavurl when he's telling me to be quiet, although I suppose with him it's hard to tell when he's using his powers. The cabin we're in is empty but looks as if it could be another private dining room. I stand on a pretty, patterned carpet, paneled kelpwood walls surround me, and on my left, several bright windows look out onto the upper deck.

"What do you want?" I retreat to the furthest corner of the cabin, putting as much space between us as I can.

Cressit reaches into his pocket. "I have something for you."

He offers me a crumpled scrap of paper.

I move close enough to snatch it, and then I scuttle back to my side of the room. There's something written on it, yet despite all my reading practice with Shara, I don't recognize the symbols.

My confusion must show because Cressit says, "It's a number code—the one Douglen used to relaycall your friend."

I close my fingers around the paper, wanting it to be the truth. "How did you get this?"

Cressit isn't wearing flashy stage clothes today, only a plain shirt and seacotton trousers. He hasn't styled his hair either, just tied it back. I find it strange to see both of his eyes.

"The crew likes me," he says, "so I had a serveman unlock Lord Osperacy's cabin while everyone dined last night. It took a while to go through Osperacy's papers, especially in a way he wouldn't notice, but I found it."

Of course the crew likes Cressit.

"Thank you," I say stiffly.

"It's the least I can do. Tomorrow in Gatreijan, I'd like to help you find a relayphone and make sure your call connects."

I don't want to talk to Sande with Cressit standing next to me, but I suppose Lord Osperacy or Douglen would be worse.

"That way the two of you can talk freely. You can tell him that I'm willing to help, and then you'll know where he is and how safe he is. Maybe he can hide someplace until we reach him."

I look down at the paper again. "What if Sande says he'll be in immediate danger if I leave the Osperacy's?"

"Then I won't take Melily," Cressit says. "I'll rescue Sande first. Listen, once I'm done performing tomorrow, I'll find you. We can slip away and make the call. Afterward, you can tell everyone you got lost in the crowd."

That's right, he's singing tomorrow at the Laeros Light Festival. Melily hasn't stopped talking about it because somehow she's convinced Lord Osperacy to let us all attend.

I nod. "All right."

"Tomorrow then," Cressit says, reaching for the door handle.

"Yes, tomorrow," I say, hating that now I feel like I can trust him again, hating that my anger is less intense then it should be. His wavurl really is dangerous.

"SO DO YOU HAVE your gunnerife?" Melily asks. "Father wants to know."

"Yes," I say, touching the weighty holster that's strapped to my thigh and hidden beneath my clothes. Apparently gunnerifes aren't allowed in Gatreijan. Lord Osperacy still wants me to carry mine, though, so I'm keeping it well hidden.

The city looms above us, forming a metallic crust on the spire of steep rocky cliffs that no one would choose to live on if it weren't for the roaming ocean. Massive stone pillars support ledges crammed with buildings, while other homes and structures jut out from the mountaintop. Winding around it all is a tangle of what looks like flat, metal ribbons that are truly a type of motorliner track. Every so often I see one of the long vehicles race by, and they are so different from the motorliners of Varasay. The ones in the deeplands had big, rectangular linercarts that the uppies used to haul goods in from distant farmlands and then up to the city. The Gatreijan motorliners have sleek and rounded linercarts, with open windows and rows of benches, and they appear to carry people.

And where there aren't curving motorliner tracks connecting the city levels, I see large, basket-like devices moving along cables that stretch from peak to peak.

"Ugh, I wish there was room for automotors in this city," Melily whines as we approach a group of smaller vehicles on the pier that the Osperacys call triwheels. "Everything is so wet! My costume will be ruined."

I look down at my outfit—a dark red gown that shines orange wherever the fabric gathers or folds. The dress belongs to Shara, and it's so loose and billowy that for once our size difference doesn't matter.

Melily isn't pleased with it, though. During the Festival of Laeros, everyone is supposed to dress like golden celestial warriors, the way she and Jeck have, or in blues and greens to represent water demons, like Shara and Douglen. But since there were no extra Laeros outfits on the *Trident*, and Melily wanted me to wear something festive, I'm dressed like an avenging spirit from the Festival of Shale.

I like my red gown, though, and the matching mask and beaded combs that go with it. It makes me feel separate from the others, which seems appropriate today.

Yet Melily is right about the damp. The waves smashing against Gatreijan's rocky shore make the air misty and wet. Tiny beads of water even cover our triwheel as if it's been raining. The little vehicle and its matching cart must have been bright green at some point, but most of the paint has chipped away leaving blooms of rust.

Shara and Douglen share a second cart that's hitched to an equally battered triwheel, and Jeck has the third cart all to himself and his gangly legs. Lord Osperacy isn't with us. Douglen says he's busy arranging upcoming tasks and reviewing current charts with Captain Gedwick. But I suspect the real reason Lord Osperacy isn't here is because he doesn't want to wear a sequined costume.

For that matter, I'm surprised Douglen put on a glittering tide-green jacket and matching mask. However, I suppose we'll be watching the musical performances in the high city, and whenever there's a gathering of wealthy uppies, Douglen seems to have business with someone.

"Make sure you hang on tight!" Melily cries as the triwheel drivers start their sputtering engines, and we rattle off across the pier. The small, three-wheeled vehicle moves far faster than I expect. It's also far noisier; although everything in Gatreijan is loud—the waves crashing into the rocks, the motorliners scraping along their tracks, and even the people shouting in the streets.

I cling to the triwheel cart's narrow bench as we careen through the lower city—or I suppose I should say one of Gatreijan's many lower cities, for there are so many different levels here. We shoot past housing towers, tiny shops, and tall, thin storage halls. Between them, I catch glimpses of the festival—gold and blue banners, clumps of people waving ribbons tied to reeds, and cookery wagons that smell spicy and a little daring.

Our juddering triwheel ride ends with a sudden stop at the base of one of those cable lifts. According to our drivers, the lifts are the quickest and least confusing way to reach the higher city levels. They tell us there isn't a motorliner that goes there directly. We'd have to switch trundles, whatever those are, at least twice, and one man tells us that the routes are "more complicated than tangled hair."

I was already nervous traveling in the triwheel, but the cable lift alarms me even more. Even though it's essentially a sturdy cage, locked doors and iron bars won't save me if the cable snaps. So I sit rigidly on a steel bench and cover my eyes as we sway up into the winds and lurch over some very sharp rocks.

"Oh, Nerene." Melily prods my shoulder. "Don't be such a minnow! Just look! The view is incredible! Ooo, I can see the *Trident* from here!"

"That's nice," I mutter between my fingers.

"Want me to hold your hand, sludge?" Jeck's voice warms my ear.

I swivel away. At least I'm finding it easy to tolerate him today—or well, easier. All I have to do is focus on the folded paper tucked into my shoe, Sande's number code.

Cressit is already in the high city. He left this morning with a slew of instruments, sound equipment, and luggage. I didn't have the chance to speak with him alone, but when he told Melily he'd sing her favorite songs, he gave me a quick, intense look that seemed to hold all of his promises.

I'm beginning to get the troubling feeling, though, that I'm not the only person with a hidden plan today. Douglen and Jeck keep whispering to each other behind Shara's back.

Finally, thank the Water Goddess, our elevated trip ends. The cable lift jostles into a brick building on the edge of a high cliff, although unfortunately it doesn't come to a complete stop. Instead it jolts sideways, and I grip the bars tightly with a little cry that makes Jeck laugh. Our cart, or basket or whatever this death cage is called, must have wheels on the bottom for it seems to lock into a track. It then rolls in a slow, jerking half-circle, turning so that it can descend again. During this bumpy little trip, Douglen unlatches the door and shouts, "Jump! Now!"

There's wavurl in his words, and for once maybe it's a good thing. I'd probably be too scared to move otherwise. Helpless in the grip of his command, I follow Shara out of the cable lift with my billowy dress bunched in my arms.

Aside from the machinery powering the pulley and a few benches, the brick building is empty. However as we pass through a passage leading outside, a city guard stops us and checks our passbooks.

After that, we step out onto the street, and it's almost as if the lift carried us to a different mountain city. Motorliners still roar across curving tracks overhead and below, but the sound of the waves has vanished, and the air is drier, colder, and windier. I fold my arms, thankful that my red dress has long sleeves.

Gatreijan must usually be a bleak, unfriendly place. Everything is built out of colorless stone and welded metal, and there are only a few scrubby plants. Yet the festival has splashed color and cheer across the city. Braided blue and green ropes wind around girders, while garlands of painted shells clatter in the wind. A huge amount of people in beautiful Laeros costumes surround us too. Some of them hold mugs of ale while others nibble on skewers of fish and baskets of steamed clams. They laugh and joke, and like a slow-moving river, they stream away from us and pour over the ornate metal bridge in the distance.

We join the crowd, and as we walk, I stare at the cliffs that rise even further above us. Clusters of houses cling to the steep rock, and some of the buildings perch so high up they're half-hidden by clouds.

On the other side of the bridge, we come to a huge gathering area. There must be a name for this type of structure, but I don't know it. Whatever it's called it resembles a metal and stone flower with circles of balconies instead of petals, and a flat, grassy lawn in the sunken center. I imagine that lawn serves as a park or market on most days, but today there's a pressed-reed platform on it that's decorated with blue and green fabric and surrounded by electric lights.

That platform is surely where Cressit will perform, although right now there is a group of different musicians there. They play a song that feels dramatic and exciting and makes me think of our recent wild triwheel ride.

We climb many metal staircases, moving from petal to petal, and eventually we reach one of the highest balconies. It's connected to an impressive house made of painted black metal and flat green stones.

Shara tells me that this house belongs to one of the seven chancellors that jointly govern Gatreijan. "Sir Finscini is a regular client of Lord Osperacy's," she adds.

I can't see Douglen and Jeck anymore. They seem to have crept off. And although I'm sure they are probably doing something awful, I'm also relieved. If they're gone, I can make my secret relaycall more easily.

Melily leads Shara and me through a crowd of costumed uppies toward a table draped with golden lace and covered with platters of fussily arranged food.

"This will not be as fun as the swingshow in Beth," Melily tells me, plucking up a skewer of salt biscuit, cliff peach, and scallop. "Gatreijan always hires these great performers for their Threegod festivals, but then they have them play for boring old people who aren't even listening." She pops the food into her mouth, pulling out the skewer. "At least there's skyfire later."

Skyfire? I smile, genuinely excited about that. I've seen skyfire before but only at a distance. We'd watch from the deeplands whenever those colorful stars flew up from Varasay to burst with soft rolls of thunder and shimmery light.

As Shara heads inside Sir Finscini's house to find a drink of water, Melily sighs heavily. "I can't believe Cressit's really leaving. I guess I'll just have to find a way to go to all his swingshows from now on. I was thinking I could command him to stay, but I suppose…" She eyes me. "That wouldn't be right, would it?"

I'm surprised. It's a real question for me as her balance, and she looks like she wants an honest answer. I feel fonder of her than I usually do, and I wish I could tell her how important she really is to Cressit. I also feel guilty that I've linked her rescue to Sande's. It's true she's not in immediate danger like he may be, but it still doesn't seem fair.

"No, commanding Cressit wouldn't be right," I agree. "But I'm sure you'll see him again."

Even though Melily seemed convinced that this crowd won't pay attention to the musicians, people certainly notice Cressit. At sunset, as horns blare and lights flash, he strides across the platform. On every stone balcony, uplanders surge against the railings, and their cheers echo up against the cliffs.

Melily seems excited too. "Ah! Marto's back! He's the drummer! I haven't seen him since Beth!"

I feel strangely tense as Cressit struts across the platform, flipping his dark hair into the wind and playing elaborate melodies on a chorder—which is what I've learned his narrowstring-like instrument is called. I can feel the emotions he's sending out into the crowd now that I'm trying to sense them. His wavurl feels like a pleasant warmth trying to slip between my ribs. It's an inviting blend of joy, excitement, and longing.

I eye Melily. She wouldn't feel his wavurl, and yet she still likes his songs. I wonder if Cressit would have adoring crowds at his swingshows if he didn't use his siren powers—maybe.

Cressit belts out song after song until he finally grabs the voice amplifier, his lungs heaving, his hair curling up with sweat, and says, "This will be my last song tonight. It's new."

He then plays a soft, delicate melody, a tune that's just his fingers dancing across the chorder strings. The song has no words, and despite not wanting to like it, I find myself enjoying the slow rhythm.

"Aw, why is he ending with this?" Melily grumbles. "It's depressing."

Finishing the song, Cressit waves to the crowd and leaves the platform, vanishing into a nearby blue tent. My breath quickens. Soon he'll find me. Soon we'll slip away from the Osperacys and relaycall Sande. But as I watch a dozen new singers climb onto the pressed-reed platform, and as I listen to Melily complain about how she used to like these women but then a few of them left the group to get married and their replacements aren't that good, I realize I've made another mistake. How can I sneak away with Cressit while I'm wearing my bright red Shale costume? This dress will look like a splash of blood in the surrounding sea of green, blue, and gold. The Osperacys will be able to spot me anywhere on this level of the city.

After the women on stage sing a few songs, someone bumps into me and, to my surprise, squeezes my arm. I turn to see a figure in a hooded, gold cloak walking away.

Cressit. It has to be.

"I'll be back in a moment," I tell Melily and Shara. "I have to use the washing closet."

"Don't worry, you won't miss anything," Melily says, slumping on the railing. "The Corals are so terrible now."

I think the ladies on stage sound lovely—each of them seems to be singing a different melody and somehow those melodies blend beautifully together. But there's no time to linger. The hooded person stands beside the entrance to the Chancellor's house, waiting for me.

The stranger glances briefly my way as I approach, giving me a glimpse of his face and confirming that yes, he's Cressit. I follow him inside across gleaming drybark floors, past fine furniture that looks as if it belongs in Beth's museum, and then through a cookery full of serveworkers. The men and women there are so busy shifting pots of boiling broth and slicing fruit, they don't seem to notice us.

On the other side of the cookery, Cressit begins opening doors in a narrow passage that's much less luxurious than the rest of the house. This corridor seems like a place that's usually only seen by servants.

"I'm sorry about the red dress," I say.

"It's fine," he whispers. "As long as my hunch is right, and... ha! It is."

The door Cressit's just opened leads to a chamber with a metal staircase that tunnels into the house's rocky foundation. He starts down it.

"What is this place?" I ask, following him. The excessive fabric of my gown and my stiff heeled shoes make it difficult for my feet to find each small, triangular step.

"A lot of rich people here build lodging for serveworkers on a less expensive, lower level," Cressit says, his voice echoing. "And then they connect them with stairs like these."

I wonder why Cressit knows about these passages, but only for a moment. Surely this stairwell would be a good way to escape a subs raid or sneak off with a beautiful servegirl.

Only a few electric lights hang on the walls, but even though I can't see much, I feel the walls change from neatly arranged brick to roughly carved rock as we descend. The stairs have no railings either just a central pole supporting the winding steps, which I cling to with both hands.

We've climbed down and around maybe four or five times when Cressit's voice emerges from the stale air. "I added that last song for you. I remember you liked the slower one at the end of my swingshow in Beth."

"Thank you," I say.

We're both quiet after that, listening to the sound of our shoes meeting the metal steps. Every few moments, a motorliner roars past somewhere outside too, sending tremors through the rock and shaking the stairs.

After we've descended what feels like a thousand steps, we reach the serveworker house. It's a sparse, clean place with a large laundry and even larger cookery than the one I saw in the house above. We thankfully don't meet any serveworkers as we hurry through the building, and outside we join yet another crowd of uppies celebrating Laeros in blue, green, and gold costumes.

This city level may not be as wealthy as the one above, but I still find it impressive. Although the houses are a little smaller, and I see no fountains or elaborate gathering places, everything is in excellent repair. Smooth stones cover the ground, arranged in complicated patterns, and the occasional triwheel I see looks brand new.

The sky's grown dark now, and electric torches gleam on top of tall poles. Music competes with the hum of the crowd, and there are lots of merchant booths on this level. Many of them seem to be selling dumplings stuffed with prickle crab and salt cabbage, but others have displays of glittering outfits, brightly colored flags, and Threegod knickknacks such as prayer bracelets, spirit candles, tide pipes, and holy songbooks.

"Now where can we find a relayphone?" Cressit leads me through the crowd. "Sleeperhouses, perhaps, or maybe private homes will let us use theirs if we offer money or…" he eyes me with uncertainty, "…I'm being charming. But those places would surely only be able to make local calls. A better option might be a motorliner station. Those are noisy, but we could manage. Worst case, we head down to the *Anchor*—that's my ship—and connect the relayphone there. But that trip would take a while, and we want to get you back to the *Trident* tonight."

He seems so confident. I wish I felt the same. I suppose, though, this isn't as risky for him as it is for me.

"I have the number code," I say.

"Good." He taps his pocket. "I brought a copy too. Now all we have to do is find the nearest motorliner station." He looks around, and so do I. And as I scan the area, I see Jeck.

No.

He's walking away from a shop built into the side of the mountain, and although he's not facing us, he'll easily see me in these bright clothes if he turns his head. I duck behind Cressit and whisper fiercely, "Jeck!"

"Where?"

I point to the shop.

"Wonderful!" Cressit says.

"What?" Why would he say that? I hunch down even more, trying to pull all the bright red folds of my dress in behind Cressit's gold cape. If Jeck sees me here, he'll think I'm running away.

"I mean the shop," Cressit says. "The shop is wonderful. Jeck just left a mechanic repair shop, and if anyone has a relayphone able to make tide-wide calls, it'll be that place."

I suppose that makes sense, and I suppose it also makes sense that Jeck would visit a shop like that. I remember the explosive metal devices he once made, and I saw him testing an invention the other day up on deck—I think it was a clockwork alarm. He surely needs a regular supply of parts and tools for his projects.

"Don't worry..." Cressit says in a hushed voice. "He's not coming our way."

I risk peering over Cressit's shoulder, and thankfully I see Jeck's short brown curls bobbing off into the crowd. "All right, let's go," I say. "Quickly."

We hurry up the metal stairs that lead to the repair store, and what an interesting store it is. I see shelves of timekeepers as we enter, as well as electric lights, mechanical toys, and plenty of uppy devices I don't recognize. Some of the machines are quiet or in pieces, while others whir and click loudly. Beneath the shelves lie rows of baskets full of parts and tools, and on the far side of the shop, somber music crackles out of a music machine much like Melily's.

"Is anyone here?" Cressit calls.

A fluffy ridge cat with tufts of silver and white on his spine leaps onto the counter and greets us with a solemn "M'row" as if he runs the place. But several seconds later, a gentleman with gray hair and the dark skin common in Gatreijan emerges from a doorway.

"Good evening, I'm not offering any festival discounts," the shopkeep says dryly as if he's repeated this all day.

"Good evening to you too." Cressit smiles. "Do you have a relayphone?"

"I do, absolutely," the man says and turns to show us several relayphones hanging over the shop counter. "So these two are top of the line, with electric lights and buzzers. That one is more old-fashioned with a bell—but it's extremely well made and the best of the lot, and that last pair are serviceable, but they are the most beautiful—if that's important to you. They have drybark sides, rather than pressed reed, and as you can see, brass accessories."

"Actually we aren't looking to buy a phone," Cressit tells him. "We simply need to make a cross-tides call."

The shopkeep gives us a closer look. "Well now, that's an interesting dilemma. Relayphones 'round here are only supposed to be set for local calls."

"Do you know of anyone who can change a local relayphone to have wider settings?" Cressit asks, and I can feel the friendly wavurl rolling off of him.

"Do *I* know of anyone who can reset a relayphone?" The man smiles, showing a glimmer of warmth. "There might be something in the back I tinker with sometimes. You can use it... for a fair price."

"Wonderful!" Cressit eyes me happily. "How does ten shells sound?"

"Yeah, I suppose that'll do." The man nods and flips a lock on the front door. "Well then, follow me."

He leads us up another stairway that cuts into the mountain, and we enter a cave-like room reinforced with metal beams. I see a bed and small cookstove, so this must be the man's living quarters. Otherwise, though, the space looks like a messier version of the shop. I see more shelves of noisy machines and piles of parts and tools. There's also a worktable and three relayphones hanging on the wall that look battered and made out of mismatched parts, but they seem to be in working order. Wires run out of them and into the wall.

The shopkeep tells us to use the first, largest machine, and then leaves us be, returning back down the stairs.

Sande. I'm about to speak with Sande.

Nervously holding my passbook bag, I watching Cressit twist a knob on the call box in different directions.

"Seven, eight," he says, and *click-click* goes the knob. "Zero." *Click.* "Six." *Click.* "Five…"

As he enters each number, I dread that something will go wrong with the call like it did in the Hill Kingdoms.

When Cressit's done turning the knob, he hands me the listening cone, which is connected to a curling, fabric-covered wire.

I press the cone to my ear and hear a soft sound, like cracking eggshells. After that, it's almost as if someone's whistling a single, endless note. Finally a tinny, distorted voice says, "Goren Industry Island."

My thoughts seem to lose their balance and tip sideways. I don't know what an industry island is.

"Anyone there?" I hear a man's voice, rough and sharp and not Sande. "You looking for a shipment? Place'n an order?"

"No." I suppose that wherever Sande is, he probably doesn't have a personal relayphone. It seems silly now that I assumed he would answer the relaycall. "I'm looking for someone—a worker," I add because that's most likely. "His name's Sande Olin… and he's a deeplander from Varasay."

Cressit watches me with an expression of concern. He points to himself, surely offering to help.

"Yeah, I don't know 'em all by name." The distant voice sounds impatient as if he'd like to end the conversation. "We don't let slaves touch the relayphone either."

246

Slaves? My insides quiver. Sande should not be a slave. That isn't the agreement I have with Lord Osperacy; he promised to keep Sande safe, and slavery isn't safe. "Wait!" I cry. "This young man—he spoke to me before. You or someone there let him."

"Ain't possible. Look, I got work to—"

"Don't go, please!" I cry. Did Douglen somehow use his wavurl over the relayphone? I didn't think that was possible. But then a solution comes to me; perhaps Douglen used a different type of power. "Lord Osperacy sent Sande to you," I say. "And Lord Osperacy wants me to speak to him."

On the other side of the shopkeep's work table, Cressit nods in approval.

"Osperacy?" The man's voice cracks and breaks as if a storm rides the tide between us. "Oh, all right… yeah, I know the kid."

I exhale heavily. "Wonderful! Let me speak to him. Please."

"Well, tell your boss that ain't possible 'cause we lost him. We lost him and a good near fifty others—and one of my best rafts."

"Lost him." I feel like someone's forcibly pulled my brief happiness back out of me. "What do you mean?"

Across the small room, Cressit makes a quick movement of dismay. But I'm not focused on him, I'm pressing the rounded, copper edge of the listening cone against my ear.

"We had a stretch of big storms," says the voice. "Like real big, and one of the barges snapped free of its groundin' chain. Bad luck all 'round, but that happens sometimes."

I don't know what to say. I feel like something in my chest has snapped free—some essential part of my lungs or heart.

"Listen, I gotta go. You tell Osperacy I still owe him that favor."

I hear a clicking sound and then nothing at all. I stare at the chipped edges of the relayphone box, and I feel like I can't move. I don't even have the strength to put the listening cone back in its bracket.

I knew today might go wrong, but all the many problems I imagined didn't include losing Sande.

"Nerene…" Cressit says gently. "What's wrong? What happened?"

I want to sob and just surrender to sadness, but I suppose I should try to understand the more confusing parts of this terrible news. "He was somewhere called Industry Island," I say, my eyes stinging. "And he was on a barge—what is that?"

"A type of factory," Cressit says. "They're chained to the Sea Spread and they float while the tide passes. Then they sit in the deeplands for the rest of the year; it's cheaper than buying mountain city land. But since most cities don't like factory barges nearby, they're not usually in the trade routes but further starways or skytide."

"Sande's barge," I say. "It broke free in a storm, and the man on the relayphone… he said it's lost."

Cressit doesn't look alarmed, he looks grim.

"I don't understand what that means. Lost how?" I wipe tears off my cheeks. "Surely people would try to find a lost factory."

Cressit sighs. "Those places often have a whole group of barges linked together. If one breaks free, it's cheaper for the owners to build a new one than to tow the other around the tide. The barges are like big floating platforms… they aren't meant to travel."

I'm freshly horrified. "So Sande…" Sande and fifty other people. "He's just drifting out there? And no one's trying to find him?"

Cressit nods. "Most likely. I'm so sorry."

Fresh tears fill my eyes, and I suddenly find the tick and clang of timekeepers and mechanical toys unbearable. I have to get out of here.

We return to the main shop. Cressit stops to thank the owner and pay him, but I walk straight out the door. "I'll wait outside," I say, nearly stepping on the poor ridge cat who seems hopeful that I'll pet him.

Once I'm out of the shop, I rush down the stairs to the street and take deep, unsteady breaths. I fought to keep Sande safe, but it didn't matter. His whole life and the possible life we could have had together just drifted out of reach.

A hand falls on my shoulder, and I shrug it off. Cressit isn't my friend. He should stop pretending he is.

But the fingers tighten, and Douglen, not Cressit, says, "Don't scream or shout or call for help. Let's start with that."

I swallow and try to twist away, but he hangs on tight.

"Stop fighting and don't run," he keeps piling commands on me, and his wavurl feels like cement, weighing me down. He carefully inspects me. "I came to meet Jeck, and yet here you are. Is he still in the shop? Tell the truth."

"No, he already left." I can hear the distant sound of Cressit still talking to the shopkeep. He'll come out of that repair store at any moment, and then what will happen? Douglen can't command him.

"Are you saying Jeck found you but then... left you here?" Douglen looks confused. "Answer me."

"He didn't see me," I say, wincing as Douglen's command burrows into my mind. If only Cressit would leave the shop.

"Follow me," Douglen says, and kraken, I have to.

I feel frantic. In seconds I'll be out of Cressit's reach and beyond help. At least I'm wearing this bright red dress. Now I'm glad that I'm easy to spot in the crowd.

"So why were you blubbing? And why are you here? You're supposed to be with Melily." Douglen turns, fixes his dark eyes on me, and commands, "Tell the truth." I think he's been drinking because his wavurl feels soft around the edges. Maybe I can escape.

I try to resist his question, but an honest answer still fights its way out of me. "I tried to relaycall Sande."

Douglen tilts his head sharply. "You had his number code?

I nod.

"How did you get it?"

I have to answer, but since his commands feel weaker than usual, I manage a partial truth. "A serveman helped me."

"Which one?"

At least this I can be honest about. "I don't know his name."

"Does Melily know where you are?"

"No," I'm forced to admit. "But I wasn't running away, and I was going to—"

"Be silent," Douglen barks, and again my words are trapped inside.

But if I can somehow escape Douglen, *should* I return to Melily? As bad as things are for Sande, at least Lord Osperacy can't threaten him anymore, and that means he can't threaten me either.

Douglen brings me to a large, stylish building with black motorliner tracks curving out of it like tentacles—it must be a stationhub. We pass through a low rotating gate to enter, and Douglen gives five paper shells to a woman behind a window. I'm surprised he's using money rather than wavurl. Perhaps he can't stretch himself too thin while he's drunk or he'll lose control of me.

There are three levels of platforms inside, all with motorliner tracks stretching across them. Towering metal pillars also rise up and branch out like mighty trees to support the massive, peaked roof.

The motorliner hub is just as crowded as the city level outside. If escape is possible, I'm sure my chance will be here and gone in an instant, so I do my best to stay alert and ready to act.

Unfortunately as I look around for an opportunity to free myself, I see Jeck jogging over to us. "There you are. What's the sludge doing here?"

"I stopped by the mechanic shop to find you," Douglen says, "And there she was, crying."

Jeck chuckles as if my grief is funny. "Crying? Why?"

"I don't care, to be honest." Douglen shrugs. "But she's breaking Father's rules yet again. I told him after that business in the Hill Kingdoms that she's not worth the trouble. But he's so hung up on his balance theory, he won't do what needs doing to protect us."

Jeck nods in eager agreement, and I tremble because "do what needs doing" surely means *kill me*. It's torture to be in danger in a crowd and yet unable to call for help. Douglen's wavurl command to be silent still clings to me.

Jeck lowers his voice and hunches down so he's closer to Douglen's ear. "Did you run your errand? We could use that on her."

"However we do it, we can't do it up here," Douglen says just as quietly. "There are too many eyes. We'll take her to the lowest city level."

Oh Water Goddess, they are going to kill me.

They turn toward the motorliner platforms, and Douglen snaps his fingers at me. "Keep up."

I stumble after them. I have my gunnerife, but I'm pretty sure that by the time I pull it out of my leg holster and untangle it from my skirt, Douglen will tell me to drop it. Jeck surely has a weapon too. And even if I could somehow shoot them both, and somehow bring myself to do something that violent, the Gatreijans would consider me a murderer with a forbidden weapon.

I hate that I'm hoping Cressit will save me—like he did in Pre'Enity. I wish I didn't have to rely on him.

Besides, maybe he'll think I ran away and feel relieved. He'd no longer have to bother with my complicated demand to help Sande. He could simply take Melily home.

"I know we should deal with her quickly—but how quickly?" Jeck asks, and his question has an oily coating that makes my shoulders tighten.

Douglen eyes him, then me. "We'll get her to the lower level first. If there's no one around, you can say goodbye however you want."

I long to risk everything and kick or hit them, but challenging Douglen's power will only make him more vicious; I learned that in the Hill Kingdoms. So instead I gaze down at the diamond-shaped tiles covering the floor of the stationhub and try to appear defeated. If Douglen thinks I've given up, his wavurl hold on me might weaken, and maybe, just maybe, I can escape.

It's a challenging act, though. I'm still so upset about Sande, and his precarious situation hangs on my thoughts and slows me down. Jeck also puts a heavy hand on my lower back, and his wordless threat makes it even harder to think clearly. Most distracting of all, the stationhub is extremely noisy. Motorliners scream their way on and off platforms, buzzers and bells ring to announce which lines have arrived and which ones are leaving, and sometimes a garbled voice speaks through a sound enhancer too. The confusion makes me feel like I'm trying to read an uppy book while standing in a waterfall.

"Tell me which motorliner will take us to the merchant wharf," Douglen commands a man who is wearing the odd combination of black suit and tasseled, blue festival hat.

The command doesn't seem to stick, though, because a motorliner rushes behind us at the same time. Its many metal wheels are far louder than Douglen's words, so the man with the celebratory hat just shrugs and climbs onto the nearest linercart.

And there it is. My salvation.

Douglen can't command me if I can't hear him over the noisy motorliners.

I'm filled with sudden hope.

When the next line arrives or leaves, I could run and hide from view, and then perhaps I could hurry back to the mechanic repair shop. But of course Douglen and Jeck would chase after me, and even if I wasn't wearing heeled boots and a dress made of far too much fabric, I can't outrun Jeck. His legs are just too long.

I glance at an increasingly irritated Douglen. He's still trying to figure out which track will take us to the docks. And then I hear another loud buzzing sound, and the motorliner on my right starts crawling out of the station, slowly picking up speed.

Three steps is all it takes, three steps of still being in reach of Jeck's long arms, three steps where I expect hands to grab me, yank me back, and Douglen to drown me in so much wavurl I can never break free.

But those hands don't find me, and if siren commands come my way, I can't hear them as I lunge into the moving motorliner.

My dress is an afterthought as I dive through an open side door and onto a bench. My leap isn't graceful either, and I crash into a woman. But the linercart catches me and sweeps me along, faster and faster. I recover quickly enough to twist around and watch an enraged Jeck race down the platform with a shouting Douglen close behind. Then they're gone, and moments later, the huge stationhub disappears too. I'm surrounded by cliffs, stars, and wind that tears my hair out of its fancy uppy knot and flutters my dress into another traveler's face.

The woman I dove into mutters something along the lines of "can't stand these revelers" and "too much to drink!" And as she grumbles, I cling to the bench, feeling a strange mix of relief and fear. If Douglen and Jeck want me dead, I can't return to the *Trident.* What will happen to Sande now? What will happen to me?

Boom.

Orange-white skyfire spins up into the darkness.

And *sizzle-crackle.*

It brightens and burns the sky.

PART THREE — NERENE

I'M TWO STATIONHUBS AWAY before I decide what to do, and what I decide to do feels so reckless it would probably shock Sande.

"How do I go back?" I shout over the rushing wind to the woman I dove into.

"Back?" She looks at me like I've spoken to her in a different language.

"Yes, back," I ask, my heart thumping with both fear and determination. "Back to the stationhub I came from."

The woman's frown lines remind me of Parsita from the tea shop —she looks as if she were born disapproving of something. "It's simple enough," she says. "Just get off this liner at the next stationhub, then cross the tracks, and ride the motorliner going in the opposite direction."

"Do I need to pay for the trip again?" I ask, worried because I don't have any paper shells.

She shakes her head. "Not as long as you stay in the building."

That seems simple, but when I climb off the motorliner at the next stationhub, I see that there are four different tracks here. At least this building is much smaller and less crowded than the one I just escaped, and at least I'm not being wavurled silent. I ask a man how to find the festival music, and he points to a sign with a blue flower on it.

"Ah, you must mean the Sonorous Arena," he says. "All you have to do is wait over there and take that motorliner when it comes in."

I hesitate, eyeing his long, dark coat—a coat that could easily cover my bright red gown. "If I gave you my hair combs, could I have your coat?" I ask, and I'm glad that the combs stayed put when the wind pulled my hair loose. I also suspect that they are worth far more than his coat. They gleam with red jewels, and they have a delicate, feathery shape.

But the man gives me a suspicious look as if wondering why I'd offer something so valuable. "I don't think so, sorry."

"Dearie, I'll trade my jacket for those pretty combs," a nearby woman says. Her jacket is shorter and has well-worn hems, but perhaps a shabby jacket is exactly what I need. I don't want to draw attention to myself. So I pull the combs out of my hair and hand them to the elderly woman, and as I do, I think about the person I need to find—the person I hope will help me—Melily.

Pulling on my new, threadbare coat, I twist my red dress up and under it as much as possible, making a few knots. Then I drape my long, dark hair forward to hide my face, and I hope I look different enough to fool Douglen and Jeck when I return to the other stationhub. Maybe they won't even be there anymore. Time has passed, and it's probably more likely they'll appear here.

Thank the Water Goddess, a motorliner soon rolls in beneath the blue flower sign, and I clamor onto it. As it shudders noisily out of the stationhub moments later, whooshing upward, I realize I'm heading in a different direction than I expected. But of course... I asked how to reach the festival music, which is a level above where I ran from Douglen and Jeck. I didn't think that through in my frightened, flustered state. Well, this is much better. Not only is it less likely that I'll stumble into danger at a different stationhub, I also won't have to sneak into the serveworker house and climb all those stairs.

As the motorliner speeds up, I feel hopeful. Melily is just as powerful as Cressit is, and I'm not affected by her wavurl. I hope I can convince her to help me, or rather, I hope I can convince her that we should help each other. And if my plan fails, I can always find Cressit's ship. As much as I don't want his help, he did offer it.

When I reach the huge, basin-like gathering place that I now know Gatreijans call the Sonorous Arena, I see lots of twinkling electric lights hanging in garlands off the balconies. I suppose the lights were there before, but I didn't notice them because they weren't turned on. The arena also still rings with music as a man with a deep, growling voice belts out a song that sounds angry. I wonder if it's about revenge.

And then there she is, Melily, all alone and leaning against a railing in her glittery festival dress. I'm glad Shara isn't with her because even though Shara can be understanding, it's Melily I need— Melily and her wavurl.

"I'm sorry I've been gone so long," I call as I cross the balcony. There aren't as many people around as there were before. The Laeros Light Festival must nearly be over.

"Nerene! You should be sorry!" Melily doesn't seem to notice that my hair hangs down or that I'm wearing an unfamiliar coat. "You've been gone for, like, three hours. Shara and I looked everywhere for you. My feet hurt."

I glance around, not wanting to stay where we are for very long. "Is Shara here?"

"No, she went to the ship to look for you." Melily finally seems to notice my tattered jacket and gives it a confused look as if she can't quite remember what I was wearing before. "She wanted me to wait here in case you came back. And I hope you're grateful because I can't stand this boring music."

I feel tense, already doubting my plan. Melily can be so selfish; she might refuse to help me. But I don't have any other good options, so I take a deep breath and start talking. "Douglen and Jeck just tried to kill me."

I expect Melily to say I'm lying, but to my surprise, she just stares at me.

And so I continue, painfully aware that Douglen and Jeck could find us at any moment. "I left earlier because Cressit promised to help me relaycall Sande. But then I ran into Douglen and Jeck, and they were really angry that I wasn't with you." I emphasize certain words to make sure Melily is following my story. She's giving me such an empty look it's as if she's in a trance. "So they decided to kill me," I continue, and the next bit is harder to say, "and maybe do shameful things to me too."

Melily flinches, but otherwise, it's like her face is a door she's slammed shut.

"There's more," I say, wishing I could take her hand and pull her away from our vulnerable spot on Sir Finscini's chilly, dark balcony.

"Cressit's also a siren, and he's been looking for you—for many tides. He says Lord Osperacy kidnapped you when you were a baby." Nothing. Still no reaction from her. "And Cressit used his wavurl to make me lie with him—that's what happened when we were separated in Beth. He's apologized, but it's complicated, and—"

"Wait—Cressit's a siren?" Melily says, and finally I'm getting some sort of response from her, although I'm not sure what it is. Her mouth shifts, her eyes focus on me, and then a stricken expression spreads across her features. I almost expect her to use wavurl to call people over to restrain me, and if that happens, could I escape? But instead she says, "I think Douglen and Jeck killed Elgin."

I blink. "What?"

"I think Douglen and Jeck killed my old balance, Elgin," Melily says. "I mean, I never had proof, but the way Elgin vanished was strange."

I take her hand. "I want to talk more. You have more to tell me, I'm sure. And I need to tell you everything I just told you with more detail, but—we can't stay here."

Melily nods and, thankfully, lets me lead her away from the balcony. We walk behind several ornate houses and up a sloping road crowded with still more elegant homes. I'm not sure where we're going or where we should go, but I hold onto her hand tightly, and she squeezes mine in return.

After a while, Melily starts talking again. "I think something was happening between Father and Elgin. Like... something romantic. I didn't really understand. But Father kept giving Elgin presents, and when we'd have long city stays, he'd take him on special trips—like just the two of them. And they'd be gone for a couple of days."

I feel an uncertain prickle at her story. I've heard rumors about romances between two men or two women. They were often connected to stories about the Threegod priests banishing people from Varasay—which always seemed so cruel to me. And yet there would have been a large age difference between Elgin and Lord Osperacy. "Did Elgin want to go on those trips?"

"Oh, I don't know." Melily folds her arms, shivering. "He never talked about it, but I do know that Elgin liked boys not girls. Anyway, Douglen thought Father was telling Elgin important things, and he was jealous. They were arguing a lot—like, Father and Douglen. Then one day in Lellev, Elgin just disappeared. Douglen gave me this note from him saying he was sick of being my balance, but it just didn't make any sense. Elgin and I were best friends." She takes a deep, shuddering breath.

It's very quiet where we are now. There are only a few lights on in the nearby windows, and even though I see dark, ladder-like tracks curving overhead, no motorliners have rumbled by in a while. We're far from the Sonorous Arena now, but I still feel like Douglen might step out of any shadow. And when I hear the occasional putter of a distant triwheel, I think about how he and Jeck might use those vehicles to search for us.

"I'm tired. Let's find somewhere to sleep," I suggest, wondering if there are any sleeperhouses nearby.

"All right." Melily immediately walks toward the nearest house. As she holds up a fist to knock, I feel like I should stop her. It's wrong—and rude—to wavurl our way into someone's home. But perhaps for tonight, staying in a privately owned building is wiser than finding public lodging where Douglen and Jeck might look for us.

So Melily wavurls us inside a tall, green house, past a finely dressed family who think they've suddenly and inexplicably decided to welcome festival guests for the night.

"Do you need to keep them in your control until morning?" I ask once we're alone in a little bedchamber with a high ceiling. "I can slip free of Douglen's hold if I'm far enough away from him."

"It'll be fine." Melily shrugs. "I only have to hang on tight to my commands when I'm making people do things they really don't want to do. Those people down there will just be confused and wonder why they made a stupid decision. And they'll also be too polite to tell us they changed their minds. That's usually how it goes."

Now that we're alone, I peel off the worn jacket I used to cover my red dress. It's also a good time to better explain everything I told Melily in a panicked rush before.

It's hard to know where to start, but I settle on telling her more about the night we met Cressit. I skip the personal, embarrassing details, but otherwise I'm honest.

"I'm so stupid that I didn't realize he was a siren." Melily frowns, her face illuminated by the dim light of electric lanterns hanging on the wall. There is only one bed in the room, but it's large. We sit cross-legged on the shiny, dark blue coverlet. "I mean of course he's a siren, and how awful that he used wavurl on you in that way." Melily makes a face. "I'm sure Douglen's done things like that too. He'll always go off with Jeck, and he often won't tell Shara or Father where they went."

I shudder because she's probably right. "I think it was a misunderstanding with Cressit," I say. "But even so... if he hadn't used his wavurl on me, it wouldn't have happened."

Melily nods and wipes away a few tears. "I can't believe I liked him so much. I'm an idiot."

"You're not," I say. "He tricked me too." And I feel sick about that night in Beth all over again.

263

I also wonder where Cressit thinks I am. Was he worried when he lost me or relieved? I'm a complication he surely doesn't want.

I try to tell Melily about my relaycall to Sande and about his missing factory barge, but she doesn't seem interested. I suppose I'm not surprised—she may have taken a big step today by running away with me, but she's still Melily. She's only paying attention when I talk about her or, at the very least, about something scandalous.

Thankfully though, Melily believes me. She even believes me when I tell her that Lord Osperacy kidnapped her.

"I used to ask him about my real parents," she says. "I'd beg to meet them and promise not to use wavurl on them, but Father always said it was best to keep our distance. Does Cressit know who they are?"

I shake my head. "He didn't say. But he did say most sirens live in one place—so I'm guessing wavurl is something you inherit. He also said his favorite city is Ellevah and that he hadn't been there in a while... so I think that might be where you're from."

"Ooo, maybe!" Melily leans forward. "You know, Father—Lord Osperacy, I mean—he never wants to go to Ellevah, like ever. He says it's too tiny and not worth our time, but maybe he's avoiding it for other reasons." Her eyes sparkle.

My half-formed plan is now propped up by the fragile hope that Melily just might agree to it. "Ellevah is also where Sande wanted us to live. If he survives, there's a good chance he'll go there."

Melily bounces on her folded knees. "Threegods, this is so exciting. If we travel to Ellevah—"

"—we might find Sande *and* your family," I finish.

"But Father and Douglen will come after us, and they are both going to be really mad." Melily's shoulders droop. "We also won't have the *Trident* or money or clothes or servegirls..."

"That's true," I say, trying to be patient. Melily's probably never lived without luxuries, at least not that she can remember.

But she gives me a firm, somewhat-resigned, somewhat-excited look and says, "You know what? It doesn't matter. Let's do it. Let's go to Ellevah. But I'll have to use wavurl to get us there, so you can't get fussy when I do things my way. Promise?" She thrusts out her hand.

I frown because I don't generally like "Melily's way." But I also don't want to be stranded in Gatreijan, so I take her hand and shake it.

"I promise."

IN THE MORNING, Melily "borrows" clothes from our hosts
—which I hate to do—but it's not as if we can keep wearing our
bright festival gowns. So with our shiny dresses bundled in my coat,
and we ride the motorliners to a different city level, a lower and
poorer one.

"All this dust is choking me," Melily complains as we leave a run-
down stationhub. But she knows as well as I do that we can't stay
near the Sonorous Arena. We must hide in a part of the city where
the Osperacys are unlikely to search for us.

"And I don't think we should travel right away, either," I tell Melily.
"Douglen and Jeck might be watching the harbor. And when we do
leave, let's travel on a small boat. They won't expect that."

Melily grumbles about my suggestion, and she doesn't seem to
stop grumbling for the rest of the day. When I suggest we trade our
festival gowns for simpler clothes, she moans, "Do we have to do

that down here? Everyone looks like they're wearing underoot sacks." And when we eat at a humble cookery shop; "I almost want to find a bug in this soup because at least dampflys have flavor." And as we wait on a crowded motorliner platform; "These people smell like they've been rolling in onioncones."

But the hardest part of the day for me is when we replace our luggage. Melily has a few shell papers, but we agree (me reluctantly and she eagerly) that she should save them. Therefore, we have to do what Lord Osperacy would call *acquiring*—and I call stealing.

"All right, so the best way to do this," Melily tells me, "is for me to distract shopkeeps with my wavurl, and then you grab what we need."

I frown, which makes her laugh.

"Unless you want to wear the same underclothes all the way to Ellevah," she says, "you'll have to get your hands dirty."

And I know that, but I still hate stealing. For every hat I stuff into my shirt and for every vest, muffler, or knit wildwool sweater I tuck under my jacket, I think about the shopkeep working hard to support their family or the craftsman who spent hours making whatever it is I'm taking. Sometimes people stole herbs from Gren and me at the barracks market, and every time it happened, I was furious.

Melily enjoys herself, though, and she acts like we're shopping. In the cobbler's store, she even tries on several boots and then winks at me to let me know which pair fit best.

I try to explain Cressit's subtler method of using wavurl to her. "He makes people like him, and then people want to help him."

But Melily dismisses my suggestion. "So you don't mind doing bad things to people as long as they feel good about it? That seems worse."

"I think I'm explaining it wrong," I say, but then I stop talking because am I going to defend how Cressit uses his wavurl? No.

That night we find a smaller, humbler place to sleep. Melily wavurls an elderly book collector into sharing his spare room.

"I can barely fit on this bed," she says, wiggling from side to side as we tuck ourselves into a small cot. "Why don't you sleep on the floor?"

"There are too many books on the floor," I counter, which is true.

So Melily huffs and rolls away from me, taking all the blankets with her.

Even so, I'm sure I'll sleep well. We have a plan now—travel to Ellevah—and I haven't seen any sign of Douglen or Jeck either.

But before I drift off, Melily says, "So… what's it like?"

"What's what like?" I whisper.

She rolls to face me again, keeping the blankets bundled around her. "Sex."

I don't know the word, but I think I know what it means.

"You know, letting a boy lie with you," she continues, quickly adding, "but you don't have to tell me if you don't want to. I mean, it's not like I don't already know most everything."

I think about her question, though. "It can be uncomfortable, but it can also feel good. And it's wonderful—and exciting—to be that close to someone."

"Did Cressit…" She trails off as if she's not sure she wants to know. "I guess all boys do it the same."

"There are differences," I say. "Cressit had done it with a lot of girls, I think. It wasn't like that night was special or anything."

"And your sludge friend?"

"His name is Sande. And we didn't really know what we were doing the first time. But I didn't mind; it was still… wonderful." I feel sad thinking about Sande. Maybe I'll find him in Ellevah, but it seems unlikely that he'll be able to travel there. Even if his barge reaches dry land, he surely hasn't befriended a siren who can use wavurl to provide clothes, food, and places to stay. But looking for Sande in Ellevah still seems like the most likely way to find him. Searching for him on the vast tide would be an overwhelming, probably impossible task. Even if I had my own boat and crew, where would I start looking?

As I hoped, I sleep well that night, despite Melily kicking me, throwing a heavy arm across my face, and talking in her sleep about pickles—I think; she was mumbling. And the next morning, over a furtive meal in the back of a cookery where I think several people are shell gambling, Melily and I try to decide if anyone else should join us.

"I wish we could tell Shara our plans," I whisper. "I'm sure Douglen treats her badly."

Melily shakes her head. "She'll never leave the *Trident*—trust me."

"Maybe not, but I would have said the same thing about you a few days ago."

"Well, that just proves you don't know me," Melily says, sipping her salted coffee. "Shara might stand up to Jeck, but she *always* does what Douglen tells her."

I don't have salted coffee; I have tea, and it's surprisingly good. There must be some local plant in it that I'm not familiar with. I suppose there are probably lots of different herbs and spices Gren and I would discover if we explored the deeplands around other mountain cities. "I'd still love to give Shara a choice," I say.

Melily shakes her head. "It's too risky. If we return to the *Trident*, they won't let us leave. Maybe we can send a secret message to Shara once we're in Ellevah or something."

"So what about Timsy and Dorla, then?" I ask, thinking about the youngest siren on the *Trident* and his little balance. "They were probably kidnapped from their families too."

Melily shakes her head dramatically. "Threegod, absolutely not! You aren't a siren, so I'd have to deal with Timsy's tantrums, and napper changes, and all the crunchy stuff that comes out of his nose. Sorry, but no."

I'm not surprised by her response, but I hate leaving children anywhere near the Osperacys. I suppose if we can find the other sirens, they can help rescue Timsy and Dorla as Cressit once suggested.

So we wait in Gatreijan for five more days, always afraid that we'll be caught and hoping the *Trident* will set sail. We venture down to the lowest level of the city every afternoon to see if she's still in port, and to our great frustration, the huge *Trident* stays in her berth.

I don't like booking our passage to Ellevah with the Osperacys still in the city, but how long can we wait? The ocean keeps flowing past, and every day Douglen has more opportunities to find us. I feel as if we're in a trap that's slowly clamping shut. I want to run free while there's still time.

"We should leave," I tell Melily on the sixth day. "Ships are always coming and going. Douglen and Jeck can't watch them all."

"Finally!" she says. "Another day here, and I'll catch some disease."

So with Melily's wavurl to ease the way, we ride motorliners to the lowest city level. Once there, we hire a triwheel driver to bring us to the cave wharf where smaller steamships dock. Unfortunately no passenger boats travel directly to Ellevah because it's not in the trade routes, so we settle for a ship that will take us to Leistelle, a mountain city slightly skytide and countertide of Ellevah. I convince Melily to use her saved paper shells to pay for our passage because I don't want to risk drawing attention to ourselves in the crowded transport office. Douglen and Jeck might search for us there. Melily mutters that I'm wasting her money, but she still opens her purse and digs out her embroidered wallet.

We book passage on a ship named the *Wanderlea*. And after we carry our newly acquired travel cases through the maze-like cave harbor, we find a small, rusty steamer waiting for us. The shipsmen on deck look as if they've just emerged from cohol taverns, with scruffy beards, tattoos, and mismatched clothes, but they end up being very friendly. They are quick to carry our luggage, and they show us not only our cabin but all around the boat. A colorfully dressed, frizzy-haired man in the ship's cookery even asks if we'd we like something to eat.

"Yes! I'm starving!" Melily says.

I'm not hungry, though, I'm exhausted. Now that we're finally on a ship and hopefully will soon be much safer than we've been since the Laeros Light Festival, I long to rest. I also feel like I haven't really let Sande's situation soak in, and I've put off a lot of crying because I didn't want Melily to see.

So leaving her chatting with the ship's cook, who introduces himself as Pavoya, I return to our cabin and pull off my boots in the narrow space beside our bunk beds. Then I climb onto the top bed and fall asleep.

Melily wakes me hours later, or at least what I hope is hours later, while loudly arranging our belongings. "Next port, I'm buying better blankets," she announces. "I'll get a rash from these—they are so scratchy."

I put my thin pillow on top of my head, hoping to muffle both her voice and block out the light she's turned on. But I'm pleased to feel trembles and shudders—the *Wanderlea* is moving. If we've left Gatreijan, we've left the two older Osperacys, thank the Water Goddess. I soften in relief. Traveling also means I'm parting ways with Cressit Scale, which is for the best.

I try to roll over and hunch further away from the light, but I find it difficult on such a narrow cot beneath such a small blanket.

"Oh no, are you awake?" Melily whispers, even though she spoke out loud moments before.

"I am now," I murmur.

"Well good because I have something to tell you."

Her tone wakes me up. There's worry in it, real worry, not scratchy-blanket-worry. I roll back to my original position and lift the pillow. "What is it?"

"Brindy." Melily stands so that she can see me on the top bunk. "I saw him on the docks as we were leaving. I was on deck. He was really far away. But he did this tilty thing with his head, so I think he maybe saw me."

It takes me a moment to remember that Brindy is the servemen who drove us to the museum in Beth. I try to sit up, but my bunk is too cramped.

"What do you think seeing Brindy means?" Melily asks.

It can only mean one thing; the Osperacys might know which ship we're on. And with all my worrying and fretting, it never occurred to me that Douglen and Jeck might not be the only people searching for us. Since Gatreijan is such a large city, of course the Osperacys sent a lot of the *Trident's* crew members out to hunt for us as well. And it would make sense to have people watching all the harbors.

"Well, if he ran off to tell the Osperacys, there's nothing we can do about it now," I say, and I still feel sleepy. "We have that one stop before we get to Leistelle. I can't remember the name of the city, but let's switch boats there."

"I'm pretty sure the next city is Tak Ceseren." Melily's eyebrows crumple with worry. "You know, you shouldn't have made us wait so long. We could have left Gatreijan right away."

"I will accept all the blame," I say, rolling away from her, "as long as I can keep napping."

But now I can't sleep, because we didn't really escape from the Osperacys—not yet. We'll have to try again.

ABOUT SIXTY PEOPLE travel on the *Wanderlea:* twelve crew members and the rest of us are passengers. One couple even journeyed all the way from Varasay, and I'm careful not to talk to them too much. Since most everyone has a tiny, airless closet of a cabin, we all spend our time either up on deck or in the gathery, where we read and play games like Slide 'n' Pass or Pick-a-String. One of the crew members even has a wooden chorder, and although he's no Cressit Scale, he often plays songs and passengers sing along. I spend a lot of my time mending people's clothes in exchange for shell coins, and I feel good doing honest work after stealing in Gatreijan.

Since the *Wanderlea* isn't a luxury steamship like the *Trident*, none of the passengers are wealthy. Most of them seem to be from mid city levels, and I think a few are from lower city levels too. Because of that, we have an unspoken agreement that we should all help out. And although the ship has a cook, Pavoya, a rotating group of people help him in the cookery, including myself. Another group of travelers do laundry, while a third group cleans the washing closets, the gathery floors, and our cabin floors if needed. Melily doesn't help with anything and anyone who suggests she should is wavurled away. She spends most of her time sulkily pacing the deck, and although I saw her with a book once, it lay closed in her lap.

"When we change ships in Tak Ceseren," she tells me one evening. "I want to ride on a proper steamship. I think this one sank and was salvaged from the deeplands. People do that, you know. And don't you think our cabin has a weird, moldy smell?"

But during our third day on the *Wanderlea*, her attitude suddenly changes. Her mood shift happens at dinner. At first, Melily is complaining about how there's no space at the gathery table and how she doesn't want to eat her meal sitting on a window bench. But then the ship's first mate passes us, stops to listen, and says, "I have a table in my cabin. Why don't you ladies dine with me?"

"No thanks, we're fine," I say quickly, for I don't want anyone paying too much attention to us.

But Melily leaps up with her plate of fish and peak potatoes. "Yes! We'd love to dine with you. If I'd known you had a table, I would have insisted on it." And she gives him a bright smile despite her siren threat.

Leading us through the ship, the first mate introduces himself as Sharles Grunner, and although his cabin is not much larger than ours, it does have a small table with benches on either side. I think the benches are meant for one person each, but Melily and I squeeze onto one while Sharles sits on the other.

He's older than us by at least ten tides, and unlike the rest of the scruffy crew, he wears a fine canvas jacket with a swordfish embroidered on the sleeve. He also has a neatly trimmed mustache, and he's talkative, which I don't like.

"Someone told me you two were sisters," he says as we eat. "But you don't look like you are, so why are you traveling together? And where are you going?"

And oh no, even though Melily and I agreed to use the false names Mollifae and Novie, we haven't thought of an imaginary history for ourselves.

"We're dear friends from Beth," I blurt, since that city is often in my thoughts. "And we're traveling to Leistelle."

"Leistelle? Ugh," Sharles groans. "Why go there? That city's nothing but port taxes, trust me."

"Oh, it's not our final destination," Melily says. "We're actually going to—"

"—continue to traveling for a while," I interrupt, giving her a firm look. We promised each other that we wouldn't tell anyone we were heading to Ellevah. Has she forgotten already?

Sharles smooths his mustache. "Well, if you need any ideas, I know all the good cities to visit. I've ridden the tide loop so many times I've gotten dizzy." He chuckles.

"I'm an experienced tide traveler too," Melily says proudly. "I've visited a lot of cities, and then of course, I always return to Beth where my family lives. I have *five* older brothers—five… and one is blind!" She grins at me as if confirming that she too can lie about who we are.

I frown back, hopefully letting her know that she's being a bit too creative.

"Blind. Tough luck, huh?" Sharles leans over the table, toward Melily. "If you could live anywhere on the tide, where would it be?"

"Lellev!" she says. "I just adore the garden fountains, and the hot springs in the royal palace are just the crab's claw."

"You're not wrong," Sharles agrees, taking a bite of peak potato. "But have you ever been to the hot springs in Fathra? It's outside of the trade routes, so a lot of people haven't heard of it. Those springs aren't as pretty as Lellev's, with that big waterfall, but they're less... how do I put it? Formal. It's like a party in the water. Anything can happen."

Melily giggles. "You mean like people not wearing clothes?"

"That and more." He raises an eyebrow.

And right then I know Sharles is trouble. I can't seem to get us out of his cabin before he tells a crude story about a traveler vomiting in the gathery. However I do manage to pull Melily away when he offers us some of his secret cohol stash. "This one's real spicy," he says, pulling out a dark green bottle with a silver label. "Apparently it's banned in Kyrani."

"I like spicy things." She holds out her empty water glass.

I give her arm a squeeze. "Cohol makes you sick, remember?"

Melily sighs and says to Sharles, "Nerene—Novie, I mean. She's never any fun."

But at least she leaves the cabin with me.

However after that meal, Sharles is the shadow we can't shake. He's constantly either sitting with us in the gathery, joining us up on deck, or inviting us to dine in his cabin again. Melily always accepts his invitations too, and since it doesn't seem right to let her eat with him alone, we both see a lot of Sharles. At least my concern about Melily saying too much about who we truly are melts away because Sharles would rather talk than listen. Most of his stories are about him cleverly breaking rules, or tricking someone he thought stupid enough to deserve it, or women he charmed away from other men.

And since we won't reach Tak Ceseren for another eight days, nearly a sunpeak, it's going to be a long trip.

Talking to Melily doesn't help either. "Perhaps we could spend less time with First Mate Grunner," I try one evening as we're changing into our seacotton nightgowns. "I find him a bit... tiring."

"I can't believe you'd say that!" Melily sounds scandalized beneath the underdress she's pulling over her head. "He's so funny! I mean, his story about accidentally knocking that ridge cat off the ship was hilarious." Her head pops out from beneath the fabric. "I was laughing so hard I spilled my coffee."

"The cat probably drowned."

She rolls her eyes. "You just don't have a sense of humor."

Two days later, after I help Pavoya make scallop rolls in the cookery, I can't find Melily. I search all three decks for her, worried that she's sick since a couple of passengers have been fighting a cough. But no— I find her in the stern of the ship, wound up in Sharles's long arms, her mouth pressed against his mustache.

"Don't fall for him," I tell her that night. "I'm your balance, remember? Please trust me. He is not a good person."

"Well, he's good at kissing." Melily flops onto her bed and smiles to herself. "And you know what he said? He said my mouth feels like pearlsilk."

Eagh, gross, and I can see where this is going. I feel like I'm watching a snapper dart fly toward her, and it's moving too quickly for me to stop.

Not ready to give up though, I climb down from my bunk and crouch beside hers. The floor is so narrow, I have to turn sideways to be able to bend my knees that deeply. "Melily, you also need to protect yourself. We aren't going to keep traveling with Sharles; we're changing ships in only five days. I don't want you to have your heart broken."

Her face hardens as she props herself up on an elbow. "I knew you'd be like this. Just because all of your boy stuff has turned out awful, doesn't mean it will for me."

"That's not it. I'm worried."

Melily reaches up and clicks off the single electric light in our cabin. "Or you're jealous."

The next day she won't speak to me, so I try a different approach and corner Sharles. "You should know that Mollifae hasn't had a lot of male friends, and she has a powerful and protective father."

"This isn't any of your business." He tries to walk past me.

I block his way, which is easy because I'm as tall as he is and the passage is small. "Maybe not, but I've been in trouble before, and I don't want that for Melily."

Sharles looks at me with half-closed eyes. "There are ways to avoid that sort of trouble, and trust me, I know all the tricks. You worry about yourself, all right?" And then he has the nerve to pat my head.

To my deep horror, although I'm not surprised, Melily doesn't sleep in our cabin that night.

And the next morning I find her curled against Sharles in the gathery with his hand on her thigh a little too close to her hip.

She flashes me a proud smile.

And I feel like I failed her.

She doesn't sleep in our cabin after that, and I worry about her the rest of the way to Tak Ceseren. At least we'll be switching ships there.

But when I remind Melily of this, she says. "Um, so… about that. Why don't we just wait and see if there's a reason to change ships. I mean, we've already paid for our whole trip on the *Wanderlea*. And it was just Brindy who saw me. He's harmless—and who knows if he even really recognized me or saw the name of our ship?"

"Melily," I say, trying not to let my frustration show. "It's very likely that Douglen and Lord Osperacy know where we are. Douglen wants me dead, and they both surely want you back. And if they take you back, that will end your friendship with Sharles—and," I add, with a stroke of inspiration, "it might put him in danger too."

"My *friendship* with Sharles?" Melily repeats with narrowed eyes. And we are thankfully alone on the windy prow of the *Wanderlea* because she raises her voice too. "I can't stand you sometimes, Nerene! What I have with Sharles is deep and meaningful and worth risking everything for. And if I can spend twelve more days with him, I want to. He says he doesn't want to travel the tide forever and that he eventually wants to settle down somewhere. Maybe that could be with me. Maybe that could be in Ellevah."

"Melily," I say weakly, feeling our safety slipping away. "Please just think about it."

She puts her hands on her hips. "You know sometimes I feel like I'm your balance—the person who has to talk sense into you. How about this; we'll find a sleeperhouse in Tak Ceseren, and while we're in port, I'll have Sharles watch for any strangers that visit the *Wanderlea*. But if no one from the *Trident* comes looking for us, then can't we just stay on this ship a bit longer?" Now Melily's looking at me in a pleading way. "No one's ever liked me like this."

Her pitiful expression softens my frustration, and I find myself saying, "Fine." And hopefully it will be fine if we take those precautions. I wish I could simply leave on my own. I wish I didn't feel so responsible for Melily and, at the same time, dependent on her.

"I think I'm in love with him," Melily says, her cheeks pink. "I know it hasn't been that long, but I really think I am. I've never been so happy."

"Well, I'm happy for you," I say, and knowing that she's never had anyone pay so much attention to her, it's not a complete lie.

TAK CESEREN, our only stop on the way to Leistelle, is a flat, structured city. Aside from a stretch of forest on its starways shore, there's nothing about it that looks like a mountaintop. I only see straight walls, square edges, and neatly-arranged housing towers. Pavoya, the cook, tells me that in order to make the city larger, the people here broke down the mountain peak and used the rubble to build up the surrounding land.

We'll be in Tak Ceseren for five days because if ships travel too fast, they run out of tidewater. And as promised, Melily uses wavurl to find us a room in a local sleeperhouse, and Sharles stops by daily to let us know if any strangers visit the *Wanderlea*.

"All I've told him," Melily assures me. "Is that some tide travelers threatened us in Gatreijan."

Whenever Sharles arrives at the sleeperhouse, Melily is, of course, eager to spend time alone with him, so I end up going on a lot of long walks. But as much as I worry about her, I also love exploring a new city. I've never experienced this sort of freedom before—simply being able to roam without having to worry about Gray Straps or the Osperacys or the many Threegod rules we had in Varasay.

On our second day in Tak Ceseren, I decide to find the city's Weather Service Office. I'm fairly certain each mountain has one, and I hope the people who work there will know where a loose factory barge might drift.

As I walk through the flat city, the square balconies, perfectly straight walls, and carefully trimmed hedges remind me of the miniature city I saw on display in Beth's museum—the recreation of an ancient deepland city. Hugging my arms to my chest, I imagine water seeping in and around these roads, and I picture the market stalls floating up, and people climbing onto roofs, afraid. The first tide must have been so terrifying. It's amazing anyone survived at all.

The people in Tak Ceseren don't wear white robes like the tiny figures in the museum's city did, but their outfits are still very unique. The women wear pale, frilly gowns with huge skirts, and the men stroll around in layered coats, elaborate jewelry, heavy boots, and decorative, feathered hats.

A few people glance curiously at my simple, belted seacotton dress and wildwool sweater, but like all cities, most everyone seems used to seeing tide travelers.

It takes me all morning to find the weather office because not many people in Tak Ceseren speak Equitorian, the common language of the trade routes. I can't read the street signs either, for they use a different set of letters than the ones Shara was teaching me to read.

I'm finally led to the weather office by an older lady who seems to understand me, although I have trouble understanding her. The office, I learn, is on the top floor of a box-shaped building made out of white bricks. Inside I find people wearing more familiar uppy clothes, like suits, blouses, and skirts. They're also working quietly at large drybark tables, marking charts, and using relayphones and other mechanical devices.

"Excuse me," I say to a mild-looking man with a lot of hair running down the sides of his face; it's somewhat like a beard, except his chin is bare. "Can you help me?"

I expect he won't understand my Equitorian and that I'll get the same confused stare I've been getting all day, but instead he smiles wide and says, "I know that accent! Are you from Beth? Me too! Currentways peak, grove park? You?"

"Oh," I say, surprised. "No, I'm from Varasay."

He nearly bounces around his table. "Close enough! I've heard Varasay isn't a nice place to visit these days, except for the puppetry competitions of course. Those are always a treat."

Puppetry competitions? That must be something that happens in the high city.

"My name's Fesro," the man says. "And do I ever miss Beth. The big boss transferred me here two tides ago because she wanted workers fluent in Equitorian to handle all the relaycalls, but let me tell you something..." He lowers his voice. "She promised I'd be temperature tracking supervisor when I agreed to take the job, but then old Marsrin over there decided not to retire."

I'm not sure what retiring is. Dying maybe? "I'm sorry," I say, attempting to be polite. "But, um, my friend is lost on the tide, and I'm trying to figure out where he drifted."

Even though Fesro seems to be a positive person, he can't give me any good news about Sande. After spending a long while unrolling charts and examining the currents, he looks at me sadly. "Since you don't know exactly where your friend's barge started, this is only a guess. But most factory barges are far starways or far skytide, and the way the currents move around Noret and the UPT... If he started there, that barge probably slipped into frozen waters."

Fesro even calls over several other workers and asks for their advice. After looking over the charts, their predictions are just as dire. Unless Sande's rescued by a ship that's late on the tide and far outside of the trade routes, I'll just have to hope he can survive a year stranded in the ice forests.

It's hard not to cry in front of these strangers.

Fesro rolls up his charts. "Listen, Novie..." he says, and it's so strange to hear people use my false name. "I don't think..." He squeezes his eyes shut for a moment as if overcome by grief. "I don't think it's possible to rescue your friend."

First Cressit thought Sande was dead and now these people. I refuse to believe it. I know Sande. I know he won't just give up.

"Thank you for your help," I say stiffly. "I should be going."

While we wait for the *Wanderlea* to set out on the tide again, Sharles shows us around the city. Melily pays for our outings because she suddenly seems to have more money in her purse, and I suppose I shouldn't be surprised by that.

Sharles brings us to a couple of stageshows, which are new to me, like so many uppy things. Apparently, during a stageshow, groups of costumed performers pretend to be other people in order to tell stories. The performers often act these tales out in front of painted screens that show all sorts of places, like kelp forests, ships, or caves.

The first stageshow we see has a lot of singing. It tells the sad story of a girl who marries a prince, only to discover her love is really a fire demon who wants a human baby. The second stageshow is all about fish-like sirens who rescue a drowning child. They think the little girl is an orphan and enchant her, turning her into a siren. In the end, her mother appears, but it's too late to bring her daughter home because the enchantment can't be undone. Thinking of Maam and Gren, I cry as the two say goodbye forever.

Sharles also brings us to a paddlebat game, which is the water sport I heard about in Beth. It takes place in a floating, oval pool built out into the tide. Around the edges of the water are seats for spectators, shaded by huge canopies, and in the pool, two teams of eight players kneel on floating boards and hold double-ended, scoop-like paddles.

"The goal of the game," Sharles tells us, "is to knock the balls off those poles—" He points to three large pillars in the middle of the pool, each of differing heights. "And then move the balls to the team poles." He points to slightly lower pillars that stand further away. "I used to play when I was young. People said I was good, and that I should join the intertide leagues."

"You should have," Melily says. "I'd love to cheer you on."

As she proves this by kissing him—a kiss that goes on and on—I examine the crowd, and I'm amazed by its size. We're surrounded by at least five hundred people, maybe a thousand. And everyone seems very excited; I see lots of children waving flags and adults wearing colorful hats.

A pretty woman strikes a gong and the game starts, and at first, I find it tremendously confusing. Players churn up the water and shove opponents off their boards. But at least the teams wear different colors—green and orange—and I slowly realize that the players move the balls around in clever ways. They either wack the balls across the top of the water or use their paddles to scoop up a ball. And sometimes, if a player has scooped up a ball, he'll ride on another player's board to move faster.

I decide to cheer for the team wearing green, and although they don't win, I still have a lot of fun. My favorite part of the game is when players scale the notched pillars to balance the balls on top. Climbing the pillars looks like it takes incredible strength and agility.

Sharles also offers to take us to a swingshow, but I manage to talk Melily out of that. "I know it's not a Cressit Scale show, but we could still run into him or some of his musician friends. I think it's better to stay hidden—we don't know who Douglen and Jeck are talking to."

And then, although I'm deeply reluctant about it, we return to the *Wanderlea* to finish our trip to Leistelle. Sharles is adamant, though, that no unfamiliar men have come by the ship asking questions. He also seems to think that the reason Melily and I are being so cautious is because we've run away from our families—which I suppose is somewhat true.

"I've met girls like you before," he says as we carry our luggage back onto the ship. "You want to go on a wild adventure before you get tied down. I don't blame you, and I hope I'm helping."

Melily laughs as he kisses her neck. "Just keep an eye out until we are on our way, okay sweets?"

And it seems she's still hoping that Sharles will leave his job on the *Wanderlea* and continue on with us to Ellevah.

"Imagine if we got married and had babies!" Melily tells me as we unpack in our cabin. It seems silly for her to leave her small, blue luggage case here, though, for I'm sure she'll be sleeping elsewhere.

But all that soon changes because new passengers boarded in Tak Ceseren, and when Sharles invites the golden-haired sisters to dine in his cabin the next evening, Melily is livid.

She tries to hide it, of course. "He's a friendly person," she says lightly, joining me on the window bench to eat in the gathery. "It doesn't mean anything."

Melily sleeps in Sharles's cabin that night, but the next evening, I find her lying on her bunk with her arms folded, staring at the wall. "Sharles thinks we're spending too much time together. He says on such a small ship, we should give each other space." She turns to me, looking helpless. "And I guess that makes sense, but whenever I'm not near Sharles, those stupid Tak Ceseren girls appear. They like him, I can tell."

The next day, things get even worse. After Melily and I eat our midday meal in the gathery, we go for a walk on deck and find Sharles with his arm around the oldest golden-haired sister. He's also standing in the exact same spot where I first saw him kiss Melily.

"Don't touch her!" Melily cries, and Sharles's arm drops away because it's a wavurl command. "What are you even doing with her?"

"Duckling," Sharles says. "Maryasa's just nervous about traveling on the tide. Not everyone's as brave as you."

He walks Melily below deck, and since I'm left standing with this Maryasa person, I say, "Sharles is involved with my friend. I don't want her feelings hurt."

Maryasa shrugs, says something in the Tak Ceseren language, and walks away.

And as stormy as things are on the ship, a real storm swallows the *Wanderlea* later that day. I experienced bad weather on the *Trident*, but nothing like this. Maybe the storms weren't as fierce, or maybe Lord Osperacy's steamship was just so large it was easy for passengers to ignore everything beyond the boat's wood-paneled cabins. Here on the *Wanderlea* though, we spend our afternoon suffering through ceaseless, sickening motion, and that night, I can't sleep. Thank the Water Goddess, my bunk has a sturdy bar along the open side, or I'd surely topple out.

"Sharles is helping the captain," Melily shouts over the booming noise of waves slamming against the hull. "I bet he's soaked through, and what if he needs something? I'm gonna check on him."

I try to talk her out of leaving the cabin, for the crew made it very clear at dinner that no passengers should be underfoot during the storm. Melily ignores me, though, and stumbles out into the dark passage.

She returns not long after, slamming the door shut, locking it, and climbing back into bed, breathing hard.

"Melily, what's wrong?" I ask.

Seconds later someone pounds on our door.

"Molli?" Sharles shouts her false name, his voice raw and enraged. "Mollifae? Open up!"

"Go away!" Melily screams.

And he does because he has to—because she's using wavurl. But he'll be back, I'm sure.

"What happened?" I cry, climbing down from my bunk and fumbling for the light. Moving around is much harder than usual because the ship's rocking from side to side.

Melily doesn't answer, and when I click the lights on, I find her bunched up at the end of her cot with her hands covering her face.

"Talk to me," I urge. "What's going on?"

Melily just shakes her head and keeps her hands over her face. She then heaves with a sob.

Only one thing could make her this upset. I'm sure of it. "You caught Sharles with that girl, didn't you?"

She nods, her face still hidden.

"I thought he was on deck," I say.

She shakes her head. "He wasn't there. Found him in his cabin with *her!*"

"Then why is he so angry?"

Melily gives me no response.

I hear a key in our door lock. Someone is entering our cabin.

"Don't use wavurl," I hiss at Melily, afraid of what she might do. "Don't. I'll sort this out."

Sharles opens the door and he's with the Captain—a sopping, tubby man I've only ever seen at a distance. I'm not even sure what his name is.

"What happened?" I ask, and I stand in the doorway, feeling protective of Melily. "She won't tell me anything—she's too upset."

"She attacked a woman," Sharles says, bracing himself against the tilting door frame. "There was a woman in my cabin, and we were just talking…"

That's a lie. I can see it in his eyes. I can see the Captain knows he's lying too.

"Then Mollifae came in," Sharles continues. "And she's angry because apparently I can't spend time with anyone but her." Sharles glares at Melily, and although she still has her hands up near her face, she glares back. "Then, *then* Mollifae tells Maryasa to smash her face into the wall. And Maryasa does! I've heard rumors about people like you."

And now he speaks directly to Melily. "You're some kind of water demon. You can make people do whatever you want! It's terrifying! Evil!"

"You weren't just talking to that girl, you liar!" Melily screams from the bed. "Do you want me to force you to bite off your own tongue, 'cause I will! You just tell one more lie, and I'll make sure you never lie again!"

"Captain, we should throw her off the ship," Sharles cries.

This is getting bad. "Melily," I shout, forgetting to use her fake name. "Calm down."

"She's crazy!" Sharles says, but now I can't see him because he's backed down the passage—afraid, it seems, of losing his tongue.

"Enough!" The Captain says, and I notice now that unlike the rest of us, he's steady and stands tall even though the boat keeps rocking. "I'm needed up top, and Sharles, that's where you should be too. You ladies will stay in this cabin until I sort things out, or I will indeed throw you both into the tide."

He reaches forward and shuts our door with a clang. I have just enough time to step out of the way.

I crawl onto the lower bunk with Melily.

"Sharles was..." she sobs. "He was with her! I saw it all!"

"I know—I believe you," I say, squeezing myself in beside her. "Did you really hurt that girl, though?"

"Yes," Melily whispers. "But I was angry, and I wasn't thinking. I did make her slam her face into the wall. I should have made them both forget, I guess, but... I can't make someone forget an injury like that. I didn't know what to do, so I just ran." She sobs again and wipes her snotty nose onto her nightdress sleeve.

I cringe. "Is she hurt badly?"

Melily nods. "She definitely broke her nose and at least one tooth came out. She screamed and screamed, and I saw a lot of blood, and it was awful."

I feel like a hole has opened beneath us, and we're in danger of being sucked down out of the ship and into the tidewater.

"Melily, this is bad," I say. "And Sharles called you a water demon too. He must have heard rumors about your family—or at least about sirens." Will the Captain believe him too, I wonder? But what other explanation could there be? Why would Maryasa willingly hurt herself?

"I thought Sharles loved me," Melily whispers, hugging her knees to her chest. "I'm so stupid, but I really thought he did."

I hug her tightly and let her cry. And not that I approve of stealing, but I wish we'd acquired more handkerchiefs in Tak Ceseren.

Kindly Pavoya brings us a message the next morning. He tells us that although Melily and I can use the washing closets—which is a relief—we must otherwise stay in our cabin. "And if you don't, the Captain says you'll be locked in the hold until we reach Leistelle." He adds an, "I'm so sorry," while peering in at Melily who's still sleeping. "He also let me bring ya this food." He hands me a basket of seed crackers, vine apples, and smoked fish, as well as a bottle of water.

I'm amazed Melily can sleep at all. The storm is weaker, but the tide still tosses the ship.

"How is the girl?" I softly ask. "The one with the broken nose?"

"Not good," Pavoya says, tapping his own nose. "It's never gonna heal right, and her front teeth are out too…"

"Both of them? Oh no." This feels like my fault. If only I'd found a way to stop Melily from falling in love with Sharles. I certainly tried.

"Is it true?" Pavoya asks. "Does Mollifae have dangerous powers?"

"No, of course not," I say, hating that I'm lying to Pavoya who is always so nice.

Pavoya nods thoughtfully. "Women troubles aren't new for Sharles, but—I was thinking about how he said Mollifae told that Tak Ceseren girl to hurt herself. And you know, I think something like that happened to me."

"Really?" I say, glancing back at Melily who seems to still be sleeping.

"While we were in Tak Ceseren," Pavoya says, "this man told me to show him and his friend around the *Wanderlea*, so I did. And I wouldn't have usually."

Fear bites into me.

"Nothing bad happened—I don't think," Pavoya continues. "They just walked around for a spell and left. Maybe they wanted to buy the boat? But still… I never let strangers on the ship, so it confused me, you know? Like, why did I do that?"

I probably don't need to ask, but I do anyway. "What did they look like?"

Pavoya thinks for a moment, frowning. "Well, one was real skinny with wavy hair. And the other was short and thick, wearing a real nice suit. Why? Do you know them?"

"No," I lie.

And when I shut the door, Melily rolls over, wide awake. "So they found us."

I nod. "But they're not here now—at least I don't think they are. The ship's so small we'd know. None of this makes sense."

"No." Melily frowns. "It doesn't."

TWO NIGHTS LATER, I wake up suddenly. I think I heard a loud noise, and although the storm passed yesterday, I suppose it could have been thunder. I'm not sure what time it is either. My thoughts feel thick and sluggish as if it's the middle of the night, but since our cabin has no windows, I can't be sure.

And then I hear strange sounds: footsteps, voices, the thuds and wallops of doors being flung open and closed.

I push off my blanket and drop down from my bunk so that I can listen at the door. I don't fully understand what I'm hearing, but I'm pretty sure people are moving through the ship's passages. I risk the Captain's wrath and crack open the door.

Fellow passengers hurry past in nightclothes. A few wear jackets and sweaters, and many of them carry luggage: chests, bags and latched travel cases.

"What's going on?" I cry.

"Yeah, what *is* happening?" Melily calls groggily from her bunk. "I was having a nice dream."

A woman who I think is from the UPT pauses long enough to gasp, "We either hit something, or a ripperblast went off, I dunno!" She rushes off, leaving me wondering what a ripperblast is.

I turn around and see that Melily has sprung up out of bed.

"That wasn't a ripperblast," she says. "That was a mechbomb. That's what Douglen and Jeck were doing on the *Wanderlea*!"

My fear swells, pressing against the inside of my chest. "What's a mechbomb?"

"A ripperblast with a timekeeper," Melily tells me, and I can barely see her in the dark. "Stupid Jeck is obsessed with them, and—"

She's interrupted by groaning sound coming from the hold. Our cabin tilts away from the door.

"What if the *Wanderlea* sinks?" Melily grabs both of my arms. "I don't want to die!"

"Uh…" My thoughts feel like they're slipping off a ledge. "It's probably fine. If it's a real emergency, the Captain will send someone for us."

"You just want to wait here? That's crazy." Melily turns away from me. "We have followed their rules long enough. We need to get out of here."

I'm scared of crossing the Captain, but I also don't argue. Melily turns on the light—it flickers for a moment but then shines steadily as we grab passbooks and shoes. I also, very reluctantly, take the gunnerife out from beneath my mattress and buckle the holster under my nightdress.

The floor slopes even more steeply now, and I don't hear people moving past our cabin door anymore. Instead, the sound of footsteps and voices trickles down from the deck above.

As we leave our cabin, our bedside light shuts off and so do the passage lights. Therefore, hand in hand, Melily and I struggle through the dark ship, and thankfully when we reach the gathery, dim moonlight shines through the windows. We clamor up the central stairwell, and soon we're on the upper deck surrounded by a confusion of noise, passengers, and crew. Several shipsmen struggle to lower a saveship, while others hand out musty-smelling floatvests. As I pull a floatvest over my head, Melily and I are jostled over to the railing. I see a few passengers give Melily wary glances, especially the Tak Ceseren sisters—bandages hide poor Maryasa's entire face —but no one speaks to us. I look down at the tidewater, and it looks different tonight, darker and thicker, like the oil used in factory machines. I also smell smoke.

"I can't believe Douglen decided to just kill us both," Melily hisses. "That's so like him!"

I nod, tightening the waist strap on my floatvest and glancing around at the frightened, shivering passengers and the frantic crew. "He won't just be killing us," I breathe. "He'll be killing everyone here."

"Oh, he won't care about that," Melily says, and I notice that she hasn't buckled the waist strap on her floatvest yet. "Trust me, there was this—"

Another blast tears through the *Wanderlea*. Skyfire seems to rupture under my feet. An unseen hand slaps me through the air the same way I'd swat a dampfly. I see white light, then nothing but black, and then I hit the tidewater so hard I lose all of my air.

Things go briefly dark and quiet—like I've fallen asleep—and then Melily is splashing toward me, yelling, "Nerene! Nerene! Nerene!"

She sounds far away, and there's a high-pitched whistling in my ears.

I'm in the water, and I see fire. Orange blankets of flame unfurl and break apart. I hear people screaming, crying.

Douglen and Jeck didn't just put one mechbomb on the ship—they put two.

Are there more?

I cling to my floatvest, which has risen uncomfortably up under my jaw. The water is cold too—so, so cold.

Melily's still yelling. She's pointing at me, and then pointing at something else, jabbing at the air, giving me instructions I can't hear.

My ears pop and now everything goes silent.

I look to where she's pointing, and I see a dark, floating hunk of something covered in wet ribbons of reflected firelight. Is it a raft?

No, it's part of the *Wanderlea*—something torn off.

My hearing returns with a roar. "Climb on!" Melily shouts. "Climb on! And I'll see if I can find the saveship!" It's so strange to have her directing me like this, but she doesn't seem to be as dazed as I am.

I swim weakly through debris: a travel case broken open, a wooden bowl from the cookery—an arm. I quickly look away so I don't recognize who it belonged to.

"Climb on! Ugh, you're so slow!" Melily shouts, shoving me against the floating piece of ship.

I scramble over hard and sharp edges, and my heavy, wet boots make it so difficult to move. If I could stop to unlace them and let them sink into the cold water, I would. Whatever I'm climbing on is also unsteady and partially submerged, which makes dragging my soaking wet self up on top of it even harder.

I shiver when I'm finally out of the water, although something warm drips down my upper arm. Blood. My blood.

And I'm not alone on this tattered raft either. Pavoya slumps against a triangle of broken boat, hugging a framed image that I can't see. "Oh hey," he says as if we're meeting in the gathery to prepare a meal. "Lousy way to wake up, huh?"

"I'll be back," Melily shouts, already swimming away. "Once I find us a saveship!"

But will she return? I watch her, concerned, as she vanishes into the slick, black shadows.

I should dive into that darkness and try to help her and other people too.

But my arm feels like it was stabbed. I prod the cut—it's deep.

And if I leave this hunk of ship, I might not find it again.

I snag something in the water, a length of broken shelving. Using my good arm, I start paddling the raft back toward the burning *Wanderlea*. But before I make much progress, a third boom sends streams of water into the air, scattering the flaming remains of the ship and sending out huge waves that push us even further away.

"Melily!" I scream, and is she dead? I hear a few faint voices, but they seem to be drifting further away. I paddle harder. "Help me!" I cry to Pavoya. Why isn't he helping?

"It's no use," he says.

So he's just admitting defeat? "If we're going to help anyone—or save ourselves—we have to do it now!" I say.

"We're in the current." He's not talking loudly, but it's suddenly so quiet it seems like he's shouting. "Even if we had a whole group of people paddling with real paddles on a ship that was, uh, ship-shaped, we're at the current's mercy. Or I suppose you could say merciless… cy." And he laughs. How dare he laugh? There's nothing funny about this.

I stop paddling, though. I'm too sore. Instead I hunch over the splintered chunk of shelf and shiver. In my wet clothes, the air feels even colder than the water. And I'm so frustrated with Pavoya.

But when he makes a gasping-whimper that I've only ever heard come from a dying amphib deer, I realize he's in worse shape than me. The framed picture he's cradling covers an ugly gash across his ribs, and even in the moonlight, I see red flesh, bone, and lots of blood.

"Oh, I'm sorry," I say, immediately forgiving him for laughing.

I can't see any sign of the *Wanderlea* anymore, and even more frightening, I can't hear anyone calling for help either. The silence above the water seems to reflect the more terrifying, suffocating silence waiting for us below.

Poor Pavoya's injuries look fatal, but I try to help him anyway, because what else can I do? I tear off the bottom of my nightdress, squeeze it as dry as I can, and then pack the fabric into his wound. He seems to be in shock because he doesn't cry out in pain—instead he sings.

The song sounds familiar. "What is that?" I ask, trying not to think about his soft, misshapen middle or the loose, broken bits of bone I feel through the fabric.

"It's the Threegod song of mourning," he tells me. "I always liked it cause it has a part for all the gods, and they're not all the same you know. They have different personalities... they're..." And then his words sink back into his song.

"I don't like Threegod," I say, unable to act like I do even now. "The Threegod Priests are terrible."

"True, true. Many are," Pavoya says. "But they aren't the gods."

"It's hard to separate them," I say.

"Well, I don't go for…" Pavoya continues, pausing to groan in pain. "Reverence and rules… not much fun." His eyes close halfway, and then he says, "What about you? You want to sing? Pray? I feel…" Again he takes a long, thoughtful time to say anything else. "It's worth a try."

I look down at my blood-covered hands—all Pavoya's. I want to comfort him by agreeing with him, but it also seems wrong to pretend. "If Threegod exists, they only love uplanders," I say. "I'm a deeplander. We belong to the Water Goddess, but we're not allowed to worship her anymore."

"You're allowed here. And calling on four gods is surely better than just calling on three. Fourgods…" Pavoya chuckles in a raspy sort of way. "Sounds good. An improvement."

I nod. "But I don't know any Water Goddess songs or prayers. I don't know how to… find her."

Pavoya startles me with a horrible sounding belch, and for a moment, he doesn't seem to be able to talk at all. But then he says, "This… this is how I think about it; if there are divine beings out there, even the finest temple song would sound like a toddling singing to them. And do you care if a toddling sings poorly? No. It's all sweet to hear. So just… make it up." He gestures gently with his left hand, but even that small movement makes him gasp in pain.

I like his perspective, but I'm not the sort of person who can just make things up. And the Water Goddess, if she is out there, feels far away. Maybe she's sleeping in that statue in Beth's Museum, trapped inside.

Pavoya doesn't wait for me. He makes up his own prayer for her—or rather a song. And as he warbles it, we hold hands. I should be comforting him, but it's the other way around.

There are only a few stars out and only one waning moon, so I can barely see him in the dark. Our ragged raft bobs gently, the tide sloshes around us, and the steady wind is surely pushing us further away from anyone who can help.

Pavoya's soon too weak to keep singing, and he eyes the gunnerife holster on my leg. The buckle glints in the faint moonlight, visible now that I've torn away half of my nightdress to pack fabric in his wound.

"I think... maybe," he says. "You should use that on me—or let me use that on me."

I put my hand on the weapon, hiding it from view. "Someone could still help us." It feels like a feeble thing to say because how likely is it that a ship will cross our path? Even on the *Trident* we rarely saw other boats, and when we did they were often far away. And yet it seems too soon to do something drastic. I know Pavoya's wounds aren't going to heal on their own. But at the same time, only a few hours ago we were sleeping peacefully, unharmed, and safe on the *Wanderlea*. If things can go horribly wrong so swiftly, it seems oddly reasonable to imagine that our situation can be set right just as fast. "Not yet," I say. "Please."

Pavoya gives me an understanding look. "In the morning then."

I nod bravely. "In the morning."

He rests his head on my shoulder, and I rest my head on his gray hair, and when dawn stretches blister pink across the water, there's no need to use the gunnerife.

At some point while we were shivering and trying to sleep, Pavoya must have quietly become a death shadow and wandered off into the dark.

I cry, wishing that I'd known him better, and I'm also distraught that now I have to deal with his body. A part of me feels like I should keep him here because he'd probably want to be burned in a Threegod temple. But it doesn't seem bearable or a good idea to share my raft with a corpse for a long time.

Even though Pavoya was a small man, his body is still heavy and the raft unsteady. Therefore it takes me a long, grisly while to manipulate him over the side of what I suspect is a piece of the main storage hold. The cut in my shoulder hurts when I try to drag him, so I end up mostly shoving him into the water with my feet.

"I hope Threegod welcomes you," I say as kindly as I can, and I kiss his brow before giving his shoulders a final push that sends him sloshing off into the waves.

It seems right to keep the wooden frame he cradled safe with me, though. I didn't take a close look at it the night before, and now I see it's a small ink drawing of a lighthouse. I wonder if Pavoya drew it, and instead of watching his colorful clothing drift down into the darkness, I watch the blurry reflections of clouds in the rectangle of glass that protects the drawing. Those fuzzy shapes are soon even more distorted by my tears.

I hope Melily reached one of the *Wanderlea's* saveships. I hope she's with good people who will be patient with her. I hope we both survive.

It's strange to think that Sande still drifts on the tide too, and it seems like such bad luck that we're facing similar troubles and can't face them together.

So I drift, and I wish Pavoya were still alive and with me. It's much worse to be alone. The sun blazes down, cruel and hot, and my tattered, shortened nightdress doesn't give me much protection. The cut in my shoulder stings, and I'm unbearably hungry and thirsty. I would have thought I could last a day at least without longing for food as well as water, but I'm already desperate to eat.

Time stretches out around me, shapeless, vast. Hours pass, and then a day. I ache for water. I hate the sun. I grieve for people I'm not sure are dead but probably are. I also huddle where Pavoya once sat because depending on which way the raft is facing, the fragment of hull that juts up casts a small shadow. It's also something to lean against.

That night the stars seem unusually bright and low. It's as if electric uppy lights dangle on wires around the raft. I lie on my back and watch the wind ripple through them, making them sway in unison.

I feel alone, but maybe I'm not. The Water Goddess could surround me. She could be in every wave, in every drop of the tide. If so, that would mean she's holding me up, cradling me, carrying me along.

Hugging the floatvest, I whisper. "Mother Tide." And what did Sir Mauricen call her in Beth? "Oro-Lemah."

As if answering me, the stars glow brighter and brighter, until it's almost as if they blaze down daylight. I squint. The tidewater has also become thick and cloudy like seaweed milk. Then silently, even though water pours off of her in great torrents, the Water Goddess rises out of the waves, huge, terrible, and beautiful. She's larger than the *Trident*, and she bears sharp, gleaming teeth and the fins on her elbows stretch out like sails. She looks down at me, calm and serene.

I feel a rush of love and bone-deep comfort, and I feel as if I could ask her for anything. When I open my mouth, though, I find I can't speak, and yet I feel my wishes being drawn from my heart, unspooling in a way that is purer and more honest than if I used my voice.

The Water Goddess then reaches up into the stars, causing them to shift and ripple as if they float on the surface of a different ocean. And when she brings her hand back down, someone rests on her palm—a person I know.

Melily.

She lies sleeping, perfectly healthy, dressed in a silvery, shimmering gown, and her short, dark curls spread out from her head like a shiny, black halo. The Water Goddess lays her on the raft beside me.

And then slowly, massively, Oro-Lemah leans down. Her face draws nearer, huge and vast, until all I can see are her shimmering, dark eyes, long nose, and sharp, pearly teeth. Is she going to devour us?

I feel a surge of joy.

And then there's scraping pain in my shoulder again.

And hot sunlight.

And the horrible, scratchy desert that is my tongue, mouth, and throat.

The sky is blinding. The tide goes on forever. But as my vivid dream recedes, I hear a peculiar, soft noise.

I let my head loll to one side, and there sleeping, her skin scratched and covered with angry burns, is Melily.

I OPEN MY MOUTH. It's impossible.

My insides feel dry and brittle, firewood that could instantly ignite, but I manage to roll weakly toward Melily and put my hand on her arm.

Her skin is warm and peeling in places. She's really here.

My eyes twinge and twitch, wanting to cry, but I'm so dehydrated tears won't come.

Is she curled around a ball? No, it's a waterpod. But what's a waterpod doing here?

None of this makes sense. Now the rest of my body tries and fails to cry. I gasp ragged breaths.

Melily's eyes open. "Nerene," she says, and she sits up. She may be battered, burnt, and covered in splotchy bruises, but she seems to have more energy than I do. "Nerene, oh wonderful, you're all right." She hugs me. "I'm so glad. You said some strange things last night. I was worried I hadn't found you in time."

I can barely talk. "But... how?" My voice sounds like a crushed, dried kelp leaf.

She gives me a look that seems out of place here on this broken shard of *Wanderlea*—as if she has a secret—but she says, "Oh, how I survived is really interesting, and you'll be so shocked, but first you probably need this. Aren't these what you sludges use for fresh water?" She rolls the waterpod forward, and it's a large one, nearly the size of a coast melon. It's surely full of enough liquid to last us a day, maybe even two. "So how do we open it?" she asks.

With an awl, ax, sometimes a knife, or maybe even a sharp stone. But we don't have any of those things—and really, where did this waterpod come from?

I moan. I'm so close to water, and I still can't drink it.

"Hmm, maybe a rock?" Melily says suddenly, and a bit stupidly I think, for we won't find a rock floating on the tide.

But then I think of something more powerful. I hit my leg, trying to show her where the gunnerife is. And oh, it's so hard to move.

Her eyes brighten. "Of course!"

It takes some thinking to figure out how to fire the gunnerife into the waterpod and not hurt ourselves at the same time. In the end, Melily holds the heavy fruit high with trembling arms, and I summon enough strength to reach up and shoot.

There's a loud crack, and then fresh water trickles down on us. Thankfully Melily is quick, and she twists the waterpod sideways so that we don't lose too much of the precious liquid. I laugh scratchily for suddenly everything seems absurd. I'm on a broken piece of steamship with a spoiled uppy who reappeared after vanishing for two, or was it three days? And now we've shot a waterpod? I half expect a fringed bear to rise up from the tide and serve us shallowberry cakes.

I'm so weak Melily has to help me drink, holding the waterpod so I can I sip from the hole in the side.

I want to drink a lot, but I stop, coughing, when my stomach begins to hurt.

"Do you want some?" I gasp, wiping my mouth on my arm and feeling bad that I drank first.

She shakes her head. "Nah, I'm fine." It's a strange response, but I'm too weak to question it.

After a few more sips, my neck stops feeling like it's full of crumpled paper, and I'm able to speak more easily.

I keep expecting Melily to vanish. I'm surely losing my sanity, or...

"You're a siren," I say, realizing it all at once. "You're a water siren —like in the stories."

"I am! And I'm just as surprised as you!" Melily smiles brightly. "I mean, I don't have a fish tail—I suppose everyone had that part wrong—but otherwise can you believe it?"

"But... but how did you figure it out?" I say.

Melily clunks the waterpod down beside her. "Well, the other night, I was trying to find the saveship for us because I knew it was the only way to survive. And I took off that ridiculous floatvest because I couldn't move in it, but then there was this other blast, and I woke up way down deep in the tide. It was all dark and cold, and I got scared because my chest was full of water, and that felt awful at first, but then I realized I wasn't dead or dying, and that I was actually breathing—breathing the water."

I stare at her in amazement. "And you didn't know you could do that?"

"No! I mean I've always been an extremely good swimmer," Melily says with a little eye roll as if I should already know that. "But what sort of person tries breathing water? I mean—that would be very stupid."

I suppose she's right, and I feel stunned. All the sirens I've met don't just have siren-like wavurl then, they *are* actual sirens. "So... Lord Osperacy, Douglen, Cressit... all of them, they're from the tide?" I manage to take another drink from the waterpod. "Do you think they know?"

"Father must," Melily says, frowning. "I suppose he never told me so that it would be impossible for me to find my true family."

"Cressit must know too," I say, feeling freshly betrayed by him, although I do remember him hinting that he had secrets that were too dangerous to share.

"It's beautiful down there," Melily says, peering over the edge of the raft. "Like a very expensive painting. But it's scary too, and you wouldn't believe the things that tried to eat me. And you know how your eyes adjust to the dark? It's like my whole body did that in the water. I could see and hear differently, and I wasn't as cold as I probably should have been. And there are all these little currents down there, and when I found the right ones, I swam really quickly."

I'm happy she's made such an interesting discovery about herself, but I also feel like everything I know to be true has tipped onto its side. For a while we sit quietly, rocking up and down on the waves and leaning against the jagged triangle of decking. I drink more from the waterpod, which Melily must have brought up from the flooded deeplands. It's strange to imagine her swimming down there through the icy darkness.

"It was hard to find you," Melily eventually says. "I almost gave up. I just hoped your raft was following the same currents I was, and then, there you were—a tiny smudge, way up on the surface."

"Did you see any other sirens?" I ask, wondering if they would be kind to her or not, and wondering if they'd be kind to me. I try to imagine the hidden places where they live, curious about how they dress and where they sleep. I also think of the ancient artwork I saw in Beth's museum, of the people on the mountain, the people in the deeplands, and the mysterious people who seemed to be standing in a lake—those must have been sirens. Long ago, maybe we were all friends.

"What's this?" Melily asks, picking up the framed ink drawing.

"It was Pavoya's." My heart feels heavy thinking of him. "He might have drawn it himself; I don't know. He died."

"I don't know if Sharles reached a saveship either," Melily says somberly, handing back Pavoya's ink drawing and wiping wet eyes. "I swam around the wreckage for a long time, trying to find him, but I couldn't."

It's hard to muster up sadness for Sharles, but I'm sorry Melily is grieving, and he certainly didn't deserve to die—no one on the *Wanderlea* did.

Melily swims back into the depths of the tide for another waterpod, and this time she returns with a sharp rock to smash it with. She leaps up out of the water in a powerful, graceful way, landing on the raft with the waterpod in her arms, but then she spends a few moments gagging, coughing, and spitting up a lot of water—and I suppose she's emptying her lungs. "That part isn't as much fun," she tells me in a strangled voice when she can finally breathe air again.

She kindly dives down a second time and returns with several huge kelp leaves that are far larger than the kelp leaves we have in Saltpool. First we lie beneath them as if they are wet, leathery blankets. Then when they're dry, we create crude, wide-brimmed hats for shade. Melily quickly gets an angry, red sunburn. And although my brown, freckled skin usually takes a while to burn, after two days of unrelenting sunshine, it's tender and peeling.

"Can you catch us something to eat?" I ask.

"I've tried," Melily says. "But it's so hard! Just imagine trying to grab a diver rabbit with your hands. Small fish and amphibs are really fast. Large ones are really fast and dangerous." Her leaf hat can't block out all of the bright sunlight, and her skin seems to glow yellow-green. "Also, ew, I don't want to hold a fish. It would be squirmy and disgusting."

"Can you drink the tidewater?" I ask.

She looks thoughtful. "I don't think I need to drink when I'm breathing the water. I only feel thirsty up here." Adjusting her leaf hat, she sighs heavily. "Do you think we'll be found?"

"I don't know," I say. "But do you want to be rescued? You belong somewhere down there, and your family's there too."

Melily frowns. "Well, I haven't seen any sirens yet. And… I don't know. I don't think I'm ready to stop living up here. All the things I like are up here. You're up here."

And she says it so casually, but it almost makes me cry. "Well, I think we're still in the trade currents," I say. "So that means thousands of steamships travel this way. Hopefully we'll be found." It's hard to be positive though. I haven't seen anything but endless tidewater since the *Wanderlea* sank. I also wonder if that's why the ocean is so empty below us. Maybe the sirens avoid the trade routes.

That night, the air is cold and we huddle close together, and in the morning, Melily does catch a fat, yellow fish. She breaks the surface of the tide making a very odd, yet happy, shrieking noise while holding her prize high in the air. She's so proud of herself that—after she hacks up a great deal of water—she gives me a detailed account of how she slowly swam over and surprised the fish, snatching it with both hands. I do the unpleasant work of killing our meal, while Melily covers her eyes. Then I cut the fish up as best I can with the sharp rock, and we eat it raw, which is something I'm more used to than Melily. She looks ill but is hungry enough to eat her share. "I mean I've eaten raw fish before in fine cookery houses," she says. "But those are marinated or seared, and there are, you know, really tasty sauces and things."

For the rest of the day, we weave and build a better shelter. Melily gathers armfuls of reeds, and each time she swims down out of my sight, I'm nervous. She could be attacked by a shark or dragged off by something worse, and who's to say that if she did meet sirens, they'd be nice to her? They might trap her and keep her down there, or even kill her.

I see a group of fur-covered amphibs swimming in the distance once while Melily is down gathering reeds. I think they might be fog raccoons, and I wonder if I could shoot one with the gunnerife. If they come closer, I'll try. I also spot a ship, but it's too far away to shout to, and it soon vanishes.

A storm gusts in a day later. It first unfurls dark clouds on the horizon, then as it prowls closer, it rumbles thunder at us and lashes out jagged wires of lightning. And when Melily says, "Just keep your head above the water, and I'll keep us together," I know it's going to be bad. At least I still have my floatvest.

The wind hits first, an invisible wall that not only rips away our reed shelter but then maliciously shreds it, twisting it off into the dark sky. The water turns on us next, rising in sharp blades that curl and slam into our raft. I hug Pavoya's ink drawing to my chest with one arm, as I also cling to the upright, triangular shard of our raft and splutter and cough out the saltwater that keeps slapping into me.

"Let go of it!" Melily shouts over the waves, eyeing the frame.

"No!" I howl back.

But when our raft flips over, I'm plunged into forceful whorls of water that rip the drawing out of my arms anyway. I can't even cry out with sadness because my mouth fills with water. Hands grab my ankle and then my left arm, and I'm hauled in a direction I think is upward. My head breaks the surface of the water, thanks to both Melily and the floatvest, and I gulp in air as the storm keeps stirring the ocean up into watery cliffs.

Melily clings to my arm, shouting, "Ship! There's a ship!"

And yes! I also see red and white lights glancing off the ragged surface of the water.

"Help! Help!" Melily cries. "Please!"

I join her with wordless screams—the loudest noises I can muster. Waves keep smashing over us with the lung-popping force of felled kelp trees, but no matter how many times I'm forced underwater, Melily somehow finds me, and with the help of my floatvest, yanks me upward again.

The ship moves closer and closer until it looms like a mountain over us, blotting out the dark clouds and sounding like a mechanical giant. Melily and I keep yelling, our cries growing hoarse and frantic, but finally, miraculously, distant voices shout back.

And even more amazing, ropes and ringfloats drop down. We struggle toward the white circles as lights skip over the waves, surely searching for us. A saveship lowers with impressive speed and burly shipsmen haul us into it. Then as Melily and I shiver and cling to each other, shipsmen winch the swaying little boat back up the side of the massive hull.

Once we're on board, the crew hurries us across the wet deck into an unfamiliar, large gathery. The bearded shipsmen then wrap blankets around our wet shoulders and speak to us excitedly in an unfamiliar language.

The man with the biggest beard seems to be the captain, and thankfully, he speaks Equitorian. "First catch of the day, huh?" he booms.

That's when I stumble and fall. The maybe-captain grabs me and barks something in the unknown language to the rest of the shipsmen. Two younger crew members then help Melily and me down stairs to a small cabin. One brings us some soup while the other bandages my shoulder, then they leave us alone to rest.

"That was incredible," Melily says. "Did you see me swimming through that storm? I'm so good at being a siren."

And I'm glad she's feeling proud, but for some reason, even though we've been rescued, I don't feel relief—I feel despair. At first I'm not sure why. We're much safer than we were hours ago. But after lying in my cot for a while with sadness clinging to me more tightly than ever, I finally understand.

Sande is surely dead.

After what I just went through—and I had Melily to help me—I don't think he could have survived.

Tears collect in my eyes, and I try to cry quietly, but I can't.

Melily shifts, and I tense, expecting her to tell me to be quiet. Instead though, she surprises me by saying, "What's wrong?"

"Sande is dead," I say between sobs. "He has to be."

And just like I cradled her when she cried about Sharles, Melily crawls into my cot and wraps her arms around me.

AFTER A QUIET DAY of recovery, Melily and I learn that we are still traveling to Leistelle. Melily says this isn't surprising because Leistelle was the next major city currentways when we were on the *Wanderlea*. She also says that even though it felt like we were stranded on the tide for a long time, we probably didn't drift that far.

Therefore we arrive in Leistelle about two days after we're rescued, and ringed with walls, the city reminds me of Varasay. The walls here seem both older than Varasay's and more imposing, though. They are made out of huge, tide-rounded, deepland rocks, and I see spikes and plenty of towers with stern, pointed roofs. The city is also surrounded by smaller islands with similar rocky defenses. Inside those walls though, stand tall green trees and simple kelpwood buildings. I ask Melily why the city is so fortified, but she doesn't know. "I never pay attention to boring politics," she says.

Yet the Captain of our rescue ship, the *Brectsteer*, explains it to me. Apparently the deeplanders used to fight the uplanders in Leistelle, sabotaging and stealing their food during the dry months. Eventually the city agreed to give the deeplanders the smaller mountain peaks.

"They still bicker and argue," the Captain says. "So I hate stopping here. There are twice as many port fees too."

I look at the little islands as we navigate the sunny, warm harbor, and I wonder what Varasay would be like if deeplanders owned tide-safe land. The Threegod Priests wouldn't have as much power over us, and there wouldn't be any forced factory work either.

At least twelve Leistelle port officers board the ship when we dock because some represent the uplanders while others represent the deeplanders. Melily lost her passbook when the *Wanderlea* exploded and I lost mine in the storm, so Melily uses wavurl to makes sure the officials aren't troubled by our lost documents. It takes some careful wavurling to hide my gunnerife too.

And then it's as if we're in Gatreijan all over again. Melily and I spend the morning stealing new clothes and travel cases, and that night Melily convinces an old woman to let us stay in her home.

The next day, we are about to step into the Sea Spread Travelers Commission to request new passbooks, when I catch hold of Melily's hand. "Wait."

She turns to look at me.

"We need new false names," I say. "Douglen and Jeck think we're dead. Let's stay dead."

Melily nods, and after some delicately-worded commands, we leave the huge, stone building with two passbooks; one for "Delina Cue," which is almost-but-not-quite the name of a singer Melily's fond of, and one for "Voreska Mynd." Voreska was the name in the passbook Sande bought for me in Varasay, and although I wasn't fond of the name then, I hope it will bring me good luck now.

We leave for Ellevah the next morning, and before we depart, I'm happy to overhear that a shipping vessel found a saveship of *Wanderlea* survivors.

"I hope Sharles is alive," Melily says, gazing at the tide as we carry our travel cases through the harbor. Stretching a gloved hand out to the foggy horizon, she whispers, "I'll never forget you, my love."

"I thought you were angry with him," I say.

She gives me a lofty look. "Anger and love are connected, Nerene. That's what passion is. Someday you'll understand."

I manage to nod without frowning. And although I'm still very sad about the lost *Wanderlea*, I'm pleased that Sharles isn't traveling with us to Ellevah as Melily once hoped.

And then we're off on the tide again, sailing starways on a little-but-lovely passenger ship called the *Reflection*. I couldn't talk Melily into traveling on a humbler boat, but at least it's a short trip of only two days.

When we arrive in Ellevah, I see at once why it's Cressit's favorite city and why Sande longed to travel here. It's small—about half the size of Varasay. The island is also covered with pretty little cottages and has a unique shape. Since it's the top of an old volcano, it's roughly a large circle. It has a spring-fed, freshwater central lake, which remains when the tide passes, and along the lake's shoreline floats a lattice of houses and bobbing, kelpwood walkways.

The people of Ellevah are kind and friendly too, and almost everyone seems to be artistic and creative. Several languages are spoken, and it's not just Threegod who's worshiped here, but other gods too—many of whom I've never heard of. Ellevah also seems to be the sort of place where no one asks too many questions, and I have the oddly comforting sense that we aren't the only people hiding here.

After selling a handful of jewelry that "somehow" appeared in Melily's pocket when we left Leistelle, we rent a small, floating cottage on the lake. I love everything about it—the warped and weathered walls, the colorful front door that creaks when I open it, and the flower boxes I can't wait to fill with herbs. Gren would also love this house. Maam would love it too.

"So, no more stealing," I say to Melily as we clean our new home.

"But that's what I do best," she says. "It's the only thing I'm good at—other than being a spectacular siren."

"It's the only thing you're good at so far," I say, scrubbing a stubborn spot on the floor with a wet rag. "But now that you're no longer traveling the Sea Spread, you have to change your ways. If too many things go missing in Ellevah and then reappear in tradershops, people will get suspicious. And we want to be able to stay here. There are other ways to earn money, honest ways."

So after selling the last of Melily's mysterious pocket jewelry, we open a herb and spice booth at a nearby market. And inspired by both Gren and Parsita, I blend the herbs together in a variety of ways. I buy most of our supplies from deeplanders or tide merchants, and I look forward to visiting the deeplands myself when the tide passes. It seems like Ellevah's deeplanders and uplanders get along well. While the ocean passes, deeplanders live in various uplanders' homes.

Melily finds the process of grinding, measuring, and packaging spice blends tedious—and I find it tedious to listen to her complain and frequently correct her mistakes—so we're both happier when she decides to organize our money instead, which she's good at. We soon realize that she's also good at making sure our landlord never raises our rent and finding us the best spots to set-up our booth in the ridge market. And whenever customers try to talk me into a discount, Melily dashes over and insists they pay full price. She says I'm too softhearted. I say she has to make sure she doesn't use wavurl to force people to buy things.

In general, though, we're happy.

Melily also gets a bit better at befriending young men. She often chats with guild apprentices she meets at the market, sometimes joining their families for meals or walking with them along the tide's edge. She never seems to get serious about anyone, though, at least not like she was about Sharles.

And as for me and love, that part of me seems to have died with Sande.

Melily often introduces me to apprentices she thinks I might like, to my great embarrassment, but I'm never interested.

However, well into our second tide of living in the remote, starways mountain city, I'm packing up our market booth one evening when someone says "Nerene" in a way that seems to fill my heart with boiling water.

I look up and see Cressit walking toward me.

"It's really you," he says. He's not wearing bright swingshow clothes or even expensive clothes, just a dark green jacket and brown work pants. His also wears his hair much shorter than he used to—cropped to his ears. He looks different, maybe thinner, although he's still handsome.

"So you're here," he says, looking stunned. "I thought… I thought you died."

"Nerene died," I say in a low voice. "I'm Voreska now."

"Well, for that matter, please call me Tedry," he whispers. "But I'm so relieved. I thought the worst had happened to you. How did you find your way here?"

"It's a long story," I say, and then I realize that the tide left this part of the Sea Spread two months ago. "Why are you in Ellevah and not on your ship?"

Cressit walks around the cart I'm arranging packets of spice blends in, and standing nearer to me, he says, "Maybe we shouldn't discuss this here." And he's right. A lot of people and other merchants are still milling around the market. "I could stop by early tomorrow morning," he offers.

"Or you could come to my cottage," I say because I want to know why he's in Ellevah, and I'm too curious to wait until tomorrow.

Cressit nods. "If that's all right."

"It's fine," I say, but I feel an uncertain tingle at the base of my neck because I never invite anyone over—and this is Cressit. Melily also won't be home. She's off wandering the docks with a baker's assistant.

But I ignore the tingling, and I lead Cressit along the lane that circles Caldera Lake. Since we would both rather tell our stories in private, we don't talk much. The sun's setting, so elongated, shadowy versions of ourselves keep us company. Birds chirp sleepily as well as if too tired to properly sing. And it's that beautiful time of year when bright orange leaves cover the savor pear trees.

"Would you like me to push your cart for you?" Cressit offers.

"No need," I say quietly, and then I add, "You know, I'm not here alone. That someone you were once searching for? She's here too."

"She is?" he says, looking surprised and happy.

When we reach my home, I squeeze the cart into the shed next to the cookery door, and I invite Cressit inside. The cottage is mostly one cozy gathery room, but there's also a cookery hidden in a pocket of cabinets on one end and a small sleeping loft.

I consider offering Cressit food, but I'm not sure I want to be overly welcoming. I'm not that angry about what happened in Beth anymore, it's an old wound—only tender when I think about it too much. Mostly, it's just nice to see a familiar face. But I still feel cautious. Melily can't use wavurl on me. Cressit can. I haven't felt that fear in a while.

"Does Melily live here too?" he asks.

I nod, sitting in one of the mismatched chairs at our table. "She'll probably be home soon. We thought Ellevah was where her family might be—at least when we first ran away. But that's not true, is it?"

Cressit hesitates before answering, but then says, "Surely you understand why I kept certain secrets. How did you figure it out?"

So I tell him about what happened on the *Wanderlea*, and when I'm done, he blows out a long breath.

"That's awful."

"It was," I say, and I want to change the subject. I'm always sad when I think about Pavoya. "Are you performing swingshows here?"

Cressit shakes his head and joins me sitting at the table. "All of that's over now. The Osperacy's thought I convinced Melily to run away, and so they hounded and tormented me. Eventually Douglen tried to wavurl me into killing myself. When I resisted, he realized what I was. Then things got worse, he started terrorizing my musician friends and the performers I traveled with, and I just couldn't protect everyone. After Douglen almost killed my drummer, it was time to… I don't know… stop fighting. Our group disbanded, I sold my ship, and I gave up performing. It seemed to make sense to hide myself away here. I've always loved Ellevah."

"I remember," I say. "And how horrible about Douglen."

Cressit runs a finger across a knot in the table. "I'm just sorry I didn't fight back—I had a few chances, and I didn't take them. But I don't regret giving up the swingshows. They weren't the same anymore. They seemed like a lie after what happened with you."

I feel like something heavy rests on my shoulders. "What are you doing now?"

"Trying to learn how to build chorders," he says, leaning back in his chair. "I'm terrible at it, though. Playing them and making them are apparently two very different things." He stands and looks around my little home, examining the herbs in pots, the blanket I'm weaving, the blanket Melily gave up weaving—which lies in a tangled heap—and Melily's wardrobe. It's the largest piece of furniture in the cottage, and it's bursting with clothes. A mound of hats, purses, and shoes also lies to one side of it. Even though Melily insists she only trades for clothing now and doesn't steal anything, I'm not sure her exchanges are always fair.

"You have a lovely home," Cressit says. "I'm sharing a housing unit with four fishermen—it's much different. What's this?"

"Oh nothing." I leap up and snatch away the stack of paper he's looking at. "I'm writing a book about herbs because I couldn't find a good one."

"Can I read it?"

I shake my head. "It's not at all finished—I'm still learning how to write properly."

"I could help," Cressit offers. "I don't know much about herbs, but I can write fairly well."

I look down at the paper piled in my arms. "Melily said she'd look it over." But that was several months ago, and she still hasn't started.

He holds out his hands. "Can I see what you already have?"

So we spend the next hour spreading my notes across the floor, and I also show him my drawings of silvany weed, moss sage, and whorl chives.

"These are wonderful," he says

"I'm focusing on common herbs," I tell him, hovering self-consciously at his shoulder. "The book would be better if I knew more about the rare plants that grow around other cities."

"Well, if your book sells well, maybe you can travel the Sea Spread to study," Cressit says. "In the meantime, you make spice blends, don't you? I bet people would love it if you included recipes for those."

"That's a great idea," I say, feeling a rush of warmth towards him. I didn't realize how nice it felt to have someone take an interest in my work. Melily usually just complains about how annoying it is that I'm always writing when she wants my attention.

Melily finds us two hours later; huddled over pages that I've spread across floor, drinking tea, and discussing ideas for a book title. I've had trouble coming up with a good one.

"Cressit!?" she exclaims.

He looks up uncertainly.

I'm not sure how she'll react to him being in Ellevah, but all she does is rush over and hug him. I feel even more warmly towards him when as she does this, he sweeps my notes out of the way of her boots, protecting them.

Then we all tell our stories a second time, Cressit his and Melily ours—and she adds way too many personal details about her romance with Sharles. Cressit asks if she would like to find her family in the tide, and when she says no, he seems relieved. After he finally bids us goodnight, Melily wraps an arm around me and says, "So he's clearly in love with you."

"What? No." I swallow. "Besides, Cressit wronged me—badly."

"But that was an accident, wasn't it? And it happened a long time ago, *and* he just spent hours reading your boring herb book. Who else would do that?"

I feel myself flush, and I'm not sure I like it. "Let's get ready for bed."

AND SO OUR LIFE changes again. Now it's the three of us at the market booth. I'm usually mixing and preparing spice blends, while Cressit measures out equal portions to package in glass bottles and paper packets. Melily keeps a record of our sales, calls people over to our booth, and chats with anyone she finds interesting. And if we're not too busy, Cressit plays music on an old drybark chorder while I sketch herbs, and that often interests passersby too.

In the evenings Cressit and I work on my herb and spice book, and when Melily's around, we play games. I've gotten really good at Slide 'n' Pass—matching amphib cards faster than anyone else. Melily often grumbles that I'm surely cheating, and even Cressit looks at me sideways sometimes.

Before we know it, it's summer and time to gather plants in the deeplands, and this tide, I'm hoping to search for mushrooms too.

Melily decides to stay up in Ellevah City to keep our market booth open, though. "I went to the deeplands last tide, and there is just too much mud down there. It gets on everything and in everything and ruins everything."

And so it's just Cressit who travels with me.

I'm nervous about that at first, and it's not that I don't trust Cressit by now—I do. It's more that I don't trust myself. My feelings for him always seem like they're swinging on a pendulum that I can't control, shifting from old pain to fondness, then over to happiness, but then back to caution. Our first meeting in Beth seems so far away now, but it's still there, a hidden hurt inside me.

At the tree-covered foot of Mount Ellevah, Cressit and I pass through two deepland villages. There we buy many of the herbs we need and arrange to pick them up on our return. We also buy several snappers and carry them further into the kelp forest—which is dryer, cooler, and rockier than the jungles surrounding Varasay. We spend a sunpeak foraging, and there are many fascinating local plants to gather; we pluck the threads of the intensely flavored invol flower and dig up grimewort roots that have to be soaked and mashed as soon as they're picked.

Thankfully there aren't too many vicious amphibs near Ellevah, so all we have to worry about are roaming fringed bears and the rare pack of velvet wolves. I'm not too concerned about them, though, because I have my snappers. I try to teach Cressit how to use the little darts too, but he doesn't make much progress. He can shoot them really far, but his aim is awful.

"There's some secret to this that you're just not telling me, isn't there?" he says, after losing yet another dart in the dense, leafy surroundings.

"There's no secret," I say with a grin. "You just have to start practicing when you're five tides old."

Cressit raises his eyebrows. "So your village had children running around with weapons? That seems like a bad idea."

"They didn't have poisoned darts," I laugh. "At least not until they were ten."

"Ten," Cressit says, still looking incredulous. "Well, that's much safer."

He's a much better companion than Melily was last tide. He works hard and stays cheerful, even when it rains on us for two days. He also assembles a clever, reed platform to put our tent on, which helps us stay dry.

And one evening, while we're sitting around the cookfire, my pendulum-like feelings stop swinging around and settle on affection —and quite a lot of it. I watch Cressit for a while as he trims the flat-topped, purple-brown mushrooms we collected that day and hums one of his old songs. Then I take the trimming knife out of his hand, and when he looks up at me surprised, I kiss him.

It's like he's been waiting for me to do that for ages because he kisses back enthusiastically, pulling me onto his lap. And it's not long before we're doing more than kissing as the cookfire crackles and sparks beside us.

When our nine-day trip is over, we return home holding hands, and Melily welcomes us back with a gleeful, "I knew it!"

Months pass and eventually the tide returns, which in Ellevah happens in the spring. Its arrival means that I've now been living in this remote city for three tides. Cressit and I finished our herb manuscript, although we're still creating a final draft using a typing machine we saved up to buy. We're going over our work one rainy evening when Melily rushes in.

"The *Trident's* in port," she cries, yanking off her canvas rain cloak and sending water droplets flying.

Both Cressit and I leap up to protect the manuscript, and he says, "Are you sure?"

Melily nods, wide-eyed. "A friend of mine loves steamships for some boring reason, and anyway, he told me this big ship came to port with a trident painted on it. So I ran up to the ridge to check, and it's the *Trident*. It is."

And of course the *Trident* would stand out. Since Ellevah is outside of the trade routes, large ships rarely come to our city.

I turn to Cressit, immediately afraid. "Why would they come here? Do you think they know where we are?"

"Surely not." But he puts an arm around me. "They're probably here for some other reason. We'll just lay low—shut down the booth for a few days."

I nod. "My snappers. I might need them. They're at your place." I used to hide them beneath Melily's wardrobe, but since we now store our herb gathering tent at Cressit's housing unit, that's where they are.

"I'll get them." He pulls on his jacket and then turns to me. "What about that gunnerife? Do you still have it?"

"Yes," I say with some hesitation, resting my hand lightly on the cookery drawer where I hid the weapon far in the back behind the drying cloths. "Do you want to take it with you?"

"You're the one who knows how to use it." Cressit reaches for the door. "I'll just go quickly."

I nod, thinking about how many times I nearly dropped that awful gunnerife into the lake, but then kept it—just in case. "Hopefully there won't be any trouble," I say, watching Cressit splash away into the rainy darkness.

And as I turn off the electric lamp in the cookery, Melily says in a small voice, "There might be some trouble."

I peer around our tall pantry cabinet to look at her. "What do you mean?"

"Well, I..." she hesitates, cringing. "The thing is, remember how you wanted to bring Shara and Timsy and Dorla with us when we first left, and I said no? Well, last tide I was feeling really, really guilty about that, so I sent Shara a letter."

"Melily, oh no!" I say.

She slumps across the table. "I tried to be secretive, and I never put our names on it, but... I did tell her to run away with Timsy and Dorla and come here."

I feel a flutter of pride because when we first met, Melily never worried about other people's safety or happiness. But it's just a flutter of pride because I mostly feel dread. "Well, even if the Osperacys know we're in the city, they'll have trouble finding us. We never use our real names."

"No, but I suggested visiting Delina and Voreska's spice booth in the letter," Melily says. "I'm so sorry, but I wanted Shara to find us."

I sigh, but I also take her hand. "Maybe this is Shara's doing somehow."

"Maybe," Melily whispers.

As we sit quietly in the darkness, I think about how long it will take Cressit to hurry around Caldera Lake, find my snappers, and return.

We listen to the rain. We listen to the sound of our neighbors in the distance, talking, laughing, arguing. And we keep holding hands. I wonder if Cressit's struggling to find my snappers. I think I tucked them in the bottom of my large carrypack, although maybe I left them in the canvas tent bag. I probably should have gone with him.

And just when I convince myself that everything will be fine, and we should probably start getting ready for bed, I hear a sharp knock —a knock that is definitely not Cressit's knock. I cover my ears tightly, crushing them against my head, but it doesn't matter. I still hear Douglen say, "Unlock the door."

There's wavurl in those words, grabbing at me, clamping onto my will. It's been so long since I felt that grip, and I try to resist, but I still stand up and move toward the door.

"No-no-no," Melily whispers, wrapping her arms around my waist and using all her strength to hold me back. "He didn't say which door! He didn't say! Unlock the cookery door!"

She's right, and her logic loosens up my thoughts up a bit. I stumble around the large pantry cabinet into cookery, and I slide the bolt back to unlock the side door. Douglen's wavurl sloths off of me, and I quickly bolt the door again.

It doesn't keep them out, though. I hear a sudden bang as the main door to our cottage breaks open. Melily shrieks.

I duck below the cookery ledge, out of sight

"Here alone are you?" Douglen snaps at Melily.

"Yes," she squeaks.

"She's lying," Jeck says, and I hear them walking around the gathery —the heavy footfalls of wet, grimy boots that we would have taken off at the door.

I feel awful about leaving Melily to fend for herself, but I'd only be a puppet out there—a body for Douglen to control with wavurl. And what if he made me hurt Melily? Fathoms, that would be a nightmare.

"I'm not lying," Melily says. "Look how tiny this place is, of course I'm alone—don't be idiots. But it's not as if I owe you any honest answers anyway. You tried to kill me—blowing up that ship."

The drawer with the gunnerife is directly across from me. I reach over and slowly, ever so slowly, ease it open.

"Are you expecting an apology?" Douglen says. "Because you don't get that. You ran away. You betrayed us. And you survived, didn't you? How'd you like that long swim?"

"You killed a lot of people—innocent people," Melily says, and her voice trembles.

I hope she'll stay strong. She knows Cressit will return soon. I reach into the drawer, past the folded cloths, past a little box of matches; and then I feel the cold, weighty metal of the gunnerife. My heart feels like it's bashing around inside of me, bruising and battering itself. Our happy life here might end tonight.

"Well, don't you worry," Douglen growls at Melily. "I've changed my mind about killing you. Come back to the ship."

"So your power's finally fading then," Melily says. "That's it, isn't it? You need me now."

"It's not gone… yet," Douglen says sourly. "But, yeah, I can feel it changing. Do you expect me to grovel and apologize? Because that's not going to happen. You come back, or I drag you back."

I see motion through the rain-spattered cookery window, past my tiny forest of herbs. Cressit's returned! He must have heard Douglen's voice because he usually uses the front entrance. I silently ease the bolt back on the cookery door, and he slips inside.

"You just try dragging me back to the *Trident*," I hear Melily say.

"I'll scream the whole way, and it won't even matter. I'll just tell Father I'm done stealing because I am. No one can *make* me use wavurl."

I hold out my hand for the snappers, but Cressit hesitates and nods at the gunnerife I'm already holding—an unspoken suggestion that I use it instead.

I'd much rather use my snappers. They aren't deadly or loud or illegal. So I carefully, quietly lay the gunnerife on the wooden preparation ledge, and then I point at it and shake my head, no.

Back in the gathery, Jeck snorts, and Douglen says, "Oh you'll use your wavurl or be in a great deal of pain. And you can't go whining to Father anymore either. He's dead."

"Dead," Melily repeats, and even though Lord Osperacy kidnapped her and used her, I hear sadness in her voice.

And to my increasing frustration, Cressit *still* doesn't hand me the snappers, so I reach over and take them, shooting him a confused, frustrated look.

He surprises me by giving me an intense, argumentative glare in return, and he mouths, "Gunnerife."

"How did father die?" Melily asks, as I hastily untie the leather cord binding the snappers and select two of the little darts.

"He was sick," Douglen says, emotionless, and I hear him move across the small room with decisive, heavy steps. "The *Trident* is mine now, along with everything and everyone on it."

"I bet you killed him," Melily says. "Just like you killed Elgin."

Douglen snorts.

I peek around the pantry cabinet, thankful that I'm in the shadows, and now I can see them. Douglen stands near Melily, with his tightly-packed muscles wrapped in a gray suit. Jeck leans against the now cracked front door, and with his spindly arms and legs looking like they always do—unspooled. Melily is almost out of sight, standing behind our round table and the typing machine as if they're a fortress. She looks tiny compared to Douglen and Jeck. She also looks terrified, and that makes my heart sting.

In a steady voice, though, she says, "You murdered Elgin. Admit it."

"Fine," Douglen says. "Yeah. I killed that little sea foam. I made him write you a goodbye note, and then I made him stand on the motorliner tracks in Lellev. And I'll do that to everyone you care about if you keep crossing me."

Jeck laughs.

Melily's hands fly to her mouth.

Douglen moves around the table and grabs her arm.

I lift my snapper, pulling the resin back, but Cressit catches my elbow. I try to shake him off, but he's pulling me further back into the cookery.

"Jeck, don't let Douglen hurt me!" I hear Melily shout.

But just as quickly, Douglen says. "Jeck, don't move." And then there's the meaty, thumping sound of a punch, and I hear one of our chairs fall over. Melily wails.

"Jeck's not really my balance," Douglen growls. "Tricked Father with that one years ago."

Cressit's locked his arms around me. "Use the gunnerife," he whispers, pressing the weapon into my hands. "Shoot them in the head."

"No," I breathe. Douglen hits Melily again, and she makes a horrible sound—like a ridge cat caught in the wheels of an automotor.

"Use the gunnerife," Cressit repeats. "Shoot Douglen and Jeck in the head." And this time, there's wavurl in each word.

I want to stop myself. I want to do things my way, which I know is the better way, but my body won't listen.

I step out of the cookery and into the gathery.

Jeck looks up seconds before his face explodes in a burst of red.

My doing.

No, Cressit's doing, as he forces his will through me.

Douglen sees me. His eyes narrow, and I realize he's holding a gunnerife too. He must have pulled it out of his jacket. He opens his mouth, surely to command me. "No!" I shout. And we both shoot.

He dies in a spectacular, gruesome, stomach-turning instant that will forever ruin the rugs, table, and typing machine.

And I'm unhurt. He didn't have the chance to raise the gunnerife and aim.

There's a terrible silence, but it's not a complete silence. The rain patters gently against the roof, water sloshes around the floats supporting our floor—soft, irregular, and almost musical. And I hear a wheezing sound as if someone is trying to suck air into their lungs and failing.

"Melily!" I gasp, rushing to where she huddles beneath the table.

Douglen did aim, just not at me.

MELILY IS COVERED in blood by the time I reach her. She's fighting to breathe, unable to speak, and staring at me with wide, teary eyes.

"It's all right," I soothe, but that's an extraordinary lie because I just stepped over two corpses to reach her, and an immense amount of dark blood drenches her chest. I crouch down and search for the wound.

"Nerene!" Cressit tosses me several cookery cloths.

And there it is, an ugly hole in her ribs with blood streaming out of it. I press the fabric against her chest—just like I did when I was helping poor Pavoya.

Melily tries to speak, wrenching up her face and wheezing, "Elgin... Father... dead."

"I know. I'm so sorry." I drape a hug around her, careful not to hurt her more.

"We have to get her to a healer," Cressit says.

"How?" I whisper. The nearest healing house is up on the ridge, the closest thing Ellevah has to a high city.

Cressit kneels. "I'll carry her."

So the three of us, all soaked in blood, hurry out of the house and across the shifting, floating walkways. Melily struggles to breathe in Cressit's arms, and I shove more cookery cloths against her ribs.

Sleepy neighbors peer out of their homes. Surely they heard the gunnerife shots. I don't want to imagine what will happen when they find Douglen and Jeck's bodies either. They'll probably call Shore Control and Shore Control will want an explanation, but I can't worry about that right now.

Melily is light, yes, but even someone small is difficult to carry after a while. By the time we reach the healing house, Cressit's breathing is almost as ragged and uneven as hers.

The healing house is an ancient, solid-looking building held up by massive stone pillars, which are covered in spirals of carved fish. I'm used to everything in Ellevah being worn and a little grimy, therefore it seems strange that the healing house is so clean. The healers who come running into the entryway when Cressit calls for help wear trim, fernflax uniforms and their hair is either cut short or pulled back into neat buns.

"She's been shot," Cressit huffs, and the healers whisk Melily away on a wheeled cot.

"Take care of her!" I cry.

We watch them vanish down a white brick hallway, and we stand like statues in the waiting area, surrounded by people coughing, clinging to feverish children, and pressing rags against minor wounds. We must seem injured ourselves with all the blood on us.

"You're angry," Cressit says at last, soft and under his breath.

I don't even know if it's anger that I feel, but whatever it is, it's destructive and sad.

"I had to do it," he says, "It was the only way to stop them—to make sure they never come after us again."

I look at him, and I feel like I'm looking at the polished and famous Cressit I first met. "It wasn't the only way. I had snappers. You didn't give me a chance."

As if we are of one mind, we move to a quiet corner of the waiting area, where a kelpwood bench is tucked into an alcove. We don't sit on it, though. We stand at either end.

"So you're saying you didn't want them dead?" he hisses. "I find that hard to believe."

"That's not the point," I whisper back, trembling with anger. "If I'd stunned them, we could have thought things through, maybe come up with another option. Instead I killed them in a way that all of Ellevah heard. What now?"

My thoughts churn—I'll have to stand trial, I'll have to prove that I killed Douglen and Jeck to defend myself... and if I can't?

Cressit rounds the bench and reaches for my hand. "I'm sure we can figure it out."

I pull away and fold my arms.

He sighs angrily.

"You knew I didn't want to use the gunnerife," I softly say.

"It was an unusual situation," he counters. "I did what I thought I had to."

"And you used *wavurl* on me," I add in an even softer voice.

The accusation hangs between us, a betrayal I wonder if I'll ever get over.

"Surely you know I won't do it again," he says after a long pause.

And I don't answer.

We're broken or breaking. All the blood on our clothes seems like our own. It hurts, and I want to cry about what I know is happening, but I'm still too shaken and worried about Melily.

Time passes, too much time.

"We should check on her," I say.

Cressit nods.

We make our way to a small kelpwood desk where a woman sits among piles of charts and folders. She won't tell us anything about Melily or maybe she just doesn't know what's happening in the rooms and passages behind her. I storm past her impatiently and march down the tiled hallway.

"Uh, excuse me. You can't go that way!" The woman struggles to stand, knocking over a stack of paper.

"Let her do what she wants," Cressit wearily commands and follows me.

The first healer we find is a startled woman carrying a tray of glass vials.

"How is the girl who was shot?" I ask. "We're her family."

"Oh," the healer pales. "Oh," she says again, her eyes darting between us. "Well, the surgeon's doing his best. He removed the bullet, but it did a lot of damage. And her body... it's *so* strange inside. Everyone says operating on her is fascinating. Well, and tragic, of course," she hastily adds, flushing. She then ducks her head and scurries away.

Cressit curses, and I turn to him. He has a stricken expression.

"What is it?" I ask.

"They can't help her," he says softly. "Of course they can't help her. I never thought about it, but we sirens must be different inside. We have to be."

And I feel stupid because Cressit and I have talked about such things before, just in a different way—Cressit's never fathered a child, not with me or anyone else. We assumed that although we seem to be built the same, we're different enough that having children was impossible.

"What do we do?" I say, but the answer is both frightening and obvious.

Melily needs someone who can fix her. Cressit has to take her home, truly home.

The surgeon doesn't want to close her up. She's dying anyway, he says, and he wants to study her. Cressit has to use wavurl and command him every step of the way.

I see shore controllers gathering in the healing house entrance as we slip out a side door. It sends a chill through me because they're surely looking for us, but Cressit doesn't seem to notice. Then we're rushing back out into the night with Melily in Cressit's arms. At least this time she's wrapped in bandages and wearing a clean hospital gown. The healers also gave her some sort of medicine that's put her to sleep, so even though she's still struggling to breathe, she looks peaceful, beautiful even.

The rain is still falling as we leave the healing house, and all the water makes the streets curving down to the tide look as if they're coated in glass.

Carrying Melily downhill isn't as hard on Cressit, and we reach the trade inlet quickly. Soon we're standing on a slim walkway, looking down at the dark, rain-puckered waves.

Cressit turns to face me. "The sirens… they'll make us stay in the tide."

"Will there be any nearby?" I ask.

He nods. "I hope so. Will you be all right?"

I nod, although I'm not sure. And then I kiss Melily's raindrop spattered cheeks and stroke her hair, and I tell her, "Cressit's going to take care of you. He will." I wish she was awake so I could say a proper goodbye.

"I love you," Cressit tells me.

"And I love you," I say.

We kiss briefly and unhappily, and then he climbs over the rail with Melily in his arms and jumps. For a moment they seem frozen, hanging over the water; a blur of white healing-gown, dark clothes, pale skin, and red blood. Then with a splash that seems too small and insignificant, they're gone, and there's nothing left but the tide.

I WATCH THE WATER for a long time, feeling stunned and disconnected from everything that just happened. I'm hardly even aware of the cold rain still streaming over my shoulders and soaking my hair.

I'm sure I'll be arrested for Douglen and Jeck's death, and the trial will be complicated. No one will believe a girl with a hidden gunnerife is innocent. Ellevah's shore controllers will also want to know where Cressit and Melily are, and they won't like it when I don't have an answer.

The more I think about my situation, the more danger I realize I'm in, and for a reckless moment, I wonder if it would be best if I disappeared into the tidewater too.

But maybe there's still someone who can help me.

Blood-soaked and shivering, I walk along Ellevah's curved shoreline. I cross brick walkways and kelpwood docks, and I also follow several dirt pathways that skirt the drybark forest reserved for tide-trapped landrunners. Eventually I arrive at the stone pier where larger ships dock. The *Trident* is definitely the biggest ship in port, tall and massive; with familiar red and black funnels, a bright white anchor, and a trident emblem on her side.

The shipsman standing guard won't let me up the gangway though, and considering my bloody nightclothes and bare feet, I don't blame him.

"I'm Vores—Nerene Keel," I say, not used to using my real name. "I used to work for Lord Osperacy. Can I speak with Shara, please?"

"Nerene? We lost that girl ages ago," the man says, but he gives me a closer look, and I can tell by the way his eyes move across my face that he recognizes me.

"Douglen and Jeck are dead," I say, taking a risk. He could be one of their friends. "Please, can I speak with Shara?"

"Dead? Really?" The man says, sounding surprised. "How?"

I hesitate. "Someone shot them." My voice cracks. It's not really a lie, but it doesn't feel like the truth either.

"Huh." He nods silently for a moment, surely thinking. "Well, Captain Gedwick will need to know. Follow me."

"Would you take me to Shara first, please?" I ask, hurrying up the gangway after him. "She should know before anyone else."

He glances back at me uncertainly, but thankfully says, "All right."

The *Trident* looks different. I see stains and wispy smears of dust on the carpets that used to be so clean, and at least a third of the electric lights are dark.

It takes a long while for Shara to appear at her cabin door, and when she does, she looks different. She was always thin, but now her joints seem too obvious. She also has dark circles beneath her eyes, and some of the pearl buttons on her nightgown have been replaced with simpler, glass ones. She cries "Nerene!" and although she looks at my bloodstained clothes with concern, she doesn't hesitate to hug me. "I must be dreaming!"

If I'm dreaming, this is a nightmare. I was happy in Ellevah. Losing Cressit and Melily all in one day feels like one of Jeck's mechbombs has exploded inside of me. If I didn't need to act quickly to save myself, I'd curl up somewhere and cry.

"Where did you come from?" Shara asks as she releases me.

I swallow back the threat of tears. "I was living here in Ellevah with Melily and another friend."

"Melily was here too?" She looks surprised and happy, so I'm guessing she never received Melily's letter. I suppose it makes grim sense that Douglen would read or steal Shara's mail. She frowns as she looks at the blood on my clothes again. "What's happened? Are you hurt?"

"I'm fine, and I have a lot to tell you, but first..." I hesitate, yet there's no point delaying the most important news. "Douglen and Jeck are dead."

"Dead?" she echoes.

"Yes."

"Have you seen their bodies?"

I nod.

"How did they die?"

I glance at the listening shipsman, who stands only a few paces behind me. "They were shot."

Shara starts to cry, leaning against the doorframe.

Now I'm worried. Did a part of Shara love Douglen? Maybe it was wrong to come here.

But then she smiles at me, and I understand—she's crying in relief. "Now I know I'm dreaming," she whispers.

She encourages the shipsman to speak with the captain and beckons me into her cabin. I'm shocked by how empty it is. She used to have two bookshelves with latched glass doors, as well as a lovely writing desk. Sitting down on the end of her bed, the only piece of large furniture left, I quickly tell her about my evening because I don't have much time. The longer I stay in Ellevah, the greater the chance that I'll be arrested by shore control and, most likely, charged with murder.

The stickiest, most complicated part of my story is when I try to explain what happened to Melily. Yet Shara seems to already know about the siren's tidewater home. Perhaps I shouldn't be surprised. Douglen surely knew—he mentioned that Melily survived the *Wanderlea* wreck by swimming—and Shara lived with the Osperacys for far longer than I did.

"Will Melily survive, do you think?" Shara asks.

"I hope so," I say. "If anything, she can breathe differently down there."

Shara dabs her eyes with a foamsilk handkerchief. "It's probably best that we tell everyone else on the *Trident* she's dead."

I nod, grateful that Shara wants to keep the Osperacy's true nature a secret. It protects Cressit too.

Thinking about him makes my throat tighten. "So are you really Douglen's balance?" I ask.

"I am," she says, "I always thought Jeck was too—but I'm not surprised that Douglen found a way around Lord Osperacy's control." She then tells me everything that's happened on the *Trident* since I last saw her. Lord Osperacy, she confirms, is most definitely dead. "Douglen said he died of a fever, but I knew it was poison." She folds her hands in her lap and looks frail. "Douglen always wanted to be in charge of the ship. But with his power about to leave him and Timsy not old enough to help, he got desperate. He sold all of Lord Osperacy's treasures. He used wavurl to cheat at gambling in sloppy ways, and he made a lot of enemies. We aren't welcome in many of the major cities anymore. I thought that was why we came here—because we had no other port options in this part of the tide—but I suppose Douglen had other reasons." She sighs. "Well, how about you clean yourself up in my washing room? I'll get you some clean clothes, and I'll talk to Captain Gedwick as well. And please don't worry about the crew. Douglen and Jeck treated everyone terribly, especially after Lord Osperacy died. You're surrounded by friends."

Thankfully Shara seems to be right, and hardly three hours after Cressit and Melily disappeared into the tide, I'm sailing safely away from Ellevah on the *Trident*.

Marthes, my old servegirl, helps me settle into my old cabin, and I'm so glad to see her again. I do find myself wondering why Douglen and Jeck didn't dismiss her like they did so many others, and I hate to think that the scars on her neck and wrists are the unsettling answer.

She greets me warmly though. "So you were in Ellevah all this time! I was so worried about you. You know, it was good that you left when you did."

"But that's when everything went wrong."

Marthes nods. "Exactly. If you'd stayed, you would have just suffered along with the rest of us."

Almost all of my belongings are gone, except for a few simple dresses and a pair of shoes. Blushing, Marthes admits that she and the other servegirls took my things when it was clear I wasn't coming back. They either sold or altered them.

"I can return what I still have," she assures me.

"No, please don't bother." I cross the cabin and pull aside the curtains covering the windows. White moonlight shines in, and both moons are in the sky tonight. It's strange to be back on the *Trident* after so long. Could I have somehow stopped Douglen from poisoning Lord Osperacy? Probably not, but it's odd to think that as harsh as Lord Osperacy was, he was keeping another monster caged.

"I tried running away once," Marthes says softly. "Me and a few other girls. It didn't go well. Douglen and Jeck caught us and hurt us and after that, they took our passbooks."

Fathoms! I left my passbook in the cottage. And then I realize something that pains me even more—I also left the herb manuscript behind.

At least Shara is able to sort out the passbook situation. Douglen had locked the crew's passbooks up in Lord Osperacy's old cabins—which he'd taken over—and Shara is able to find them. And as for me, when Captain Gedwick begs his way into one of the bigger port cities, Shara shows me that passbooks can be purchased with enough money.

Captain Gedwick, who I hardly knew while I was traveling on the *Trident* before, turns out to be a gruff but friendly man. He gives the crew generous shore leave, and he also encourages Shara and me to think about what we want to do now that the Osperacys are gone. He says he'd like to buy the *Trident* and make her more of a passenger ship. He reasons her current owner is Shara, for she was Douglen's wife, and he offers to pay for the *Trident* in installments through the equatorial banks.

Shara is more than happy to sell the ship, and she decides to return to her childhood home.

"I'll take Timsy and Dorla too," she tells me. "Timsy and I get along well enough, so I think I can manage his wavurl. And you're welcome to come with us. You'd like Kell Theer. It's well outside of the trade routes, like Ellevah, and the people there are kind to deeplanders, at least that's how it was when I left."

I thank her and tell her I'll think about it, but I'm not sure it's what I should do.

The next few months are quiet, and for me, they feel melancholy and aimless as we sail from mountain city to mountain city. Captain Gedwick hires new crew members and employs guild workers whenever we're in port to make repairs and upgrades. He also renames the ship to help shake off its poor reputation, and so we soon travel in the *Lady Alonia*—she's apparently a famous warrior from Captain Gedwick's home city. Because he's eager to take on more paying passengers, Shara and I move our things into the smaller cabins in the bow. We also take the remainder of Lord Osperacy's treasures, and there isn't much left—mostly just jewelry that, for whatever reason, Douglen hadn't sold yet.

Shara and I spend most of our time either walking Timsy and Dorla around the upper decks or letting them run through the cavernous hold, depending on the weather. The children are five tides old now, and Shara says she's learned, following several ugly, siren temper-tantrums, that it's easiest to care for Timsy when he has plenty of opportunity to roam.

"Why did you marry Douglen?" I finally find the courage to ask her one morning.

She pulls her shawl close as she watches Timsy and Dorla chase each other around a funnel. "Lord Osperacy made me. He wanted Douglen to have a wife. He thought it would make him seem more trustworthy. Lord Osperacy also threatened to stop sending money to my family if I refused, and…" She gives a little shrug. "I'm a lower city girl. My family needed the money."

Shara reaches for Dorla's hand, steadying the child as she climbs over a deck chair. "The worst part is, I don't even know if Lord Osperacy ever sent my family money. He never let me visit them, and they never responded to the letters I sent—or, at least, I never received their replies."

She frowns, surely thinking about how Douglen took Melily's letter about Ellevah.

Timsy and Dorla go to bed early each evening, and once they're settled, I organize what's left of Lord Osperacy's treasures while Shara sorts through his papers. We hope she'll find information about Dorla's family, but in the end, I make the most interesting discovery. Opening a plain drybark box, I find brilliant white gems—the arctic stones Melily and I stole in Beth. I pick up one of the sparkling rocks. It seems as if it should feel ice cold, yet it isn't. I watch the shifting, soft inner light reflect onto my fingertips, and I think I finally know what to do.

We eventually pass Varasay, and I long to go ashore. Yet considering how I left, it probably still wouldn't be safe. Shara bravely visits the deeplander barracks, though, to see if she can learn anything for me. Some of her news is sad; Gren Tya passed away during the past summer, and Giron rebuilt his terrible factory. But some of her news is good; Carnos married a girl from Pirock and they already have twin baby girls, and twins are a sign of blessing from the Water Goddess.

Shara also brings me a package of cinniflower tea from Parsita's shop. "She's an interesting person, isn't she? She wrapped this up nicely and said it was for you—like it was a present—but then she made me pay for it."

The seas beyond Varasay are calm, and I feel calm as we arrive in Beth. With Shara's blessing and some of her money too, I hire an automotor and travel to the high city. Apparently there aren't any automotors on the *Trident* anymore because Douglen sold them.

I feel particularly anxious as I pass through the long, dark tunnel that cuts up through the countertide mountain. I squeeze the fabric seat coverings and drum my shoes on the floor. I'm not sure what's bothering me the most—that this is where I first met Cressit or that the museum will want to know why I have the arctic stones.

The tide always passes Beth in winter, and so the city looks a lot like it did the last time I visited. Snowflakes even dance down from a white sky as I climb the museum steps.

I hug the box of arctic stones to my middle. If the museum accuses me of stealing them, I have no siren here to save me.

"Welcome to the Royal Museum of Beth." A man wearing dark clothing greets me in the museum's entrance hall. "It costs fifteen shells to visit the museum today."

I rummage through my handbag for the uppy money Shara gave me. Nearby, other museum visitors stand in groups, shedding fur coats and speaking softly.

"May I see Sir Mauricen?" I ask the greeter, handing him the folded paper shells.

He looks mildly surprised. "Is Sir Mauricen expecting you? He's a very busy man."

"No, but I found something I think belongs to him." I don't want to give this man any more details than I have to, but I also don't want him to send me away, so I add, "It's very valuable."

The man inspects me with raised eyebrows, but my steady gaze seems to satisfy him. "Very well, follow me."

He leads me to Sir Mauricen's office, but the door is locked, and no one's there. I try not to let my disappointment show. I want to return the stones personally. Thankfully my guide says that there are a few more places the museum director might be, and after we wander through several exhibits, another museum guide suggests that we look for Sir Mauricen in the "glass house."

The glass house turns out to be a large hall made of windows, sheltering what looks like a patch of deepland jungle. For a one heartsick moment, I feel as if I'm home in Saltpool. The air is humid with the tangy, citrus smell of kelp and brinewood trees. I can even hear a few familiar bird calls. Yet there's no seagrass or smooth, mossy rocks at my feet, only pebbles and tiled pathways.

Sir Mauricen stands in the center of the hall with drawings and plans strewn around him. As we approach, he looks from diagram to diagram, tapping his mouth thoughtfully with a ringed finger. He looks just like he did when I last saw him, wearing a suit and a few elegant accessories—this time a deep green necktie and gold eyeglasses. He's also combed his white hair back, and he has his cane, the one topped with the starfish trapped in glass, tucked beneath an arm.

"Pardon me, Sir Mauricen," says my guide. "This girl insisted she speak with you."

I frown because saying that I insisted makes me seem so rude. And when Sir Mauricen looks at me expectantly, there's no spark of recognition in his eyes. Melily truly made him forget us.

"I don't mean to bother you," I say. "I just… may I speak with you privately?"

"Of course. Garby, do you mind?" Sir Mauricen waves the guide away.

Garby leaves, but not before giving me a suspicious look.

I search my thoughts for the right words. I should have planned what I was going to say. Instead I awkwardly hold out the box. "I believe these are yours."

Sir Mauricen uses his walking stick to steady himself as he steps over the diagrams, crosses the room, and takes the box.

Opening the hinged lid, he draws back in surprise and blinks several times. He then looks at me. "Why yes, these *are* mine."

There's an awful silence. He's waiting for an explanation, and I can't give one. "I'm sorry," I finally spit out. "I can't tell you why I have them, it would… I just… The thing is, I knew they belonged to you, and that it was right to return them."

He must sense my discomfort because he graciously says, "Well thank you… Did you tell me your name?"

I shake my head. "It's Nerene Keel." Now that Douglen and Jeck are dead, I hope it's safe to call myself that again.

Sir Mauricen watches me thoughtfully before saying, "Thank you for returning the arctic stones, Nerene Keel. I can't tell you how upset I was when these went missing. It was baffling and rather embarrassing, to be honest." After another long silence, he adds, "Do you know your way out? I'm afraid this hall won't be open for a few sunpeaks, and I'm—" He looks down at the drawings and makes an exasperated noise. "Still working out the details."

I swallow. I'm not *just* here to return the arctic stones, and I know that what I want to happen won't happen unless I'm brave enough to ask for it, so I blurt, "Would you hire me?"

Sir Mauricen looks up in surprise, but he doesn't immediately say no, so I ramble on.

"It's just, you seem kind, and I'm a hard worker. I don't want to just… follow the tide anymore, I'm ready to find a place to stop and stay." And now I'm sure I'm no longer making sense. "Please. You won't regret giving me a job, I promise."

Sir Mauricen still looks startled. "What is it that you do?"

I hope the few skills I have matter in the uppy world; "Well, I know a lot about deepland plants, especially herbs—I once tried to write a book about them. And I'm very good at catching flier hens and visconeys. I can also shoot a snapper, and I know how to make them too, so long as I can find urchin root. I can weave almost anything out of reeds as well." I swallow, hating how my words echo in the vast space.

Again it takes a while for Sir Mauricen to speak, but eventually he says, "Are you from the deeplands? You weren't born in Beth, surely?"

"I'm from the deeplands near Varasay," I say quickly, trying not to let on how unhappy I was there. "I've also lived in Ellevah."

He gives me a keen look. "How did you get a passbook?"

I hesitate.

He quickly raises a hand. "No, don't tell me. I don't need to know."

I smile. I knew it was the right decision to come here.

"Well then," he says, smiling too. "How interesting. I would actually love to hire you."

It seems too good to be true. I stand there, my heart thumping, waiting for him to elaborate.

"You see, my friends and I have wanted to travel to the ruins of a pre-tide civilization for a long while now, but we've had trouble finding deepland guides. They're hard to come by in Beth, as you can imagine, with our shameful slavery laws. Would you be willing to help us travel through the kelp jungles?"

"Yes, of course," I say, thinking fondly of my herb gathering trips in Ellevah.

Sir Mauricen smiles. "How wonderful! And I'm sure I can find something for you to do here until the tide passes too. There's always *something* that needs doing." He waves a hand at the scattered diagrams.

"Thank you," I say. "Thank you so much."

Sir Mauricen holds up the drybark box. "No, thank you. And perhaps when you are ready, you can tell me where you found these."

My hesitation surely must show in my face, because he gently adds, "If, of course, you are ever ready."

SAYING GOODBYE TO SHARA, and even little Timsy and Dorla, is heart-wrenching. Shara and I hug and hug, and we promise to visit each other and send letters, even though we both know how difficult that will be.

Then all of a sudden, the tide passes, along with the winter, and I'm on my own. I move into a small housing unit—a spread in the high city not far from the museum—and I do my best to create a quiet, stable life for myself. Every day I fall more in love with the museum, and Sir Mauricen proves himself to be the trusted friend I hoped he would be. The rest of the museum staff is also kind, and when summer comes, our expedition goes well. As always, I adore hiking through the deeplands, and I'm fascinated by the ancient settlement we visit too. When I'm not exploring the old buildings that are draped in vines, I look for and sketch interesting plants. I also do my best to learn all I can about the statues, tablets, and pottery that we'll be bringing back to the museum. When we do return to Beth, Sir Mauricen asks me to help plan future expeditions, and I soon realize that I'm good at it.

Time slips by, tides pass by, and it starts to feel as if things will go on unchanging until my skin wrinkles and my hair silvers. But one winter, four tides after I said goodbye to Shara, I'm marking routes on a map of the Suthrellon deeplands when there's a knock on my workroom door. I open it and find a museum guide waiting in the passage, a young woman named Maralee.

"There are people outside with a package for you," she says. "I offered to deliver it, but they said they'd rather give it to you themselves." She frowns apologetically.

"Package?" I say, while imagining what Maralee means when she says "people." I picture a crowd of uppy strangers. I also think about how I once arrived at the museum with something I wanted to personally deliver. "I'll come down."

I find only two people on the museum steps. A child with bright red hair grasping a large, square parcel wrapped in paper, and a man wearing well-worn clothes, who has a short beard, eyeglasses, and... and a face I know.

"Sande!" I cry.

"Nerene!" He rushes forward to hug me, and for an instant, I dive back seven or eight tides to when I last saw him. He even smells the same. Yet when he lets go, we're washed forward to the present. And here in the present, we're strangers.

"How?" I say, feeling flustered and unsteady. "And please, come in out of the cold."

The doorman steps forward saying, "It costs fifteen paper shells to enter the museum today."

But I wave him off. "They're with me—it's fine." And again I look at Sande, still shocked that it's really, truly him. His face seems rougher now, or maybe harder. He's skinnier too and missing a bottom tooth. "How did you find me?" I say.

"Someone asked me to bring you this." He nods at the parcel the little girl's hugging. She gives me a beaming smile and holds it out to me. I accept it—it's heavy—and I wonder if she's his daughter. I can't quite tell how old she is. Six tides? Or maybe seven? She doesn't look like him at all, though, except for maybe her curls.

"I was so happy to know you were still alive" Sande says. "And the package came with an envelope of paper shells. I thought the money was simply for postage, but there was so much of it, as well as passbooks for myself and Klariah. It seemed whoever wanted you to have this package wanted us to bring it to you in person, and we were quite happy to take the trip—it wouldn't have been something we could afford otherwise."

Klariah, so that's the child's name. "Is she yours?" I ask.

"Sort of." He winks. "A lot has happened since I last saw you."

"A lot has happened to me too," I say faintly, looking down at the package in my arms. I feel as if I've slipped down an icy hill and now the world is speeding past me. Sande is alive. My name is also on the parcel, and I recognize that compressed, angular handwriting. "Who gave you this?" I ask, even though I already know.

"I can't remember," Sande says. "Strange, isn't it? Whoever they were, they must have been very unremarkable."

Of course he doesn't remember. "Well, it's so good to see you," I say. "And I want to know everything that's happened since we left Varasay. There's a good place to talk nearby, a tea shop. But... do you mind if I run this up to my workroom?"

"Not at all," Sande says, looking impressed that I have a workroom. "Do you mind if we..." He eyes the main gallery where the exowhale hangs on wires. The little girl, Klariah, has already skipped several paces away from us and is peering longingly into the huge hall.

"Yes, please, explore the museum," I say. "I'll be back in a moment."

And of course, I can't bear to just put the strange package in my workroom. I shut the door, cut the strings tied around it, unwrap the outer paper that reads, "Nerene Keel, Royal Museum of Beth", and pull back the waxed canvas inside.

It's a hand-bound book with a leather cover that reads: "Common Sea Spread Spices."

I wipe away a tear. It's our manuscript; Cressit's and mine—the one I lost. It never had this cover before, though. I open it, and as I hoped, I find a letter tucked inside. I unfold the paper with trembling hands.

Dearest Nerene,

I'm afraid I'm writing in haste, so this will be short. I'm also sorry that I'm not bringing you this book in person, but I thought if I did, it might be hard to leave. Yet after using my wavurl inexcusably on you twice, it doesn't seem right to risk making that mistake a third time.

Melily is well, and she would send her love if she knew I was writing you. She survived, but her lungs were permanently damaged, and now she cannot walk where you walk—if you understand what I mean. She found her family, and last I heard, plans to be married.

Deepest love to you, and maybe I will visit when my wavurl fades. I hope you are happy. I also hope this was hand-delivered. I went to great lengths to find just the right person to bring it to you.

-C.S.

I tuck the letter back into the book, and I dab my eyes with a handkerchief because I suddenly have so many things to cry about. I have happy tears because I've finally heard from Cressit, and now I know Melily survived. I have sad tears because it seems that Melily can no longer breathe air, which means I'll never see my dear friend again. And I have sad tears because I won't see Cressit any time soon either. It could take another fifteen or twenty tides for his wavurl to fade. Do I think it best that he stay away until then? Yes, I suppose I do, but hearing from him still makes my chest feel tight.

And yet, I'll have to think all of these things through later, because I have visitors—interesting visitors—and they're waiting for me.

Hoping my skin isn't too red and blotchy, I walk back down the museum's marble staircase having imaginary conversations with Cressit about Douglen and Jeck's deaths, and about our book—which he must have gone back and rescued at some point.

But he's not here now.

Sande is.

I find Sande and the mysterious Klariah where I left them in the main gallery. She's calling out to him in a language I don't know, and he answers her in that same language, sounding as if he's spoken it all his life.

He waves when he sees me crossing the hall, jacket over my arm, and he smiles. "You opened the package, didn't you?"

"I was curious," I admit. "I'm sorry for taking so long."

"Don't be, but you have to you tell me what was inside." He laughs. "I've been traveling with it for months, and you have no idea how many times I nearly tore it open out of curiosity. It was torture."

The old Sande would have torn it open, and I find his restraint interesting. "It was a book that I wrote with a friend. I thought the only copy was lost, so thank you for bringing it back."

He raises his eyebrows. "You wrote a book? That's amazing."

"Well, it's not a real book, not yet. There's just the one copy, but who knows?" I'm holding my coat, hat, and muffler because I thought I'd take Sande to a nearby tea shop, but seeing that his small companion is happily skipping around the main gallery, perhaps staying here is better.

My story seems too difficult and complicated to begin with, so I sit on a bench near Sande and say, "So where have you been for all these tides?"

He smiles in a bittersweet way. "Are you sure you want to know everything?"

I nod.

So he sits down beside me and begins to talk.

ACKNOWLEDGMENTS

A BIG THANK YOU to everyone who encouraged me during the (long!) process of sending this story out into the world.

Thanks in particular to Alexis Lantgen for always being willing to talk through plot problems, and to Gerardo Delgadillo for giving me such great feedback.

Additional thanks to the many other amazing people who's insight and advice have helped me grow as a writer: Dani Baxter, Diana Beebe, Mervyn Dejecacion, Sean Easley, Jason Gurley, Ann Hasseler de Carrasco, Kellie Patrick-Getty, Jared Pope, Holly Rylander, and my editor, Thalia Sutton.

Thank you, Mom and Dad, for letting me subject you to lengthy discussions about my publishing plans. And thank you to my sisters; Christine for being so encouraging even when your life is busy, and Laura for being a great beta reader and my first beta reader ever.

Thanks also to my awesome kids who know that when Mom is hunched over her computer, they should ask questions two or three times—and to never assume that they can eat candy if I vaguely say, "Yes."

And above all, thank you to my wonderful, amazing, supportive, dashingly bearded husband, Stephen, who reads all my messy first drafts. You told me once this was your favorite book, and more than anything else, that helped me find my way when I got lost in the Sea Spread.

I love you.

ABOUT THE AUTHOR

Sarah Mensinga was born in Toronto, Canada, and now lives in Texas with her husband and three kids. She often works as an artist in the animation industry and has had short comics published in various anthologies, including Flight 4 & 5.

Find her at www.sarahmensinga.com or on Instagram and Twitter.

If you would like to experience an audio/visual exploration of this novel, visit the Chattersketch channel on YouTube.

Made in the USA
Monee, IL
22 April 2021